Judith Cutler, like her heroine, Sophie Rivers, lives and works in Birmingham. She taught for many years in a big inner-city college, but is now a part-time lecturer for the University of Birmingham's Continuing Studies Department. She is also a trustee of the City of Birmingham Symphony Orchestra's Benevolent Fund and on the committee of the Birmingham Chamber Music Society.

Judith has enjoyed considerable critical and popular success with her novels featuring Sophie Rivers, which all have a Birmingham setting. She has also written a number of short stories, most notably for the BBC Short Story slot. She is currently at work on a new Sophie Rivers novel.

Also by Judith Cutler

Dying Fall
Dying On Principle

DYING TO WRITE

JUDITH CUTLER

Acknowledgements

I would like to thank the following: the Arvon Foundation; Tim Priestman for the chocolate pudding recipe; David Stephenson for his teaching and especially for Matt and Hugh's poetry; Graham Townshend for his cures for teacher's throat and ideas for poisoning people; Edwina Van Boolen for her constant support and criticism; West Midlands Police for their polite and ready help.

First published in Great Britain in 1996 by
Judy Piatkus (Publishers) Ltd of
5 Windmill Street, London W1

First published in paperback in 1996

A catalogue record for this book is available from the British Library

ISBN 0 7499 3004 7

Phototypeset in Times by
Computerset, Harmondsworth, Middlesex
Printed and bound in Great Britain by
Mackays of Chatham Plc Ltd, Chatham, Kent

For my parents

Chapter One

Sunday afternoon.

August rain dripping down my neck.

A rat regarding me from the reception desk.

And a man confessing to murder.

Anyone else winning a raffle might have picked up a snappy car. A trip to Disneyland – stateside or in France. Even a bottle of whisky. What do I win? A course for would-be writers. In Birmingham.

Birmingham's trying to reclaim its heritage. Where it merges with the Black Country, there's a large tangle of grass and heathland. They describe it euphemistically as a Country Park.

And, sure enough, it comes complete with a country house.

Eyre House is not a stately home. It may once have been a gentleman's residence. Now the eighteenth-century stuccoed house is attached to a sixties block: concrete, blue panels and aluminium-framed windows.

I found the reception desk in the umbilical corridor connecting the two. Apart from the door I'd come through, there were three others, one in each wall. From the half-open one on my right came two voices raised in anger.

'I told you I put paraquat in Phil's tea,' a man shouted. 'And you should have been teaching the bloody course anyway – after you were short-listed –'

'No!' came a woman's voice.

The rat, honey-coloured with brown eyes, shuffled to the end of its cage and pricked its left ear. I pricked my right.

'So you have to, Kate!' the man continued.

'No!'

It occurred to me that I ought to announce my presence, though it would clearly be much more interesting not to. I coughed, mildly. In response, the door slammed, reducing the voices to no more than a murmur.

The door on the left opened. A huge typewriter appeared, Remington circa 1930, at a guess. It settled on the desk, edging the rat's cage perilously close to the edge.

'Hello,' said a diminutive Asian woman emerging from under the Remington. 'I'm Shazia. I'm the administrator here.'

'Hello. I'm Sophie. Sophie Rivers.'

Shazia picked up a pencil and reached for a typed list. The door to my right opened.

'Shazia!' It was a man's voice.

'Excuse me.' She disappeared in his direction, punctiliously closing the door behind her.

The rat shrugged its shoulders and set about exploring its cage. I looked round the reception area. Neither of us would be occupied for very long.

The rat, its tour completed, embarked on a minute examination of the fur at the base of its spine.

The door to our right opened again. Shazia's voice – and the other woman's. The rat looked pleased and stood up, pressing a stomach of comfortable proportions against the bars. I put out a tentative finger to tickle it. Then Shazia reappeared, with a woman in her forties. She had a rather lived-in face. She wore the sort of suit you can dress down with a T-shirt or up with a silk blouse. At the moment she was playing safe with Marks and Sparks poly-cotton.

'Oh, you don't mind Sidney? Thank goodness! I thought people might be afraid of him.' She put down the sheaf of papers she was carrying and chirruped at him. He abandoned my finger for hers.

'I'm Kate,' she said at last, withdrawing her hand from Sidney and offering it to me. 'Kate Freeman. I seem to be one of the course tutors.'

'Sophie Rivers,' I said, rather shyly for me. I'd not met a real writer before.

A man now emerged. She half-turned to smile at him.

'And this is Matt Purvis, the other tutor.'

Matt smiled, an open, friendly smile. Like Kate, he was in his forties and wore depressingly normal clothes: jeans and a heavy sweater. I suppose I'd hoped for eccentricity in the form of bare feet and baggy cords. At least he sported a beard, but it was as neatly trimmed as his hair.

'Kate, I'll shift your cases while you get that list retyped,' he said. 'Which room, Shazia?'

'Number twelve. On the ground floor.'

Matt pushed through the door on the left, into the newer part of the building. He reappeared a minute later, a key between his teeth, carrying a suitcase and what appeared to be a state-of-the-art computer notepad. 'Another couple of bags,' he grunted, dropping the keys neatly into Shazia's outstretched hands. 'Bloody hell, Kate, never heard of minimalism?'

'OK, I'll get them,' said Shazia.

Matt disappeared through the door on the right.

'Bloody French farce,' he muttered, as all the doors sighed. Kate meanwhile was busy with the list.

'There: will they be able to tell I was originally supposed to be a student?'

I peered at her paper. Two undeniable blobs of Tipp-Ex.

'I'm afraid they might,' I said hesitantly. 'And you know what people are like if they think they're not getting the real McCoy.'

'Difficult?'

I nodded.

'Oh, dear. And, well, I helped train people when I was in Customs and Excise but I've never actually taught before –'

'Maybe we'd better keep quiet about that. Here – there's a couple of cars coming up the drive. Let's retype that list before anyone else arrives.'

Altruism doesn't pay. That's what my thirty-five years should have taught me. If I hadn't been sorting out the Remington's temperament, I'd have bagged the nice end room with the window overlooking what could one day become a garden again. As it was, I found myself relegated to one in the row of identical hutches whose only view was the kitchen bins.

The decor was no more inspiring than the view. It didn't take me long to settle in – I travel more lightly than Kate. I'd go and confront my destiny in the form of my fellow students.

Shazia had mentioned tea or coffee. That meant retracing my steps across the gusty hall and into the old building. I found the lounge without difficulty, and strapped on a convivial smile. But even that minor effort was in vain. There was no sign of any of the people who'd arrived while I was lurking behind the reception desk. Except one: a woman a good ten inches taller than me. She was dressed – most unsuitably for the weather, which I braved in a winter-weight tracksuit – in a skirt shorter than you could buy anywhere in Birmingham. When she heard me come in, she turned from the window. She turned back again. The clear implication was that even the sodden lawn was more interesting.

I shrugged and padded over to the tea urn. It rumbled with the same menace as one we'd had at the college I work at. Periodically it would shudder and breathe steam. We'd christened ours Vesuvius. You'd expect something more literary in a place like this.

'Have you had some tea?' I inquired, squirting water into a mug. 'Or did the Balrog defeat you?'

'Tea rots your teeth, darling.' She sounded ineffably bored. Then she put on her party manners. 'What did you call that thing?'

'The Balrog. As in *Lord of the Rings*.'

'Bloody Wagner or something?'

'No. A book by –'

'Oh. A book.' She turned back to the window.

Her posture was impeccable, despite the high heels which the course prospectus had expressly forbidden, in order to protect the wooden floors in this part of the building. Her legs, evenly tanned, stretched up to her waist. Mine merely reach my bottom. To my provincial taste, the gold anklet made her look a little on the cheap side.

Clearly she did not want to talk about the original oak panelling or the badly foxed prints on the walls.

Sipping the surprisingly good Assam, I slipped off my shoes to toast my toes at the fire some kind soul had lit.

'What lovely feet!' said a Birmingham accent. And a hand

grabbed one of them.

I nearly fell into the fire.

'I'm sorry. I didn't mean – oh, please . . .' Crouching, the speaker dabbed at the tea I'd slopped on to the hearth. I attended to that on my thighs.

All I could see of him was one of those Oxfam sweatshirts with a giant frog on the back. There was one on the front, too, as I saw when he eventually stood up. I was to wish he'd chosen another design. Whenever I thought of him after that, I saw a frog. No, a toad. His pale bulgy eyes and rather wide mouth didn't help. But he hadn't any warts or anything. Really he was quite a normal-looking man. Young – well, mid-thirties. Broadly built, but not heavy. Rather pale skin, and mousy hair which was quite distinctly thinning. Nothing remarkable. Except for his sweatshirt and the way he was clasping my right foot.

'Quite lovely. Lovely straight toes. No corns. Lovely!'

Not surprisingly, the woman at the window turned. She held out one of hers. Not for attention. Just worship.

I thought the colour she'd painted her toenails was common. But Toad leaped across the room to kneel before her, resting her foot on his knee and removing her strappy sandal.

'Look at that arch,' he breathed. 'The line of that arch!'

But he came back to me. I knew he would. There he was, clutching a custard cream and smiling at me.

'You see,' he was saying. 'I always loved feet. I wanted to be a chiropodist. But I couldn't pass the A levels. Couldn't even get on the course.'

The trouble is, I always ask sensible questions. 'Couldn't you do an access course at a further education college?'

What if he evinced a sudden desire to try William Murdock College? And ended up in my English class? But I needn't have worried.

'Oh, no. I'd want to do it properly. Real exams.'

Ah. That sort of person. The sort who wouldn't do any of the writing exercises the tutors here might set because he wanted to write *War and Peace* straight away.

By now there were plenty of other people dunking their teabags. Shazia was busy distributing name badges. 'Just put your first names on – nothing formal.'

'Christian names,' said a voice with too much emphasis. I watched him write, ostentatiously, Mr Gimson. I eyed him: what kind of man insists on using his title? This one came with a beautifully cut sports jacket and immaculate brogues it would take Toad several minutes to unlace. And I thought Mr Gimson might expect a little adulation: although he was short, he tried to look down his nose at everyone. Literally and metaphorically. I'd make a point of pouring hot water on his fingers if he came near the urn.

Matt came and stood my me and cleared his throat gently. No one took any notice. He eyed me. 'How d' you do it?'

Sometimes I think they must brand teachers' foreheads.

'Call an unruly mob like this to order?' I said. 'Oh, cough portentously and waggle some papers. That usually works – eventually.'

Red Toenails – Nyree, according to her badge – lounged possessively over to a sofa. All eyes turned to her.

Matt coughed again, more dramatically this time. It had the desired effect.

'Ladies and gentlemen, welcome to Eyre House. We want you to have as free and productive time as possible while you're here, but we want to say one or two things that will make the running of the course easier for everyone.

'First may I say how fortunate we are to have Kate Freeman with us. Philip Doyle has had to drop out –'

A general sigh.

'Because he's been rushed to hospital. It's quite serious, I'm afraid.'

It would be, wouldn't it? Isn't paraquat irreversible? No. He'd been joking, hadn't he?

'So Kate has kindly agreed to take his place. You'll recall that Kate was short-listed for the Whitbread last year, and you may have heard her plays or stories on the radio. And there's a television series coming up in the new year – right, Kate?'

Kate blushed in acknowledgement.

Then she started her part of the spiel: 'We've been asked to remind you of just a couple of rules. No smoking and no high heels in the old part of the house. Sorry.'

Matt pulled a face and ritualistically tapped out his pipe. 'Food,' he continued, 'is up to you. Shazia's prepared tonight's supper –'

'Bloody curry, I dare say,' muttered Mr Gimson.

Matt overrode him: 'But for the rest of the week you good people will take turns cooking the evening meal for the rest of us. Perhaps you'd divide yourselves into teams during supper.'

'I assume we're allowed breakfast and lunch?' Gimson again.

'Only if you forage for them,' Matt replied. 'Then you can organise your days to suit yourselves. Your time is your own; we only claim it for individual tutorials and for group activities. The first will be after supper, which is now ready. What writers in a more gracious age might have called a cold collation, I believe.'

And he gestured us into the dining room.

The beautifully proportioned room still tried hard to be elegant. Unfortunately much of the decorative plasterwork was blurred by layer upon layer of paint; it would take hours of patience to restore it. Rather sadder, however, because someone had obviously tried so hard to get it right, was the wallpaper, which aspired desperately if anachronistically to Regency stripes and ended up looking like something from a bar parlour or a cheap restaurant. Crimson flock does, especially if decorated with a gold motif and dabs of food.

No one wanted to lead the stampede to the table. Gimson, however, got things moving, taking Kate's elbow, the better to establish her – and himself – at the head of the table. He would clearly have liked Nyree on his other side, but she had already claimed Matt, down at the far end. I hung back because I wanted to put space between me and Toad: there must be more interesting people. Since a little male pulchritude never comes amiss, I fell in beside a young Afro-Caribbean man called Courtney, who grinned at me with a pleasant degree of malice as a loud young woman told anyone willing to listen that she was not here to write but to see how writers worked, since Daddy had got her a job in publishing. I did not intend to become her research material. We sat opposite an elderly man. He had also put his surname on his label: Edward Woodhouse. But there was neither white soup nor Emma in prospect.

Next to him sat a trio of greyish ladies, who had attempted to reinforce summer polyester with winter woollies – and indeed, who could blame them?

'Those greens with those beige stripes!' whispered Courtney. 'That old dear looks like a parsnip!'

But then whoever it was on his other side claimed his attention, and I turned to my other neighbour, a young man with John Lennon glasses. I tried to draw him out. I like students and enjoy their company. This one had a premature scholarly stoop. Alas, I shocked him back into catatonia when I confessed that I did not read science fiction. Beyond him were a couple of young girls, one giggling, one morose behind a brace.

Courtney nudged me. 'If Kate and Matt can make this lot work together, they'll be earning their corn and no mistake.'

We started our first exercises after supper. We were in the lounge again, with all the chairs pushed back against the wall, and we were to work in pairs. We had to stare into our partner's eyes and learn to act in concert with him or her. Whatever our partner did with his hands, we were supposed to do with ours. It was inconceivable that Nyree would want to look into my eyes, and I'd no intention of gazing into Toad's. Mr Gimson had stomped off for a smoke. For a while I mirrored Mr Woodhouse, but not very successfully. Then I linked up with Courtney.

They gazed dutifully, his dark-brown eyes and my blue ones. And our hands tracked one another obediently. Then Courtney spoiled it.

'I'm glad I got you again,' he said. 'You're nice and safe.'

'Gee, thanks. And middle-aged, too, I suppose.' I'm always having this problem with my students – they think you're way past it by the time you're thirty.

'I didn't say that. You're younger than Nyree, I should think. But at least your hands – I mean, what's a guy s'posed to do when a woman – I mean . . .'

I shook my head: what had she done?

He dropped his voice to a confidential whisper. 'Her hand,

Sophie. She had her hand straight on my you-know-what. I mean!' For a second his voice was camp: 'On to a bit of a loser with me, though.'

We grinned at each other. It was nice to have a potential ally.

Then we had to change partners. Soon I was staring into Matt Purvis's eyes. They were grey, within a tangle of crow's-feet. Our hands circled in parallel swirls and dips. We were very good. Until he broke all the rules and looked away.

'Jesus!' he said. He nodded at Mr Gimson's crotch.

Nyree must have groped him, too. Or perhaps he just wished she had.

'I know there's a novel in me,' someone was saying earnestly. The girl with the brace, I think.

We'd moved the furniture back and were allowed to sit down and relax. A glass nestled closely in my hand. Nyree had produced a litre bottle of gin, and it seemed the only way we'd prevent her sinking the lot was to discover a little cache of glasses in a top cupboard. Some of us saw it as a positive duty to make up for others' lack of dedication. The result was that not only the names but also the name badges were by now a little hazy.

'So why are you here, Sophie?'

Blast Matt.

'I won a prize.'

There were aahs, both appreciative and resentful.

'In a raffle. The head of English at my college sold me a ticket. He said if I won, he'd come. But he had to change a tyre on the principal's car and now he's having his hernia repaired. So here I am.' After a close encounter with death earlier in the year, I'd resolved to grab every new experience that came my way. So I added, terribly earnest with gin, 'Now I'm here, I'll try anything.'

'So will I, darling, so will I.'

'Ah, Nyree. Why have you joined the course?' Matt succumbed to *force majeure*.

I could have told him the answer to that. It wasn't so very different from the one she gave.

'Because it's easier than the OU, darling.' She tipped

forward to show him more of her left breast.

'The OU?' repeated Matt, foolishly.

'Of course. You know, darling: summer schools.'

Yes. That sort of education.

Having silenced him, she continued: 'Not that I don't mean to write. I've started on my memoirs, darling. Married to a secret agent. And now what does he do? Gets made redundant, and asks for political asylum in Viet-bloody-nam. So I stayed here. To meet a few red-blooded Englishmen. God, I'm sick of fucking pansies!'

Kate caught my eye. We sniggered into our gin.

'I've got to Chapter Seven, now, darling. Willies I have known. I'll be a very good student – I know how important research is.' She leaned back. Her breasts might have sunk to comparative oblivion but her legs hadn't. In case anyone hadn't noticed, a languorous hand lay halfway along her thigh, weighted down by a ring with more carats than should decently occupy one space.

Matt was clearly unequal to the situation. But Kate wasn't.

'Thank you, Nyree. I'm sure you'll have a very fruitful time here,' she said, the irony barely audible. But she grinned at me again before she turned to the next victim. 'Garth?'

So Toad had a name. I peered more closely at his label. Garth Kerwin. The gin and I were trying to work out whether his name suited him when something scuffed at the door.

'Is the house haunted?' I asked no one in particular.

The ghost jingled.

The door was pushed open, very slowly. Its creak was especially convincing.

'Sidney! You bad animal!' shouted Kate.

The rat poured himself around the door. He was wearing a tiny leather harness with a bell on the shoulders.

Gimson's face contorted. 'How dare you!'

'I'm dreadfully sorry. I really am!' said Kate.

Toad leapt to his feet, white showing around the pale irises. Nyree pressed close to Gimson. One of the older ladies gasped; her lips turned alarmingly blue.

All around, voices were raised. I was on my knees cajoling Sidney with a gin-flavoured finger, which he rightly ignored. The first old lady was fumbling for tablets, another for an asthma spray. Gimson was booming away about social irresponsibility, but was also keen to tell us the difference between *Rattus rattus* and *Rattus norvegicus*. And surely that was Toad's voice: 'You should be shot! Keeping an animal like that!'

Chapter Two

I suppose it was at about this point that I realised that this course and the people on it were not there simply for my amusement. There were real feelings engaged. I must sober up. Rapidly.

Water. If I drank a lot of water it would help. And there'd be plenty of water in the tap in the kitchen.

The corridor to the kitchen was occupied by Matt and Kate, both grim-faced. Kate might have been enduring a bollocking, but Matt seemed more apologetic than anything. Quite clearly they did not want me to join them.

I might as well go back and collect a few glasses from the lounge while I was at it; most of us had left them where we'd been sitting. The lounge wasn't empty, though. Courtney had found a tray and a dishcloth and was systematically gathering and mopping.

He smiled at me as I started to help. 'Funny old evening it's been,' he said.

'Some funny old people to make it that way. Jesus, Courtney, can anyone really find Nyree attractive?'

'You're asking the wrong man here, sweetie,' he said, camp again. 'But I wouldn't have thought so. Poor Matt looked scared –'

'– if not rigid,' I concluded.

Courtney's tray and my hands full, we headed back to the kitchen. The corridor was by now quiet.

I ran water and sloshed in washing-up liquid. Courtney found a cleanish tea towel, but he didn't start using it. Quite a backlog had accumulated before he spoke. Then it was merely to ask what I did for a living. I told him about my job at a big inner-city college. He listened in silence. I didn't want to upset him by asking about his job in case he hadn't got one.

He put down the saucer he'd been polishing. I felt him looking at me.

'I think I can trust you, Soph,' he began. 'I think I can. You see . . . Dear me, there's no easy way to say this.'

I waited.

'I've been there, you see. In the nick, Soph. Nice boy like me in prison.'

There was nothing I could say.

'And now this. This harassment. That's what it is, you know: harassment.' He pronounced it the American way.

'Hm?'

'Her being here like this. That woman.'

'Which woman?'

'There was this joke we used to have in the nick. There's someone in your house. Midnight, see. Not a burglar. Not the filth – whoops, pardon my French! And he's turning over your stuff and there's nothing you can do to stop him. Who is it?'

I shook my head. I don't like being called 'Soph' but didn't want to stop his flow. 'Not a clue. Who?'

'Customs and bloody Excise, that's who.'

'So?'

'They harass you. They follow you even when you've done your time. Them and the filth.'

I paused in my washing-up. To give myself time I poured away the dirty water and started to run fresh. I try to be broad-minded, always, but words like 'filth' upset me. The only policeman I know at all well is not at all filth-like. He is eminently civilised in most respects.

'Even here, for Christ's sake,' he said, quite wildly, now. 'My probation officer, he managed to get me on this course, you see. There was this tutor I had in Durham: reckoned I could write, see. And I come down here, where no one knows me, and who do I find but her?'

'Who? You'll have to tell me.'

'I bet she's told everyone. I bet she's told you. I saw you

talking to her.' His voice was shrill with ill-concealed hysteria. 'Why should she be here? She wasn't supposed to be!'

I knew by now, of course, but I thought I'd do better to ask flatly: 'Who are you talking about?'

'The one you were best buddies with when we arrived. That Freeman woman. What's she doing on a course if she's so bloody good? Someone must have told her. Harassment, that's what it is!' His voice still rose alarmingly.

I had to keep calm. 'Kate's said nothing to me, I promise you. Or to anyone else, as far as I know. Are you sure she even recognises you?'

He stared at me. 'How d'you mean?'

'I'm a teacher, right?' I tried to keep my voice as low and calm as I could. 'And because I see so many students I don't always recognise them when I see them out of college. I'm sure I've offended lots of them because I couldn't quite place them. You may just seem vaguely familiar.'

'She ought to remember me. She had me sent down for eight years.'

I don't know anything about crime and punishment but eight years suggested he might have done something pretty serious. I tried hard not to react.

'Eight years. Well, not her personally. But her evidence. So what do I do, Soph? Tell me: what do I do to shut her up?'

'Nothing,' I said.

'Come on –'

I didn't like that note in his voice.

'Honestly, Courtney. Either you can do nothing and trust she says nothing. Or, if you're really worried, you might just try asking her to keep quiet. What d'you think?'

'I don't know. I just don't know. All I know is if she talks . . .' And he shouldered his way out of the kitchen.

Then he was back.

'And don't you fucking say nothing either, Soph,' he said, pointing a hostile forefinger as if it were a gun.

I'd wanted something to sober me up, and I'd certainly got it. In fact, Courtney's transformation from mild young man to raging criminal scared me more than I cared to admit. It had been so unexpected. The question was, what to do next? There seemed to be only one answer. I didn't feel proud of myself, breaking an implicit promise, but clearly I had to say something to Kate, and quickly, too. I left the remaining glasses to drain, and slipped up the staff stairs.

The wooden treads made an embarrassing amount of noise. According to the background blurb in the course prospectus, old Eyre had installed a primitive heating system – the first since the Romans' – ducting hot air under the stairs and along what was now the staff corridor into the principal rooms. The old wood had no doubt dried and now, since the introduction of humidifiers, was expanding again, with considerable protest.

I stood in the shadow at the top of the stairs, wondering what to do next. I didn't know which was Kate's room, of course. Just that it was along here somewhere.

And then I saw Kate. She might be providing an answer to Courtney's question about why she was here. But it was clear she wouldn't want to discuss anything with me at the moment, however serious it might be. Wearing a dressing gown, she was shutting a door quietly behind her and turning down the corridor. She stopped outside another door and scratched gently.

It was opened by Matt. My warning would plainly have to wait until the morning.

The main lights had been switched off throughout both buildings, leaving emergency bulbs to cast lonely pools of light at infrequent intervals. I felt my way through the umbilical corridor, pushing at the door and hearing it sigh shut behind me. The front and rear doors to the outside world sighed in sympathy. It was well after eleven: what time did Shazia lock up, for goodness' sake?

To my rabbit-hutch.

What I hadn't realised in daylight was how deeply recessed each doorway was. The frames must have been inset by a good eighteen inches from the corridor wall, and none was lit. The next day, I resolved, I would buy a torch. Not a ladylike affair just for lighting my way – a good heavy one. An isolated building like this might well attract people other than those whose ambitions for adventure were confined to making the trip to London to pick up the Booker prize.

I didn't like the way my pulse was working after the simple matter of fishing out my key and unlocking the door. Perhaps I was missing the security lights outside my own home. Generally they do no more than irritate me by switching on every time a fox investigates, and for years I'd kept them switched off. But last spring someone had tried to murder me, and there is nothing like a close encounter with a killer for concentrating the mind on the essentials of life – such as being alive. I'd have liked a friendly glimmer now. I sat on the bed and contemplated my next move: gathering up a towel and heading for the bathroom.

After the creakings of the old house, this section was unnervingly quiet, though why on earth they should have bothered with sound insulation in such a patently cheap building as this was beyond me. There were no sounds of people moving round in the rooms to either side of me. No one padding round upstairs. And yet I had a strong feeling that not everyone was quietly reading in bed: if I were Sidney I'd have been sitting with my ears pricked and my whiskers a-quiver. I sensed movement rather than being able to identify it.

On reflection I decided to leave cleanliness till tomorrow, and contented myself with a spirited dash to the loo. When I returned, quite safely, I laughed at myself. Any nocturnal wanderings were probably merely Nyree hunting for a bed-mate.

And yet I did not sleep. I missed the noises of my quiet suburban street. I missed the hum of fridge and freezer. If I drifted off for a moment, images of giant toads and long scaly tails clustered and drifted. I wondered what had possessed Kate to buy such a creature. Then I speculated about Toad and his grasp on my feet. His gesture wasn't absurd, but distasteful. More than distasteful: unnerving. And he'd overreacted to Sidney's illicit arrival even more than Gimson and the women had.

Most of all, I suddenly realised, I was missing my duvet. I am not unusually tall – just five foot one, to be honest – and fit most beds and most duvets. Not this one. Whatever position I adopted, I found bits of me sticking out.

I'd pulled my tracksuit back on and was making sure the window was as tightly shut as it seemed when I saw the light spilling from another bedroom window on to a distant bin. Then it went out. Another cold writer, no doubt.

Breakfast. Most of the women were down, but they tended not to sit next to each other. We were all warmly dressed; some of us had already applied make-up to disguise the ravages of what seemed to be a communal attack of insomnia. Then Nyree appeared. Her face was a clear case of the triumph of cosmetics over adversity, but she still wore, not a thermal dressing gown, but a negligee which more than hinted at her admirable figure. Suddenly I wanted her out of the room before Toad appeared.

When she came swanning over and greeted me by grabbing my chin and turning my profile to the window, I wanted her out of the room for another reason.

'What did you say your name was? Sophie what?' she asked in a particularly carrying voice. 'Rivers, that's it! You're just like him, aren't you?'

It took a lot of effort not to tear her fingers from my chin, and to sit back calmly.

'Yes,' I said. 'But I don't intend to talk about him now.'

I wouldn't walk out. Not with all these people watching me. I couldn't give her that much satisfaction.

'Our little mouse has a famous cousin,' she continued. 'Guess who Sophie's cousin is!'

Not all my family are indigent lecturers. Indigent anything, for that matter. There is my cousin Andy.

Andy took to what the family always considered bad ways. He dropped out of grammar school and hitched with his guitar to Spain, Portugal and other warm and Latin countries. Somewhere he must actually have learned to play the thing, because we next heard of him going professional. Then he was having top-ten mega-hits. It was a phase, they all said. Soon he'd see sense. He could always come back and join his dad's plumbing business. People always wanted a good plumber. Then he'd never be hard up.

In the circumstances it was perhaps a generous offer. By now Andy, whom I'd taught to bowl leg-breaks on the back lawn, was headline news in the tabloids for his extramusical activities. He'd long since dried out – campaigns against drink and drugs – but there is always someone after a snippet to sell to some gutter journalist.

I care for Andy a great deal. And I won't talk about him. To anyone.

'Come on, darlings – guess who Sophie's cousin is!'

But then the door opened to reveal a god. A macho Rudolf Valentino. Tendrils of black hair fell across an olive forehead. Without looking, I knew his eyes would be dark pools of passion. He stood there, tawny brown in a sudden patch of sun.

Nyree lost interest in me.

There was a preoccupied silence.

He stepped inside and closed the door.

I wish that his voice had been deeper, or his words more meaningful. 'Found 'em, Shaz. Two more setts.'

'Get those wellies off, Naukez! I'm not having mud all over this floor again. By the way,' Shazia added in a public voice, 'this is my husband, Naukez. He's in charge of wild life on the Eyre Estate, with particular responsibility for badgers.'

He smiled bashfully, she proudly.

I suddenly felt very lonely; it was a long time since I'd had anyone to smile at like that. And then I knew incontrovertibly that the relationship with a colleague I'd slipped into a couple of weeks before the holiday would have to end. I'd never smile like that at him.

Meanwhile Nyree was trying to insert herself into Naukez' consciousness, and again I saw my relationship in perspective. Perhaps my first piece of creative writing should be a letter ending what I now saw as a grubby little liaison, and returning him giftwrapped, if somewhat shopsoiled, to his wife. I pushed away from the table. In the doorway I nearly ran into Kate; her face was as sober and preoccupied as mine.

'Are you all right?' we asked each other simultaneously, in voices of equal concern. And we gave matching brave but grim smiles.

Matt, breezing along as if he might actually have slept,

stopped to give me a friendly and unexpected hug. But I resolved not even to think of fancying him. One of the great romantic composers – was it Brahms? – had as his motto, 'Lonely but free'. I suppose I could do worse. I continued on my way whistling – there's a bit of Brahms' Third Symphony which picks up the 'lonely but free' motto in music. I felt better immediately. Especially when Gimson greeted me with a scowl and the muttered information that a whistling woman and a crowing hen were pleasing to neither God nor men.

As a lecturer I always like observing my colleagues, not just to score points off them, but to pick up new approaches. As I lay on the lounge floor alongside my fellow students I did, however, find myself hard-pressed to imagine a use for this particular exercise. Matt had talked briefly about trying to unlock the creative, as opposed to the critical, part of the brain, then handed over to Kate, who, he explained, was an experienced practitioner of the relaxation techniques involved.

'One good way to relax,' she was saying, in a low, persuasive voice, 'is to take yourself on an imaginary journey. A walk. Notice where you're going. Notice the colours, the smells, the sounds . . . Open up the creative part of your brain –'

'My good woman,' Gimson said, his everyday voice harsh after Kate's, 'I've seen more brains than you've had hot dinners, and I've never come across one unlocked by lying on the floor with its head on a pile of paperback books.'

There was a tentative murmur of agreement.

'You're all paying Kate and Matt a great deal of money to help you to write,' I heard myself saying, 'so why not let them help you?'

So we were all flat on our backs when we first heard the voices. One was Shazia's; she was speaking quickly, as if remonstrating. The other was more gutteral – heavy, insistent.

Footsteps. Then the lounge door was flung open.

'Charrotte Brontë!' demanded the gutteral voice. 'Charrotte Brontë!'

There was a rapid scrabble as we all returned to the vertical.

Kate moved forward quickly, as I would have done, to protect her class. Matt, who'd been on the floor with the rest of us, joined her to confront the intruder. Shazia waited by the door, as if to show him courtesy when he finally left.

'Charrotte Brontë! Jay Eyre!' the man repeated, more loudly.

There was no reason why he should have been threatening. He was an ordinary Japanese tourist. Five foot two, very thickset, very bad skin; thousands of pounds' worth of cameras round his neck. But there was something about the way he scanned the room that chilled me.

'Jay Eyre!' he shouted.

The four of them stood there.

God knows why it took me so long to fall in. But when I did, I started to laugh. And I joined the group by the door.

'I think you're at the wrong place,' I said slowly. 'You want the Brontë Museum. For *Jane Eyre*.'

He nodded. But he continued to look around the room.

'You're way off course,' I continued. 'You need to head a hundred or more miles northeast.'

Eventually Shazia took him off to mark Haworth on his road map. But as he left the room he looked round again. And I'm sure the person his eyes sought longest was Nyree.

Without doubt hers lingered on the door until Kate quite sharply told her to lie down with the rest of us.

But the moment was destroyed. Soon a querulous voice was saying it had no idea what to write about, and soon we were all sitting up again, bleating our agreement.

'Surely,' said Matt, bracing and positive, 'you've all had some moment in your life, some feeling –'

'Love, I suppose,' said Gimson.

'Why not? Or any other feeling. Fear. Hate,' said Kate.

'I nearly died once,' said one of the elderly ladies. 'And I think my main feeling was outrage. Perhaps I could write about that.'

'Excellent,' Kate said. 'What better than an experience like that? Now, what we could do is –'

'– have a coffee,' Matt suggested.

We started to drift from the room. I hung back to avoid Nyree, and found myself alone with Gimson and Kate. But they obviously didn't realise I was still there. They were talking in urgent under-voices: I didn't want to eavesdrop and headed briskly for the door. But I couldn't avoid hearing some of what they said.

'I nearly died once too,' she was saying. 'A pulmonary embolism –'

'Embolus.'

'A pulmonary *embolus*, then – often is fatal. I might have died. Because of you.'

I was almost at the door. But I couldn't miss what Gimson said next: 'If you try to put it in some book, I promise you I shall take every step possible to silence you.'

After mid-morning coffee we were allowed free time. I jogged down to the depressed mining village a couple of miles from the estate to buy a torch. I found an old-fashioned hardware shop with exactly the heavy, rubber-covered type I wanted. I could have bought Kilner jars and a jam kettle if I'd wanted, and enough poison to exterminate all the rats and weeds in Birmingham. I restrained myself, and strolled up the main street. There was a new Peugeot 205GTi parked neatly outside the chemist's. I winced at the thought of the insurance premiums but soon drifted into covet-mode. It was certainly sleeker than my van. George's van, really. He'd left it to me, half-converted to combine transport and accommodation for the world tour he had planned for when he retired. When I collected it, his tape measure was still half open on top of his toolbag. The tools have gone now, to a charity that specialises in refurbishing them and distributing them to African workers. But I have the van, and I bought a new tape measure for Africa.

The van itself was a problem.

I ought to have paid to have the conversion completed. But I didn't want a motor-caravan. It was a liability in a city like Birmingham. Since it was too big for my garage, I had to tax and insure it, so I did occasionally drive it. But my main mode of transport was a cycle. Hitherto I'd been quite happy to augment that with public transport, but an occasional foray into self-indulgence had given me the taste for something better. A Peugeot like Kate's, for instance.

But then, I could never, ever sell George's van.

Kate emerged from the chemist's and opened the car door.

'Hi! Want a lift? I can wait, if you have shopping to do.'

'No, I've finished, thanks.'

'Sure? There's no hurry.'

I convinced her, got in, and we set off up the long hill to Eyre House.

She drove well, confident despite the fact that the odometer showed only 998 miles.

'How are you enjoying the teaching?' I asked, in what I hoped was a supportive voice.

'It's OK,' she said doubtfully. 'But I do find it hard to deal with some of the individuals. Like Garth. He insisted on changing his place on the cooking roster. Has to do it tonight, he says, or his creative juices will evaporate. And he has to make a chocolate pudding. Nothing else will do. He'd already browbeaten the rest of the team by the time I got involved, so I could hardly refuse when he asked me to pick up some of the ingredients. And then he held me up by coming and admiring the car. Sat and told me how he wanted to be famous and buy a Maserati.' Her voice suggested he wouldn't achieve fame through his writing.

'I thought Shazia was responsible for stocking up,' I said, returning to a subject which would soon affect me intimately, since I'd be cooking too.

'She'd left ages before the rest of their order. And I was coming here anyway with a prescription. Though how I'll be able to face food from the same source as Tampax and toilet rolls I don't know. God knows why it has to be liquid glucose. Rum I can understand. Continental chocolate. Amaretti biscuits. Double cream. But liquid glucose?'

I couldn't help.

'Thank God there's this wonderful delicatessen down the main street. Goodness knows how they keep open in times like these, but they seemed to be doing a reasonable trade. Ah! Excuse me if I sing "Happy Birthday!"'

'I'm sorry?'

She tapped the odometer: all the figures were rolling

round.

I not only excused her, I joined in. One thousand miles must constitute a car's birthday, surely. And I certainly hoped it would be happy. I decided to postpone the Courtney business till after lunch.

Lunchtime didn't seem especially auspicious, however. Although there was no fixed hour, most of us had gathered in the dining room by one. The talk was general and subdued. Then Gimson strode in, smoking.

Shazia stared silently at his cigarette.

He moved it to his side so that it was level with my eyes. I waved the smoke away, not so much elegantly as ostentatiously.

'Let me tell you, my good woman, I shall smoke where and when I like.'

'So long as the where isn't here and the when isn't now, that's fine by me,' I said.

'I think tobacco makes a man smell masculine,' Nyree observed.

'Hmph,' I said, unconvinced.

'My good woman, you've obviously no idea that nicotine is addictive.'

'But if you're a doctor –' I didn't want a row, but I wasn't going to be anyone's good woman.

'I am Consultant General Surgeon at St Jude's,' he said, capital letters much in evidence. 'The London teaching hospital.'

I hate people who stress 'London' like that. An even nastier, dirtier city than Birmingham, if you ask me. Full of people who smoke at meals, no doubt.

'If you're a *surgeon*,' I corrected myself, 'you must have seen the likely consequences of your addiction.'

'But if it's an addiction, darling, you can't give up. That's what addiction means.'

'I know what addiction means,' I snapped. Foolishly.

'Ah, yes, your cousin was an addict, wasn't he?' She had her mouth open to tell everyone his name.

'Yes.' I overrode her. 'Yes. And he conquered his addiction. Triumphantly.'

There was a movement behind me. 'I'm sorry, Mr Gimson, but you seem to have forgotten our rules,' said Kate in a wonderfully majestic voice.

Gimson started to protest, but contented himself with an arrogant movement of his upper lip. Then he condescended to open the french door to let his smoke out.

Someone out there was playing Bach.

'What the hell's that racket?' Gimson stepped back in, but left the hand holding the cigarette outside.

'A viola?' I suggested.

'Must be Garth Kerwin's,' said Kate. 'I saw him unloading yesterday. Everything but the kitchen sink. Three cases, a word processor and a Mafia machinegun case.'

'And the biggest ghettoblaster I've seen outside Handsworth,' I added.

'Kerwin? That idiot who was holding forth about animals? What about humans, for God's sake?'

'I think he's rather sweet,' said Nyree, looking at her feet.

Sweet! That wasn't the word that I associated with him. But I was intrigued. Learning any instrument takes the sort of commitment I hadn't associated with Toad. And bringing it with him to Eyre House confirmed that.

There are times when I shame myself with my hasty judgements. I would clearly have to overcome my repugnance and get to know him better.

Chapter Three

On Monday afternoon we had individual appointments with one of the tutors to help us choose our projects for the course. I was to see Kate at three.

I thought as a teacher I'd be inured to the nerves others might feel at such a prospect. I'm generally confident in my own abilities. And I seemed to get on well with Kate. But I discovered, as I hovered in the corridor outside her study, that I was quite reluctant to tap the door and go in. Apart from anything else, I had absolutely no idea what I could possibly write about.

When Kate opened the door, I was greeted by Sidney, who darted backwards and forwards in anxious forays to sniff my feet. Kate knelt on the floor, and he finally retreated to the security of her lap. She stroked him, gathered him up in her arms, and got up to put him in his cage, a procedure not entirely to his satisfaction. She pacified him with a piece of wholemeal biscuit from a packet on her desk. He ate with gusto. When he stood to ask for more, he looked like a cuddly toy, a cone of thick fur from which apparently inadequate hands and feet protruded. Kate let me give him another sliver of biscuit. He took it gently but very firmly, and withdrew to the far corner of the cage. A perfect pet, except for the pong. Despite a litter tray, the room smelled like my grandmother's house before the council sent in the rodent man. But if Kate didn't object, why should I?

She sat at the desk and waved me to the chair beside her. She pushed away the computer notepad and its printer, and a wad of printed pages with blue arrows and scribblings.

'That's what I ought to be working on,' she said, as if

apologising for any subsequent inadequacies as a tutor. 'I don't know why I let Matt talk me into this.'

'But why should you have come as a student? You obviously don't need any tuition!'

'I wanted to master this in peace,' she began, patting the computer. 'It's time I gave up my quill pen. And it's also a sort of touching wood. It was Matt who really set me on the way, and I always show him work for criticism and advice. I'm working on a novel now and I know there's something wrong and I know he'll sort it out for me.'

'He seems very nice,' I said neutrally.

'His whole family is. His wife and both their children.'

Her tone too was carefully neutral. We both knew a question had been asked and answered. What I didn't know was how truthfully. Nor that it was any of my business anyway. Courtney was my business, though, and I still couldn't think of a way to broach the topic tactfully.

'Do you know any of the students on the course?' I asked.

'Two, actually. People from my past. The long arm of coincidence, I suppose.'

'One of them – Kate, this is none of my business but he isn't very happy to see you. I thought I ought to –'

'Neither of them is.' Her smile was grim but established her discretion. Not a word would she speak even to her fellow singer. Then, rather to my surprise, she added: 'Men! At least I knew Sidney was a rat before I bought him.'

'Funny, isn't it?' I agreed. 'The nicest, kindest man I knew got killed. Murdered by mistake. Everyone loved him and yet –' Appalled, I felt my voice break. 'George,' I continued. 'My friend George . . .'

She passed me a tissue. 'It's all right.'

'And that's what I want to write about. George.'

We talked quietly for several minutes about how I might tackle such a mammoth task. We agreed at last that a poem might fit the bill. Long or short. Rhyme or free verse.

'Now all you have to do is go away and write it,' said Kate kindly. 'Look, the sun's coming out. Get into the fresh air – have a walk. It really does seem to help people think.'

And the session was over.

* * *

All I could think of was a cup of tea. I headed for the kitchen to find it full of amateur cooks. I got grudging permission to boil the kettle.

In the lounge I found one of the grey ladies. Agnes, I think. I was to be in her team to cook Wednesday's supper. She wanted to convene a meeting for the following morning to discuss the menu. I agreed.

'What I'd really like to do,' she said, 'is shock the lot of them. Did you ever see such a collection? I've been on a course like this every year as long as I can remember, but I've never met people harder to get on with. That Mr Woodhouse: do you know how many times he's nagged that sweet Shazia about damp bedclothes? And that awful Nyree: man-mad. Old enough to know better. And that girl who says she's going to be a publisher – did you ever see anything like those skirts of hers? With her legs, too. That coloured man – black, I suppose I should say, though of course he isn't – he's nice enough, and I'm glad you've made friends with him. He's a bit out of it, isn't he? But he did talk to me about his project for this week, and it seems very interesting. Have you started anything?'

I shook my head. 'Not quite. But I thought I'd like to write about a friend. He – he died, you see.'

She looked at me hard, then started to talk about a story she was planning. It too was to involve death. In this case her own.

Apparently she'd had a heart attack after routine surgery. 'Very irritating it was, too. There I was, expecting to be in and out in two days, and they kept me in three weeks. It meant I missed a test match. The Lord's test, too!'

I'm happy to gossip cricket any day – my father played professionally for Durham and coached me for hours as if I'd been a boy – but just at the moment I wanted to hear more about her death.

'Oh, yes,' she chuckled. 'I died all right. Clinically. But whoever writes the script obviously decided I wasn't ready for my exit just yet, and so he started my heart again. With a little help from the medics. But there's nothing unusual about that. What is unusual, perhaps, is that I watched the whole thing happening.'

I listened. She talked. And then, quite abruptly, she declared she was a little tired and wanted a nap before supper. So I set off for the walk Kate had prescribed.

Eyre House has a long and impressive front drive, covered with a thin layer of tarmac. It leads, via several curves and many potholes, to an even more impressive set of front gates. Alas, however, the road they turn into is what the Ordnance Survey maps show as white – single-track and hardly used. You have to make an effort to find the place, in other words. My taxi driver had cursed the whole of the way. Yet the Japanese Brontë-lover had found it, and so, as I discovered, had another driver.

I'd been minding my own business, walking at a moderate pace, hoping to find a path round the perimeter wall. I'd stopped to look back at the house; it was good to stand with the sun on my back – the weather had changed dramatically at about three and might well stay fine till five. I was wearing a T-shirt and lightweight jeans. If I could find a cowpat-free patch of grass, I might lie down for ten minutes and soak up some sun.

But then I felt – knew – I was not alone.

I turned casually. It would be natural to look from the house to its gates.

A large red car was parked across the gateway. A man in it; just one, as far as I could see. Not looking at a map or anything; looking down the drive. Then he put the car into gear and pulled away. A BMW, 7 Series, by the look of it. And as a cloud covered the sun and turned me for home, I wondered why the driver of such a car might want to pick his way through a narrow lane hedged with prehensile brambles to look at the distant façade of an undistinguished house. And I spent so much time puzzling that I forgot to work on George's poem. As punishment I denied myself a cup of tea and locked myself in my little hutch to stare at a blank sheet of paper.

I sat so long that supper came as a positive relief. We gathered in the dining room wondering if we were supposed to sit where we'd sat last night, but I decided to link up with Agnes, and Courtney rapidly escaped from Nyree to join us.

We speculated in under-voices about the menu. I suggested we might get sausages in batter, Toad being one of the cooks. Agnes giggled like a thirteen-year-old.

But I was ashamed when the food did appear. The team had produced an imaginative antipasto, followed by spaghetti and two sorts of sauce – traditional Bolognese and a spicy vegetarian one. Then the *pièce de résistance*.

Toad's chocolate creation – to call it a mere pudding would be to underrate it – was ambrosia. No, that would be to confuse it with something out of a tin. Manna, then. There was this wonderful crunchy topping of amaretti biscuits mixed with the darkest, bitterest continental chocolate you can imagine. Then, when you thought nothing could be more blissful, you found the chilled, sweet, creamy chocolate and rum interior.

'People have murdered for less,' whispered Agnes.

We ate in silence. Then the plate came round again. I helped myself and, in a belated effort to establish better relations with Gimson, offered him the plate.

'Absolutely not,' he said, covering his plate with a well-manicured but oddly brutal hand. 'Lethal in at least ten different ways. Allow me to enumerate –'

'Oh, please don't!' Toad gulped. 'I never meant . . .'

Matt accepted another portion, but Kate declined, saying that chocolate gave her migraine.

'All the more for the rest of us,' said Courtney. 'I'm sure you'd like extra,' he said bravely to Nyree.

She managed to make each mouthful an erotic experience. Finally, with a little-girl widening of the eyes, she raised the whole plate to her mouth and started to lick.

But then, in the lounge, she became involved in an exchange with Matt. Although she should have been reeling with calories and wine – we'd started a kitty to buy a few bottles for supper each night – she wanted him to drive to the village and buy her more gin. He was scheduled to read aloud from his poems and short stories, he was saying. He clearly implied she'd had more than enough anyway.

'But Matt, darling, you know I need a drink. A real drink.' She put a scarlet fingertip on his throat, circling it round his Adam's apple. Then she tiptoed the first two fingers up to his beard. At last she hooked her little finger in lock of grey and tipped his chin towards her.

'Nyree! For goodness' sake!' he began, waving his hands as if to fend her off without having to touch her.

'Who said anything about goodness, sweetie?' She ran her spare hand down his side till it rested on his buttock. She pulled his hip towards her.

'Nyree!'

At this point, right in the middle of the lounge, she kissed him hard on the mouth. The little finger remained where it was. The other hand did not.

No one spoke; no one moved – embarrassment? Prurience? The sheer impossibility of doing anything remotely useful? Then Kate opened the door. She stopped on the threshold. Everyone looked at her.

'Ah, Nyree,' she said, 'are you going to share that whisky I bought for you this morning? I've organised glasses.'

Nyree abandoned Matt. She walked steadily, elegantly, to the door, which Gimson held open for her. I happened to look from her face to his. For the first time I understood that he might be a good doctor. Compassion, even tenderness, softened his mouth and eyes.

He didn't follow her. He quickly rearranged his features and claimed the only comfortable chair in the room.

We shuffled the rest into a circle, and begged Matt to start reading.

He read beautifully. We were all willing him to, of course, and relaxed as his voice grew in confidence and authority. But one or two of the older students fell unambiguously asleep, and I could not restrain my yawns. Neither, in the end, could Matt himself.

'That's it, folks,' he said. 'Sorry. And if you've any questions we'll save them till after coffee.'

Despite the second mug, I still felt somnolent, and had only a hazy idea of the discussion.

'But what is truth?' someone was asking.

Somehow they must have got on to the perennial discussion about the relationship between fact and fiction. Kate was arguing stoutly on the side of the writer's creativity.

Gimson insisted that fiction was only a regurgitation of what had happened in reality. Toad supported him, with more enthusiasm than intellectual rigour.

'Take Lawrence, for instance,' Gimson said. 'He seems to have a following among you – er, Brummies, is that the term? Local boy made good, I suppose.'

'He's from Nottingham, not Birmingham,' I said, but was ignored.

'He calls *Sons and Lovers* a novel, but it's pure autobiography.'

I couldn't be bothered to argue.

Then Nyree surprised me. 'Look at that Brontë woman,' she said. 'The one that Japanese man was talking about. Didn't she write that book of hers because of one of her neighbours? Married the governess while he'd still got a wife?'

Where could she have picked that up? And why had she cared enough to remember it? Tomorrow I would fight my way through the barricade of sex and personal dislike to find out more. But tonight I wanted more than anything to sleep.

Chapter Four

I fought my way up. I knew I wasn't really drowning, that I must be having a nightmare. But I couldn't explain why I was being shoved and buffeted by the otherwise calm water. Except, of course, it was a dream, and silly things happen in dreams. And then it wasn't a dream. The buffeting was someone shaking my shoulder. Someone who was yelling at me to wake up.

I made a final heave and came up shaking my head. It was Shazia, and she was calling my name, over and over. I pulled myself up on an elbow and blinked at her, fighting for breath. So I hadn't been drowning. Just fighting asthma. A couple of puffs of my inhaler and I'd live.

But I still couldn't make sense of it all. And then I could. Shazia was crying and pointing wildly. She thrust my dressing gown at me and ran out. I followed.

The door to the nice end room was open. Nyree's room. Shazia was calling me from inside.

A wave of alcohol hit me as I went in. I stepped back, it was so powerful. And then there was another smell. Vomit. My stomach rocked in sympathy. One curtain was half open. I pulled it back fully and opened the other, too. When I turned to the bed, I wished I hadn't. Nyree wouldn't have wanted anyone to see her like this. Not that at first sight there was much wrong. She might have been asleep. Her limbs lay apparently relaxed, and her eyes were closed. But her face was puffy, the fine bones almost hidden, and her skin was a reddish blue. And from the far corner of her mouth, slack and open, came a trickle of vomit.

'What shall we do?' Shazia was yelling.

'Get Gimson. And dial 999,' I said, knowing neither would help but not having any other ideas. And I retreated to the door: I couldn't stay closer to Nyree, but I couldn't leave her on her own.

Gimson came running; and he was alert and cool. He touched Nyree's neck, and then seemed nonplussed. He fumbled with the duvet.

'There's no sheet,' he said tersely, and pushed past me into the corridor.

At last I realised what he'd wanted to do.

'We'll use a clean towel,' I said, and covered Nyree's face.

The ambulance drove off. Someone switched off the flashing blue light. There was no need for haste, after all.

We stood there, sober in the grey morning light, the half-dozen who'd watched Nyree being taken away, and tried to find something to say.

Shazia was dithering; I put my arm loosely around her shoulders. 'We might as well get everyone in,' I said quietly. 'There's nothing we can do here, and we can't risk Agnes catching cold in this rain. I'll get the kettle on, while you have another go at waking Kate and Matt.'

'I don't like –' She stopped.

'OK, you do the tea. I'll roust them out.'

I could see why she should be reluctant. One room or two? I tried to work out a strategy to minimise embarrassment.

As it was, I need not to have worried. There was no reply from either room.

Gimson was talking to a policeman in his twenties when I came downstairs. I picked up the words 'inquest', 'post-mortem', 'alcohol poisoning'. Gimson spoke with cool authority; the constable listened with respect. Until he saw me.

'Were you wanting something, miss?'

'Not specially. I was interested because I found the body. Me and Shazia. We called Mr Gimson.'

'I dare say we shall want to talk to you later, miss.'

And so I was dismissed. I would go back to my own room and try to write.

My route did not, of course, take me past Nyree's room but I found myself going to it. The door stood wide open. No one was inside. But it occurred to me that if Nyree had died unnaturally – and that accorded with what Gimson thought – the room might contain useful information. Using my handkerchief in the best Agatha Christie tradition, I closed it. It would lock automatically, like all our doors, on the Yale lock. But I felt the constable had been careless, and made it my business – I wish I weren't always so damned officious – to stroll back and mention it. I would be as tactful as possible. I hate people telling me how to do my job, and I didn't want to put his back up. I need not have worried, however: his panda drove away even as I reached the front door. And then I was worried.

I went in search of Shazia. I found her coming down the stairs from her flat with an armful of bed linen.

'I thought I'd get the room straight as soon as I could,' she said.

'No! You've got to leave it as it is,' I said, and then wished I hadn't been so schoolmarmish. 'Evidence – there may be some evidence there. That's why I locked it.'

'But the smell – we ought to let some fresh air in. And the constable didn't say anything about evidence or anything.'

'I was friendly with a detective once. A rather senior one. He dinned it into me: never touch anything.'

'But there's no reason –'

'Just to put my mind at rest – please. Don't even go in there until I've phoned my friend.'

Shazia was plainly unhappy.

'In any case,' I said, groping for something persuasive, 'someone's got to decide whether the course should go on. And I'm afraid that someone's you.'

I watched her retrace her steps. A pillowcase slipped from the pile, and she had to pick it up. I made my way to the office and the telephone.

The last person I wanted to contact was the man I'd described as my friend. Not because I didn't like him; I did. But because he liked me, too much. We'd formed two sides of an eternal triangle in the spring, and I liked and respected him too much to want to stir up hopes I knew I couldn't fulfil.

I dialled and waited. I looked around: her office was neat and well organised. It put mine to shame. The plants grew, the calendar was up to date, the furniture newly dusted and the bin empty.

'West Midlands Police?'

'Can I speak to DCI Groom, please? Rose Road Police Station.'

'I'm afraid he's not available at the moment. Can anyone else help?'

'Sergeant Dale?'

But it was not Ian who answered. A voice from the heart of the Black Country spoke: 'DS Reed. Can I help you?'

'Tina! What's all this about Sergeant Reed?'

Tina and I had spent more time than either of us liked in each other's company in the spring, when she had been my minder. But although we came close to killing each other, closeted in the confines of my semi, we also became quite fond of each other in a guarded sort of way.

'Ah,' she began, 'got me promotion through at last. Imagine me sewing on all them stripes.'

'I can: I can still see you sewing all those curtains up in my spare room!'

'How's yourself, then, our Soph?'

I brought her up to date with my limited news.

'And did you know as how Chris is back from India?' she asked. I could hear the grin in her voice. 'Came back Sunday, he did.'

'He wrote and asked me to meet him,' I admitted. 'But I told him I'd be on this writing course. Wouldn't be able to get away.'

'Oh, ah,' she said, the syllables signifying profound disbelief. 'Any road, Ian Dale picked him up.'

'Does he get any leave so he can get over his jet lag?'

'Shouldn't think so. He said as how he wanted to have a couple of weeks' holiday there, when he'd finished with Delhi. Be a tourist, like.'

'Good for him.' Better than a week at Eyre House failing to learn how to write. 'So will he be taking on this case?'

'What case?'

'Sorry: I've got everything out of order. I'm on a residential writing course. Right? Out at Eyre Park.'

'Back of beyond, that.'

'Yes. Not very exciting. But one of my fellow students has just died, and the local police are very – relaxed about it.'

'Any reason for them not to be?' Her voice was suddenly alert.

'She wasn't old. She didn't threaten suicide. A doctor here reckons it's alcohol poisoning.'

'Well, then.'

'But so many people here hated her. I've just got a feeling.'

'Feeling, my aunt Fanny! Soph, haven't you got nothing to go on?'

'Nothing at all. I'd love to be proved wrong.'

'OK. Tell me what our people have done so far.'

'Nothing. The ambulance people took the woman away and then a kid in a panda turned up and went away again. Leaving her room open to the four winds. I just stopped the administrator here from giving the room a thorough clean.'

'Jesus. OK. Seeing as how I know you, I'll have a word with Chris, shall I?'

She expected me to back down – she'd seen my efforts not to get emotionally involved with him.

'Great,' I said brazenly. 'Do that.'

Shazia was in the kitchen, making coffee for everyone who was up. There was some sort of emergency get-together in the lounge, and I ought to have been there. But I couldn't face the questions they'd want to ask, questions I'd want to ask in their situation, and I drifted out on the terrace. It had stopped raining, and I wanted some fresh air to clear my still foggy brain.

If I sat down on an inviting bench I might even go to sleep. It had been a real effort to respond to Shazia's frantic summons. Normally I'm up and working at raising my level in the Canadian Air Force Exercises by seven-thirty. How I should have slept through till nine, goodness knows. Every movement was still almost as much an effort as it was to think. And why had Shazia come to me? Ah, because she couldn't wake Kate, and she wouldn't want to alarm Agnes or her friends. Why me when Gimson was the logical choice?

Perhaps Shazia wouldn't be able to think of a rational answer either.

Where should I meet Chris? How should I speak to him? I really do like the man. Like. I'm fond of him. Fond enough not to want to cause him pain. Because what he felt for me last time we met wasn't liking, but love.

I thought I'd rather meet him among other people. That way there'd be no opportunity for personal displays from either of us. A hug, a kiss, can't be neutral. Not in our circumstances.

It was time to return to the house. It was unfair of me to leave Shazia to deal with all the problems of breaking the news and deciding how much of the show would go on. But Shazia had Matt and Kate to call on. I was only a student, not a responsible, reliable member of staff. Not here. At college, maybe, but not here.

I took the long way back into the house – along the terrace, on to the gravel path at the side, and then via the drive. Through the umbilical corridor. Over the top, Sophie, I told myself grimly.

In the corridor outside the lounge the two girls were in half-resentful tears. They had each other. I looked into the library; the science-fiction student might never have heard of sudden death. One of the ladies – we still hadn't sorted out the menu for tomorrow, of course – was hurrying downstairs with an asthma spray like mine.

'I've got Thea to lie down,' she said over her shoulder. 'This is for Agnes.'

Time for you to be responsible, Sophie.

Then I heard the door from reception whoosh. Without thinking, I turned back. If I could deal with any problem without bothering Shazia I might as well.

This visitor was oriental, but not Japanese.

I'm not very good on racial types. Japanese people I'm generally OK with, and I even have a misleading amount of the language. I can greet people convincingly and I can call in a rabbit and swear when it messes the carpet, a form of specialised communication which would have been no use at all in yesterday's encounter with Brontë-man. This is a result of a live-in relationship with an angora rabbit and his associate, a serious-minded man called Kenji, now long departed to write a doctorate on the dietary habits of sumo wrestlers.

I smiled at our visitor. He nodded.

'I want to see Mrs Compton immediately,' he said, in accented but excellent English.

'Mrs Compton?' Who the hell was that? It'd been first-name terms all round, hadn't it? And it seemed a long time since I'd typed that list.

'Now.'

This was clearly a job for Shazia. I'd still no idea who Mrs Compton might be.

I produced a smile my dentist's receptionist would have been proud of. 'If you'd care to wait here, sir, I'll see what I can do.'

He started to follow me.

'Would you be kind enough to wait here, please.'

He continued to follow me.

I stopped; he tried to push past.

'I will go and ask Mrs Compton if she wishes to see you. Wait here, please.' This was the formula – and the frigid tone – I use with unwelcome visitors at college. I'd at last placed the name. Mrs Compton was Nyree.

He tried to push past again. Then he heard the sounds of feet on gravel, turned and, with all the doors whooshing in sympathy, dashed through the front door, colliding violently with the new arrival as he did so.

So Chris Groom and I were absolutely alone for our first meeting for five months.

I had the advantage of him; I'd seen him first, spinning on his heel to yell at our departing visitor. I'd taken in how thin he was, how the sun had dried his skin into a dull red with no hint of a tan. There was the start of a stoop about his neck and shoulders that might have been fatigue but was more likely in his case to be stress.

Then he saw me: heavy-eyed, certainly. And Shazia had been so distressed when she woke me I'd had no time to apply make-up or brush my hair. The T-shirt and jeans he'd expect.

I wonder how much he noticed after all. Perhaps he was

too busy controlling his own face to see anything wrong with mine.

'Hi,' I said, too brightly, as he stood irresolute on the threshold. 'Come along and have a cup of coffee and I'll tell you all about our murder.'

At last, however, he managed to gather the shreds of protocol, and he said, his voice almost under control: 'I think I ought to talk to the administrator first. And, of course, you realise the officer who came earlier thinks you're wrong.'

I smiled. 'I hope I am wrong, Chris. Because if Nyree has been murdered, I might be one of the suspects.'

I would use that as my exit line; it was time to fetch Shazia. I did no more than put my head round the lounge door to summon her. Then I introduced them briefly and watched them retire to her office. One of them shut the door quite firmly.

Duty called me back to the lounge. I'd have to face them sooner or later. I slipped in quietly. And my ploy worked. I had ten uncomfortable minutes not enduring their questions, as I'd feared, but listening to their complaints about Kate and Matt. And I began to feel that they might after all have some justification. Now Shazia was no longer in the room to support them, they needed someone with some authority. Not me, as I reminded myself again. At least I had enough initiative to do something. Maybe if I rousted them out before an official deputation demanded they get up and teach, I'd defuse the situation. So I slipped out as quietly as I'd gone in, and headed for the staff corridor.

As I crossed the hall I nearly collided with Matt, hurtling down the stairs.

'Where's Kate?' he demanded.

'Still asleep, I suppose,' I said. 'Matt, there's been –'

'No, she isn't. I've just checked her room.'

'But it was locked.'

'Still is, for all I know.'

'Then how –'

'The bathroom doors connect, and no one's got round to finding a key. Found that out a couple of courses ago when I locked myself out. That was before Shazia's time, of course – I can't imagine ever having to tell her anything twice. Ah, here she is. Shazia, my love, I have something to confess!'

Shazia was plainly concerned; but then she remembered something of much greater importance.

I wondered if they both realised that Chris, from the office door, was listening and watching.

'Matt,' she began, 'something terrible has happened. To Nyree.'

'Got the DTs, has she? Delirium tremens,' he added, as if Shazia might not understand the term. 'Serve her bloody right.'

'Nyree's dead, Matt,' I said quickly. 'Shazia couldn't wake her this morning.'

He stared at me and rubbed his hands over his face. 'None of this is making sense,' he said at last. 'I need a coffee. Then perhaps you can start at the beginning and tell me what's happening.'

Chris stepped forward, nodding at Matt without apparent interest. Matt might have been deceived. I introduced them briefly. Neither seemed much impressed by the other.

For some reason I led Chris not to my room but into the grounds. We soon found a bench where no one could overhear us. Perhaps it was the sun, now quite warm, but I couldn't stop yawning; I felt as if I'd had a heavy night of it, but I counted back and couldn't total more than a glass of wine and half a finger of Nyree's cherished scotch. You wouldn't call the air here relaxing, as if it were some genteel spa. It wasn't any different from the air I always breathe, down the road in Harborne.

Chris too seemed subdued.

'Jet lag,' he said briefly when I showed concern. And then he half turned to me as if he were imparting bad news. 'I really do think you're overreacting, Sophie. I've spoken to young Speller, who's nobody's fool.'

'The PC, you mean?'

He nodded. 'And then I had a word directly with Gimson. He struck me as the sort of man who might say one thing to a woman and something slightly different to a man.'

I beamed; this sort of distinction had seemed beyond Chris's range when we first met, and I wondered if my influence had made him think more subtly. I hoped so.

'Overreacting?' I repeated, though with undue fire.

'After the spring. Trauma of the sort you experienced must take its toll one way or another. For you even to consider coming on a course like this –'

'Like what, Chris?'

'You know – poetry, writing . . . I wouldn't have associated you with anything like it.'

'Please, DCI Groom, sir, I teach English. For my living.'

'But it's not the same as writing it,' he said.

And again I was surprised by his perceptiveness. I might shock him by agreeing for once.

'You're right, Chris. But to get back to our *moutons*, Nyree does seem to have attracted a lot of attention from us students and from outsiders. And I'm alarmed at some level I can't make sense of that no one knows where Kate is.'

'So you think Kate might have killed her and run?' he said. The serious tone was belied by the crow's-feet of amusement he couldn't conceal.

'No. She'd have run in her car, surely, and it's still in the car park. Are you going to take it away for forensic examination?'

'Not until we have grounds to believe a crime's been committed. Or should we be alerting all forces to look for a serial killer?'

I wished he'd try to be serious. Or perhaps he was. 'No. I don't know. God, I hope not. Jesus, Chris –'

'Slow down. I was joking. Tell me, why did that Asian woman – what's her name?'

'Shazia.'

'Why did she call you?'

'No idea. I don't even know why she went into Nyree's room in the first place – do you?'

'To call her to the phone,' he said briefly. He probably shouldn't have told me.

'Chris, she must have acquired enemies like other people attract mosquitoes. Please, don't just assume it was an accident.'

He looked at me, holding my gaze for longer than I found comfortable. 'OK. There has to be a PM. I'll get them to prioritise her. Get the results through quickly.'

He was doing it to indulge me, not because he believed it was necessary. Today it was easier to let him.

'And, just to be on the safe side, mind, I'll get the room sealed. So if necessary the SOCO –'

'Sorry?'

'Scene-of-crime officer, Ms Rivers. So he can have a ferret-round if necessary.'

He grinned and got up. We walked to his car in silence.

'What will you do for the rest of the day?' he asked at last, as he slipped the key into the ignition.

'Go back to my room and try to write,' I said. 'And pray the shock's unblocked me!'

Although lunchtime took a long time to arrive, when we gathered in the dining room people were able to talk with remarkable verve. Some played the *nil nisi bonum* game, but there was a good deal of enthusiastic bitching going on too. Normally I would have joined in gladly, but it was dawning on me that Nyree could not have been a happy woman, and that I had made very little effort to stop her drinking – except, of course, to help share her booze. The other thing that worried me was Kate's continued absence.

My usual means of restoring brainpower is to go for a jog. Perhaps it would work today.

Naukez would no doubt have been the best person to ask about good routes, but he was nowhere to be seen, and I hesitated to disturb him in the staff flat. But Shazia was in the kitchen, and I asked her instead.

'Oh, dear – I'm hopeless at giving directions. Got a piece of paper?'

As a nonwriter, I had no notepad tucked in my pocket. In desperation she reached down the kitchen blackboard. Really it's there for people to jot down items that are running out, but she wiped it clean and sketched out a possible route for me.

'That bit's a bit steep,' she said. 'And that part's quite exposed.'

I thanked her and went off to change.

I thought of Toad and chose not my running vest and shorts but a tracksuit. In any case the wind justified it. It was whipping my hair quite fiercely into my eyes. I stopped; there was bound to be a rubber band in my trouser pocket.

Someone else stopped too.

No. I was imagining it. Surely?

I took an unconscionable time to fish out the band and loop my hair through it, but no one moved.

I started again.

There was a well-defined track from the house, through scrubland, to the far end of the park. Then, beyond the motorway, were some old pit mounds.

The twig that snapped was not one I'd trodden on.

I pretended my lace had come untied: I knelt, waiting for someone to come close, poised to bolt if I had to.

Two magpies flew up, cackling. Two for joy. I pressed on.

It was easy running. There was enough of an undulation to make it interesting, but no fierce gradients. The surface was good, too, with no vicious roots lurking to ensnare the unwary. I padded on, perfectly at peace for the first time since I'd arrived. The scientists say it's all to do with the chemicals you release in your brain by hitting your feet on the ground. Endomorphs? Endorphins? Pheromones? No, one of those is the name for the smell that attracts mates.

The sound of the motorway was becoming obtrusive. If I could I would turn away. There was nothing down there anyway but some derelict buildings, according to Shazia. I found a narrow track which would take me through the woods. I would have to slow right down but it was better than all that noise. Not that the woods were silent, of course. The birds were busy telling all the others to keep off their patch. Some blackbirds were excavating the undergrowth. An untimely owl hunched on a tree stump.

And someone was watching me again.

I stopped, and scanned a hundred and eighty degrees.

A shadow moved. A twig snapped. Then there was a definite rustle, but the sound might be moving away from me.

For a moment I wanted to chase whoever it was. No. Much more sensible to head in the opposite direction. I told myself I was there to write, that the sole purpose of my run was to clear my brain so I could write, and that I was heading back to base to write.

For once I listened to myself.

I took a path to the right and accelerated. Anyone wanting to catch me would have to be pretty fit. I lengthened my stride. The breaths came easily. Another three hundred yards and I'd be in sight of the house.

Practically.

Thirty yards away a figure emerged from the shadows. The ground shelved sharply to my left and I hadn't noticed him there. I realised, as my feet carried me closer and closer, that I couldn't reproach myself for not spotting him before. In his camouflage jacket and muddy jeans, Naukez was practically invisible.

He stared at me as I slowed to a halt. 'Wrong time of day,' he said, 'for the badgers.'

'I'm just going back to the house.'

'Ah. That's OK then. Wouldn't want anything to disturb them.'

We nodded at each other. I set off gently – he wasn't going to know how much he'd rattled me. But I could feel his eyes on my back the whole way.

The first person I saw when I'd showered and pottered along to make a cup of tea before trying – again – to write, was Matt.

He was staring at the kettle as if willing it to boil. I reached across him and flicked on the switch.

'She's still missing,' he said. 'All they do is rabbit on about that stupid bitch Nyree, and I can't get them to listen. A woman like Kate doesn't go walkabout, Sophie – does she?'

'Is that what Chris – the policeman – is saying?'

'You know he buggered off hours ago. Nothing to do till they get the PM report on Nyree, he says. And it's twenty-four hours before they consider someone missing. That's a long time, Sophie.'

I made the tea.

'Is anything missing from her room?'

'How should I know?'

'Just wondered. And – Christ, Matt, has anyone fed Sidney?'

'Sidney? Oh, the rodent. Never thought. Come on, bring your tea and we'll go and see.'

'You're not keen on rats,' I observed as we went upstairs.

'It's their tails. Don't mind their front ends, and I quite like their starry little feet, but it's their tails. Come on, we'll go through my room.'

The tutors' rooms were impressive, now I had time to look round. There was a study-bedroom, larger than an average bed-sit and comfortably furnished. Then there was a private bathroom, luxurious with mahogany and brass, with a dense carpet and a proliferation of towels.

Then Kate's bathroom, a mirror image of Matt's, and into Kate's room.

Sidney's cage was empty.

Matt groaned. 'Why didn't I think of that before? The bloody animal's got out and she's looking for it!'

That seemed to be the logical explanation; I wanted to accept it. But I couldn't stop asking myself: 'Why didn't she leave a note – ask us to keep an eye open for him? And surely she'd have been back by now?'

'She may have lost track of the time.'

'She must have left before the Nyree business. It's – what? – three twenty now. That's a long time to be hunting a rat with no help.'

'So you think she might have gone looking and been taken ill?'

'I wish I knew what to think, Matt. My brain's still fuzzy; I thought running would help but –'

In my mind's eye I suddenly saw Naukez, heard the invisible presence in the woods.

'I think we should talk to Chris Groom again,' I said.

Chapter Five

Although I knew it would be impossible, I tried to make myself write for what little remained of the afternoon. I sat in my room and stared and doodled and achieved not even a kind memory of George. Eventually I gave up and went in search of strong coffee. The kitchen was full, of course: I made myself scarce as soon as I could. But I didn't want to go back to the silence and the unyielding pen and pad. I went out on the terrace again, to find Shazia with a watering can and a grim expression, staring at Toad's back.

`And when I want your advice I'll ask for it,' she muttered.

After a moment she started moving regularly across the paving stones. I decided not to make a joke about weedkiller. Instead, without preamble, I launched into my worries about Kate.

Shazia agreed with me: Kate was simply not the sort of woman to go off for such a long time without telling anyone. As soon as Chris returned – he'd left a message with her saying he'd be back by seven – I should talk to him, she said. With or without her and Matt in support. I was to decide.

I retired to a bench in the watery sun to think. Somehow. I still felt hazy, as if I were missing on one of my cylinders. It would be terribly easy to drowse off, even now.

But something was executing a tap-dance on my left foot. I made my eyes focus downwards. Sidney!

I looked around hopefully: maybe Kate was somewhere in view. She was not.

Sidney continued to tap.

His fur was sodden, and lay in dark feathers across his

flanks. He must have been burrowing through the wilder parts of the estate – there were bits of grass and a couple of dandelion petals garnishing his head.

Now it came to it, I wasn't sure how I felt about picking up a rat. How would the rat feel about being picked up by me? He was even less sure than I was, and struggled. There must be quite a lot of muscle to struggle with, and rats come equipped with needle teeth. But clearly I had to return him to the safety of his cage. I pressed him to my chest.

He struggled more purposefully. Then he slipped clear. But instead of diving to freedom, he clawed up my shoulder and on to my neck, where he lay, heavy, warm and wet. Presumably this was what rats considered first-class travel.

I simply walked into Kate's room via Matt's, which happened to be empty and unlocked. But there was no food around, apart from a sprinkling around the edge of the room, a giant parabola of brightly coloured confetti. The packet of digestive biscuits had gone from Kate's table too. I thrust the rat with some loss of his dignity into the cage, balanced the litter tray on top, and retreated to my own room, where it would be easier to keep an eye on him. Food? A rapid raid on the kitchen produced cheese, the heel of a granary loaf, an apple. The biscuit barrel was empty.

Sidney eyed the apple and cheese with disdain. It was a good job I'd thought of the bread. Plainly there was more to rodents than I'd realised.

I nibbled the cheese and apple myself, and started to feel better.

Chris had made his own plans for the evening meeting. He'd asked Shazia, Matt and me to join him in the staff flat above the rabbit-hutches, then he wanted everyone together after supper so he could make a general announcement.

Shazia welcomed us politely and showed us into her living room. The room contained a genial mixture of Impressionist prints and Islamic art. There were a number of holy texts in Arabic lettering; Shazia followed my gaze and said quietly, 'Yes, we made the hajj two years ago.'

I was impressed – they were very young to have made the expensive pilgrimage.

Chris gestured at the dining table: it might be more businesslike to sit there.

'The pathologist's report,' he began, in his official voice, 'confirms that Mrs Compton –'

'Nyree?' asked Matt.

'Mrs Nyree Compton died of a mixture of alcohol and barbiturates,' Chris finished. 'Specifically, as you saw, she choked on her own vomit.'

'So it's what we thought,' said Shazia, visibly relaxing. 'We all warned her about her drinking.'

Or thought about it. I'd never spoken aloud.

'Stupid woman,' said Matt.

'Or a very sad one,' I said.

'Oh, there's no suicide note,' said Chris. 'Don't think we didn't check,' he added smugly.

'Her whole life was probably a suicide note,' I said, thinking of the Stevie Smith poem about drowning. 'You can't behave like that if you're happy,' I continued. 'I wish I'd made an effort. I just let her make me mad. If I'd tried –'

Chris looked at me sharply. 'Any particular reason? For you to be mad with her?'

'She was unkind.' I stopped. I didn't want to tell him about Nyree's ogling Shazia's husband. Nor did I want to introduce my cousin Andy at this stage of the conversation. 'I might be unkind myself at times, but I don't really like unkind people.'

'I think you're very kind,' Chris said, 'for all you pretend to be waspish.'

'I am waspish. I'm waspish because I should have found other ways of dealing with my irritation. I could have hidden her sleeping tablets, rationed them or whatever.'

Then we remembered we had an audience. Chris coughed slightly and resumed his official voice: 'The pathologist reports she took round about the standard dose. So you probably wouldn't have done any good if you had tried to interfere.'

'She wouldn't have thanked you for trying,' said Matt.

I tried to imagine myself acting as night nurse, doling out a pill at a time. And failed. I tried to imagine Nyree being sober enough to shake just one tablet out of a bottle. And failed. She'd have dropped them all over the floor and had to scrabble for them. There might even be a couple under the bed for the police to pick up.

'Are you all right?' asked Shazia.

'Yes. No. I was just wondering what would have happened to Sidney if he'd chanced on one.' And I remembered with a flush of guilt I'd told no one about the rat's recent adventures. Now was certainly not the time. I'd waylay Chris later.

'They'd come in a bubble pack,' said Chris, dismissively. So I caught his eye, to be rewarded with a long, slow flush. His expression changed from complacency to pure panic, taking in horror on the way. Chris had not yet seen the tablets, had he?

Which meant, of course, they hadn't been in Nyree's room.

I let him talk on: he had no objection on the course continuing –

'Well, I bloody have,' said Matt. 'How can the course bloody continue when one of the tutors has gone missing and you lot aren't even interested?'

Chris's expression was opaque. So they were interested, but he wasn't admitting how. I would probe a little.

But Matt pre-empted me.

'She leaves her room without telling anyone, is missing all day – bugger it, it's time we had a search party out for her. She may be lying out there sick or injured, and all we do is talk about Nyree and her angst. And whether the course will go on. Do something about Kate and then I'll talk about the course!'

He pushed away from the table. We heard him slam out of the flat and could follow his footfall until the sound insulation mopped it up.

It was better not to remark on it. We smiled our thanks to Shazia and left.

'We have to talk, Chris,' I said, as we reached my corridor.

'Later.'

'Now. There are things you need to know to help you make your decisions. Apart from finding those tablets you assumed were hers – you could get one of your underlings to check for that, surely?'

He flushed. 'I've had the room sealed to preserve the scene. Anything in there will turn up.'

We walked past my room to Nyree's. Beyond the police tape, the door was open. Someone had put boards down on the floor. I pointed at them. 'What on earth?'

'So people don't have to walk on the carpet, of course. With modern technology we can actually lift footprints off carpets. If,' he added, grinning like a naughty schoolboy, 'they haven't been hoovered off first.'

It was the nearest he'd get to thanking me.

He spoke to a plain-clothes officer with a video camera; she nodded – she'd look for the tablets at once, she said, beaming winsomely. Chris rewarded her with a very warm smile. She blushed.

We went back towards my room.

'OK, what do you want to talk about?'

I opened the bedroom door and pointed at Sidney.

'That, for starters,' I said.

Chapter Six

I settled Chris in the only chair. I sat on a pillow on the floor. I didn't like having to look up at him, but preferred it to the alternative – sitting on the bed. Before we could began talking, Sidney started to pound up and down his cage, which I took – rightly – as demand for his litter tray. He then settled down to consume with rather unpleasant enthusiasm another bit of bread.

Chris watched the whole procedure with distaste. 'How long have you had that?' he asked, getting up and ostentatiously opening the window.

'Since four this afternoon. Chris: this is Sidney. Sidney: Chris.'

'What on earth possessed you –?'

'He did. He possessed me. He's Kate's. He went missing and came and found me. Since there's no sign of Kate, I thought he'd be safer here. What are you going to do about Kate?'

'Nothing. Not yet.'

'She's been gone twelve hours. Her rat was wandering around –'

'She probably went looking for it.'

'Him. And then –? She's a professional woman, Chris. Here doing a job for which she'd get paid. She wouldn't bunk off without letting at least Matt know what she was up to.'

'Hmm.'

'Do you intend to wait till something nasty happens to another woman? There are a lot of us on this course for someone to choose from.'

He shook his head. Kindly. I could have hit him.

'Tell you what,' he said at last, 'if she doesn't turn up for supper, I'll reconsider. And I'll have a word with everyone after you've eaten. Put them in the picture.'

He got up to go, weariness in every movement. Even his smile was tired. I wished I could suggest we had a drink together. But there was no bar, he had work to do, and I had to face the others at supper. I followed him out of the room.

Supper was a silent and unappetising affair. Mr Woodhouse had been teamed with the aspiring publisher and Jean, the third grey lady. Her menu reflected her experience as a school dinner lady in the days when they'd had them: cottage pie, diced carrot and mashed potato. Toad, who was improving the shining hour with a buttercup yellow T-shirt bearing a bilious green message that fur looked better on animals, left the meat in a greyish ring round the edge of his plate. I had to draw myself up short. Mostly I avoid red meat, and I wouldn't dream of wearing fur; why should I find his behaviour objectionable? Perhaps it was his air of complacent ostentation that irritated me. Certainly it annoyed Gimson, who stared testily at him and seemed only to be searching for an opportunity to say something truly scathing.

Rice pudding followed. Not, I'll admit, your average school pud: she'd used golden syrup to sweeten it. Matt, despite his testy anxiety, scraped and ate the crusty bits from round the top. Toad and he had tossed for the golden-brown skin; Toad had won. Courtney did no more than push his food from side to side of his plate. He'd tied back his hair in a fashionable if miniscule pony-tail, but the style made him look not trendy but gaunt. I kept thinking about Chris. I wanted to talk about his experiences in India before he could bury them in the matchless police prose of the report he'd no doubt have to write. But all I'd done was talk about Nyree and Kate. At least the gloom on my face would match that on the others'.

Would Chris make a grand entrance into the lounge after supper, or would he simply stand there waiting for us? I favoured the more theatrical option; so, it transpired, did he. His style was so good, one or two people started to their feet like punctilious third-formers. I caught his eye in approval. But I was sure the slight grin he flashed me included guilt.

He didn't need a cough, portentous or otherwise, to gain our attention.

'I know that in a group like this rumours gather and spread like colds,' he began, with a smile to fetch the ducks off the water. 'So I thought you all ought to know what few facts we've gathered. And if anyone has anything they think I ought to know, perhaps they'd reciprocate.

'First, as you all know, Mrs Compton – Nyree – died this morning. Mr Gimson examined her as soon as Shazia found her. That was at about nine. There was nothing anyone could have done. She'd been dead several hours by then. The cause of death was alcohol plus barbiturates.'

Gimson, who had been casually inspecting his nails, was galvanised. 'I beg your pardon?'

'Barbiturates.'

'Sleeping tablets,' Jean explained kindly.

'As I said, she was a stupid woman,' said Matt.

'Anything special to look at?' asked Thea.

'Tiny little white ones. My aunt used to take them,' Jean said. 'We found whole bottles full of them when she died. Ever so careless, her doctor. Oh, no offence, Mr Gimson, please – I didn't mean . . .'

Gimson permitted himself a frosty smile.

'Bottles?' I repeated. 'I thought,' I pursued, not looking at Chris, 'that drugs tended to come in bubble packs, these days.'

'Those are still dispensed loose,' said Gimson, apparently bored again.

'And, unfortunately, we haven't yet found any trace of a pill bottle in her effects,' Chris confessed, studiously avoiding my eye.

'Have you looked in the bathrooms?' asked Mr Woodhouse. 'I'm always leaving things behind in these bathrooms. And you never remember until someone else is in there.'

'How typical of the woman to leave dangerous drugs around,' said Agnes. 'To take them to the bathroom and be so – so –'

'– drunk,' Matt supplied.
'– she forgot to pick them up.'
'Quite,' said Chris.
'And a couple of times I've picked up someone else's toothpaste,' Woodhouse continued. 'D'you suppose someone might have picked up these pills of hers?'
'That's a distinct possibility, sir,' said Chris, as sincerely as if the idea were new to him. 'Maybe you'd all be kind enough to check when you return to your rooms. And if you find anything in your spongebags or whatever that doesn't belong there, perhaps you'd be kind enough to tell one of my colleagues. One or two of them will be on duty here all night.'
'What about Kate, for Christ's sake? There's that lovely woman who might be lying sick or injured anywhere in the grounds. Damn it, her computer's still plugged in – she can't have meant to go anywhere for long. And all you do is rabbit on about some obnoxious gossip-mongering nymphomaniac lush's dentures!'
'Dentures?' wailed Toad. 'Nyree wouldn't – she didn't . . .'
'Of course, not,' I said briskly. 'Matt's joking.'
'*Joking*, when she's –' Toad broke off, covering his face and lurching from the room.
After a moment, Shazia followed. So did a policeman, who'd been barely visible through a crack in the door.
There was an embarrassed silence.
Chris broke it. 'As far as Ms Freeman is concerned,' he said, not looking at me, 'a search of the house and grounds is taking place at this moment.'
'What about that dear little animal of hers?' asked Jean.
'I'm looking after him,' I said, wondering whether she was being brave or hypocritical.
'Will you be setting up a what-do-you-call-it?' asked Mr Woodhouse. 'Like they do on TV? You know, with all the computers and polythene sheets round the body.'
'An incident room,' Jean said. 'But they've taken the body away.'
'Unless they find Kate's,' said Mr Woodhouse.
'These days of excellent communications we tend not to

need an on-the-spot incident room,' said Chris. 'Rose Road Police Station is the place where I have my office, and they're geared up for everything we should need. But I may ask if we could use somewhere as a base – cups of tea, taking statements and so on.'

'The stable block? That's self-contained,' said Matt.

'But that's where I like to write,' said Mr Woodhouse. 'All the sounds of nature so close. So inspiring.'

'Perhaps you could move to the conservatory,' said Matt.

'If that's OK, then, that's where we'll set up our control point. So you'll all know where to find us if you need us. Thank you, ladies and gentlemen. I hope you'll be able to get on with your writing and won't find this unpleasant business too obtrusive. Oh,' he said, as if he'd genuinely forgotten, 'one small thing. We shall have to speak to each of you and ask you to make short statements. Just a formality. One or two of you might like to get it out of the way now, and my colleagues and I are ready to help. Shazia suggested we use the library for this evening. Tomorrow you'll find us in the stables. Thank you all. Good evening.'

I fell quite casually into step with Chris as he left the lounge, and we walked amicably to my room. Chris strode straight to the window, which I'd closed before supper.

'I just didn't want any surprise visitors,' I said apologetically, as he opened it to its maximum.

'A child of three couldn't get through that,' he replied. 'And I'm sure you've no need to worry. Not this time.'

He smiled.

If only I could have responded by walking into his arms! I smiled back, sadly. He sat down on the foot of the bed, this time. I took the chair.

'If no one hands in the bottle of pills, what then?'

'I search. With or without a warrant. You don't expect anyone to produce them?'

'Do you?' I shrugged. 'Why did Gimson prick up his ears when you mentioned barbiturate?'

'I thought you'd notice. Thanks for not asking.'

His smile was sadder than mine; I would have to move into bracing mode.

'Come on, Chris, you've got me better trained than that.

All that undercover work we did together! Tell you what, you couldn't find an excuse for us to go undercover at the Music Centre again? I'm finding this place quite claustrophobic. And I've not written a single word yet.'

'Did you expect to?'

'I thought I'd try. When in Rome, you know. Anyway, these 'ere tablets – what's wrong with them? Why did Gimson leap to life?'

'Because they're unusual these days. Most doctors prescribe drugs without such drastic side effects: diazepam-related ones, usually.'

'But they can have side effects!' I'd once had a week on some. 'They can give you unimaginable nightmares.'

'Unpleasant side effects, true. But not as fatal as those Nyree experienced.'

'OK. So why did she take them?'

'I'm trying to locate her GP now. But she's been all over the world, according to her passport. She could have picked them up anywhere. God, Sophie, you should have seen the drugs you could get in India just for the asking. Steroids, antibiotics – the whole caboodle.'

'But the bottle – you're absolutely sure it is a bottle?' I grinned.

'It's a bottle of very small tablets, perhaps five millimetres across,' he said stolidly. 'And I could wish,' he added, perking up again, 'that that wretched, noisome rodent had found one and put us out of our misery. Do you really propose to sleep with it stinking the place out like this?'

'There is, as the lady once said, No Alternative. No one else would be fool enough to take him in.'

He stood up. 'You said it; not me. What are you planning to write about?' he asked, looking at the desk with the blank pad and unused biro.

'About George,' I said. 'I still miss him, Chris, more than I could have imagined. I want to phone him for a natter. If I leave my tapes or books in a mess, I expect him to be there putting them in order. And he's not there for me to phone, and when I turn round he's not there. It's as if part of me is missing. Something inside.'

I'd never spoken to Chris like that before; I wondered how

he'd react to such a change of gear.

'I wish I could say you'd soon be over it,' he said. He looked me straight in the eye. 'But you won't. Not if my experience is anything to go by.'

Then his radio spat out a rude summons, and he was gone.

One day I'd ask him what he meant by that. Meanwhile my mind was full of George. I felt closer to him than ever before. Maybe, if I couldn't reach out with my hand, I could reach out with whatever part of my brain and write about him. Kate had recommended lying on the floor. I would lie on the floor.

It was not George's face but Courtney's that appeared before my inner eye. Courtney, camp and funny; Courtney, succumbing to hysteria; Courtney, taut and silent at supper.

I was on my feet and halfway down the corridor. Number six? Number seven? Number seven!

Yes, and he was in there. I could hear the scrape of a drawer, the suppressed mutters of someone wrestling with uncooperative inert matter.

I tapped the door. Sudden and complete silence.

'Courtney? It's only me. Sophie. Can you let me in?'

I tapped again.

This time there was a metallic sound, ugly in its implications.

In the moment before he flung the door open I had time to wonder whether he'd gesture me in with what I was sure was a gun or would merely threaten me once I was inside.

It was the former. And since what I'd heard was presumably the safety catch being slipped, I was terrified to see he was shaking as much as I now was. I slid in and sat heavily on the bed. I knew this was a mistake – I wouldn't be able to make a quick dash. But I wouldn't anyway. I'm not up to that sort of heroics. If I were to survive – and if I were to get Courtney out of this too – I had to use my brain.

For a moment he took his eyes off me, but it was only to lock the door. The gun was wobbling around all over the place. Poor Courtney!

'The key's on the floor,' I said, as prosaically as I could. 'Just by the waste bin. Near your sock, Courtney. The one by your shaving kit.'

He bent, the gun still pointing roughly at me, picked up the key and straightened. But he couldn't fit the key with his left hand. And he needed the right to hold the gun.

'Oh, put the bloody gun down,' I said. 'I don't want to go anywhere. I came to see you – remember?'

'Why?'

'Because – oh for goodness' sake, put the gun away. Lock the door if you like. Just to ruin my reputation.'

He forced a half-smile. 'With me, dear? You're joking!'

'Everyone knows you're a very handsome young man, Courtney. Does anyone besides me know you're gay?'

'I might be ambisextrous,' he said, and this time smiled properly. 'OK. Why'd you come and see me?'

'Intuition. I suffer from it sometimes. I just had to come. You tell me why I had to come.'

He pushed the gun towards me, then retrieved it and ejected the clip of ammunition. He balanced the gun in one hand, the clip in the other. I watched his face. He was relaxing.

'I was going to flit, Sophie. Because of that Freeman woman going walkabout. Everyone'll think it was me.'

'Why should they?'

'Oh, not the people here – I wasn't saying you've blabbed, Soph. The filth. They know I'm on parole and what for, they know her job, they can look up the trial records and even they can put two and two together.'

'Flitting would convince them if nothing else did.'

'So I wait for them to do a room search – sure as God made little apples that pig'll get a warrant if no one comes forward clutching Nyree's pills in their hot little hand.'

I couldn't deny it.

He got up, shoved the gun casually into an open holdall, and flipped the ammunition on to the bed beside me.

'Not supposed to have a gun, am I? Not a con on parole. Straight back into the nick, that's what'll happen.'

'It'll certainly happen if you flit and get caught or wait for the fuzz –' I couldn't get any more colloquial – 'to search your room.'

'So?'

'Courtney, you have to accept I'm saying this in good faith. I may be making a terrible mistake. But I think you ought to talk to Chris Groom. He's a decent man.'

'You're out of your sweet mind!'

'Have you any better ideas?' I allowed a certain astringency to permeate my voice.

'No –'

'Give me your ammunition, perhaps. That'd prove you didn't want to use the gun. And let's tidy this lot up – there's no point in advertising that you intended to do a runner. Courtney, I can't guarantee you won't be back in Durham before you can say knife, but any other way guarantees you will. And for a few extra years.'

'Give me more time to research for my screenplay,' he said, with a dry laugh.

'Is that what you're writing?' It was the first time he had talked about writing with me.

'Yes. That's why I was in such a tizzy when I recognised the Freeman woman, and why I was in an even bigger tizz when she took herself off. Did you see that thing she had on TV the other week? Really powerful, it was – all about this man who survives a plane crash by imagining he's somewhere else. And I wanted her to teach me.'

I smiled.

'So you work it out: would I kidnap or kill the woman? OK?'

'OK,' I laughed. 'Tell you what, I'll put these things safely in my bedroom and we'll go and have a nice cup of cocoa to celebrate.'

Chapter Seven

He unpacked the last pair of socks from the holdall, zipped up the gun, and went in search of the constable on duty in reception.

`Now, I'd like you to be a real sweetie and tell the DCI I have to speak to him.'

The constable looked doubtful. 'Sorry, sir, he's out with the search party for that writer lady.'

I should have expected it, I suppose. Chris hated delegating.

Courtney tutted, but pushed his holdall into the PC's arms. 'Well, you'll have to look after this then. Ms Rivers here is guarding the key with her life: she'll give it to her pal the DCI tomorrow. Night-night.'

We left before the PC could argue.

We celebrated with wonderfully gooey cocoa and a plate of biscuits, then Courtney escorted me ceremoniously back to my room. He watched me, embarrassed, while I fished out my key. Any minute now he would try to thank me. I put my arms round him and hugged him. Mr Woodhouse scuttled by, carrying, no doubt, his spongebag.

'There: that's your reputation shot to buggery,' said Courtney, hugging me back.

He set off down the corridor; then, as I unlocked my door, he turned.

'There's something else,' he said quietly, 'I want you to know.'

I gestured him into my room, and shut the door – he'd spoken in that sort of voice.

'I've had the test, Soph, and it was negative. You know, sweetie, *the* test. HIV. And I wanted you to know because – well, because.'

I took his hand and squeezed it. 'Thanks,' I said.

'Well,' he said, camp again, 'all the goings-on in the nick – all those queens, darling. And I promised my mum I'd keep myself pure.' His voice returned to normal. 'A nice lady, my mum. You'd get on. Now, I must be trotting: we need our beauty sleep, you and me both.'

He blew me a kiss and was gone.

I ought to have tried to sleep, but I stood by the window, watching. One by one the lights in the other student rooms had gone out. But out there the police were still searching; I could hear occasional shouts. I was left with my blank sheet of paper, my unused biro and a smelly rat. I wondered if rats got bored with cage life; presumably when he was with Kate Sidney spent his time roaming round, but I didn't relish giving him that sort of freedom. I fished him out and dumped him in his litter tray. He responded, and consented to be returned. Then he consumed the last of the bread, and had a thorough wash and brush-up.

That seemed like a good idea. A nice warm bath might make me sleepy. But I felt edgy, too nervous suddenly to want to scoot around the dark and empty corridors, even with my torch poised for action. I tried lying on the floor again. Still no poem. I went to bed.

Perhaps because he was indeed bored, Sidney decided to imitate an entire symphonic percussion section. My bedside light showed he was swinging on his water bottle.

I removed it.

What if he needed water? How often did rats have to drink? What if he were dehydrated, dying, in the morning? What time did vets start work?

I replaced the water bottle.

He turned his back on it, and arranged an apology of a bed from a few wisps of tissue.

The meagreness of my own bedding made me feel for him. I thrust a handful of paper hankies into his cage.

The sounds of his assembling his new bedding were

strangely soporific. My socks were warming my feet. My thick tracksuit – the one I'd been wearing when I first met Nyree – was dealing with the rest of me. Any moment now I would drift into oblivion, any moment . . .

A car door? At this time of night? Here? I was up on one elbow, alert.

Silence. The profound silence of a country park, despite the motorway on its distant boundary.

Go to sleep, Sophie.

Sleep?

It must have been about three when the question I ought to have asked myself finally formed itself into words: why had I slept like one dead the previous night?

Wednesday morning dawned early. At least, I presume it was early. Five-ish feels early to one who never wakes before seven. By six I was bored with lying on my back resenting not sleeping. Not writing either. When tears for George trickled across my temples into my ears, I knew it was time to do something.

An early jog was clearly the answer. I changed tracksuits, bade a tenderish farewell to Sidney, with the promise I'd find him some breakfast as soon as I could, and padded off.

I was doing some stretches in the sun on the terrace when I realised I was not alone. Four eyes were staring at me: a pair on Toad's T-shirt, and Toad's own. He too was dressed for a run.

'You have to be so careful about running shoes,' he observed to the world at large. 'Getting the fit right. And everyone trying to sell you the most expensive ones without worrying if they're going to hurt you.'

'Hurt you?'

'Well, I have this trouble with this tendon here.' He prodded the back of his heel. 'If I buy shoes with proper support, like they say, they rub summat shocking.'

He started to unlace his shoe.

If there is one thing that really appalls me about the human anatomy it is the average male foot. A woman's foot – unless it's been damaged by fashion shoes – looks like something designed for walking: springy and neat. But walking is the last thing I associate with the male ambulatory appendage. Plates of cold spaghetti, maybe, or the sort of string mops our college cleaners use.

And he was going to show me his, any moment now. I clearly had to find a diversionary tactic. Particularly as he'd no doubt suggest that we should run together.

'Tell me,' I said, 'was it you I heard playing the viola?'

He smiled coyly.

'Such a difficult instrument,' I pursued. 'I've always loved it.' Here was my chance to find out more about him. But I didn't want to.

He spread his hands. They were as broad as the rest of him, but well-shaped, with long fingers.

Go on, Sophie.

'Why did you choose the viola?' I asked.

'Don't know, really.'

'Do you play in an orchestra?'

'Not really.'

That puzzled me.

'Do you play anything?' he asked.

I didn't want to tell him anything about my musical activities. 'Not really,' I said, forgetting my Grade Eight on the piano and my singing. 'Look,' I continued, 'we're both getting cold. I know the sun's bright, but it hasn't much strength to it yet.'

'You going for a run?'

'No, not yet. I like to do my Canadian Air Force exercises in the open air if I can. What about you?'

'It'd be nicer if you came too.'

'Another time, Garth. And I'd love to hear your viola properly some time.' Thank goodness for that mysterious some time which never comes. I waved him brightly out of sight.

I'd just finished exercising when Gimson came into view. He was carrying today's *Telegraph* and a new packet of cigarettes. We hadn't spoken since yesterday morning, when I'd watched him bolt from Nyree's room.

'Before you ask, Miss Rivers, I know nothing about yesterday's events. Less than you, perhaps, given your relationship with the chief inspector.'

I let that pass. 'I bet you surmise a great deal, however,' I said.

'Surmise?' He appeared to relish the word. There was a glimmer of a smile.

'Hmm. Surmise,' I agreed.

'Like stout Cortez?'

Did he hope I'd recognise the allusion? Or did he hope to catch me out? I returned his serve, as it were: 'Perhaps Eyre House is less dramatic than a peak in Darien. You must excuse me, Mr Gimson. I'm getting cold.' And I turned and jogged to the kitchen. Bread for Sidney, a quick shower before breakfast, then I'd have to help Courtney brave Chris.

Matt was boiling the kettle when I opened the door. He looked desperately tired.

'What do I do, Sophie?'

'Do?'

'About the course. I mean, all these people have paid good money – but how can I do the work of two?'

'Reorganise your schedule. You've got plenty of time to do it before everyone else gets up. Toad and Gimson apart, that is.'

'Don't even know where to start.'

So I ended up – at the ungodly hour of seven in the morning – on the floor of Matt's room, a large sheet of paper in front of me. I divided it up neatly and fairly with names against each time slot.

'There. When all else fails, have a timetable,' I said. But he didn't want a timetable, however efficient. He wanted to talk to someone. I stood up, hoping the crack in my knees hadn't been as audible as it felt, and waited.

I might have to wait some time. I moved across to the window.

As you'd expect in a house this age, it was a sash window, deeply recessed. But whereas every other comparable room I'd seen had wooden shutters or panelling between the wall and the windowframe, this had a long, narrow mirror let into the woodwork.

'Interesting idea,' said Matt, coming to stand beside me. 'Apparently old Eyre had a daughter who was bed-bound or chair-bound. He fixed those for her so she could keep in touch with the world. Like a car mirror, I suppose. See without being seen. See who was coming to visit. Watch the comings and goings from the stables, over there. Try it.'

I sat at the desk; I could see down into the staff car park. A Land-Rover – presumably Naukez's – Kate's Peugeot, a faded Fiesta and a spruce Renault Five.

'There's a moral there,' said Matt gloomily. 'If you try to make a living by your pen, you end up with a W-registered 900-cc model. If you make your living harassing people for bringing in too much brandy, you get a snappy little number like Kate's – and, moreover, you can afford to insure it.'

'Does Kate still work for Customs and Excise?'

'No. Took very early retirement on the basis of her writing and a convenient legacy. And to be fair to the woman, she wasn't on the luggage-searching end of the job. Much too senior for that. A very bright woman. She likes you,' he added.

'I like her. I'm worried about her. They can't have found anything, Matt, or Chris would have let me know.'

'At this hour?'

'At whatever hour. Good news or bad.' I trusted Chris.

'So where does that leave us?'

'With a lot of questions to answer. And a few to ask.'

'You mean, you want to ask some.'

'Only to clarify my thinking, which seems to have been singularly cloudy for a couple of days. Can't work it out, Matt. I'm always a light sleeper, until I really go dead to the world. I hardly slept at all on Sunday night, or last night, for that matter. But Monday I was out cold for hours.'

Matt rubbed his hands over his face as if trying to iron out the creases.

'Do you know something? I was so knackered on Monday I fell asleep on the sofa. Spark out. And you saw what time I woke up. But last night . . . I know she's in some sort of trouble, Sophie. I know. But I don't know what sort and I don't know where.'

I nodded. I had the same intuition. I felt she was still alive. I certainly knew that George was dead before I had any evidence, though I didn't know the moment he'd been killed. But if I started talking intuitions and presentiments, I'd get sidetracked. I liked Matt, wanted to believe he knew as little about Kate's disappearance as I did, but wanted most of all to find Kate.

'Why did a woman as talented and successful as she was want to come on a course like this?' I asked. I could compare their answers.

'Because she wanted help, I suppose. There was a big problem with the way her novel was going. She couldn't spot what it was and trusted me to. She was a bit superstitious, too: I've always had a hand somewhere in what she's written – oh, only as a critic, don't get me wrong. And she felt showing it to me was like touching wood. And we're friends.'

I reflected on the inflexion of 'friends'. It didn't sound as if it were a euphemism. But there again, it didn't sound quite straight. I glanced at him. He turned away.

'Why didn't you tell me her rat was back?' he asked.

'I didn't not tell you. You weren't in your room when I brought him back. That's how I got into Kate's room for the cage: through the bathrooms. Which reminds me: maybe it'd be safer if you kept your room locked. Just in case, as it were.'

He nodded absently.

I looked at my watch. Seven thirty-five. A bit early for breakfast, but I hadn't anything else to do. And the interview with Chris about Courtney might be a bit fraught. I might as well eat now. And when I saw Shazia, I'd ask her to buy some rat food.

And some other food! Today was Wednesday, the day I was to cook with Agnes and Thea. An urgent meeting was called for.

'Coming down for some breakfast?' I asked.

'Not yet. I've got to read through this lot first.' He gestured at a pile of manuscripts. 'People will want a response when they see me.'

I smiled. My students are like that. Hand in an essay three weeks late, and expect you to have it marked before lunch. At least my efforts hadn't added to his stress.

'And I can't recall seeing anything of yours, Sophie, come to think of it.'

I smiled again. And left the room at a run.

What a pity I had to spoil my exit by returning for my biro. It's vaguely special. A grateful student gave it to me, in the days when students could afford to show their gratitude without getting deeper into debt. There was no sign of the biro on the floor or on the chart.

Matt patted a hand over his worktable. No joy.

'There it is: over on the windowsill,' he said, pointing. He walked across and picked it up. 'Very nice,' he said, inspecting it. 'Engraved, too.'

'You get me to write and I'll give you an entire pen-and-pencil set, all engraved,' I said. The way I was going it seemed a pretty safe offer. Then I lost interest in the game. I looked out of the window at the cars.

I was sure Kate had parked more neatly than that. Everything she did with that little Peugeot was meticulous. I'd swear she'd left it exactly parallel to the wall. Now it was at an angle of some thirty degrees to it. I suppose the distortion in the old mirror glass, maybe the whole concept of the mirrors, had prevented me from noticing. I didn't want to say anything to Matt at this point. I wanted to think about it, and maybe talk to Chris about it. He was bound to come looking for me soon. He'd probably go straight to my room. I'd better wait there for him.

As soon as I opened the door to my bedroom I saw the note. I was meant to see it. It was, after all, fastened firmly to my pillow. The haft of the penknife they'd used was crimson against the white of the pillowcase.

I managed not to scream aloud. I'd better find Chris. I backed out and closed the door firmly.

The PC in the umbilical corridor – a different one from last night's guardian of Courtney's bag – thought he might be in 'that lady writer's room'.

He was. Standing on duckboards. With him were his usual sergeant, Ian Dale, and a man in white overalls. Chris's greeting was off-hand. Perhaps he was embarrassed by my assumption that I could intrude on him when he was working. Certainly he returned to his conversation with the man in overalls so quickly that if I interrupted now I'd look like an importunate child. And the news could wait – a few moments. Then I'd have to tell him about it, and ask about Kate's car. I turned to Ian, who went so far as to shake my hand and greet me as 'Sophie'. This was emotion indeed from Ian, a dour Brummie. He had shared with Tina the tedious duty of guarding me; he'd taken me supermarket shopping, in the hope that he'd discovered at last a suitable candidate for the role of Mrs DCI Groom, but he'd been sadly disappointed by my choice of vegetables. But anyone who'd chosen okra and aubergines would have been equally suspect – there was nothing personal.

'Too thin, if you ask me,' he said, indicating Chris with a jerk of his head. 'And he could have done with a couple of days' acclimatisation leave. Look at him.'

The morning sun dug ruthlessly into every line on his face, highlighting the now quite definite stoop. I hoped Chris was sufficiently keen on pleasing me to risk an osteopath – he'd soon need one.

As if to confirm my fears, as he straightened he put his hand to his back.

'OK, Sophie, you may as well know: there was no sign of Kate Freeman anywhere in the grounds. No sign of any sort of struggle taking place. No nothing.'

'So –?'

'I've got two options: to assume – in the absence of those phenobarbitone tablets – that she killed Nyree and disappeared; or to assume that whoever disposed of Nyree has disposed of Kate, too.'

'Which do you favour?' I asked, feeling sick.

'Open mind. I'm preserving the scene in either case. I shall have it sealed off and an officer on duty outside from now on. This is Ade, by the way. He's in charge of the team looking for stuff for Forensics. The Forensic-Science Laboratory,' he corrected himself with heavy irony.

Ade and I shook hands. He was younger than me – probably only late twenties – and was unprepossessing with ginger hair, buck teeth and a slightly receding chin. But he had a brightness about his big brown eyes that suggested a great deal of intelligence.

'Before Ade gets to work,' Chris said, 'cast your eyes

around the room. Notice anything?'

'What sort of thing?'

'Anything different, out of place.'

I closed my eyes, covering them with my hands. When Chris tried to speak, I waved him to silence. What I wanted to do was see what I'd seen when I came in for my tutorial. The biscuits, the computer and printer. On the wardrobe there'd been a thick towelling robe – she'd expected to have to share a bathroom since she'd come as a student. And a little leather harness for Sidney.

I opened my eyes.

The desk was almost bare. No biscuits. No computer or printer. Her manuscript was still there.

'Have you stowed anything in those bags yet, Ade? I asked.

'Nope,' he replied, in a mellow Sheffield accent.

'In that case, someone's lifted the notepad and printer. And they've done it recently. They were there when I came in for Sidney's cage yesterday afternoon. The biscuits had gone, though.'

'What biscuits?' asked Chris.

'Kate kept a packet of digestive biscuits for Sidney. Look, there are some crumbs there.' I pointed.

'Risky, that,' said Ade. 'Small mammals can get diabetes if you give them too much sugary stuff.'

'Anything else?' asked Chris, tartly.

'Bathrobe. A thick towelling one. Thicker than I could dry in a week. It was hanging over there, by Sidney's lead. I suppose,' I added hopefully, 'I couldn't liberate the lead, could I? It would make exercising Sidney much easier, and I can't imagine that it'd provide much in the way of evidence.'

'Like a bit of exercise, do rodents,' Ade observed.

Chris handed it to me without speaking.

I pocketed it. 'Thanks. What about her bag?'

'What about it?'

'Have you found it? I think it was leather, but I only saw it in her car for a moment. Brown. A shoulder bag.'

'No bag, sir,' said Ade.

'Coat? Shoes?' said Chris.

'Coat's still in the wardrobe.'

'How about slippers?' I asked.
'No slippers.'
'Is that her nightie?' I reached to pull back the duvet, but Chris shot out a restraining hand. 'Sorry. Chris, I have to talk to you about something else, when you've a moment. Two other things, actually.'
My voice must have shown more than I meant it to.
'Give me a couple of minutes. D'you want to stay here? If not, Ian will go with you.'
'No. I'll be all right. I've got to have a word with my two fellow cooks so Shazia can get the ingredients for tonight's meal. You'll find me in the kitchen or the dining room.' I smiled generally and left.
Thea and Agnes were delighted with my rather malicious suggestion for supper. Shazia looked amused when my list involved fresh coriander, ginger and chillies, but said nothing. She headed off for her Renault. Then she turned back. 'Don't forget to cook for one extra,' she said. 'There's that poet coming tonight to do a reading. He'll be eating with us too.'
'There'll be plenty!' said Agnes. 'Poor Mr Gimson may not want any.'
Then I remembered Sidney, and hared off after Shazia: she added rat food to her list and promised extra digestives. Sidney's diet was no business of mine.

Ian was waiting for me outside my room. I opened the door, stood aside for him to go first and pointed. The note and knife were still there, the blade stabbing through a folded sheet of paper.
Ian touched me gently on the arm and knelt on the floor. He tipped his head sideways to try to peer between the folds. But he wouldn't touch it till Chris appeared.
We surveyed the room together. My make-up lay where I'd left it on the dressing table. The pad was still on the desk. I knew better than to open any drawers or touch the wardrobe.
Then I realised it was too quiet. Sidney!
His cage was empty. I joined Ian kneeling on the floor; perhaps Sidney might just be under the bed.
'Asking for divine assistance?' Chris demanded lightly.

Then his tone changed. 'Jesus! Why didn't you tell me about this earlier?'

'That's what I came for. To tell you. But I got sidetracked.'

'Get Ade.'

Ian left. I wondered why Chris hadn't simply summoned him via his radio. Then he turned to me.

'I'm sorry. I should have listened. Thank God it was your pillow, not –'

I wonder if he could have continued.

'I'm fine, Chris. Honestly. I don't like getting letters in this way, but I'll bet it's more a warning than a threat. Why don't you open it?'

'Photographs first. Evidence.' He made an effort: 'So why were you on your knees when I came in?'

'Sidney. I was hoping he'd be under the bed. But there's no sign of him. I suppose he could have climbed out of the window but –'

'No chance. And there'd be little scrabble-marks where he'd tried to jump,' said Ade, coming in with a camera bag. He took out an SLR and photographed my missive from a variety of angles. Then he passed Chris gloves, and held open a polythene bag to receive the knife, a Swiss Army one with God knows how many blades and a pair of nail scissors for good measure.

Chris opened the note, holding it at arm's length as if it were likely to explode. Then he pulled his head back. Finally he dug in his breast pocket for spectacles. Presbyopia. That's what you get when you're middle-aged.

Wearing gold-rimmed half-moons, he held the paper so I could read it too.

YOU. KEEP YOUR NOSE OUT OF MY BUISNESS.

'Didn't use his spell-check,' I said. But my laughter was shaky.

'My God, you've become computer-literate at last!' So was his.

'Nice print,' said Ian, prosaically.

'And what would our expert say?' asked Chris, smiling at me ironically.

So I decided to tell him: 'Single-sheet feed, not tractor-driven. No perforations along the edge where the strip with the little holes has been torn off.'

'Go on, Holmes.'

'Laser or ink-jet? Or an extremely good 24-pin dot-matrix?'

'Better and better. Any idea how many people have got word processors or computers?'

I shook my head. 'The one in the office has died: Shazia's been using an aged Remington. There are ordinary typewriters at one end of the library. One of the older ladies, Jean, brought up an entire BBC Master, complete with printer. But her printer wouldn't produce this quality.' Come to think of it, I didn't know why I'd bothered to mention it. Except I do tend to talk more when I'm upset.

'Anyone else?'

'Kate, of course. The little number that was missing from her desk.'

'I thought you said she had a notepad.'

'A computer notepad, Chris. Posh. Expensive. And its printer.'

'Anyone else?'

'I really don't know.'

'OK. Look here, Ian, go and do a room-to-room check, eh? Ade, roust out a few more SOCOs. I want this room quadruple-checked as soon as they've finished with Kate's.'

Ade waited for Ian to go first, then left himself.

'How would whoever it was get in, Chris? I shut the door, I know I did. Because of Sidney.'

Chris pulled out his wallet. 'Probably used his flexible friend. Or maybe they take American Express. Oh, it's so bloody easy, Sophie. You could do it yourself with a lock this old. And don't take that as a hint to go and practise.'

I think the severity was genuine.

'Are you sure you don't know more than you're letting on, Sophie? I hoped you'd be a source of useful gossip.'

'Copper's nark?' I said nastily.

'No, I know you won't talk about friends. But these aren't your friends. They're just acquaintances, surely?'

'And one of them is missing, one I hoped might be a friend. Funny, I think one or two people have struck up friendships. But there's a singular lack of camaraderie, now I come to think of it. The only other person I've had more than a passing conversation with is the person I wanted to talk to you about.' Hell, I was letting him off far too lightly. I should have dropped coy hints, dropped my eyes a little. 'Courtney, that Afro-Caribbean man. He's an ex-con. He left you a present last night. Here's the key for the padlock.' I fished in my pocket and dropped the key in his hand.

Most of my explanation was truthful. I told him I'd gone along to Courtney's room because I knew he was worrying about something, that he'd told me about the gun and then acted on my advice. Chris nodded gravely, then looked me for a moment in the eye.

'You know he's violated the terms of his parole?'

I nodded.

'Straight back to gaol. Loss of remission.'

I nodded.

'Had a grudge against Kate – wanted her silenced.'

'You've seen him already, then?'

'He was sitting on the front steps waiting for me, Sophie. He wanted to keep you out of it, but there was the small matter of the key.'

'He had every reason to want Kate alive, Chris. He's writing a screenplay and wanted her help.'

'Have you seen it?'

Chris was vacillating: I could hear it in his voice. I was glad I wasn't in his position. If he ignored a very serious offence, and Courtney was eventually proved to be implicated, Chris would be in grave trouble. But his humanitarian instincts were proving very strong.

'The screenplay? No. But I'm sure he could show it to you. Matt would be able to authenticate it.'

Chris walked over to the window. 'I've got to bloody turn him in. Got to. Haven't I?'

'You've certainly got to find out why he had a gun in the first place. I must admit, much as I like him, that's the thing that worries me. Eyre House didn't strike me as the sort of place you needed to carry a weapon. At least,' I added with gloomy irony, 'not until one woman died and another disappeared.'

'And what I now want to make sure,' Chris said, with no irony at all, 'is that a third woman doesn't come to any harm.'

'I'll look after myself,' I said. 'I promise.'

Chapter Eight

I wanted to run.

But first I had to watch the scene-of-crime team go through my belongings: Chris had asked me to before he tactfully withdrew to the stables. He wanted to know at once if anything was missing, if anything had been disturbed. Something niggled at the back of my mind, but the whole scenario seemed more like a tableau from someone else's life – more and more I felt I should be watching from the ceiling, as Agnes had done. In the end, although I knew Chris would be irritated, I did grab my running things and set off to put as much space as possible between me and Eyre House. Perhaps I ought to have tried to make systematic notes. But I knew that my brain would simply not function for a while.

I'd never had the chance to ask Naukez why he wanted to keep me away from that patch in the woods, so I resolved to explore the area. I had no real reason to, except I'm naturally nosy and I suppose I wanted to prove to myself that Naukez was not a sinister, duplicitous man. In fact, I wanted Shazia's husband to be quite definitely on the side of the angels.

I forced myself to run slowly enough to have plenty in reserve. I took the shortest approach, retracing the route I'd taken back to the house yesterday.

No one intercepted me this time. I left the main path to follow a scarcely defined track down to a largish hollow. The terrain was oddly lumpy: something else I might ask Naukez about. Some bracken grew at such judicious intervals that I expected to find David Attenborough and a film crew lurking. I found no one. Since even I know that ten thirty in the morning is an inappropriate time for badgers, I shrugged, and headed off downhill to the corner of the park furthest from the house. There was a jumble of dilapidated buildings down there – the old home farm, perhaps.

Every instinct told me to give up. The traffic noise became a physical force pressing me back. It poured into my ears, of course, and then into my nose and mouth and chest. It resonated on my bones, like loud music at a pop concert.

I had to get away.

But I had to check first. OK, I was being totally illogical: how could I hope to find anyone, anything, a team of experts had missed? Nonetheless, I couldn't do what I wanted most of all to do, turn tail and bolt back to base.

I made myself follow the outlines of what I presumed was a farmhouse – square-built, and, you'd have thought, completely impervious to the elements. But it seemed to have been defeated by the noise of the motorway. I moved on. There was a well in the far corner. The cover – crisscrossed iron bars – was rusted too tightly for me to shift. I'd have to assume no one else had moved it. In any case, there was water only twelve inches down. Anyone down there would be dead.

Dead as George.

My stomach wouldn't take it. If I didn't get away from here I'd throw up. The only way I'd do it was by making my legs work again, but they were like jelly. At last I managed an extremely sedate jog. I'd got as far as a rotting gate when I realised I was no longer alone. Some three hundred yards away, a man was climbing a stile. Probably he'd wanted a pee and pulled off the road which crossed the motorway.

Surely he was walking too purposefully for that?

I dodged into a redundant pigsty. From its cover I watched him.

He jumped lightly from tussock to tussock as if he were enjoying himself. And he was heading towards me. He was probably my age or a bit nearer forty. An embarrassing encounter or a humiliating bolt? Neither – he struck off uphill towards a symmetrical hummock.

I emerged cautiously. There was a convenient mounting block on the barn wall. If I climbed that, it would give me an extra hundred yards' vision.

The hummock was the shape of a Christmas-card igloo. He approached it, then started to drop from view. Presumably there were steps down into it. For a moment he disappeared altogether. But then he reappeared, dusting his fingers together, and clambered to the top of the mound. King of the Castle. Monarch of all he surveyed.

I'd prefer him not to survey me.

I dropped from the block and scurried to the sty. Years ago I'd read about a murder – and surely it had been real, not fiction – in which the victim was fed to pigs. The thought made my stomach heave again. It would just have to heave. The last way I wanted to greet any visitor was on my hands and knees.

He was on the move again.

Back to my ruins?

No, he was returning whence he'd come. This time he did stop for a pee.

He vaulted the stile with panache, and that was the last I saw of him. I could only deduce it was his car I glimpsed through the gap in the hedge. Red and glossy. But more I could not tell.

The mound turned out to be a prosaic little ice house. It was locked, of course, and barred. I pulled meaninglessly at one of the bolts securing it. Then I too scrambled back up the steps, dusting rust from my hands.

I jogged back slowly, and was almost at the house when I was galvanised by the sight of a police tow-truck, with Kate's car perched apparently precariously on the back. Kate's car! I should have told Chris about Kate's car! Now it was too late. Any revealing footprints – if indeed there had ever been any in the coarse gravel – would have been well and truly messed up. To prove it to myself I went and had a look. Two constables were still there, talking loudly and derisively about a colleague who'd come out as gay. I had to remind myself it was none of my business, that I shouldn't say anything. And I didn't get the chance, anyway. They ordered me away – the only men in Chris's team who'd been anything other than courteous and pleasant. Since they were stamping all over the gravel, there was no point in arguing. I turned mildly and went to hunt for a second breakfast. I went via the stables but Chris was nowhere to be seen and I suspected if I told anyone else that I thought I might have heard a car door slam, they'd dismiss it as irrelevant and not bother to tell Chris anyway.

'Out of training, Miss Rivers?' Gimson asked dryly as I pushed open the kitchen door. 'You look very pale. Perhaps you went too far?'

I reached for the kettle and filled it before I spoke. I needed something sweet. Perhaps there was some drinking chocolate in the cupboard. And Shazia should have replenished the biscuit barrel by now.

'A little further than usual, perhaps. I wanted to think.'

'I trust you found a quiet corner?'

'On the contrary, a very noisy one,' I said, foolishly. I rattled my way through the cupboard and came up with a jar of chocolate. I made it strong and milky, and added more sugar than I'd normally have gone through in a week.

'Ah, down by the motorway?'

'It was worse than being near the speakers at a pop concert.'

I burrowed in the biscuit tin. It was satisfactorily full.

'An experience I have so far managed to avoid, Miss Rivers. And so should you, in future. Low-frequency noise is known to have unpleasant effects. Nausea, for instance.'

Smiling coldly in acknowledgement, I took my chocolate and four custard creams, and passed through the reception area, where I ran into a harassed Shazia.

'We'll be having them by the coachload soon,' she said. 'I'll have to get a guidebook printed, sell afternoon teas. You lot can be official guides.'

'Or exhibits,' I said. 'What's been happening, Shazia?'

'Three more Japanese. And a very rude man who looked sort of Chinese. Fortunately Naukez was here.'

'Have you told Chris?'

'Oh, Sophie, for goodness' sake! I can't bother him with every chance visitor. You know the Japanese are obsessed with the Brontës – there are even signposts in Japanese on the moors round Haworth.'

'Whom did they want?'

'The Japanese? "Charrotte Brontë", of course.'

'And the rude Chinese?'

She looked distressed. 'Nyree. I tried to explain that she was no longer with us. He didn't seem to understand – kept on asking where she was.'

'I suppose you didn't happen to notice what sort of car he drove?'

'Why should I?'

'It seems to me that we should notice everything just now, Shazia. After all, there's one woman dead and another missing –'

Fortunately, just as I was getting pompous and didactic, Naukez put his head round the back door. The other three sighed in sympathy.

'You OK now, Shaz?'

She nodded.

'Great.'

He withdrew.

'Did the Chinese hurt you?' I asked, sharply, because I ought to have spoken to Naukez and didn't for fear of upsetting Shazia.

'No. Pushed me a bit. But I'm a bit off colour. I got all weepy.'

I nodded my sympathy. And, trying not to spill my chocolate, I legged it as fast as I could to Chris. Surely by now he'd be back in the stable block.

The stable door was the old-fashioned type. Someone had fastened back the top half. Chris was in a group of men and women near the door. He was bending over something I couldn't yet see, wearing the glasses that made him look like a desiccated schoolmaster. The sun faded his blond hair further and explored the tired lines of his face. And when he turned and looked up, it spotlit the expression of hope and joy he quickly suppressed.

'Well?' he asked, in a strongly official voice.

'Kate's car. You've had it taken away?'

'I thought we ought to check it.'

'Why only now?'

'No reason to – if you don't suspect foul play.'

'And you do now? You see, I think I might have heard

someone using a car last night, very late, and I also think it was in a different position when I looked at it this morning. I'm sorry. I should have said.'

'Pity you didn't mention it earlier,' he said, sounding parental. 'Never mind, it'll be kept at Rose Road nick and given the most thorough going-over it's ever had in its young life.'

'What will they be looking for?'

'Anything and everything. Do I have to spell it out?' He looked at his watch irritably.

I shrugged and turned to the door. Then I stopped. It was as if my mouth spoke without my mind, and I was quite interested in what it had to say.

'Chris, I have an idea that something might have been taken from my room.'

'Might?' He was at his driest and most irritating.

I hesitated. I could be about to make an almighty fool of myself.

'Sophie, what's missing, for God's sake?'

It was unfortunate that one of those random silences should have chanced to fall as I replied.

'A packet of tampons,' I said, in my carrying, fill-the-lecture-room voice.

Ten assorted police personnel can laugh very loudly. He flushed. I didn't.

'But surely you'd know for sure whether . . .' By now he was red to the ears. 'Aren't they . . . monthly?'

'Chris, I may have simply left a packet lying on my bedroom floor. But I thought I'd packed it. And it wasn't there when your colleagues checked.'

'Could you go home and find out?'

'No transport.'

'Hell – and we're in the middle of a crisis. Some royal wants to commune with nature on the bloody Wrekin this afternoon, and all our mobiles –'

'– are mobilised?' I asked sweetly. 'Or are they cars?'

He grinned. 'Bloody pedant!'

'And Courtney?'

'I've sent Tina to interrogate him. Very slowly.'

I touched his hand lightly. 'You're a good man, Chris.'

He flushed again.

'Has Shazia told you about her visitors?'

'Visitors?'

I explained.

He sent Ian Dale off to talk to her.

It suddenly occurred to me that, tampons apart, it would be very convenient to spend a few minutes at home. I didn't buy the idea that intelligent Japanese tourists who'd made their way across God knows how many time zones should suddenly fall down on their map-reading to that extent. Kenji had always urged me to phone him for a natter one day. This could be the very day. But some weird moral code dictated that I phone from home, not at someone else's expense.

But transport? I had to be back at Eyre House and on duty in the kitchen by two thirty at the latest.

'Are you too busy to run me to Harborne? It'd take hours by bus, and a taxi would be absurd. And extortionate.'

Poor Chris: he would have given much to have me on my own for the hour or so the errand would take. He wouldn't have grabbed me or embarrassed me in any way. He'd simply have luxuriated in my company. And I'd have enjoyed his.

At last he shook his head. Then he dug in his trouser pocket and thrust a bunch of keys at me.

'Here: help yourself.'

'Chris, I – your Peugeot!'

An executive Peugeot. A 605. It was still new, still smelled of leather. He'd bought it when he fancied himself in some absurd competition for my affections with an old friend of mine who'd just bought a classy Renault.

'Go on. But I could do with it about four, if that fits your plans.'

We smiled at each other. He didn't want to make any fuss that would draw the transaction to the notice of his colleagues. So I just nodded, picked up the keys and turned. 'Will you show me what's what?'

We walked to the car park together.

I live in Harborne, which is, according to the property pages of the Sundays, one of the more desirable of the Birmingham suburbs. Balden Road teeters on the edge of, and practically collapses into, Quinton, which is infinitely less desirable. I owe my presence there to the fact that one of my relatives omitted to make a will.

George's van sat patiently in the road outside, wishing its girth were small enough to let it get into my garage. I patted it gently, and then let myself into the house.

There wasn't much post – a couple of bills and a card from Carl just to say hello. At the moment it didn't seem important. I dropped them on the kitchen table and dialled Japan. Kenji answered on the fourth ring.

We greeted each other cautiously. I apologised for waking him. Kenji reminded me he was a light sleeper and admitted that he would not find it hard to fall asleep again. There was, however, a significant other in his life, who tended to lie awake if her slumber was broken, and –

'God knows how much your moans are costing me, Kenji. I'm glad you've found someone else. I hope I haven't woken her. Hell, you're having me on, aren't you? It can't be much after ten over there, can it?' I shut up. Kenji went to bed before one only if he went with someone and not to sleep. 'Having an early night,' had always been his euphemism for what usually turned out to be a protracted, inventive and often enjoyable bonk. Then curiosity got the better of me. 'Who is she? What does she do?'

'She's an American journalist. Works for CNN.'

'Better and better. Now here's what I want you to do.'

'I don't want to do anything.'

'You always said I only had to ask. I'm asking.' I explained about unwonted oriental interest in a corner of the West Midlands, and about Nyree's defecting husband. If I stopped, Kenji prompted me with a little grunt.

'You think there might be a connection between our government bribes scandal and this disreputable diplomat?'

'Do I?'

'I can't think of any other reason to ask me.'

Neither could I.

I asked after his rabbit. He asked after my marking. We bade each other a polite *au revoir*.

I watered the herbs on my kitchen window and fed them a little Phostrogen. George's thyme. George's rosemary. His coriander was long dead.

There was no packet of tampons on my bedroom floor.

I locked up and headed back to Eyre House.

The big Peugeot was such a delight to drive I didn't want to return it. I've always bought other people's mistakes, and cheap ones at that. But I love driving with a passion I find embarrassing. Now I had found a vehicle that behaved like a car, not a supermarket trolley. It went where and when I wanted it to. The radio tuned quickly to Three FM.

The temptation to whizz up the motorway was almost overwhelming. M6 or M5? Sophie, the choice is yours! But it wasn't. Chris needed his car. I had to get back. I was supposed to be writing a poem. More important, I had to tell Chris what I'd found. Or rather hadn't. Soberly I picked my way through West Bromwich, past the football ground where Andy and I had cheered the Albion as kids. I found myself going more and more reluctantly. It was as bad as driving to work.

Back at Eyre House, I reversed the Peugeot into a parking space and grinned at Chris, who emerged from the stables talking to Ian and Ade. Ade gave a thumbs-down gesture – I gathered there was no sign of Sidney. Chris walked across to me, looking ostentatiously for signs of damage to his baby.

As I locked up and passed him the keys, I told him about the tampons. As an afterthought I reported my conversation with Kenji. He laughed, and beckoned me to follow him to the stables. I was about to be patronised. I'd let him get away with it this time: a swap for the Peugeot.

An acned constable was tapping data horribly slowly into a computer. He made way for Chris, who sent him off to lunch. I peered over Chris's shoulder. Computer-literate I might now be, but I'm always fascinated by other people's expertise. And there we were. In the States, being welcomed to the files of NYPD. Then LA. I was about to make impressed noises when Matt appeared at Chris's other shoulder.

'Wonderful!' he said. 'You can fart about all over the bloody States but you can't fucking well locate one woman in sodding Birmingham. Damn it, we don't know whether she's still alive –'

Quite needlessly, Chris pressed my foot. As he did so, he said mildly: 'We've actually been using this to check Kate's past –'

'She was positively vetted.'

'Yes. A very important woman. So it may well be that someone in her past bears her a grudge.'

'Try Gimson for a start,' said Matt savagely. 'She went quite white the moment the bastard came into the room.'

I looked up sharply. I'd heard Gimson threaten her with something. When? Something about every possible step? And he'd not been happy with Sidney's presence in the house. I'd been stupid to let my dislike of him show so much: he'd hardly cooperate with me if I started to question him, no matter how circumspectly. Consultant surgeons needn't be intellectuals, but they couldn't be utter fools.

The more I tried to recall their conversation, the less I was able to. Perhaps I had to creep up quietly on the memory and surprise it.

The way I suddenly surprised Matt's reference to paraquat. Why hadn't I told Chris about it? But I liked Matt enough to want to speak to him in private first.

'We're questioning everyone,' said Chris, his voice even and calm. 'If you've got time, I'd like to talk to you myself – after lunch, perhaps. Say two thirty? After a short meeting I'd like everyone to attend at two. Would you try and get people together in the lounge, Matt? You and Shazia. Nothing startling. Just to keep everyone briefed. What's the matter, Sophie?'

'You promise it'll be short? I've got a lot of cooking to do.'

'Very short.'

So we gathered, as requested, in the lounge. Courtney was there, sitting as if by choice with Tina. He ventured the tiniest grin in my direction. The only people missing were Toad and the sci-fi buff. Shazia sat beside Matt and Chris. The rest of us were in a rough semicircle. Ian Dale slipped in after Chris had started to speak. I don't think anyone else noticed him, but I picked up the smell of his aftershave, a surprisingly sexy one for such a bastion of respectability.

'I suppose you people will insist on incarcerating us here

till you've managed to establish –'

'No,' said Chris.

I'm sure he enjoyed saying it. The monosyllable came out with great weight and gusto. He allowed himself to glance at me before addressing himself more fully to Gimson's question. 'No, Mr Gimson, we'll be operating the standard police procedure for cases like this.'

'I have the most important meeting scheduled for Monday,' Gimson said. 'Trust status for St Jude's. It's imperative I attend.'

'I'm quite sure you will, Mr Gimson. I'm trying to explain, sir, if you'll give me a chance. What we do these days is to ask you all to make detailed statements. Then we ask for your home address. Your local police will verify this for me. Thereafter you'll be free to go about your business. We'd like you to be available for further talks if necessary, so it might be a bit tricky if you wanted to leave the country.' He smiled, everyone's favourite nephew or cousin. 'We have, after all, two quite difficult problems here. Nyree's sleeping tablets have not turned up; there is no sign of Kate. We need all the cooperation you can give us.'

'What are you going to do about Nyree's tablets?' asked Shazia.

'To be honest, it's so vital we find them I'm going to ask you to let my colleagues check your rooms. They're all professionals. They won't disturb or damage your possessions. But we do need to establish once and for all that they're nowhere in Eyre House.'

We all nodded – middle-aged, middle-class people clinging to the ethos of helping the police. But I thought of my tampons and discovered I wasn't as middle-aged or middle-class as I'd thought. 'Would it be WPCs or policemen?' I asked.

'Here we go. You women and your insistence on equality. I suppose I can't demand the equality of having my male belongings searched by a male officer!' Gimson said.

'I don't see why not, sir,' said Chris equably. 'If anyone prefers their room – and it is only their room, not their body – to be searched by someone of their own gender –'

'*Sex*!' said Gimson.

'– then I'll be happy to arrange it.'

'Nyree's dead,' said Matt brutally. 'OK, I'd like her killer found. If she didn't do herself in accidentally, which is my theory. But Kate – what are you doing to find Kate?'

'Let me tell you what we've done so far,' said Chris. 'There has been a thorough examination of her room by a team of forensic scientists. The search revealed no signs of violence at all. We can only assume that Kate left her room herself, perhaps to look for her rat, or that if she left with someone, she did so willingly.'

For a moment, his eyes flickered in my direction. He was holding something back, something he might share with me when we were alone. I blinked: message understood.

'And –?' prompted Matt.

'As you know, we've searched the grounds exhaustively. We'd like to check all your cars, by the way, in case one of them might have any clues.'

Chris was sending me another message; he only used the outmoded term to me. I smiled.

'Is that OK by everyone?' he added.

There was muttered agreement.

'Isn't there anything else you can do?' Matt's voice sounded both angry and despairing. 'What about the media? Can't you get them involved?'

'We'd rather not, at this stage, just in case – you see, there is just the remotest possibility that she's been abducted, and when that's the case we have to follow very strict guidelines laid down by the Home Office. We have no option.'

'So what can you do?'

'Just talk to you all, again and again. Just in case a chance word helps us. So bear with us, please, ladies and gentlemen, if we appear slow and irritating. We're doing our best. And if anything, no matter how trivial, comes to your mind, please, please talk to me or one of my colleagues. We shall treat everything as confidential.'

The meeting was over. But he'd be in my room waiting for me when I got back.

Chapter Nine

To be precise, he was waiting in the corridor. When he smiled at me, it was with as much relief as if he'd been waiting, vulnerable on a street corner, for his girl. And yet I hadn't delayed.

'No blood, no seminal fluid, no nothing,' he said, closing my bedroom door. 'I didn't want to spell it out back there, but I was actually telling the truth.'

'But not the whole truth,' I said. I gestured him to the chair. I sat on the bed.

'All right. Not quite. And I thought you'd want to know. That bulge in Kate's bed wasn't her nightdress. It was a bag of rat food.'

'There was a ring of something around her room – no, a parabola, as if someone had thrown –'

'Right. I thought you'd probably noticed that. Yes, it was rat food. Perhaps she just wanted to make sure that Sidney was kept well fed.'

'Or perhaps she was trying to do what that little boy in the fairy tale did.'

'I'm sorry?'

'He was getting lost so he left a trail of breadcrumbs so he could find his way out of the woods. OK, not very apposite. But she was trying to tell us something, possibly.'

'Not to go into the woods, perhaps. And what does Ian tell me but that you went trotting round the woods yesterday and again today?'

'Exercise, Chris.'

'Balls, Sophie. Come on, what did you find?'

'Bugger all. Apart from a man in a red car, and I kept out of his way. He only wanted a slash in the hedge, anyway.'

'Sure?'

'Sure. He had a bit of a walk round and then got back in his car. What about Courtney?'

'Tina and I are reasonably convinced, but he wants to tell you himself. He sees you as –'

'Safe!'

'That. And as a friend he ought to have trusted from the start. You've made a conquest there, Sophie,' he said with care.

'I'm safe all right. Haven't you spotted it, Chris? He's gay.'

'Oh?'

I could have laughed at the relief he tried to suppress: instead I nodded casually. 'And now I must go and cook.'

'Hang on. Matt.'

'Very anxious for you to find his friend.'

'Or –?'

'Or?'

'Is he just being very clever? Trying to con us that he knows nothing? I'm not sure he's as pure as the driven snow, Sophie.'

'He can be as randy as Don Juan but that doesn't mean he's done her in. And I've only seen him as being a nice, affectionate, friendly type. Speak as I find, Chris. But if I do find anything, I'll let you know. But only if you let me go and cook a pile of samosas and pakora.'

'OK. If you tell me when we can expect the honour of a formal statement. I don't recollect your giving us one yet. And God knows you've enough to tell us.'

I wouldn't even ask him to let me off. 'If I can get the first half of supper under way. I'm way behind schedule. Say about five thirty? Six?'

We smiled at each other, stood up together and left the room. When I locked the door, he turned and pushed it. 'Just making sure.'

And we walked in silence to the end of the corridor, where we parted company.

Before I reached the kitchen, however, I decided it was

time to clear up one silly niggling worry and to do that I might as well phone Carl. He was the friend who'd sent the postcard. Not exactly friend. The man I'd been seeing at the end of term. Despite my resolution on the first morning at Eyre House, I hadn't got round to writing to bid him farewell, and for the moment I was glad I hadn't. He might have his uses, as a keen gardener and as a pharmacy lecturer. The phone call could scarcely be anything other than strictly business anyway, since his wife was likely to be around. She might even be the one to answer. I hoped not. I knew enough about Paula not to like her very much, but that didn't justify what I'd done. Or what Carl had done. There'd been two of us, after all.

It was Carl who answered. When he heard my voice he sounded so furtive I nearly laughed. I made my voice as brisk and neutral as I could and came straight to the point. How, I wanted to know, could I kill someone with easily available garden products? It was for this course, I explained – part of a story I might be writing. That was why I'd phoned him. Surely his wife wouldn't object to that?

To do him justice, Carl was not a man to come up with that sort of information irresponsibly, and he hummed and ha'ed for ages.

'OK, Carl, let's simplify the proposition. I have a man I want to dispose of and a supply of paraquat –'

'No good. Contains an emetic, these days. But you have to be very careful anyway – a single splash in the eye and you can cause major damage to the cornea. No, I'm afraid what you really ought to do, but it certainly wouldn't be undetectable – Jesus, Sophie, you're sure this is only for a story?'

'Honest, Carl. But my money's running out. I'll be in touch, OK?'

I managed to put the phone down on anything more personal.

So Matt had only been joking! But what would he tell Chris about his colleague's illness? Whether or not it was in confidence, I was dying to know.

Three o'clock. I was alone in the kitchen, and badly behind

schedule. Agnes had already done her share. She'd had a short story commissioned by Radio Four – plain, ordinary Agnes could write to order – and wanted to work on it in peace. So she'd prepared a couple of summer puddings this morning, and left them to chill on a marble shelf in the pantry. The fridge was full of raw chicken pieces for me to stir into a big biryani.

I had to be systematic. The vegetable curry to go with the biryani would take hours to mature. I'd better do that first. Then the messy business of the pakora. I wanted to get them done before the slightly easier job of the samosas. Thea should be up and around by then; she was still having her afternoon rest, and in any case I didn't know if it would be wise for someone with her heart condition to stand around peeling vegetables.

Toad popped his head round the door just as the onions were at their most vicious. Tears simply dripped off my nose. He muttered something about returning later, and withdrew. Perhaps it was the unlikely possibility of his playing the viola that made me start singing Berlioz's *Harold in Italy*. I know I wasn't designed for the voice but George always went on the principle that anything with a good tune ought to be sung, and *Harold*'s nothing if not tuneful.

At last the onions were frying. The vegetables were chopped. I'd given up counting the number of garlic cloves I'd peeled ready to mash. The spices were vivid in Shazia's mortar.

Life felt good, as it always does when I'm cooking. Maybe I could even write a poem about cooking. Then, as I was pounding at the spices and raising wonderful fumes of chilli and ginger, someone opened the kitchen door, very quietly. And shut it again, equally quietly.

By the time I'd reached the door and flung it open, the hall was deserted.

I was so scared I could hardly raise the pestle. Then the door opened again, and it was Thea.

She was amazingly deft with the pastry for the samosas. She'd borrowed from Shazia a plastic ring which cut six samosa shapes at a time. We became a good team, cutting and filling and deep-frying. The pakora already sat in a delectable heap, which diminished every time anyone decided to come in to make a cup of tea, an occurrence which increased with suspicious, if flattering, frequency.

Five o'clock. We were back to schedule.

We couldn't cook the rice too much in advance in case it went soggy, but we wanted to make sure the chicken pieces to go in it were thoroughly cooked. Neither of us wanted to give Gimson the pleasure of diagnosing mass salmonella poisoning. We decided to cheat by frying them first.

'I'll get them,' said Thea, reaching into the fridge. She screamed; grunted; and keeled over.

There was no pulse.

I flung open the door to yell for help, and dashed back to start mouth-to-mouth. A few quick thuds against her chest, and then I yelled again, more loudly and desperate than I'd ever yelled.

Shazia – one look, and she was off again, screaming for Gimson and Naukez.

I never thought I'd be pleased to see Gimson. He knelt beside me.

'Keep going,' he said.

I did as I was told. I don't know how long.

Suddenly people came running, and then slammed out again. And I was elbowed aside by a slender youth who turned out to be a paramedic; Thea was stretchered out, accompanied by Gimson; and all was quiet again. But not for long.

Once again the kitchen was full, and everyone was talking, except me. I was trying to piece it all together. Shazia pressed a mug of vile, sweet Co-op tea into my hand while explaining to Tina how Naukez had saved the day by making Ian, with all his police authority, call the ambulance. Naukez stared at his muddy wellies. Matt was leaning on the door to the kitchen, white and shaking. Courtney appeared at the other door, furtive as a schoolboy saved by the fire-bell from the head's wigging. Chris was immediately behind him, but was clearly trying to push in ahead.

'What made her ill?' he asked me casually.

I shrugged. 'The sight of the dead chicken?' I opened the fridge door.

And then I too keeled over.

It wasn't Sidney amid all the chicken pieces, although I'd thought at first it was. It was another rat, its feet tied together and its head cut off. It was now in one of Ade's bags, and I was wiping tears from my face and pushing away the smelling salts Chris held ready to apply again at any minute.

I pulled myself up. Agnes had heard the commotion and abandoned her short story. She held a flask that looked as if it might hold brandy. I reached for it. It did.

'I want you checked over,' Chris was saying. 'You shouldn't be drinking alcohol after shock.'

'I'm not drinking any more of that bloody tea,' I said, ungraciously.

'Of course you're not,' Agnes agreed. 'Go on, young man, clear everyone out of here and then go yourself. We've got a job to do here – supper won't cook itself, you know.'

'But surely –' he protested.

'The chicken pieces are all sealed in polythene bags. They can't have been contaminated. And before you say anything, there's no point in sending your crew in here and hunting for fingerprints or whatever. We all use the place. Shazia wipes down all the working surfaces every morning. Just leave us to it. I promise not to put cyanide in the summer pudding.'

'I think we might notice,' I said, as she shut the door on Chris.

She shook her head. 'Not until too late. The cherries and the kirsch I put in – they have the same sort of smell as cyanide. Sweetish, almondy. I always used to disguise my children's medicines on that principle. Sickly-tasting stuff in jam, and the converse. Easy.'

As promised, I made my statement, of course. After the rat business there was no getting out of it. But I went through it like a dose of salts, to the great irritation of Ian, whose normal pace is thorough to the point of ponderous. But I had, as he admitted, nothing to add to what I'd already told him or Chris informally, and he knew where he could find me if he wanted to clarify any details.

It might make supper late, but I had to have a shower and

wash my hair. Then I found the only way to make my dryer reach from the power point to anywhere near the mirror was to lie flat on my stomach on the bed.

I was ready to cry again. Especially when someone tapped on the door.

Courtney. I ought to want to see him, to hear what Tina and Chris had decided about his future. I did, but not now. I wanted to get my hair dry and decide what to wear and go and be chatty and efficient and serve supper while all the time I was wondering about Thea.

Some of this might have shown in my face. Enough.

'Here, I'll do that for you,' he said, taking the dryer and brush. 'You poor sweetie, you haven't half had a busy day.'

He smoothed and lifted and smoothed again. I could feel myself relaxing as his hands found a rhythm.

Then he stopped. 'Where's your spray, Sophie? Ah – no, I'll get it. You sit still.'

He sprayed not my hair but the brush. 'There. Take a look. D'you think it's OK? Because I've never done it to anyone live before.'

There are questions you don't want the answer to but have to ask.

'Live? You mean you've practised on . . .' Say wigs, Courtney. Please say wigs.

'The clients like their loved ones to look nice. Make-up, too, some of them have.'

I looked in the mirror. He'd transformed my bob into something worthy of Princess Di. I wanted to say something truly appreciative, grateful. What came out wasn't.

'We're talking about corpses here, are we?'

'I hope you don't mind?'

I shook my head. The hair swung and glimmered and settled back easily. How could I mind? I smiled at him in the mirror. He smiled back.

'Courtney: Nyree – would someone make her look nice for her funeral?'

'I should hope so.'

'They say . . . they say people's hair keeps on growing. What about her roots?'

'It doesn't grow that much. The old facial hair – you have

to shave the men, sweetie. But you'd style hers so the roots don't show. You wouldn't let her go out showing any grey, not when she was so particular about her looks. I'd comb it maybe like this. And what's more, she wouldn't be able to you-know-what while I was doing it, would she?'

We grinned at each other in the mirror. Then his face became serious.

'I should have told you, shouldn't I, Soph? About why I was in the nick, why I'd got that little shooter. Drugs, you see. All to do with my job, actually. The funeral care work. It was a big firm, see. International.'

'International?'

'Of course. I mean, say that husband of hers wants her buried in Vietnam or wherever, who's going to do everything? All those rules and regulations. Someone's got to take care of everything. The poor dears can't book their own tickets, you know. Anyway, this is where Kate came in. The boss had the idea that no one would ever check inside, see. In the caskets, Soph. And there's all that padding and quilting and stuff.'

'So the coffins provided an ideal means of transport for other things than, er, bodies?'

'Right. Currency. Drugs. Even an oil painting or two, would you believe? Which reminds me, Soph: you don't look too bright. What about a spot of blusher?'

I gestured at my cosmetics bag.

'OK, you put your foundation on – haven't you got a sponge? You naughty girl! – and I'll do the rest. Turn round. There, that's better.'

'So how did you end up in Durham?'

'Kate and her friends. Someone sang. Not as loud as I did, though, when they caught me. Scared witless I was, Sophie. If you get my meaning. But they never caught the boss. And he got the message round that if he ever caught up with me . . .'

'Hence the gun?'

He nodded.

'And the last thing you wanted was to turn up here and find Kate?'

'Absolutely. And then having Nyree drop off her perch,

too – seemed like a conspiracy.'

'What about all those foreigners who keep turning up? They wouldn't be anything to do with you, would they?'

'That's what that DCI of yours wanted to know. God, I've had a day and a half of it too. Better than going back inside, though. Though he's made no promises about that. He wants to talk to my probation officer, he says.'

'What's he like in action?'

I shouldn't have asked; it was like asking how good a colleague was in the classroom.

'Didn't see much of him, Soph. Mostly some woman. Hard as nails, but fair. Then she hands me over to the DCI. Mostly he's very quiet. Then there's a sort of hiss. And every so often he gets up and bangs the table. Then he goes and stares out of the window, and this older bloke with a face like a tired horse, he comes over and starts telling you how upset the DCI is about you being involved, Soph, and why don't I make it easy for everyone and tell them all I know? But I already have. I just don't know about any Chinese or Japanese or any other-ese you care to mention. Honest. And you don't really believe me either, do you?'

I looked at him frankly. 'You know I do. But it's all so much of a coincidence.'

He gave one last dust to my nose. 'There. Have a look at yourself, and then go and wow that poet who's doing his reading tonight.'

'Poet!'

'Hugh Someone-or-other. The guest reader. Really something, he is. I'll fight you for him!'

Chapter Ten

'Is there any news of Thea?' I asked as soon as I reached the kitchen. Agnes was stirring the vegetable curry reproachfully, and permitted herself a glance at her watch.

'Mr Gimson phoned Shazia,' she said. 'She's going to live, and it's thanks to you, she says. No, don't you dare touch anything until you've got one of those aprons on. There – behind the door. Curry's indelible stuff.'

I was gracing the occasion with the only two silk items in my wardrobe: a camisole intended to make the wearer look sexy and a coordinating overshirt. White jeans, and some strappy sandals that would make Toad salivate. But I did not intend – much as I wanted to explore his dedication to the viola – to sit anywhere near Toad this evening.

I tested a forkful of Agnes's rice. Beautifully *al dente*.

'And Mr Gimson says she watched the whole affair, Sophie. From a spot near the ceiling – just up there.' She gestured with the spoon. 'I'd have loved to see Gimson's face when she said that. Oh, and he sends his apologies – he won't be joining us for our meal tonight. He's met some old crony at the hospital and he'll eat with him.'

Our colleagues had already gathered in the dining room. We could hear their voices: the publisher-elect laying down the law; a murmur from Shazia; the giggly girl and the brace-girl; Mr Woodhouse quavering a little. Matt sounded perilously forbearing – he must have got landed with Toad. And another, rather deep voice, talking to Courtney, no doubt the gorgeous poet. Hoping his appearance would match up to his calling, I positively demanded a bearded man with holey jeans and an inadequate T-shirt.

Agnes had already laid out plates for the first course, and now she staggered off with the plate of pakora. I picked up the larger plate, laden with samosas. One slid off.

It disappeared under the china cabinet, but not, I was sure, of its own volition.

'You might as well come out, Sidney,' I said. I should have been grateful for his safe return; as it was, I wished he'd waited until after supper. 'You won't enjoy that. Too spicy. You'd be better off with a biscuit. Come on, try a custard cream.'

I fished one from the biscuit barrel and held it not quite close enough. The whiskers moved a little closer. I could now see a pair of eyes.

Then the door opened.

I didn't shift my gaze from Sidney's.

'Close the door very quietly and don't speak,' I breathed. 'Come on, Sidney. You know you like biscuit. I've spent a long time sprucing up and I'm damned if I'm going to lie on the floor to talk to you. You're a civilised creature. You understand.'

He did. He crept out. A quick rush, and long teeth sank purposefully into the biscuit.

It would be a gross exaggeration to say he leaped into my hands; but he certainly consented to my picking him up without having to crawl all over the floor.

He'd kept himself respectable, but he'd lost weight and smelled more strongly than ever. There would be no separating him from his biscuit. On reflection, it would keep him usefully occupied while I transferred him back to his cage. I rather thought he might be kept in the stables tonight, under police protection. Perhaps if they kept the top half of the door open, he wouldn't stink the place out.

'OK, young man, it's straight back home for you,' I said, reaching for the door.

'Matt was right,' said the young man who opened it for me. 'You really are an interesting woman.'

I suppose to describe Hugh Brierley as a young man reflects my view that although I'm well into my thirties I'm by no means middle-aged. Hugh was about Chris's age –

thirty-eight – but he was altogether sleeker and glossier. In normal circumstances such a man might not have attracted me, and I might not have welcomed his offer to escort me back to my room. But who could refuse the chance to have doors opened when she is carrying a nervous rat?

We accomplished the journey safely, and re-installed Sidney. He'd left no more than a rat's-bottom-shaped set of creases in my shirt, and perhaps the faintest trail of fine crumbs. He drained his water bottle as we watched. I slipped out to replenish it.

Hugh was standing my the desk when I returned. He glanced ironically from me to the blank sheet of paper and the ball-point pen poised to record my poetic thoughts, as and when they should deign to flow.

I shrugged with equal irony.

What I could have done with at this point was a stiff drink. Like Sidney's, but with gin. What I had was a social situation I was by no means sure I could deal with. Particularly when Sidney demanded his litter tray.

We stood solemnly side by side and watched him use it. Then I gathered him up and once more returned him to his cage.

'The trouble is, I said, to fill the silence and get us back to supper as fast as I could, 'I bet Sidney's filling you with all sorts of poetic inspiration, while all he does is make me feel sick with the smell of him.'

'I'll let you know,' he said solemnly. 'But before we eat I'd certainly like to wash my hands.'

Not an auspicious beginning, then, to our relationship. I'd liked his opening line, but marked him low on effort and artistic achievement for the rest. I didn't sit next to him for the meal, either. The publisher-elect grabbed him, almost literally. Matt, at the head of the table, patted the seat next to him, but without enthusiasm. I joined him, with a perfunctory smile. I still craved that gin. Matt looked grey, and ate his way through the first course, the one I'd hoped would stimulate lots of favourable comments, in total silence. So did I. At last, seeing that Agnes was now deeply engaged in discussion with Hugh, Matt offered to help with collecting plates and distributing the larger ones warming in the kitchen. Then he carried in the rice – two big platters, requiring separate journeys. I took in the bowls of vegetable curry, one for each end of the table.

Still no opportunity to talk to Hugh, of course. I was irritated that I wanted to: surely I was at an age where someone's brain mattered more than his looks? And he'd hardly been charming – except for his opening comment, of course. Perhaps he was now being charming to the publisher, whose name I ought to use, if one could ever decently refer to someone as Tabitha. She was certainly laughing a great deal, though possibly at her own wit. Toad, who was opposite them, was holding forth about Madame Tussaud's for some reason.

And I ought to be talking to Matt. Even listening to him wouldn't be a bad start. I turned apologetically.

'I wonder what Gimson will eat,' I said idly. 'Perhaps he engineered Thea's attack just to avoid an ethnic meal.'

'Is that what you've been worrying about for the last ten minutes?'

'What else?'

He grinned, but then turned to look at me more fully. 'You did well there, kid,' he said at last.

'Couldn't have done anything without Shazia and Naukez. Not to mention Gimson.'

'Any idea who did it?'

I shook my head. I didn't want to point out that whoever had killed the rat had probably killed Nyree. I wondered if he'd killed Kate, too. If she'd been killed. The tampon business might suggest otherwise.

'I mean,' he pursued, 'it's not the nicest thing to do.'

'Agreed. I don't suppose either the rat or Thea enjoyed it.'

'You're being very cagey, Sophie.'

I winced extravagantly at the pun. 'Cagey? Just shit-scared!'

'They've been putting pressure on Courtney,' he continued. 'Do you think they really suspect him?'

This time I was cagey: 'I noticed he looked pretty grim – in the kitchen, just after – after . . . When I was having gibbering hysteria.'

'Such a cliché is not worthy of you. You simply passed out,

quite unobtrusively. And I'll bet those tears were caused by those stinking smelling salts that big Boy Scout of yours kept shoving up your nose. What's he got to say about it, anyway?'

'Nothing. I suppose he's been too busy detecting. That's his job.'

Matt pushed his plate away. 'Jesus, Sophie, what are we going to do?'

'Talk to Chris? Hang on, didn't he want to see you this afternoon? Did he say anything to you?'

'What didn't he say! Jesus, he's supposed to be a friend of yours, isn't he? How did you fetch up with someone like him? D'you know, he practically accused me of raping her and then disposing of her body. Me! As if I could ever harm Kate!'

I wasn't quite sure which line to take. Mostly I wanted to remain silent in the hope he'd continue. 'Did he tell you why?' I had to ask, eventually.

'The sodding glasses, that's why.'

'Glasses?'

'I had a couple of glasses in my room. And the whiskey. Irish.'

'So?'

'I'd drunk out of one, see, and Kate out of the other. I didn't try to hide them. In fact, I never even washed them up. You know how it is. And now they've confiscated them, *and* the bloody whiskey. Good job I've got another bottle. Hey, why don't you come and share it later?'

'Sounds nice,' I said, temporising. 'But why should an innocent drink make Chris think –?'

'God knows. She's a friend, Sophie. A dear, dear friend.'

'And you didn't rape her and dispose of her body?' I said, smiling grimly to show I was joking. If I was.

He dropped his voice so low I could hardly hear it above the chatter and the scrape of cutlery. 'She was my friend. We've been friends for years – nice, platonic friends. Then – I don't quite know when – I fell in love with her. I think. At least, I wanted to go to bed with her.'

'Is that why you wanted her to be a tutor? So you'd have rooms next door to each other?'

'I don't know. No, I don't think so. I thought she'd end up enjoying teaching.'

'She didn't.'

'No. And maybe if she'd stayed in the student corridor –'

'No ifs, Matt,' I said sharply. 'Being in the student wing didn't help Nyree, did it?'

'OK.'

'What about the other tutor – the one you're supposed to have poisoned?'

'Phil Doyle? He had a gall-bladder attack and needed an operation. I might as well have poisoned him – we went and had fish and chips together, and he was supposed to be on a fat-free diet. You must have heard me and Kate – it was a joke, Sophie. Honest. And I thought it would be a great chance for Kate. She . . . she loved me before I loved her. She came willingly to my room. Don't ever doubt that. And would have come to my bed. But I fell asleep. I bloody fell asleep, Sophie, with this warm attractive woman there in front of me. When I woke up, she wasn't there, of course. But before she left, she'd taken my shoes off and covered me with the duvet. And now God knows where she is.'

I touched his hand gently. He turned to clasp mine. 'The one you have to watch for,' he said in quite another voice, 'is our friend Hugh. Got a bit of a reputation, has Hugh. Mad, bad and dangerous to know.'

I pulled back my chair to peer under the table.

'Just looking,' I said to Matt, 'to see if he's got a club foot. I'm just in the mood for a Byronic hero.'

It was just as well no one had prepared Hugh a giant hollow cake for a nude woman to leap out of: there'd have been too much competition for the role of cake-filling. Both the brace-girl and the giggly girl were now craning right forward to gain his attention. Tabitha had leaned round to obscure anyone at her end of the table. Poor Courtney was feigning an interest in wax models so he could gate-crash the conversation with which Toad was still persisting.

'Being a writer is its own aphrodisiac,' Matt observed tartly. 'Hey, world! I've been published too!'

I laughed, and went round the table collecting plates. Agnes didn't notice – she was too busy burrowing in her bag for something. So it was up to me to bring in the summer pud.

Agnes hadn't found a basin big enough for all of us, so she'd used two smaller ones. She'd tipped them on to plates some time before supper and decorated them. She'd sliced strawberries round the circumference and then plonked a whole strawberry on top of each. Commissioned writer she might be, but she didn't have as dirty a mind as mine. I was shaking with silent giggles as I carried them in – chest-high, a plate in each hand. My quivering made the puddings quiver too. Matt was staring into his glass; most other people were engaging Hugh's attention or were trying to.

But Hugh looked up and caught my eye. When he smiled, slowly, erotically, I'm afraid my pulse beat distinctly faster.

I returned demurely to my place. Then, because, after all, the room was quite warm, I took off my overshirt, slipping it over the back of my chair. Perhaps the camisole would do its stuff and make me look sexy. Perhaps, even better, it would make me feel sexy. Meanwhile, waves of dejection kept washing over me. For all the brilliant cerise of the camisole and a whole tropic of colours on the overshirt, I felt bleak. Chris ought to have made some effort to come and see how I was; he shouldn't have been put off by Agnes's mock anger. He should have tried to comfort me, even if I'd rejected any attempts to do so. Kate would have cuddled Sidney. If I'd been at home I'd have dug out my old teddy bear.

I was on my own in the kitchen. The team of cooks was also supposed to wash up, but Thea was in hospital and Agnes wrestling with an asthma attack which one or two people were ready to ascribe to the presence of Sidney in the kitchen. I rather hoped other people might offer to help out, but on the assumption that I'd stay on my own, I scraped and stacked systematically. Then I thought of my silk camisole. I'd have to wear that disgusting apron again, and maybe rubber gloves.

I could feel my hair collapsing in the steam from the washing-up water; I could almost see the glow from my shiny nose, my make-up having gone wherever make-up goes. Perhaps it was a good job everyone else was dancing attendance on Hugh, I thought bitterly. Was it Mary or Martha who got stuck with the chores while her sister was listening to Jesus? And then got told off for her pains? I felt for her. And for me. And I still wanted that gin. Especially as I could hear the deep attractive laugh rumbling in the distance. At this rate, Hugh's reading might start without me.

I'd better sing.

One thing I will lay claim to is a good voice. It's not all that strong but it's true. I filled my lungs and let rip. Schubert, the Octet. All eight parts, if not quite at once.

So I jumped – literally, it seemed – when a hand lifted a plate from the drying rack.

'Sorry to hear about the rat business,' said Ade. 'Nasty thing to do.'

'Very.'

'I thought you'd like to know they'll be doing a postmortem.'

'On a rat!' I exclaimed. 'They'll be having a bloody inquest next! Doesn't having your head cut off usually result in death?'

A different hand took the next plate. 'In a case like this you can't afford to make assumptions like that, Ms Rivers,' said Chris. 'In any case, I thought you and Ade were rodent-lovers.'

'I'm more a gerbil man myself,' said Ade, who'd obviously missed the sarcasm. 'Less smelly, if less intelligent. I keep mine in a big aquarium, with a deep layer of peat and sawdust, so any smells they make are quickly diffused. And I bath them, very occasionally. You could bath Sidney, of course. That might help.'

'Bath him?' Chris asked, pausing, his hand suspended over the plate rack.

'Some rats jump, so you need to close the doors and windows. Lukewarm water, then towel them dry.'

'Not a hair dryer?' I asked, keeping my voice particularly serious.

'Only if you're very careful. Low heat. And make sure you blow the fur the right way.'

'That goes without saying.' All this talk about bloody animals when I could hear that laugh again, responding, I was sure, to Tabitha.

I emptied the washing-up water and ran the taps again. Glasses, now. But it was nice to have assistance. And I was enjoying Ade's conversation. So, I suspected, was Chris, who was gaining an insight not only into rodent care, but also into one of his more promising colleagues. I hoped he appreciated it.

'Any news,' I said, after a reasonable interval, 'of Kate?'

'The news is bloody well full of Kate,' said Chris. 'God knows who snitched to the press. We wanted to maintain the blackout another twenty-four hours at least. Haven't you seen – oh, of course, no TV, right?'

'No radio either. Just newspapers. And she wasn't front page this morning. In any case, there can't be any real news or you'd have told me – wouldn't you?'

He laughed.

'So the news is no news?' I prompted.

'The news is we're still looking. Roadblocks. We've extended the search to Cannock Chase and all public parks in the area, big and small. A check on all ports, of course. The press'll be baying round here any moment. Hell, the last thing we want is unauthorised bloody poking around. Jesus!'

I'd had enough of the press after the debacle of the spring. The only consolation was that news is a very evanescent phenomenon, so that after three days of what felt like persecution I had suddenly and completely disappeared from the headlines.

'I've briefed Shazia,' he continued. 'She's agreed to lock all the doors to the outside world. My people will stop any harassment. Let me know if . . . if –'

For once I looked straight at Chris and held his gaze. Ade dropped the spoon he was polishing. Chris and I jumped. I think we'd both forgotten he was there.

'– if you have any problems,' Chris concluded in his official voice.

Then his radio barked and he and Ade left. Ade ducked back for a moment to shake out and hang up their tea towels.

At this point the other kitchen door was opened by Toad, his hands full of glasses. We'd drunk water with the curry and apparently they'd now been drinking the surplus wine. I could easily have become either lachrymose or vicious. I hummed a little more Schubert while I decided.

'That's nice,' said Toad. 'Mozart, is it?'

'Schubert,' I corrected him gently.

'I like Schubert,' he said. 'Nice tunes.'

'Wonderful. Do you play his Sonata? The one for the arpeggione? You know, that defunct string instrument. It's been adapted for the viola, hasn't it?'

Toad stared at me. 'You do know a lot about music, don't you?'

I wondered if I detected a note of resentment. 'I just like Schubert,' I lied. 'Who's your favourite?' I know this is the sort of unanswerable question people usually put to six-year-olds, but Toad was having that effect on me. And it was better than feet.

'Oh, Mozart,' he said. 'He's so soothing, isn't he?'

That was not the adjective I would have chosen.

'Wonderful melodies,' I said mildly. 'Think of the *Sinfonia Concertante* – that slow movement.' I wished I hadn't said that. It was one of George's favourites. He said the work was the apotheosis of friendship. I bit my lip till I could taste blood. I wouldn't let Toad see me cry.

'You do know a lot. Hey, you teach English, don't you? You could tell me what I ought to read. And maybe you'd like to look at my screenplay. Give me your expert opinion.'

'I'd love to read it. But I'm not an expert.'

'I'll just go and get it. I'll read it to you while you wash up.'

'What about the reading?'

'Oh, I came to get you. And bring you these glasses.' He clearly thought I should be grateful.

'Could you swill them while I go to the loo?'

'Oh, it won't take you long. And you've missed some cups.'

'Couldn't you –'

'No.'

'Please? Won't take you a second.'

'Washing-up's women's work,' he said, with unbearable smugness.

The words came out before I could stop them: 'If I wasn't

on my best behaviour, my very, very best behaviour,' I said, 'I'd knee you in the groin for that. And as your head came down I'd tip the washing-up water over you.'

I swept out of the room.

While I was in the loo, I wondered what on earth had made me overreact so badly.

I slunk back to the kitchen. No Toad. Then the door opened.

'There you are!' said Hugh Brierley. 'I've been waiting for you.'

Chapter Eleven

The Reading.

It had certainly acquired a capital letter from somewhere. The students were sitting in a reverent circle; an old master could have used them as models for a particularly melodramatic depiction of the disciples. There was a flutter of applause as Hugh re-entered. I held back until I could scuttle into the group as unobtrusively as a cerise camisole will allow.

Toad was nowhere to be seen; my rudeness must have upset him. Gimson would still be avoiding my cooking. Naukez was no doubt counting badgers. Shazia was looking anxiously at Agnes, whose chest was still heaving. She was dragging at an asthma spray.

'Empty,' she gasped.

'And I can't find the one she says is in her bedroom,' added Shazia. 'Don't you think we ought to call a doctor?'

'Hasn't anyone else got a spray?' Hugh asked.

'Of course,' I said, forgetting, in my anxiety, all about unobtrusiveness. 'Will you try mine, Agnes?'

She nodded.

'I'll get it. Hang on.'

I ran to my room. Sidney's smell greeted me – I'd forgotten to foist him on to the police. He padded over and stood hopefully on his hind legs. I rewarded him with a tickle to the tum and a bit of biscuit.

His odour gave me another idea. In my case was some Gucci 3: I sprayed a little cloud into the air, then walked into it. That should improve both the room and me. Thirty selfish seconds doing that. Then to business. Asthma spray. Where the hell had I put it? It wasn't in my case. Then I remembered. It was in the pocket of my thicker tracksuit – I sometimes get an attack while I'm running.

I closed the door carefully. It seemed to be general knowledge that Sidney was back and it might not be mere self-interest to give him police protection. I'd try and find Ade as soon as the Reading was over. I dodged into a bathroom and washed the inhaler's plastic outer case carefully; then it occurred to me that she might find an antihistamine tablet useful, so I took extra seconds to go back to my room and dig a bubble strip from my toilet bag.

Then I legged it – via the kitchen so I could get her a glass of water – back to the lounge. Toad was now in the group. He glared at me resentfully and hunched a shoulder when I tried to catch his eye. A couple of gasps at the spray gave Agnes enough breath to agree that a tablet would be useful. Shazia pressed one out of the strip and held the glass to Agnes's lips.

Matt coughed quietly. Not to attract general attention – just mine. Without a word he burrowed under the big cushion at the back of his chair and out came at least half a bottle of rioja, followed by a glass. Then he put the cushion on the floor beside him.

'I'll give you a hand with the washing-up and tidying afterwards,' he said. 'There were a couple of plods in there when I looked in, and I'm afraid I wasn't in the mood for light conversation after this afternoon.'

I nodded. I understood, and was grateful for his offer.

'Before we start,' he continued, in his public voice, 'I thought you should all know that incoming calls are being intercepted to save us being harassed by the media. The Bill are stopping traffic at the main gate. Shazia has agreed to keep the house doors locked to keep out any more energetic paparazzi who might've walked from the access point down by the motorway. If you want to talk to the press, that's up to you. But remember to respect everyone else's privacy.'

Whenever Matt spoke, people seemed to murmur agreement. They murmured now. I almost wished for a Gimsonian interruption.

At last, Matt introduced Hugh Brierley. 'He's a poet who

appears in many of the small literary magazines – *Iron* and *Stand*, for instance. Many people think he deserves a wider audience. Perhaps he'll get it in the autumn, when Bloodaxe publish his first collection. Ladies and gentlemen, Hugh Brierley.'

Hugh smiled, much less tense than I'd have expected him to be, and started. He projected his voice well and without apparent effort. While he read, I tried to make sense of the man. He certainly didn't have the air of someone starving in a garret; payments from small presses for occasional poems wouldn't buy shoes or a shirt like tonight's. His lean, elegant build suggested regular weight training or running. He had slender hands with rather heavy veins and tendons, and used them economically to emphasise the occasional point. His head was interesting, too. He might be losing that fair hair, but his skull was the sort designed to be shown off. His facial bones were good, but then, I've always liked heavy brows and wide cheekbones, and jaws untrammelled by jowls. In this light his eyes were so blue as to be navy. How could I fancy such a visual cliché? And yet there was a saving grace – one of his teeth, the second incisor, protruded slightly. I wondered why he'd never had an orthodontist treat it, but I was glad he hadn't. All in all, he'd certainly be decorative company. Perhaps I should invite him to join me if I went for my constitutional tomorrow.

His poetry was so easy to listen to I suspect he must have spent hours polishing it. Politics; erotica; desolation in the Black Country; a curiously moving, unsentimental poem or two about his handicapped brother. A funny one about growing old. As encores, two about food.

Then questions. I've always found that many people at this sort of gathering ask not to discover anything but to show how clever they are. This group was no exception. Most questions were longer than the answers. Once or twice I suspected him of trying to catch my eye. More likely it was Matt's: I could feel suppressed chuckles shaking the seat I was leaning against.

Inevitably, when the Reading was over, he was mobbed. Matt stood up slowly, rubbing his back.

'OK, let's attack that washing-up. Much left?'

I looked around: there were still some glasses and coffee cups.

'Hardly worth bothering you. I'll soon –'

'You gather these up,' he said. 'I'll see if there's anything left in the dining room.'

Matt's formula for effective washing-up included glasses of triple-distilled Irish whiskey for the workers, so progress was not especially fast. Matt was silent and his face grim. But I was content just to have company.

The door from the hall opened and Hugh came in. Without speaking he took a glass and poured himself several fingers' worth. Then he took a tea towel and started polishing. Very domesticated.

'They're still in the lounge,' he said at last. 'Is there anywhere else we could sit?'

'The terrace? But it might be a bit chilly,' I said. 'Maybe I should get my overshirt.'

'No need. A perfect summer evening,' said Matt emphatically. 'What are we waiting for?'

Perfect, but chilly. I needed my overshirt. Matt too was dithering, and plainly uninterested in Hugh's disquisition on the different colours of streetlights in the industrial West Midlands. As he talked, his Black Country accent grew more perceptible; so, I'm sure, did mine. Quarry Bank and Oldbury, respectively.

'Let's go in,' Matt said abruptly, interrupting Hugh in mid-sentence. 'My room. Come on.'

'I'd like to find a policeman first,' I said. 'To protect Sidney. I'd hate him to end up in a fridge.'

Rather to my surprise, Matt and Hugh fell in beside me, one on either side. Ade was nowhere to be seen. Matt and Hugh were absolute in their rejection of my idea that Sidney could join us in our drinking party. We compromised eventually. I would see if there was any other police officer with a tender disposition and no sense of smell. When we saw a young PC on duty at the far end of the student corridor, our problem was solved.

'The Gaffer's asked me to check off each of you as you retire for the night,' he said.

'Singly or in pairs?' asked Matt.

'In threes, if that's what takes your fancy,' said the constable, winking lewdly.
'Thank you, constable,' I said, deciding it was time to take control of the conversation. 'But I'm not retiring yet. I came to check on the rat.'
'No one's been in your room since I came here at ten, miss.'
'Thanks. But I'll just make sure.' Perhaps Matt's tension had infected me. My hands were sweating so much I could hardly turn the key, and I fumbled clumsily for the light. But the smell reassured me – and there was Sidney stretching and asking for food. Matt cautiously jiggled a bit of biscuit for him, but Hugh shoved his hands ostentatiously in his pockets and stayed close to the door.

Matt's room might have been much more luxurious than the students', but it was short of chairs. Matt made for his sofa. I found my natural level on the floor. Hugh hesitated, at last plumping for the other end of the sofa, whence he must have had an unparalleled view of my camisole and thus my braless chest. We had another slurp of whiskey, Hugh leaning well over me to fill my glass.
'God, what a course!' said Matt. 'Missing tutor, sudden death, illness and stinking rodents. I'll be glad to get back to my allotment.'
'Funny group, too. Not much sense of unity,' said Hugh. 'And those questions. Jesus! "How do you write a poem?" Bloody hell!'
'Surprised you didn't ask that, Sophie. All these people dripping with useless ideas, Hugh, and the only person who's blocked is Sophie. She's the only one with anything to say, of course.'
'Am I?'
'Can't have less than the others, love. And Kate said you were writing some sort of requiem.'
'Requiem? Are you sure? I thought I wanted to write a goodbye poem, but requiem sounds better, doesn't it? I shall be able to go back to college and pass a hand wearily across my forehead and sigh, "No, I didn't get away this holiday – I've been too busy working on my requiem."'

'So long as it isn't for you,' said Hugh, with an intonation I found promising.

I smiled, dismissively.

'Not till she's put something on paper, anyway. Come on, Sophie – let's get you started. Hugh, how do we get her started?'

'A drop more whiskey, for a start. And I'd better have some too. And you.' He poured, generously. 'There. Now what shall we write a poem about?' He settled back on the sofa.

'Something profound and significant of course,' said Matt. 'Really serious. But it's difficult to find anything to rhyme with sex.'

'We're going to write about sex, then,' I said, reaching up to Matt's desk for his notepad. This was clearly a meeting to be minuted. 'Does Matt have a seconder?'

Hugh and I raised our hands.

'Any abstentions?' I peered around the room.

'Only if we haven't any condoms,' said Matt. Then he looked embarrassed.

'Don't worry, you won't need condoms,' I said. 'Drink provoketh the desire but taketh away the performance.'

'Food doesn't,' said Hugh. He felt round for a nonexistent cushion, rubbed his back, and then shifted from the sofa to the floor.

'Food provoketh the desire and increaseth the performance? OK, so we write a poem about food. And sex,' Matt added, but not as an afterthought.

'We'll start with tonight's meal, then,' said Hugh.

'But what'd rhyme with curry?' I demanded.

'We don't try to rhyme with curry. We find other words associated with curry.'

'Like fart,' said Matt. 'Art, heart, cart, tart: they all rhyme with fart.'

'I can think of words to rhyme with sick,' I said, 'but I don't think any of them are poetic. Is poetic.'

'Rice,' said Hugh firmly. 'We had rice. Saffron-flavoured rice. Voluptuous mounds of saffron-flavoured rice. And with rice we rhyme spice.'

'It was a good biryani,' said Matt. 'The cardamom, the

cumin – and that sauce was perfection.' He kissed the tips of his fingers in my direction.

'Don't thank me,' I said. 'Thank Bashurat Ali. When he passed his GCSEs, his dad took me and all the others who'd taught him to his restaurant. Taught us how to cook. And then treated us to a wonderful meal he'd cooked himself.'

'Bashurat Ali won't rhyme. Sorry. More whiskey?'

'Hell, Hugh, you're knocking back that stuff as if it's wine,' Matt protested, inspecting the bottle.

'Well done! We can rhyme wine and dine. And we've got to mention Sophie's wonderful pair of puddings.'

'Agnes's puddings. I merely –'

'Sophie, nothing you do is merely anything –'

Matt banged his glass on the table. 'Order, please. I think we have a first line. You were talking about voluptuous rice, Hugh. Mounds of the stuff.'

'*Voluptuous mounds of saffron-coloured rice*: yes!' yelled Hugh. 'Come on. How about: *Richly something sauces, every single spice* –'

'Richly oiled?' said Matt.

'*Richly oiled sauces, every single spice* – new line – *A separate something on the tongue*.'

'*A separate explosion*, I said. 'Hey, I didn't know you could write poetry by committee.'

'Make sure you minute it all,' said Hugh.

I did.

I gave up counting the glasses of hooch. I gave up wondering how we'd come to write a poem, most of which was now recorded on Matt's pad, if illegibly. I knew there was some reason why Hugh had to try Kate's relaxation technique, the one involving paperbacks and the floor. I knew there was some reason why I was wearing one of Matt's sweatshirts. I might as well do the obvious thing and go to sleep. After all, Hugh was fast asleep on his pile of books, and Matt had lapsed into total silence, broken only by occasional rumbling snores, rapidly cut off as he struggled back to consciousness. With a certain amount of effort I could possibly have tiptoed to the door and back through long, dark corridors to bed. But it seemed easier to reach for the light switch and simply doze for a bit.

I woke up sharply at three. But there was no point in staying awake. Awake would be cold and stiff and sensible. Asleep was warm and friendly.

Five thirty was much chillier and more uncomfortable. I had a crick in my neck and an urgent need for the loo. At first I tried not to move, less I disturb the others. I could concentrate on thinking about a poem of my own. A requiem. I looked round the room. I peered at the sky.

Matt moved slightly. His head fell with its full weight on my bladder. I had to move now.

Moving Matt's head as gently as I could, I eased myself up and tiptoed round Hugh to the bathroom. But if I used the *en suite* one I might wake the others. Since I didn't expect to sleep again, and I might well chase that elusive poem more successfully now, I would go back to my own room. I reached the door and shut it quietly enough, but the corridor screamed out under my feet as embarrassingly as if I were leaving a lover's arms.

Chapter Twelve

I might as well go back via the dining room and pick up my overshirt.

The curtains were still drawn, of course. I opened them, and threw open a window, for someone had violated the house rule by smoking what smelled this morning like a compost heap. It was a nice day out there. Too bright too early, maybe. I guessed it would rain later.

Automatically I picked up a couple of used paper napkins and threw them in the bin, and straightened a chair.

Then I saw the back of my overshirt.

The first thing to do was hold back the bile rising in my throat. I grasped the back of another chair and breathed deeply. That was better. Now I could walk back and take a proper look.

What had looked like a splash of blood was in fact part of the multicoloured pattern. But the corkscrew was undeniably there, driven deep into the back of the chair, through the back of the shirt. The implication was horribly clear.

This time the shock made me think properly, if very slowly. This was evidence. The police had to see it. If the police were to see it, I had to find a policeman. Or woman. And then I had to get the hell out of Eyre House.

Back in the student corridor, the PC was asleep. I had to shake him awake.

Normally I'd have laughed. But something – my fear, perhaps – made me unreasonably angry. Anyone could have got past him and attacked Sidney. Or, come to think of it, me, if I'd spent the night there.

'Get your fucking arse out of that chair,' I found myself yelling. 'And get on that radio of yours. Tell them to seal off the dining room until DCI Groom's seen it. Tell DCI Groom I'm OK but I'm making myself scarce. And sit here, with the rat in his cage on your bloody lap, until someone takes him into protective custody. Got all that? Go on, then. While I'm fetching the rat.'

Sidney was still there in his cage in my room, safe and hungry. He demolished a peanut while I threw on some more sensible clothes and grabbed my bag. I shoved my make-up bag inside it: I couldn't face the day without it, but wouldn't wait around here to apply it. Then I piled Sidney's food and litter tray on his cage, and dumped the lot beside the PC.

'Anything happens to him and you answer for it: get that?'

He nodded.

'And don't forget to tell your gaffer I'm all right. I just can't stay here any longer.'

'Miss, I – shouldn't you – we could . . .'

But I was halfway down the corridor and didn't hear anything else.

I cut through the student car park, wishing I'd got more rapid transport than a pair of legs and a blue and cream bus. Perhaps I might even get as far as home and come back in George's van. But it would look out of place among all the neat cars. Gimson's Rover was back, I saw. I wondered what he'd eaten instead of the biryani.

I was nearly at the main gates before I realised I'd scarcely be able to get through unnoticed. Matt had told us the police were guarding us, but the mention of Chris's name should get me through.

As it happened, I needed no open sesame. The gate was swarming with officers, but they were all engaged in deep discussion with the driver of a large silver Mercedes. The ladies and gentlemen of the press were so enthralled with this that they took no notice of me. I didn't want to alter this state of affairs, so I didn't try and find out what was going on. But I did see that the driver was probably oriental, though the car was British-registered.

At least this gave me an idea of how I might spend my day profitably. Nyree, Japanese tourists, another oriental – there must be some sort of connection. Must be. Money always seemed a good reason for people to start chasing other people. It must be big money for people to hurtle round the world. Big money and Japan: was that unlikely? And yet Kenji hadn't phoned me back.

Like the little red hen, therefore, I'd have to do the work myself.

I sat on the bus slapping on make-up and thinking hard. I needed a refuge. One place no one would think of looking for me, surely, was a library. I could bury myself in the stacks and dig through endless copies of old newspapers. There were two libraries to choose from. The Central Reference Library, the one Prince Charles condemned as looking more like a place for burning books than one for reading them, and the one at the college I work at – William Murdock. William Murdock is a desperately poor inner-city college, with a library budget of £20,000 a year. But it retains all its old newspapers so students can photocopy items for projects and other work. And as a refuge it was even safer than a public library. So I got off the bus a couple of stops earlier than I'd planned and set off briskly up the hill to the college. Too briskly. A rattle of asthma tightened my chest. Blast! Relax. Breathe out slowly. Lower the shoulders. And put out of your mind the fact that your asthma spray is safe and sound in Agnes's handbag.

I knew the solitary porter on duty well enough to ask him to phone up to the library if any stranger should appear, and pressed the lift button. Normally I walk up the stairs to the seventh floor, but this time it was better to appease the chest than exercise the legs.

The librarian was wearing a pair of workman's overalls and greeted me from the top of a stepladder. He was lifting books from the shelves and banging them together to shift the dust. This was not going to be a comfortable place.

'Morning, Mark. Nice to see you doing some deep academic work!'

He threw a book at me. Then he came down, and we spent a few depressing minutes reviewing our holidays and the prospects for the next term. Eventually I asked where he'd put all our old papers.

'Out there,' he said, pointing to the window.

I peered out. Seven floors down were two skips.

'Mark! I needed – Hell, I'll have to go off to the Central Ref.'

'They've only got microfiche there,' he said smugly.

'Only got –'

'And I've just got a CD-ROM system.'

'Congratulations. What does it play?'

'Sophie, I thought you were supposed to have been on all the computer courses going. Come over here and sit down.'

I followed him to a quiet corner with a new computer. He inserted a compact disc.

'There! All the *Guardians* for the last two years. Up till the end of June, anyway. We'll get the update for the summer round about mid-October. What do you want to look up?'

'You mean all the news for two years is on that one disc?'

'Everything the *Guardian* covered, anyway. There are other papers available, but we could only afford one. Go on, tell it what to look up.'

I typed in 'Japan'. Pages of references appeared on the screen. I accessed one idly. Whale meat. Not much help. But not disappointing – not on this twentieth-century miracle toy.

'Give it some more factors,' said Mark, grinning. 'Or try something different. You can browse or look up specific stories. Go on. Poke it. See what it does.'

He stayed with me for ten minutes or so, as we pursued increasingly unlikely references. But the library assistants threatened mutiny if he didn't return to the spring-cleaning, and so he left me to it.

In the next hour or so I concentrated so hard I forgot my asthma. I knew a great deal about Japan, about Vietnam and about Nyree's husband. But eventually I had to admit that there was absolutely bloody nothing that helped. I learned that apart from his idiosyncratic politics, Nyree's husband might have been an exemplary capitalist. Nyree had been, in fact, not Mrs but Lady Compton. Her husband was Sir Magnus Compton. He was a keen yachtsman. He liked opera. He'd played in a pro-am golf tournament alongside some professional golfer I'd never heard of. He'd been on several company boards. He'd never been ambassador to any of the Western states. He'd fled to Vietnam. Period.

I told myself that there might be something in the last two months, but of course for the next thrilling instalment I'd have to resort to leafing through the Clover Index.

By now the book-banging had reached the next aisle. The dust was reaching me. I started to wheeze. And I had no Ventolin.

You can't buy that sort of asthma spray. It's available on prescription only. So I had to hope I'd got a spare at home, or talk my way into the doctor's for an emergency appointment. Home then. Maybe what I jokingly call the fresh air of Birmingham's Inner Ring Road would clear my chest.

I was actually beginning to feel better by the time I reached Five Ways, a fiendish traffic junction. On Broad Street, one of the roads off it, is the 103 bus stop; the 103 would take me home. First, however, I popped into Boots to buy some antihistamine tablets. They would help my asthma, as they'd helped Agnes's. I'd left my tablets back at Eyre House, of course. The change from my fiver would help get me on the bus – you had to give the driver the exact fare.

I was out on Broad Street, at the bus stop, counting it out, when a voice called my name. At first I took no notice; then, as the voice got nearer, I looked up. And smiled in disbelief. Hugh!

The Mondiale, a big hotel among other big hotels on Broad Street, would not have been my choice for morning coffee. But to demur when Hugh suggested it would have been to engage in all sorts of explanations that would have embarrassed me at this stage in what appeared to be a nicely developing relationship. The place had bad memories, of sexual humiliation and what I now suspected was an attempt to kill me. But there are times when bad memories can be replaced with good ones, and I hoped Hugh might work this sort of magic.

The omens weren't entirely good. He drank his coffee black, and gestured away the cream cakes with a shudder that suggested his liver was still resentful after last night's alcohol. I was now on good terms with mine, however, and consumed more than my share. Hard work always makes me hungry, and my stomach insisted it was lunchtime.

'What time – what time did you . . .?' Hugh hesitated charmingly.

'About six. I had an early breakfast – that's why I'm so hungry. What brings you into Brum, anyway?'

'The car. One of the warning lights keeps flickering on and off. I don't believe this theory that alarm lights are there just to alarm. I don't want to find I've run out of brake fluid or something. So I've dropped it off at Rydale's for a check-up.'

Rydale's suggested an up-market car, but I didn't want to appear inquisitive.

'They say it'll be ready mid-afternoon. So I've got some time to kill. Maybe we could kill it over some lunch?'

'That would be lovely. But I have to get home first.' I patted my chest. 'Agnes still has my asthma spray, and I daren't be without one when I run.'

'You run, do you?'

It sounded as if I might have acquired a brownie point. But there was something else in his voice that might have been – no, it was too fleeting for me to allow my expectations to be raised.

My asthma rattled again, and he earned several points. Why hadn't I thought of a taxi?

George's van was sitting patiently in front of my house. The taxi pulled up behind it. Hugh paid. The neighbourhood curtains shimmied.

It should be made clear at this point that though I found Hugh increasingly attractive, and though I had every reason to believe he reciprocated, not a caress, not a kiss had been exchanged. Sooner or later I hoped to remedy this. But later might well have to do: I needed my spray quite badly now.

I left Hugh in the living room and walked slowly upstairs. I knew I had a Becotide spray, but that works more as a preventive. I needed a quick spurt of Ventolin to clear the tubes. If I started to panic and throw things around in my efforts to find a spray, the asthma would get worse.

There was nothing on the dressing table, nor in the bathroom cupboard. But I'd taken a new one away. I remembered taking it out of its packet at Eyre House. I sat down on the bed. I hadn't stripped it before I went away.

So there was the old one, tucked under the pillow. Two long sucks. And then two at the Becotide. I was a new woman. Shoving them both in my pockets, I ran down lightly to Hugh.

It seemed quite natural to squat beside him on the floor. He was picking his way through my tapes, commenting occasionally on a particular interpretation. A man who liked Brahms in my living room. Life might be looking up.

We had more coffee and he looked at my books. My asthma had cleared completely. My stomach was ready for a proper lunch, although the rest of me would infinitely have preferred an improper one. What I had to do was work at maintaining without break the tension between us. On one level we might have known one another for years, on another we both seemed shy enough to suggest a sexual interest. As we sat at my kitchen table, we were mirroring each other nicely. Eye contact was being made. From personal tastes we were beginning to talk about each other.

'It's amazing,' he was saying, 'how much someone's house, someone's home, shows about them.'

'What does mine tell you about me, then?' I leaned forward, my chin in my right hand.

He responded by leaning forward, chin in hand too.

'Oh, apart from the obvious things like music and the nineteenth-century novel, there's your paintings.'

'Not mine. I'm no artist. They're all by friends, though. I used to collect china until an enterprising burglar smashed the lot last spring. Perhaps these will be less vulnerable.'

'Unless your burglar slashes them,' he said.

Suddenly I felt cold. 'What about some lunch?' I said, just to make my mouth move again.

We decided to go out for our meal, the contents of my freezer being generally unlabelled. One of these days I'd get a proper system, I said. I knew what most things were, but there was always an element of serendipity in my frozen meals.

He grinned. 'I'll bet your whole life is serendipity.'

'I wonder how the other people on the course live. Agnes,

for instance – she'll have a clock in every room, and probably a timetable. An organised woman.'

'What about Matt?'

'A man of good intentions, surely. Bottle banks, that sort of thing.'

'And?'

'No. He's a friend of yours, isn't he? I won't be lured into discussing friends.'

'Not a close friend, but I take your point. What about some of the others?'

'Your turn,' I said. I leaned against the front door. That was as far as we'd got.

'All right. That publisher woman. Loud paintings, loud music and a loud car. And a wardrobe full of short skirts that are really quite embarrassing with those thighs. Why don't you wear a skirt, Sophie? I suspect you're covering things that deserve a greater public exposure.'

My smile was meant to be enigmatic, but it probably looked smug. I thought I'd better change the subject. 'OK: how about Mr Woodhouse?'

'The elderly man? He'd have slippers, a cupboard full of vitamin tablets and a pile of gardening magazines. Come on – we can shred your colleagues over lunch. Where shall we eat?'

'Somewhere local?' I opened the front door and held it for him. 'How about Valentino's? That's pleasant enough and literally just down the road. And there's a car park just behind it.'

Shyness seemed to return while we waited for our order. We drank Perrier sip for sip; half a bottle only of the house red with our meal. What we ought to do was let our fingers touch, not quite by chance. But neither was ready to make the move. My voice sounded, to my ears, a little strained. He stuttered occasionally. How fortunate that teachers are used to plugging conversational gaps. In I plunged again.

'We never finished speculating about people's houses,' I said. 'I've been trying to work out what sort of place you'd occupy.'

It was the wrong thing to say. I could sense him fending me off.

'Oh, it's very ordinary. Victorian. High ceilings, huge heating bills. Untidy.' He stopped. What on earth had he been about to say? 'Now, there was a surgeon on the course – modern luxurious or period luxurious?'

'Expensive spartan, I'd say. Those knobbly Jacobean chairs that are wonderfully carved but fiendish to sit on. A big, big bathroom with black and white tiles. But something surprising. Like his smoking's out of character. A huge tank of tropical fish – big enough to occupy a whole wall, perhaps.'

'I'll tell you who'd keep fish,' said Hugh, relaxing again. 'That man who sat opposite me last night. He'd keep piranhas, and enjoy watching them eat live goldfish. Or snakes that consumed mice. God, he gave me the creeps. He went on and on about Madame Tussaud's. About Nielsen and Neilson and how odd it was two criminals should have nearly the same unusual name. Over and over.'

'He's supposed to be keen on animal rights. Would that square with nasty pets?'

And then our first course appeared.

He'd chosen a minestrone so thick he could nearly stand his spoon up in it. I'd remembered the plentiful food at Eyre House and been virtuous with a Galia melon. Swordfish *pizzaiola* for his main course, a succulent and surprisingly large breast of chicken in lemon sauce for me. Then a wonderful sweet, the name of which I never caught, but which came with cream cheese and liqueur and chocolate and more calories than I cared to contemplate.

Over the coffee, I brought the conversation back to Toad. An idea had been growing, burgeoning throughout the meal. It blossomed as we simultaneously produced our credit cards.

'The DCI in charge of the Eyre House case,' I said carefully, 'is convinced that someone broke into my room using one of these. Have you ever done anything like that?'

'Good God, no. I'm a respectable – poet.'

'The last thing a poet should be is respectable,' I said. 'Poets should have adventures. Think of Byron.'

'I don't want to go and fight anywhere,' he said. 'Or be pursued by a latter-day Lady Caroline Lamb.'

'There are other sorts of adventures,' I said. And I flexed my flexible friend.

Chapter Thirteen

It was raining heavily by the time we left Valentino's at about three, and my enthusiasm for burglary was appropriately dampened. Perhaps I had meant it as a joke and certainly Hugh took it that way – or perhaps it was an offbeat substitute for what I really wanted, which was an afternoon in bed with Hugh. I was destined not to get that, either.

Lunch, which we took late, of course, had been a leisurely affair, if that is not a misnomer. Hugh said his car would be ready by three thirty. I offered to run him into the city centre on my way back to Eyre House. I'd resolved to take George's van back there. If I couldn't do any burglary, I might do some spying. It was scarcely an unobtrusive vehicle, but it would provide shelter in a stakeout: that was the term my TV heroines Cagney and Lacey would use. I had a vision of myself huddled in the van drinking coffee – though I'd forgotten, of course, to provide myself with a flask – watching a villain lead me to Kate. It was quite a pleasant scenario. Unfortunately it led to my hopping across the lights at the Green Man when I could have just stopped, and I soon found a flashing blue light in my rear-view mirror.

I pulled over immediately and got out of the van, looking suitably apologetic. I was prepared for a bollocking, and for a charge of careless driving if the fates were against me.

It looked as if I would get away with it. Hugh corroborated my truthful denial of having had too much to drink, and so I was even spared the public humiliation of a breathalyser, which disappointed the people in the nearby bus shelter. And after a telling-off, which I accepted with very good grace, I was allowed to go on my way. So I drove at an exemplary thirty towards Five Ways, the police car twenty yards behind me. Surely I'd proved by now I was a good, law-abiding citizen? But then they flashed me again. I pulled over. I got out, at least as irritated as I was puzzled. I walked towards them, spreading my hands in innocence. They ignored me.

But they pulled Hugh from his seat and thrust him hard against the side of the van, arms and legs spread-eagled.

Both officers continued to ignore me.

'May I ask what you're doing?' I demanded. My voice carries, remember – all those years of teaching and sounding confident when you're sick with terror. 'What's going on?'

For answer, one of the policemen dragged Hugh's arms free of the van, twisted them up his back and handcuffed them. The other officer yelled the standard caution. They were arresting him! Then they dragged him to the patrol car and threw him face down on the back seat.

'Officer,' I shouted, 'what are you doing? Leave him alone!'

The machismo appeared to be over for a while. One of them took my arm quite gently and propelled me towards the car's front passenger seat.

'It's all right now, Sophie.'

'On the contrary, it plainly isn't.' How dared they use my name? Because I'd shot the lights, that's why. And it was another form of power, that's why. I shook my arm free, but, because he kept stepping towards me, was forced into the front passenger seat. 'What are you doing to Mr Brierley? I've never seen such brutality.'

'Now don't you worry yourself, please. We'll go off to Rose Road nick – PC Clarke here'll drive your van if you give us your keys – and then we'll have a word with our friend.'

His voice was irritatingly soothing, as if he were genuinely concerned for my wellbeing. The only way I could react was with an extra spurt of anger. 'What the blazes for?'

The officer leaned back irritatingly in his seat and ticked off his fingers: 'Abduction – that's kidnapping –'

'I know what abduction means. Who's he supposed to have abducted?'

'Hear me out, Sophie. Abduction. Murder. Resisting arrest. Don't even think he had his seat belt on.'

More power. Smug power. The men smiled impregnably. I felt like a fly hitting a window. A vast, impotent anger gathered. This fly must crack the window.

I got out of the car and removed my shoe.

'Come on, Sophie, what d'you think you're doing now? You ought to be sitting down having a nice cup of tea. And we want the police surgeon to check you over.'

'If you do not release Mr Brierley I shall smash your windscreen,' I said. 'That'll take some explaining when you get it back to the pound.' At least I had their attention now. 'You think Mr Brierley is connected with the Eyre House business: yes? Why don't you get on the phone to DCI Groom? Then we can clear up this mess now.' The authority in my voice grew. 'And don't think I don't know you, Constable Kevin Bennett. I remember you as a sweet little police cadet trying to abseil down from the fifteenth floor at William Murdock and nearly getting the sack for it. If I hadn't begged them to give you a second – or was it a third or fourth – chance, you'd be one of the three million on the dole.'

'And you –' I wagged my shoe at Clarke before slipping it back on – 'had better release Mr Brierley. Now! And if you apologise nicely he may limit himself to suing for wrongful arrest rather than assault.'

'Can't release him now, miss,' said Bennett, a touch sheepishly, getting out of the car. 'Once he's been arrested, we have to go through the formalities. And to do that we have to take him to Rose Road. And ask you if you'd be kind enough to accompany us. As the complainant.'

'I'm not complaining except about this. Damn it, you've got a crowd out here as big as if you were selling Cup Final tickets. I'm driving peaceably into town, and I get pulled over and my passenger assaulted.'

'Please, miss –'

'Get Chris Groom on the phone.'

'Got to go through the radio system for that. Much easier if you'd agree. You could phone him from Rose Road.'

'If I say no?'

'He has to go anyway. And it'd be easier for him if you were there to confirm you didn't want to press charges.'

'Get the handcuffs off him then, and let him sit like a human being. Now.'

I watched them release Hugh. He'd remained silent throughout, but from the way he shook his hands free I deduced it was because he was too angry to risk speech. The look he shot at me was hardly tender. Then he softened, and grinned.

'Thank God I'm not one of your students,' he said.

'Oh, I'm nice to them. Aren't I, Bennett?'

Bennett looked delightfully embarrassed.

'See you in a minute,' I said. And got into George's van and drove through the one-way system back to Rose Road Police Station.

Tender as if I were an invalid, they ushered me through anonymous beige corridors and handed me over to a WPC. She smiled and steered me into a green-painted room, shutting the door. Wherever I might be, I wasn't in a cell. There was a carpet, and bulgy easy chairs and a sofa.

The WPC answered the question my eyes asked.

'The rape suite!' I exclaimed. 'But I haven't been raped!'

'Just sit down for a minute, Sophie. I'll make you a coffee – or would you prefer tea? – and then we can clarify everything.'

I sat. There was no point in maintaining my blind fury. The sooner I convinced everyone that I was sane and sober, the sooner they'd release Hugh.

The WPC nodded and touched my arm lightly. Then she disappeared behind a curtain, and I could hear her filling a kettle. I looked around me. More curtains the other side of the room. They weren't drawn tightly enough to hide the sort of high bed I associate with gynaecological check-ups. And there was a supply of rubber gloves and a speculum, no doubt. There was a bathroom to my right.

'Here you are!' The WPC offered me extra sugar, which I waved away, but I took the mug.

She smiled encouragingly. If I'd been raped, I'd be able to talk to her, maybe. I'd be able to pour it all out, knowing that whatever I said wouldn't shock her out of her calm control. She'd be kind and supportive, wouldn't she? So how would she take the simple truth?

I peered at her shirt – in this clearly labelled world, I expected her to have a name badge. But the police have numbers, of course.

'Helen,' she said.

Yes. I should have remembered. They'd introduced us as if we were to become friends. She'd be one of a small team supporting me as long as I needed them. At that point I'd been too angry to do more than nod.

'Helen,' I began, 'there really has been a mistake, you know. And I do realise that your people were acting in what they believed were my best interests, but it is time to stop. Mr Brierley is a respectable man –'

At this point I stopped. I knew nothing of the man, except that he wrote poetry and that I fancied him. He was no more than a party acquaintance, was he? But when you meet people you have to take them on trust, if you like them, that is.

'If you contact Matt Purvis at Eyre House –' I burrowed in my bag for my diary to tell her the phone number. She assumed I wanted a cigarette, and had her lighter ready. I flourished the diary. 'Look, can't you just phone? Or better still, phone DCI Groom. He'd surely have the authority to release him.'

Helen shook her head.

'Not even the chief constable could do that. Nor the home secretary. Once someone's been formally arrested, there's a set procedure we have to adhere to. I'm sorry, I really am. But there's absolutely nothing we can do.'

'So where is he now? What's happening to him?'

'I'll check for you.' Helen picked up the phone, but as she did so there was a tap on the door and another woman, part of the support team, came in. She was in sweatshirt and jeans, and wore a name label: Molly. Molly sat down beside me on the squashy sofa and leaned towards me. She looked so kind I could have screamed.

'You really are quite sure you don't want to make any sort of complaint against Mr Brierley?' Helen asked before Molly could say anything.

The women exchanged eye contact.

'You're quite sure he's not threatened you – said that if you don't deny it he'll make things worse?' asked Molly. 'Because if he has, we can offer you protection as long as you need it. Up to the trial and beyond.'

'Hugh Brierley has done nothing to harm me. Last night he helped guard me. I left a message with one of your colleagues at Eyre House that I was leaving. To be honest, bolting like that wasn't the most sensible thing I've ever done. But I'd just had another threat. Nothing verbal, but someone had attached a shirt I'd been wearing to my chair with a corkscrew and I overreacted. I spent the morning at the college I work at and then I met Hugh. Quite by chance. He'd taken his car to Rydale's for repair. You can check. We had coffee at the Mondiale, and cake – the most wonderful fattening banana cream cake you've ever tasted – and then we took a taxi back to my home so I could collect my asthma spray. Lunch at Valentino's. The rest you know. Look, you could clear this up straight away.'

Molly stood up. 'You're telling the truth? OK, I'll go and talk to the custody officer. It won't make things any quicker but it might make it easier.'

I turned to Helen. 'What'll be happening to him?'

She looked at her watch. 'They should have finished the documentation procedure by now. And he'll have been allowed his phone call. I should imagine he'll have called a solicitor. If he doesn't know any solicitors, then there's a duty solicitor.'

I laughed grimly. I should imagine that a man with Hugh's assurance would have a solicitor tucked away somewhere. One who would have a wonderful time dealing with Hugh's complaints against the police.

'He'll wait for his solicitor in a cell,' Helen continued. 'Then he'll be taken to an interview room.'

'Are the cells like those on TV? Plastic mattresses? The loo in full view of the door?'

She nodded.

'And it'll take how long to set him free?'

'Two hours.'

'Bloody hell! And I was supposed to be seducing him this afternoon.'

As it was, I spent the time reading back copies of *Hello* and contemplating a pair of sexually explicit dolls. This must be where they brought victims of child-abuse, too.

We were eventually reunited in a little apricot-painted interview room just off the reception area. Neither of us said much, not with Helen there, but we managed a very asexual hug, and he ruffled my hair in what I hoped was a forgiving way. Then we shook hands most cordially with all involved, and beat it to my van.

'Don't say anything. Just get this bloody thing moving,' he said, fastening his seat belt.

I pulled into Rose Road and turned down the hill. When there was a gap in the cars parked at the kerb, I pulled into it. When I looked at him, his face was stony. He pulled away when I touched his hand.

'I'm sorry,' I began.

Whatever he'd been going to say, he'd changed his mind. And then he looked at me and smiled. 'OK. Not your fault. And you certainly did your best to stop them arresting me. Never seen such a termagant. Talk about Attila the Hun late for a invasion. Come on now, Sophie. There's work to be done ere the setting sun.'

I grinned: the Black Country expression was one way of building a rather weakened bridge.

'Work? After this afternoon?'

'I promised Matt I'd stay on. He wanted help with some of the tutorial work. And I didn't see any reason not to stay.' His smile and brief handclasp suggested he had another reason to stay on at Eyre House.

Then I plunged into the rush-hour traffic. All Birmingham's bottlenecks lay before me and Eyre House. And I had to go via the city centre so I could deliver Hugh safely to Rydale's. We didn't talk much. When I glanced at him, he had his eyes closed. And then we were at Five Ways and into Broad Street and I had to decant him.

'See you later,' was all he said.

George's van had neither a radio nor a cassette player. I had nothing for company but my own thoughts and reflections, none of which was especially pleasant. And I had them for nearly an hour.

Six ten. Eyre House at last. I flung the van viciously into a parking space and yanked on the handbrake before it was truly stationary, so the whole vehicle shuddered and jerked. I slammed the door with far more force than I needed. Chris would be expecting me to report immediately to the incident room. He would be disappointed. First I was going to have a shower and wash my hair. I might even see if Courtney would blow-dry it for me. I strode into reception. The doors gasped at my passing. A WPC tried to intercept me, but failed.

I was halfway down the student corridor before I noticed the far end was taped off. Two PCs were now on duty. There was no chair.

'Got too busy for one, did it?' I asked, in the tone of voice I use to students who forget to hand in homework.

The younger one opened his mouth to speak. The older one merely nodded downwards. I followed his eyes. On the thick, soundproofing carpet, was a chalked outline of a sprawling figure. Near the head was an ugly stain.

And then I noticed another chalk outline. Rectangular. About three feet by two.

'Where's Sidney?' I asked.

'DCI Groom wants to see you, miss,' said the older man.

'I asked you what happened to the rat.'

'I'm sure the DCI will tell you, miss.' He nodded at his colleague, who reached for his radio.

'I'm sure he's just dying to. Tell him I'll be along in a few minutes.'

'But miss –'

I let myself into my room. Nothing seemed to have changed except that the smell was less fierce. I grabbed my dressing gown and sponge bag. Chris might even hear me singing in the shower.

The water was hot and plentiful. I washed my hair, too. But I didn't sing. I found my face running not with shampoo or conditioner, but with tears. I rebuked myself sharply. Surely, surely I couldn't be weeping because of a rat?

When I emerged from the bathroom, carrying my clothes, my hair still wrapped in a towel, the two PCs shuffled with embarrassment. But it was not the sight of me in my dressing gown that caused their unease. I was sure of it. So I was half prepared. Chris Groom was waiting for me in my room. He was sitting on my bed.

I didn't speak. I merely held the door open for him in a furious parody of a courteous invitation.

He didn't move.

Neither did I.

We maintained our hostile eye contact. Whichever of us gave way would lose the battle. And after this afternoon I did not intend it to be me.

The same thought had occurred to Chris, of course. But I had the advantage that he was clearly in the wrong. I'd obeyed the police despite everything. I was in no way to blame. Perhaps – though I would never admit it – my flight had been foolish, but I had taken the trouble to tell his representative what I was doing. And the treatment to which Hugh had been subjected was deplorable. Unless, of course, he had indeed been trying to kidnap me.

Meanwhile, Chris sat staring at me. And I stood holding open the door.

The longer the silence lasted, the more difficult it would be to break it. But I would not back down. In fact, I would up the stakes slightly, as I would in a confrontation at work. I raised my eyebrows ironically, and made a minute gesture with my head: out.

I thought he was going to hit me, he got to his feet so fast. He jabbed his index finger at me.

I touched my finger to my lips, then jerked a thumb in the direction of the PCs. Did he really want an audience? I asked silently.

'Certainly, Chief Inspector Groom,' I said, in my classroom voice. 'I'll be along to the stables in about fifteen minutes.'

I had won. But as I closed the door behind him, I found myself crying in good earnest. I managed to get dressed: the skirt Hugh had requested, and a coordinating polo-neck. But then I had to dry my hair, and all I saw in the mirror was this unhappy face, blotched and puffy.

I did the only thing possible: knelt by the bed and let the tears come. Only when I had cried myself out did they stop.

I was now sitting on the floor, my back supported by the bed. Any moment now I'd be able to gather myself up, finish drying my hair, and try to match Nyree's expertise with make-up. Any moment. But not yet.

And then I thought of Hugh and the ordeal simply being with me had inflicted on him. Enough of self-pity. I pushed myself to my feet, dabbed my eyelids with toner, and finished my hair. Then I started on my make-up.

If I was going into battle with Chris Groom, I'd better get my war paint on.

Chapter Fourteen

Before I tackled Chris I gave myself five minutes on the floor with paperback books under my head. I wanted to face him calmly. Then I would have the advantage over him if he was still angry – and somehow I couldn't imagine him doing stress-reducing exercises.

At last I got up and checked myself over. New tights, clean shoes, the polo-neck neat and tidy, and the skirt – the skirt as short as Hugh could expect, if not quite in Nyree's league.

I closed the door behind me and walked coolly along the corridor, not even looking back at the PCs. All the doors in reception sighed at me. The WPC again tried to intercept me, but I ignored her and, letting the front door shut behind me, made straight for the stable block. Although it was no longer raining, the cloud was heavy enough to make it dusk at seven o'clock. All the lights were on, all the computers humming purposelessly away.

Chris sat centre stage, apparently studying a print-out. But he didn't seem to be making much progress. His shoulders were hunched and his head was too heavy for the hand that was supporting it.

Poor Chris! All this strain, and I had added to it. And I was supposed to be his friend.

On the other hand, he was supposed to be mine, too.

I collected styrofoam cups and poured coffee. Three sugars for him, one for me. I parked his and a plastic stirrer on his table, and stood just behind his shoulder, stirring mine.

'What happened to the PC I was talking to this morning?' I asked, as if we were in the middle of what we were saying.

'I take it that chalk outline –'

'– means someone socked him,' said Chris, without hesitation, though he had jumped slightly. His voice was under control too. We seemed to have arrived at the same tacit decision that there was nothing to be gained, and everything to be lost, if we kept up our hostility. 'Oh, he's all right; he'll live. Back on duty in a couple of weeks or so. But he's got a nasty cut and he was out cold when they found him.'

'"They"?'

'Mr Woodhouse, actually.'

'Did someone mean to kill him?'

'Hard to tell. Unless you're a real expert it's almost impossible to work out how hard to hit just to lay someone out. And where – the exact point. How thick the skull is. Fortunately Halford's got a thick skull.' He leaned back and smiled slightly, looking up at me.

Yes, we were to be friends still. Maybe we'd have to talk about our anger later. At the moment the bruises were too painful to touch.

I pulled up a chair. We both sat sideways on to the table.

'Did he contact anyone before he was socked? To pass on my message?'

'Message?'

'About my overshirt and Sidney and how I was running away because I was too bloody scared to stay here a moment longer?'

'Sophie, I'd bet my pension you never told anyone you were scared.'

'A palpable hit. I told him I was doing a runner but would be back. And I told him to look after Sidney. And I mentioned my shirt. Told him the room ought to be sealed till you'd seen it.'

'Shazia told us about your shirt. The sight of it brought on Agnes's asthma again. Gimson, out of purest professional etiquette, called a GP from a practice in Sandwell. When he'd sorted her out he said she'd be better away from all these alarums and excursions. So Tina ran her home.'

'Tina? Bit of a low-grade job for her, surely? And isn't she supposed to be interrogating Courtney Rabone – slowly?'

'Tina doesn't look like a policewoman; she doesn't sound

like one. That's why she's so good on a job like this. Agnes will witter away –'

'Not Agnes!'

'OK, she'll talk without realising how much Tina's picking up. Anyway, she'll be back in Leicester by now. She left you a note. Shazia's got it.'

I shook my head sadly. I liked Agnes. Maybe I'd get in touch with her when all this was sorted out. But then, I've been on a lot of courses and exchanged a lot of addresses, and can count on the fingers of one hand how many relationships have actually been followed up.

'What about Courtney? Have you decided what to do?' I prompted.

Chris crushed his styrofoam mug and hurled it into a bin. It ricocheted out. I lobbed mine in, gently and accurately.

'Well? Do I gather this is something I shouldn't ask you about?'

'It's never stopped you before.'

'What a good job I'm discreet, then. Come on. Courtney's well on the way to being a friend of mine –'

'A gay, black ex-con! Jesus, Sophie, you don't half choose some weird friends.'

'I chose you.'

Whatever he'd meant to say, that silenced him. He sighed and then looked straight at me. 'OK. And I did what I did as much out of respect for your judgement as anything. And it's a hell of a risk for both of us.'

Not sending Courtney straight back could mean the end of Chris's career if he were found out. At best a reprimand so severe it'd blight his chances of promotion for ever.

'Both of you?'

'His life, for a start. Tina managed to wrinkle out of him – told you she was good, didn't I? – that the people who used to, er, employ him wish to punish him for talking so freely. Right? Hence the gun, remember. And he had a whisper they might be coming this way. So the official deal is he stays here as bait. Then he goes back up to Durham, where he and the authorities will sort it all out.'

'If he's still alive, of course,' I said dryly. I wasn't happy at the prospect of Courtney as unarmed target.

'I hope and pray the chances of a gang attack at Eyre House are remote,' said Chris, seriously.

'His employers weren't Japanese rat-hating kidnappers, were they?'

At last we both started to laugh, properly, without any strain. A couple of officers at the far end looked round. One of them, Ian Dale, winked at me.

Then I remembered Sidney. I was irritated that such a small and smelly creature should arouse such protective feelings.

'Speaking of rat-hating –'

'Ade's been out looking for Sidney,' said Chris, smiling gently.

'That chalk rectangle represented his cage?'

'Yes. Empty. But Ade thinks he'll make his way back here, since he's done it twice already.'

'If he's allowed to,' I said.

Chris nodded. 'They say the rat in the fridge died of natural causes by the way. The business with the head and feet came later.' He looked at his watch. 'Fancy a pint?'

'Love one. But supper –' Supper and Hugh.

'OK. Another time, maybe.'

There was a lot of pain in those syllables. Friendship or lust? I compromised: 'I'll find out what time it'll be ready, shall I? There might be time for a quick half.'

By a stroke of fortune, the sci-fi freak had been so immersed in his work that he hadn't turned up till five, and the girls had not unreasonably refused to do all the work. So supper wouldn't be ready till eight thirty. Until then, Shazia said, Matt and Hugh were doing tutorial work for those students who wanted it. Tabitha would no doubt be having immense difficulties that couldn't be solved by Matt, I told myself sourly. But I applauded Hugh's decision to work after the afternoon's ordeal. The Black Country Nonconformist work ethic at its best.

So Chris drove me down to a pub: the Miner's Lamp. It was clean and warm and they served good Banks's, and I settled down gratefully with a half of mild. Chris had a pint. Our eyes met as we toasted each other across the small round table.

'To friendship,' I said.

'Friendship,' Chris repeated. 'You know, you really had me scared, Sophie. I thought he'd got you. And I know those lads overreacted, but I think I'd have done the same. And I think you would, too.'

I smiled. Perhaps he was right. It was the nearest I'd ever get to an apology, anyway.

'But why pick on Hugh?'

'Because you left at much the same time. Coincidence, maybe, but there have been too many coincidences.'

I looked at him hard. There was something he hadn't told me. 'Go on.'

'OK. Another coincidence. He drives a big red car. Not a Seven Series BMW, but a Five Series BMW. And I remember you telling me –'

The big red car at the main gates; the big red car down by the motorway. Could the man investigating the ice house have been Hugh? I drank and swallowed carefully. Perhaps it could. But if Hugh had been around Eyre House before he arrived officially . . .

'– of course, a lot of people drive big red cars,' Chris continued. 'And there's absolutely nothing in our records to suggest Brierley is anything except a decent, law-abiding citizen.'

'A very rich law-abiding citizen, if he drives that sort of car.'

'You're not going to go all Marxist on me and claim there's no such thing as an honest rich man?'

'Eyes of needles,' I said lightly. 'Was Christ the first Marxist? Here, let me get you another.'

'Just a half.'

With luck my hands would no longer be trembling when I carried our glasses back to the table. To give myself a little longer to settle after the news about Hugh, I tried to buy some crisps, but they'd run out. The barman offered two alternatives: pork scratchings, the traditional Black Country snack, or cellophane-wrapped baps. I didn't fancy the cholesterol in the scratchings, wonderful though I'd thought them when I was a kid.

Chris picked up the bap suspiciously when I dropped it on our table.

'Try it. You ought to have something to eat. Bet you missed lunch. And you're driving, remember.'

I watched, amused, as Chris picked at the cellophane which enclosed chicken tikka, according to the label. A line from a poem or song worried at the back of my brain – something about feeding your man. But one of the ways I like to show my affection is to offer my friends food; Chris was no exception.

He eyed the bap with misgiving.

'Better than an empty stomach,' I prompted him.

'My brother would quote that bit from the Old Testament about oxen and herbs,' he said.

'"Better is a dinner of herbs where love is, than a stalled ox and hatred therewith,"' I said. 'And before you gasp at my knowledge of the Bible, Brontë quotes it in *Jane Eyre*. Any more tourists, by the way?'

I refused to touch on the love part of the quotation. Even to make a joke. And the tourists still bothered me.

'There was a little fracas this morning,' he said.

'I know. I sneaked out past it.'

'But that was –' He sounded immeasurably relieved. Hugh must have left later.

'Horribly early. Anyway, these 'ere tourists,' I prompted.

'I'm sure you're right. They're not just here for the photo opportunities. But I've no idea what they do want. We've asked Lloyd House to find us an interpreter. Next time someone turns up we can question them properly. By the way,' he added, an edge to his voice, 'do you know why a CNN reporter should telephone from Japan?'

'If you try that bap, I'll explain.'

As gingerly as if he were expecting the thing to explode, he pulled apart the two halves of the roll to liberate huge chunks of chicken in what looked mayonnaise. We sniffed. He nodded, replaced the top half and bit in. He smiled, and broke off a large piece for me.

'Try it. And then tell me about CNN.'

I nibbled, and smiled. 'Yes, it's OK, isn't it? Not that I'd have identified it as tikka without a label, but it's good in its own right.'

'And CNN?'

I reminded him about Kenji, my Japanese rabbit-loving lover. Ex-lover. 'He's replaced me with an American woman who's a reporter for CNN. I asked Kenji if there was anything in the Japanese papers to connect Nyree's husband with Japan. I didn't think they were going to bother. That's why I spent the morning at the *Guardian* on CD-ROM in the college library. Ended up with asthma and little else.'

Chris spent several seconds picking up a minute crumb and parking it on the side of his plate. He was going to ask me something he shouldn't.

'Did Brierley know you were going there?' he said at last.

I picked up my glass and tilted it, as if to tip it over his head. 'I told about six people in Harborne that Hugh and I left separately for Birmingham and we met by chance while I was hanging round waiting for a bus home. I told you. I expect you to believe me, even if they didn't. I didn't even know I was going to William Murdock until I was on the bus. Dust in the library gave me my usual allergy. Agnes had my spray. Chris, she had a strip of my tablets too –'

'A bubble pack?' he asked. His eyes twinkled in self-mockery. He was clearly feeling better.

'As it happens, yes. But nice big tablets, not like Nyree's phenobarbitones. I suppose no one mentioned finding them in the lounge?'

He shook his head. But it didn't mean anything. Agnes could have put them in her bag. If she didn't, probably Shazia had picked them up. But I wanted to know what had happened to them.

I risked a glance at my watch. Chris saw me.

'Time to run you back?' he asked sadly.

'No, the car won't turn into a pumpkin yet. And I suspect eight thirty is optimistic. But I want to be there eventually. As your eyes and ears, as much as anything else.'

'Humph. And of course you'll share anything you pick up.'

'I usually do.'

'Eventually.'

'Another palpable hit.'

'Why did you bring that appalling vehicle?'

'George's van? It's not that bad. It's waterproof, thickly insulated and has an engine and four wheels. Beats my bike any day!'

He finished the bap and sloshed the dregs of his mild thoughtfully round the glass. He was about to say something else I wouldn't like.

'How would you feel,' he began, 'if I asked you to have a minder again?'

'Why me? Why not all the others? The women at least.'

'Because no one else has had threats. Someone is clearly after you. I don't want you to end up –' He stopped abruptly.

The thought of round-the-clock company filled me with revulsion. I seized on a diversion: 'I think Kate's still alive – and I reckon you do too.'

He looked up and smiled. 'OK – you tell me why.'

'Because all your best efforts haven't found her body. There have been a lot of oriental people around here giving the impression they're looking for live women, not dead ones. Because a number of things have gone missing. That asthma spray, for instance. Because – No, your turn now.'

'Same reason. Your tampons. Who'd want to nick something they could buy?'

'It could be one of the women "borrowing" and forgetting to tell me. That toothy woman, maybe. No, Tabitha!' I said spitefully.

He shook his head. 'You'll keep this under your hat? That chemist's, down the road. A man tried to buy some, then changed his mind and bought a stack of large-size disposable nappies.'

'Any description?'

Chris shook his head. 'Nope. God knows how long they'll let the pharmacist continue to practise. I'd say she was nearly blind. I suppose her dispenser does most of the work. Scared me rigid, though. Don't let her give you any tablets, eh, Sophie?'

'Nappies?' That was what I ought to have picked up on before. 'Why the hell buy nappies when you want tampons?'

'I was hoping you might tell me.'

'Only that – Christ!' I didn't even want to consider the

possibilities. Not if I wanted to sleep tonight. I pulled myself up short. Hadn't I intended to use the night to spy on whoever might have used Kate's car?

'We also have a person who is nicking biscuits,' Chris said. 'Shazia tells me three packets so far have disappeared from the kitchen before she could even open them.'

'Perhaps writers nibble for inspiration? I should try it.'

'Three whole packets seems excessive. Shazia wasn't going to tell me, but it seems you bollocked her for not passing on information.'

'Did I?' Oh, dear – if only I could escape my teacher persona when I'm not teaching. I shall turn into a flogger and hanger if I'm not careful, a blue-rinsed scourge of liberal home secretaries. D'you see me at Tory Party Conferences, Chris?'

'I'd love to,' he said.

The drive back was short and uneventful. He offered to drop me a hundred yards from the house, in case I didn't wish to be seen as his nark.

'Don't worry,' I said, staying put – the car was warm, and rain was slicing down again – 'everyone knows we're acquainted. Everyone knows everything on a course like this. Like everyone will know I spent the night with Hugh and Matt last night.'

'Hugh *and* Matt?'

'Hugh and Matt,' I said firmly. 'So rumour's got a bit above itself, has it? We all got boozed, and fell asleep writing a poem. There should be a copy on Matt's notepad. Matt and I shared the sofa; Hugh was on the floor. I woke early needing the loo, and saw my overshirt. The rest you know.'

Chris yawned. What time had he come on duty?

Then I yawned too. And my stomach rumbled vehemently. We both laughed.

'Chris, I want to talk to you again.'

'So I should hope.'

'Because there are odds and ends floating around my head, and they may tie up with things in your head. I'll try and make a list.'

'I'd be grateful,' he said. No sarcasm; just sincerity.

I wished I could hug him without raising his hopes. I liked him immensely, loved him even, but not in the sense he wanted love. Why should I fancy someone like Hugh, who was hardly more than an acquaintance and whom I perhaps ought not to trust at all, and not poor Chris, as worthy a man as I've ever met, apart from George, that is?

'Better go in,' I said.

'OK.'

'I'll talk to you soon.'

'When?'

'As soon as I've something to say!'

As soon as I'd discovered whether Hugh had any plans that might include me. I yawned again. A night safe in my own bed seemed at the moment preferable even to a night in Hugh's. And the prospect of cruising round in George's van was repellent. I ought to face it, I simply had no energy left for anything.

He stopped outside the front door.

'Thanks. And will you be working late or heading for your duvet and a glass of scotch?'

'Depends what turns up.'

Now we had the embarrassing business of saying goodbye. We'd never got it right yet. Perhaps that's why we had rows: to give us exit lines. He wanted to say something tender. I wanted him not to. I ran up the steps and turned to wave him off. As his car disappeared to the area where the police were parking, I saw another car. It was at the edge of the student car park, just where it narrows into the drive. No lights. Just for once, though, I wouldn't stick my nose in. It must have got past the police checkpoint. It was none of my business.

Chapter Fifteen

I pushed open the front door.

All the other doors sighed in greeting. The constable was answering the phone and didn't look up. On impulse, I decided to go straight to Hugh's room: I wanted to see what the afternoon's activities had done to the delicate shoots of what might grow into a relationship. Then I thought perhaps I wouldn't. Not until I'd combed my hair at least. I dodged into the nearest loo, spruced myself up, told myself to be assertive and re-emerged into the corridor. What I did not expect to see from the dark corner of the hallway was Hugh running downstairs, his hands on his hand. Matt followed him. Then came a man with a gun. He herded them into the lounge.

The door slammed on them.

It all happened so quickly I couldn't believe it. It didn't make sense. Any moment they'd all come out laughing and joking. But I knew they wouldn't because it dawned on me that the man with the gun had been wearing a stocking over his face.

I waited. Then I slipped off my shoes and padded back to the reception area. I eased the door a fraction, praying that the others wouldn't respond. I couldn't see much, of course. What little I could see brought bile up from my stomach. Shazia was lying face down on the floor, her hair streaming free of her scarf. She whimpered once, but silenced herself. Beside her stood a man I'd not seen before, his foot perhaps an inch from her head. His gun pointed at the middle of her back. Naukez was slumped against the reception desk, his chin bleeding and bruised. The door to the student corridor swung slightly – someone must have just gone through. Perhaps the sigh from that had been enough to cover my arrival.

They talk about split-second decisions. I had to choose in that moment whether to make a heroic attempt to throw myself at the man, who pointed a weapon and who had been strong enough to lay out Naukez, or to try something, anything, else.

I'm afraid I chose not to be heroic. I let the door shut as quietly as I could, and retreated to the corridor again. Plainly I couldn't stay there.

I had to get out of the building to get help. That was clear. How? I dared not risk the creaking corridors at this end of the house. The cloakroom again. Some of the cubicles had windows to the outside world. I found one that seemed a possibility, and scrambled on to the toilet seat. And froze. Someone was opening the cloakroom door. I crouched, still on my slippery perch. I pushed the cubicle door very gently. Like the others it hung practically closed. I heard footsteps. Saw a male foot, brutal in a Doc. Heard breathing. Held my own breath.

The feet withdrew.

Now escape took on a more personal note: I knew I had to save my own skin. I turned back to the window, a small version of an old-fashioned sash. The upper part was open. That meant the lower part should open too, if I had something to lever it with, like a knife or a screwdriver. I had fingernails, and short ones at that. They scraped against the paint, the sound setting my teeth on edge. The longer ones bent right back. The wood did not move. So I would have to get out of the top section. I pulled the window right down. The wood screamed. Without waiting to see if anyone had heard, I put my hands on the frame and started to pull myself up. This was one form of exercise for which the Canadian Air Force had not prepared me. I thought my arms would pull from their sockets. My legs and feet flailed against the wall. But at last I got my chest across, and rolled slowly the rest of the way.

I landed hard on gravel, my elbows and knees first. Surely

someone must have heard. I'd lost a shoe, but dared not look for it. Kicking the other off, crouching and dodging, I hurtled for the stables.

If I expected a hero's welcome, I didn't get it. I was plainly superfluous. I don't even think they noticed me for a while. Chris was already strapping on the sort of bulletproof vest I'd only ever seen on TV correspondents. Other men and women were doing likewise. If Chris caught sight of me, it might shake his concentration.

I backed out. I stood irresolutely in the deepest shadow I could find. Words like 'crossfire' sprang into my mind.

I made my way, crabwise and keeping as close to the wall as I could, back to the main building. Pressing right up against the stucco, I peered round. The dark car was still there, and now my eyes were thoroughly used to the dark, I could see it was a Granada. The driver was pulling on gloves. Such a prosaic gesture terrified me as much as anything I'd already seen. What I couldn't work out was why he'd let Chris walk away. And how had he got in past the police presence at the main gate? I'd almost persuaded myself he might be one of Chris's colleagues when I saw the unmistakeable shape of a gun in his right hand.

Around me I sensed movement. Then heard feet, in controlled little rushes. Suddenly I was grabbed from behind and thrown down. When I twisted my head, I found myself staring down the barrel of a gun. This one was about a foot from my head. Then I picked out flakjacket and a navy sweater.

'It's OK, officer,' I breathed. 'I'm Sophie, DCI Groom's friend.'

God forgive me for trying to hide behind a man's authority like that. But it worked.

'What the fuck are you doing out here?'

'Trying to warn you all; there's trouble – men with guns . . .'

The man grunted, and spoke quickly into his radio. 'Female civilian', was I?

I didn't hear the reply, but he gestured me to get up.

'Where will I be least in the way?' I breathed.

'Just fucking stay here.' He now stood watching from my

previous vantage point. He lifted his gun in both hands and aimed at something I couldn't see. I have never felt so impotent. I should have waded in to help when I had the chance, done anything rather than cower like this.

It was so quiet I could hear not just my breathing but the policeman's too. Nothing else.

We waited.

A shot. From inside the house, surely. And screams. Including a man's. Then there was a gleam of light. I couldn't place it at first, light where none should be. But then I realised it was a reflection on the side of that big, menacing car. Someone had opened the front door. The man in the car turned. He stretched his arm to aim the gun.

Surely to God someone would give the order to fire?

And then I heard – we all heard – a loudspeaker voice tell him to drop his gun, he was surrounded. And he was. Even the dark, you could see a ring of figures. And yes, very slowly, he threw down his weapon. And gunned the engine instead. The heavy car lurched forward, straight at those figures, at the men in the middle of the group. Where Chris would have placed himself. It was going to mow them down.

Without thinking what I did, I bent for a stone, picked it up and threw. The big, heavy car slewed round faster than the suspension could take. I saw it turn. I saw it hit the tree. I saw the flames. I heard the screams.

There were other screams too. From the house.

I joined the rush forward. Shazia was on the floor still. Naukez was kneeling, but not attending to her.

I outran the policeman who'd yelled at me. Beside Shazia was a still male figure, face down, the heavy Remington crushing his shoulders, his hand outstretched but unable to reach his weapon. And there, against a dreadful splash of scarlet on the far wall, was Courtney. If I had to look at that wound, touch that blood, I'd faint. I couldn't faint.

'Shazia, pick up that gun, hold it steady and shoot if he moves. You have to. Naukez?'

They'd given him a beating but at least he could walk.

'Get Gimson. Now. Tell him Courtney's bleeding to death.'

He nodded. Then pulled himself painfully to his feet and set off.

If he could make that sort of effort, so could I. I stripped off my polo-neck. It was cotton, the softest, most absorbent thing I could think of. I rolled it into a tight ball and stuffed it into the quivering mass of tissue that was Courtney's shoulder. I held it there, praying.

'Dear me,' said Gimson, 'I thought I was here to practise my writing skills, not my A and E techniques.'

The sounds were familiar, but not what I expected I should be hearing. Echoing acoustics, antiseptic smells. The light was bright enough to penetrate my eyelids. Hospital? I opened my eyes, very slowly.

Chris withdrew his hand from mine, not quite quickly enough.

'Casualty,' he said. 'Thought you might need an anti-tet jab.'

'Courtney?' My voice didn't sound quite right. Perhaps they'd given me something else. Or maybe I was just tired.

'Touch and go. He's still in theatre. They won't make a prediction either way.'

I nodded. I respected him for not trying to lie.

'Naukez?'

'Two lovely black eyes and a touch of concussion. But he's tough. And Shazia's with him.'

'The . . . the men who came for Courtney?'

'The one you know about. We'll get an ID on him later. The man under the Remington – I think he may have some damage to his ribs and to his shoulder blades. Naukez picked it up and slung it at the bastard. There was another guy too, a gofer. He's glad to be in a nice cosy police cell.'

'My shoes? I left them on the path somewhere.'

'Didn't think you'd be able to wear them.'

'I don't intend to spend the night here, Chris.'

I gestured. I was on a stretcher in a corridor. Someone had found me a police sweater, so I was decent, but I felt my location was altogether too public. I struggled on to one elbow, found it was bruised, and tried the other. That was better. I peered at my feet. A lot of Melolin and some micropore – Chris must have told them about my Elastoplast allergy. More on my knees. Some on my hands, now I had time to look at them. When had I earned all that?

'Thought you'd say that. Here.' He produced my slippers. 'I'll take you back to Harborne, shall I?'

I thought with great longing of my home. But there were other people who'd had a bad time tonight, and I suppose some vague idea of mutual support made me shake my head. 'No, Eyre House. Damn it all, Chris, it should be safe enough now!'

'I wish I could agree. But this lot tonight may not solve anything. It was purely and simply Courtney they were after. Not Kate. Not Nyree. Not Sidney. Not even you, I'm afraid. So Eyre House is just as risky. God knows where you can even sleep in safety.'

'Don't need to ask God,' said a familiar voice. 'She'll sleep where she slept last night, with Hugh and me. If that's all right by you, Sophie?'

Chapter Sixteen

There was nothing Chris could say, of course. He looked at me.

'Safety in numbers,' I said mildly. 'I survived last night, at least.'

'Numbers?' Chris repeated.

'Hugh's outside, trying to find somewhere to park,' said Matt. 'We found your bag, by the way, Sophie – it's in police custody until you get back.'

Nothing Chris could say about that, either. But he didn't want me to go, that was clear, to me at least. And he'd had a difficult enough night – I didn't want to add any more stress than I had to.

'Bless you, Matt,' I said. 'But I'd better see if they'll discharge me.' I looked helplessly round the corridor. Two more people on stretchers had joined me, both looking a great deal sicker than I. A couple of policemen in yellow jackets were looking harassed. Someone was wandering round with a polythene carrier bag. A couple of male nurses were arguing by the coffee machine. All it needed was a camera crew and we might have been on the set for *Casualty*. Except these people were bleeding for real.

'Is there anywhere more comfortable for you to wait?' I prompted Matt.

He took the hint. 'I'd better go and find Hugh.' He patted the end of my stretcher affectionately and was gone.

I turned to Chris. He was grey, with huge brown smudges under his eyes.

'I don't want to stay here,' I said. 'I don't fancy going

home to an empty house. You can't really spare anyone to keep an eye on me there. Can you?' It was hardly a question. 'I certainly don't want to share my rabbit-hutch at Eyre House with anyone. And as I said, I survived last night. Possibly, before you say anything, because no one knew where I was. They needn't know now.'

'Not very comfortable. You could always –' He broke off and looked away.

If I was going to sleep on a sofa, he wanted it to be his. I had to find something positive but noncommittal to say. I smiled. 'What I would like is a bit of police protection at breakfast,' I said.

He straightened and managed to return my smile. 'You're on. OK, I'll see if I can find someone to discharge you.'

I must have drifted off to sleep again – certainly I've no idea how long it took Chris to clear any formalities and collect a little bottle of painkillers for me. And I definitely had no warning of his plans for transporting me, until he stood beside my stretcher patting a wheelchair.

'Your transport of delight,' he said.

'Thank you but no thank you,' I said, revolted.

'Bloody walk then.'

He watched, hands in pockets, while I heaved myself into a sitting position, then swung my legs free. I seemed to have more bruises than the evening's activities warranted, and my legs screamed for the decent privacy of jeans. All they had was a very short mini. Chris parked the slippers side by side roughly where I'd land. It was not a comfortable landing. Hoping he hadn't noticed my wince, I stuck my feet into the slippers – soft fabric ones I'd bought for easy packing – and started to shuffle.

'There,' I said.

We proceeded slowly to the waiting area. And then I felt really sorry for him. Hugh, apparently in one unrehearsed movement, got to his feet, crossed the room and scooped me up. And before I could say anything, we were out through the automatic doors and heading for his BMW.

Of the journey itself I have no recollection. I woke up to hear Matt and Hugh discussing in subdued voices the possibility of carrying me upstairs. Matt was suggesting that for

Hugh to undertake any more heroics would result in a rupture.

'I'm not that heavy,' I said. 'And I'll walk.'

'But not over the gravel,' said Hugh.

I couldn't argue. He strode round to my door, watched while I eased myself out, and picked me up again. But I think he was glad when we reached the front door. It was opened for us by a WPC wearing a gun.

We went straight – if slowly – to Matt's room.

'We have, after all, a poem to finish,' said Matt.

'Precisely,' said Hugh. 'Where's the Jameson's?'

I relaxed into Matt's sofa and held out a hand. A glass arrived with commendable promptness.

'And I can't believe that a drop of this is any more damaging to the human body than those.' Matt shook the little bottle of painkillers the hospital had given me.

I was too weary to argue. And I wasn't in any particular pain, apart from a general malaise, as if I'd spent a cycle in a tumble dryer. Now I had time to look, I found the damage to my feet was minute, far less than the dressings suggested – just a few puncture marks. My knees were no worse than the average schoolchild's after a playground fall. What had really suffered was my fingernails, during my attempts to open the window. Where they'd been bent back, the nail-beds were discoloured. I stared at the broken ones in disgust. Matt produced an emery board from his spongebag – he was evidently well trained. But using it was not much fun.

There was a knock at the door, accompanied by a man's voice: 'Police.'

Hugh looked at Matt and me, and opened the door cautiously. We heard voices but no words. Then he came back into the room, locking it behind him. He was carrying a mobile phone.

'The police aren't letting anyone into the grounds in general,' he said. 'The car park's still floodlit. They've got the last writer back to his room and no one will be allowed to come into this wing until they say so. Oh, and someone called Ade reckons he's found some fresh rat droppings, Sophie, though he can't guarantee their provenance.'

'What about Courtney?'

'The guy who was shot?' He shook his head. 'Want me to find out? I've got the control-point number – hotline!'

I nodded. If Courtney died it would be my fault. He might have been safe in gaol if it hadn't been for me. Hugh tapped. Matt came and sat on the arm of the sofa and held me; the police jersey was rough against my skin, and I remembered where my top had ended. I took a deep swig of whiskey.

Hugh shut the phone. 'Still critical. Life-support system. But no worse.' He picked up his glass: 'To Courtney's recovery.'

We drank. Matt reached across to my face. When he took his fingers away they were wet.

'Sorry,' I muttered.

'My good girl, you're entitled to soak six boxes of Kleenex if you want to. But I still think we ought to finish our poem. Where were we? *Voluptuous rice*, as I recall. Which reminds me – God almighty, it's half past one, and we never had our supper!'

Bread and cheese, courtesy of the fridge and a constable acting as waiter, had never tasted better. Hugh produced his duvet to augment Matt's, but as yet no one had mentioned how they might be shared. Perhaps the men would offer some suggestion when I got back from the bathroom, whither I was heading. Matt solemnly checked that the door between his bathroom and Kate's was properly locked, though I would have bet next summer's holiday that Chris wouldn't have overlooked a detail that like. Hugh helped me to my feet, but didn't carry me this time. Perhaps he wasn't after all into weights. If I remembered, I'd ask. Remembering – that was the problem. There were things I ought to be asking myself. Maybe things I ought to be asking Chris. The only things I could remember, however, were the things I'd rather close my mind to – bits of the arrest jostled with an exploding Granada which merged into Courtney bleeding at my feet.

And now something was banging in my brain.

I fought my way up to wakefulness. I'd better make some effort, if only to spare everyone the embarrassment of forcing the door and finding me asleep on the loo.

Where Matt and Hugh spent the night I've no idea. I woke up

to find myself in Matt's bed. I stretched, and wished I hadn'
A hot bath might help.

But not yet.

Tina was standing by the bed, holding a tray.

Breakfast in bed is so rare a luxury in my life I hitche myself up with enthusiasm. But it was only tea, and glowered.

'Thing is,' said Tina, sitting at the end of the bed, 'we nee to have a look round like, and so I came to ask if you'd lik to go back to your own room.'

'Ask!' I drank the tea. Co-op tea bag. UHT milk.

'Well, you know how it is.'

'What are you looking for?' My brain was beginning t function again.

'Still that sodding bottle of pills. Or summat. Chris' turning the whole place upside down.'

Tina's a nice woman, but not a good liar. Or should it b *and* not a good liar? But it was unfair to put pressure on he I'd go and sort out Chris as soon as I was dressed – we had breakfast date, after all. And then I remembered more of th circumstances in which we'd made it.

'Tina, what's the latest about Courtney?'

She got up and walked to the window. She never liked t admit she cared for anyone, did she?

'Still hanging on,' she said to the curtain. 'Just.'

'Not your fault, Tina. Mine, if anyone's. He meant to fl but I talked him out of it.'

'I liked him,' she said, still not looking at me. 'You're n supposed to get involved. And he was a con. And black. B I liked him. Really liked him. And then Chris goes and say he's gay and all that, but I still like him.' She leaned h forehead against the window and sighed. I watche helplessly. She'd hate it if I put my arm round her. The be I could do was slide out of bed and join her at the window.

'Thought you was making a song and dance, like, whe that friend of yours died. And it isn't as if we're not used t people dying, not in this job. One of my friends in unifor bought it a couple of weeks ago. But the thought of hi dying . . .'

'Would it make it any better if you were there in th

hospital with him?' I asked at last. 'After all, someone'll be guarding him. Couldn't it be you?'

I waited a long time for the answer. At last it came, so low I could hardly hear her.

'No. I couldn't cope with it, the waiting. All those lights and bleeps and things. Give me the bloody creeps. No,' she said, straightening up, 'what I will do is escort you to your room, ma'am, and then report back to Chris. OK?' She saluted ironically.

'I'm supposed to be having breakfast with him,' I observed, as she locked the door behind us.

'What, tomorrow? Bloody hell, our Soph, it's half ten already.'

A warm shower convinced me the best way to ease all the mysterious aches would be a mild jog. Nothing very far, and nothing very fast. I wore a tracksuit so if anyone intercepted me they would assume I was merely protecting my lacerations from public display.

The most level stretches of path lie through the old ornamental gardens, now long since overgrown, but flattened, even scythed in places, by the team searching for Kate. I started very slowly, wincing not so much at the cuts on my feet as the gravel rash which flexed with my knees. But if I concentrated on my breathing, perhaps I would be all right.

The last thing I wanted this morning was company. Anyone's. Somewhere deep down I knew I'd have to submit to Chris's suggestion that I have a minder. This might be the last chance I had to be on my own. The question was, should I stay here, like Courtney a bait, or should I settle for becoming a refugee in my own home?

The pain was easing a little: I speeded up. I shouldn't even be out on my own. I knew that too. I'd shaken off Tina by saying I was going to get my bag from the stables. I would eventually, of course. I would just have to hope I didn't have an attack of asthma while I was out.

And then I saw another jogger. Except this one was a runner – vest, shorts, proper shoes and an impressive turn of speed. And a very beautiful body. He saw me from the far

end of a long straight path and lifted a hand in greeting. If
speeded up we should meet by a long-dry fountain.

The decision whether to flit or stay was made as soon as
saw the expression on Hugh's face.

For some reason we didn't, as I'd hoped, run straight int
each other's arms. Instead we turned, he to his left, me to m
right, and we fell into step. He dropped his speed sharply;
increased mine a little. We were heading towards th
summerhouse.

Then we slowed down. His hand felt for mine. We ran han
in hand, laughing like children. So there was no need to talk.

Three thick planks were nailed across the summerhous
door. In any case, as I said between kisses, the place woul
no doubt be crawling with woodlice and spiders. Literally.

'And Eyre House will be crawling with police. Literally,
he replied. He unzipped and removed my top: we would li
on that.

He made each part of my body feel desirable, kissing i
stroking it. My fingers found muscle and bone to explore, t
cherish. I pressed my hands to his buttocks. Yes, I wante
him as much as he wanted me. And then I went sane
Panting, half-crying, but sane. And so did he. He patted hi
shorts, then spread his hands comically.

No pockets to carry condoms.

I had pockets but no condoms either. That, at least, coul
be remedied the next time we ran together. Meanwhile, w
slowly gathered ourselves together and jogged sedately bac
to the house.

There was no sign of Chris when I popped my head into th
stables to ask for my bag. I'd asked Hugh to wait outside fc
me: I didn't wish to hurt Chris any more than I had to. H
agreed, after an extravagant kiss. Ian, who'd been sittin
quietly at a far desk, got up as I came in. He unlocked
cabinet and passed me my bag, grudging as if he'd had to pa
for it himself.

'Just check the contents, please, miss.'

'Miss!' I must be in his bad books for something. He'd te
me, sooner or later. I took the bag and tipped it on to a corne
of Chris's table. Purse, comb, credit-card holder, asthm

spray, a dishevelled tampon, several felt pens, a red white-board marker and three tissues. A lipstick emerged from the rest of the detritus and insinuated itself under Chris's computer.

I giggled.

Dourly, Ian bent and poked with a pencil. At last the lipstick rolled towards me and I fielded it.

'Nice throw,' he said grudgingly. 'Last night. Saved a couple of our lads. Your dad would've been proud of you.'

I nodded. Dad had never subscribed to the theory that girl's can't throw. I'd practised and practised till I could throw down the stumps from square leg. But I preferred life at cover point. More to aim at – a wicket in profile is rather too challenging.

'And Chris,' he added. 'Very impressed. Bet he hasn't told you.'

This was an extraordinary speech for Ian. It showed emotion. I smiled.

'He's a good copper, young Chris,' Ian said. 'Takes his job very seriously. Doesn't like anyone to get hurt. He's really upset about that young coloured kid.'

'Any news?' I asked quickly.

'Still critical. But no worse. And they think he's making an effort himself.'

'Visitors?'

'Next of kin only.'

'You'll let me know when he can have friends?' And I'd tell Tina. There'd be none of the conventional future of roses round the door and two point four children for them, not if I knew Courtney, but maybe learning this would help Tina. And they might become friends.

'Look here, my girl, one of these days you'll listen to what people say to you. That Courtney – he's a common criminal and a queer to boot. You go and bloody throw yourself at him and you'll be sorry, see if you won't. And there's one of the best lads I've ever come across eating his heart out for you – you should be ashamed!'

'Ian, I –'

'Look at the way you played around with that Yank this spring.'

I told myself not to react, not to get angry. I made mysel
concentrate on my breathing, not on Ian's words. Dou
phlegmatic Ian, dressing me down like an errant daughter.

'Ian, listen.'

'No, you listen to me. You just think what you're throwin
away.'

'I'm not throwing anything away. Courtney is gay: you'v
just said it. He's a friend – well, hardly more than an acquain
tance. *You*'re a friend – I think.'

He didn't laugh, just stared at me, baffled, angry.

'If I ended up in hospital, you'd visit me. Or I might visi
you – smuggle in some sherry, perhaps.'

Still no response – and, come to think of it, why was
trying to appease him? Perhaps because I knew he was tryin
to make life better for Chris, a young man whose rapi
promotion he could have resented, but didn't, because in
way he saw him as a son. Or perhaps because deep down h
reminded me of my own father, now irresponsibly retire
with a woman I loathed to the naffest bit of Spain you coul
imagine.

And then Ian's face cleared a little. 'Bet you'd brin
Cyprus.'

'I bloody wouldn't. Not after those lessons you gave me
Wouldn't bloody dare.'

'No need for language. This Matt character, Sophie – wha
d'you make of him, then?'

I pulled a face. 'You'll never guess: I like him too. He an
Hugh nannied me last night.'

'Don't forget,' said Ian, 'that protection works two ways
You may have thought he was protecting you, but all the tim
you were protecting him.'

'From what?'

'Just have to wait and see, won't we? But don't get to
fond of him, will you, Sophie? You stick to young Chris.'

I smiled disingenuously. And then, just as I was leaving,
had an idea: 'Ian, any chance you could get a minion t
phone Agnes? I'm wondering if she took away some asthm
tablets of mine when she left. No, I don't want them back,
just want to know. And Chris might be interested to hea
too.'

That would clinch it, of course. It did. He picked up the phone himself, running his finger down a list as he did so. I grinned, and backed out.

Hugh was nowhere to be seen when I emerged. I felt as deflated as if someone had hit my stomach. Couldn't the man wait five minutes? Didn't we have things to say to each other?

But he was a tutor. He might be working even now. And how would he feel about an interruption? How would I feel in similar circumstances? I walked slowly back to my room, nodding to the two officers on duty. The room was as I'd left it. After my jog I ought to shower again – maybe that was what Hugh was doing, making himself civilised. But I'd write a short note for him, remarking on Ian's loquacity and inviting some sort of response, before I did so.

My note began by asking what the hell had been so bloody important. Not the most tactful of starts. But then I didn't feel tactful. I felt angry. If I'd sung in the shower to keep Chris waiting, I could do it for Hugh. Extra loud.

And then I heard voices arguing outside my door. I opened it as one of the constables stretched out his hand to knock.

'This gentleman says you'll want to see him, miss.'

Hugh, changed into jeans and sweatshirt, was looking thunderous.

'Thank you, officer,' I said coolly. 'OK, Hugh, come in.' My tone wasn't tender. I'd been stood up. But at least he was here.

'Where the hell –?' we yelled, simultaneously. And then laughed. But his face clouded immediately.

'They've taken Matt,' he said. 'I saw them driving him away. Questioning, they say.'

'Who?'

'The police, of course.'

'Where've they taken him?'

Hugh smiled grimly. 'Rose Road, of course. What are you going to do about it?'

'Me?'

'You. OK, me too.'

'First of all we must find him a lawyer,' I said.

'The man I used yesterday seemed to work quite well. We'll go and roust him out.'

'We?'

He grinned. 'I take it you'd like a lift?'

This time I played it almost as punctiliously as Chris would have wanted. I told the constables in the corridor that I was leaving with Hugh. I told Ian I was leaving with Hugh. I left a large notice on Chris's noticeboard that I was leaving with Hugh. And I left with Hugh.

Not quite straight away.

I didn't waste time changing – he'd have to put up with me in a slightly sweaty tracksuit, which didn't worry me since he'd have been quite happy for me to be a lot sweatier with no clothes on.

We ran to his car, slamming the doors behind us and feeling suitably urgent. But I was tense for another reason. I could feel he was too. We eyed each other sideways. And then we kissed. Then, as he started the engine, he reached for my right hand with his left. The clasp felt like a promise.

Chapter Seventeen

It was impossible to make a fast exit from the grounds, of course. But the police kept the press from being too much of a nuisance, and, as we turned right into the lane leading to the main road, one of the constables gave us a sketchy wave. It might even have been a salute, given Hugh's car. New this month – like Kate's, it had the latest registration letter. This one had clocked 2,134 miles, however.

About a mile from the gate, Hugh slowed and stopped. Four or five people were gathered round a Transit van, which sprawled at an uncomfortable angle across the tarmac and tilted towards the hedge. It looked as if the driver had pulled out from a gate on the far side of the lane and thought the verge on the nearside was solid enough to bear the van's weight during an awkward left turn. Unfortunately for him, lurking under the long grass was a ditch, in which his offside front wheel was now trapped.

Hugh swore under his breath and applied the handbrake. 'I'd better go and help,' he said. 'We can't get round him, after all, and an extra pair of hands may help. Hey, what d'you think you're doing?'

'Helping too.'

'For Christ's sake, Sophie –'

'As you said, we can't move until he does. And I could try to reverse it out while everyone else pushes and pulls.'

I half expected him to insist on locking me in the car. Perhaps I half wanted him to. But instead we walked together and joined forces with the other good Samaritans.

The smell from the clutch convinced me that if anyone was

going to finish burning it out it ought to be the van driver. I didn't want that on my conscience. So I was hovering on the far side, searching for a hold that wouldn't hurt my fingers, when a couple more vehicles arrived. One was another heavy van: the driver offered a tow, if anyone could produce a rope.

'I've got one in my boot,' said Hugh, jogging off to fetch it.

And then the occupants of the car strolled up. Two of them, one either side of me. I sketched a smile, and then felt less sure. They were Japanese. And I didn't like the way they smiled back.

I followed the line of their gaze. Their gun was so small no one else noticed it. A hand covering my face prevented my screaming but permitted me to breathe. And they walked with me back to their gun-metal Mercedes without anyone giving them another glance.

I had to admit, they did a very neat job.

Then they helped, rather than pushed, me into the back seat. A man already occupying the back passed me my seat belt.

'We wish to talk to you, not hurt you, Mrs Compton.'

Since he too held a gun, I chose not to argue.

The car reversed into a gateway.

As we sped away from Hugh, I tried to make sense of the feelings that chased through my brain. There was anger. A lot of fear. An irritating but irrepressible regret that I'd not phoned Kenji back – I kept forgetting what had stopped me. And a great desire – perhaps Kate had shared it too – to scream that I was Sophie Rivers, not Mrs Compton.

They'd discover soon enough, anyway. I was a foot too short, for one thing. And since I hadn't phoned Kenji I wouldn't have a clue what they wanted her for so there'd be no stringing them along even if I wanted to. Perhaps now I was shaking less I should try telling them. It would make sense – before we hit the motorway, or the maze of Birmingham's suburbs.

I took a deep but not obvious breath; the sort you take before plunging into a vicious class.

'I do wish you'd put that thing away,' I said as mildly as I could. 'And before we go any further, perhaps you'd like to tell me why you addressed me as Mrs Compton.' I looked inquiringly at my fellow passenger.

He spoke rapidly in Japanese. The driver pulled the car down a rutted and muddy track.

When he stopped the noise was appalling, despite the Mercedes's soundproofing. We were in a culvert that ran right under the motorway embankment.

'Talk,' he said to me.

'I can't!' I shook my head, pressing my hands against my ears. 'Not here! You'll have to find somewhere quieter!'

'I said talk!'

'Please – anywhere. But not here!'

The man beside me tapped the driver on the shoulder. For a terrible moment we moved forwards, deeper into the noise.

Something cracked across my face. Then I realised some of the noise had been me, screaming. They'd slapped my face to stop me. But I couldn't stop, nor stop the tears.

At last we moved backwards. We pulled up with a jerk about halfway back along the track.

I retched. When I grabbed for the door, someone rapped an order and it opened under my hand. No one tried to stop me crawling to a bush and throwing up my early-morning tea. When I scrabbled to my feet, one of the men passed me an open packet of tissues. I took a handful, dabbing at my eyes and mouth. I gestured vaguely with them when I'd finished. All those prohibitions against dropping litter must have been dinned into them too. He held open a polythene bag for me. Even as I deposited the disgusting handful, I wished I could have shredded them and dropped them like a hare-and-hounds trail for Hugh and Chris. But I thought of Ade and tyre tracks and knew there'd be more sophisticated forensic-science methods on my tail.

Eventually.

Meanwhile, they gestured me back to the car.

'You are not Mrs Compton?' said the rear-seat passenger.

'No.'

'So you are –?'

'I'm a student on the writing course at Eyre House.'

There wasn't any reason for them to believe me, but they didn't argue.

'You know Mrs Compton?'

So they didn't know she was dead. I decided not to enlighten them, not yet. I nodded.

'Where is Mrs Compton?'

'I don't know.'

'Is she at Eyre House?'

I shook my head.

Back passenger reached inside his jacket. 'Perhaps this will help you remember,' he said.

Despite myself I closed my eyes, bracing myself ready for the pain. But there was no pain, only a familiar smell of new paper. When I opened my eyes, eight inches from them was a wad of banknotes, about half an inch thick.

'You should've taken it,' said Hugh, tenderly tucking a strand of hair behind my ear. 'Compensation for all that stress.'

I smiled, and wished the gear lever anywhere but between us.

He'd been driving frantically down the lane when I'd stepped out from the verge and flagged him down. At first he'd been at least as furious as Chris would have been, but when he'd let me explain he'd comforted me beautifully. Then he called the police on his car phone to let them know I'd turned up. I sat entranced, warm in the sun. He'd opened the sunroof, and I could smell countryside and listen to Birmingham's birds. All half a mile from Eyre House. Ten minutes away from a gun and God knows how much money. Maybe enough to buy a car like this: the notes were a denomination cash machines never fed to me. Maybe they fed them to Hugh, though. The car was more opulent than Chris's, and to me that was luxurious enough. At last Hugh passed the phone to me. I gave the policewoman at the other end the tersest explanation I could get away with. I'd save the rest for Chris. But the police would be looking for the car. I was reasonably sure I'd got most of the number right, and I didn't suppose there were that many gun-metal Mercedes saloons trundling round the West Midlands. Especially not many looking for the morgue.

'The trouble is,' I said, 'that if the Japanese lot are as keen as that to find Nyree, the other lot are likely to be equally keen. And less well-mannered, as I recall.'

'You call kidnapping good manners?'

'They were polite about it. Afterwards. Hugh, Kate . . .'

'Kate?' he prompted.

'Do you think they took her and she was less . . . cooperative?'

'She might simply have taken the money and run?'

I shook my head vehemently. 'She had plenty of money *and* wonderful prospects.'

He looked at me oddly.

My stomach rumbled. 'My God, I'm so hungry!'

'D'you want to go back to Eyre House and find some food?' he asked, without enthusiasm. 'Only a couple of minutes away.'

I shook my head. The last thing I wanted at the moment was to share Hugh, and the thought of all the explanations and exclamations made me cringe.

'But I think we ought to find you something soon,' he said. 'You're very pale.'

I probably was. I kept my hands in my lap for fear he would see how much I was shaking.

'I'm not exactly dressed for your average restaurant,' I said: I was still in my sweaty tracksuit and muddy trainers.

'I know,' he said, his smile sweetening his whole face, 'exactly where we could eat. If you don't mind eating alfresco, that is?'

But food would have to wait while we drove into the city centre, where Hugh's big-shot lawyer was based.

Whenever I try to park anywhere in Birmingham I know the whole exercise is pointless and that I ought to have caught the bus. I know that drivers of big cars don't necessarily share my scruples about parking on double yellow lines – perhaps the flashing hazard lights spell out some Masonic code to passing wardens. But I didn't want Hugh to be as arrogant as that. I wanted him to be human, and fail to find a space and have to trail on foot several hundred yards from a crowded multistorey. I suppose. Or did I want him to find, as he did, a space that was somewhat shorter than was comfortable, and park with consummate neatness?

'Well done,' I said sincerely.

'Power steering,' he said with a mixture of pride an apology. 'Would you rather come with me or stay here?'

'Come with you,' I said firmly. 'Provided you ca guarantee no Japanese in big Mercs.'

Perhaps I expected him to take my hand as we walked; h didn't, but as he held open the solicitor's door for me, he ra his free hand the length of my back.

The receptionist looked at me and my tracksuit doubtfully of course, and at Hugh with enthusiasm. She was about my age, perhaps a little older. Very svelte; very well made-up.

'I'll just tell Mr Cordingley you're here, Mr Brierley – I'n sure he won't keep you a moment. If you'd like to take a seat And perhaps you'd like coffee?'

'I'm sure we'd both like some,' said Hugh firmly.

The receptionist didn't blink. She produced a percolate brew that was too strong for me, and then a tin of biscuits. told myself not to snatch. Hugh reached for the tin and left i casually and tantalisingly on the low table in front of us.

'Help yourself,' he said quietly. 'This guy's fee for sorting things out yesterday must have paid for several hundred tins.

The receptionist smiled automatically, and then looked a me more closely. 'Are you all right?' Her tone changed fron professionally plastic to genuinely concerned.

I smiled wanly and nodded.

'We passed a road accident,' said Hugh.

They spent the next few minutes discussing details o crashes, real and imaginary. I tried to work out why he'd bothered to lie, why he needed to explain the pallor of a tota stranger to someone he hardly knew. Perhaps charm is something that needs to be practised, and he was merely giving his a bit of a work-out.

I didn't want to talk about blood and sudden death. helped myself to the last of the chocolate digestives and looked around me.

The building must have been well over a hundred year old, built when Birmingham believed that civic pride wa best expressed in terracotta curlicues and Minton tiles. Bu they'd gutted it into anonymous modernity. No mahogany desks, no wondrous cabinets for legal tomes. Just quiet simple, confident luxury.

A buzzer reminded the receptionist why Hugh was here. She smiled him through the heavy teak-faced door, and then resumed her word-processing. But she noticed when I emptied the coffee cup and was quick to offer more, which I declined. I wondered idly what makes a woman take a job like that. If you want to care for people, you could nurse; if you want a business career, for goodness' sake get on the other side of that door. Perhaps she did it for the clothes. I would bet any money that in real life Hugh would wear the male equivalent of that suit. Probably an even better one. I'd have to ask, of course, what he did. In a sense I was sure he was setting me some sort of test. Did I care for him or his money? Certainly he'd clammed up when I asked him about his home.

Hugh. Matt. What did I really know about either of them?

Then Hugh emerged, smiling jubilantly at me.

Matt was now represented. Whether he wanted to be or not.

Chapter Eighteen

Tesco's was full of lunchtime shoppers; the queues for handbaskets, cash only, were as long as the others. We had a baguette, a variety of cheeses, olives, fresh fruit, wine, paper plates and plastic cups. We had a feast. The checkout girl, who'd passed three A levels at William Murdock but then had been confronted with Tory employment policies, commented on my extravagance: all too often I contented myself with cheese and an apple, or sometimes a packaged sandwich. I smiled in Hugh's direction by way of explanation. He dug out a fold of fivers. For once I did not argue.

We didn't speak the short distance to the multistorey car park, and I wondered if something had upset him. But in the car, he kissed my hand lightly before putting the car into gear.

So many other people had had the idea that the Botanical Gardens would make a wonderful place for a picnic that we couldn't find anywhere to park, and were relegated eventually to the overflow car park.

'Don't worry,' said Hugh, as we waited to cross the road, 'the gardens are big enough to absorb even a bank holiday crowd. We used to come for our big treat when I was a kid.'

To my surprise he produced a membership card. A lot of my neighbours and friends are members, but they live locally and it's a bonus to have a dog-free park for their children. Then he ushered me through the hothouses, remarking on changes. At last, after picking our way past cockatoos, rabbits and ducks, we left the main path and found an idyllic bench by a rock pool. To reach it, we had to pass through a gate marked 'No Children'; Hugh opened his mouth to speak, then shut it. In the distance were the grounds of a private tennis club. If you wanted, you could watch more energetic people hurtling round grass courts, their expensive-looking gear at odds with their amateurish shots. The sun was now distinctly hot; already turrets of thunder clouds were piling up to the west of the city. Why I should suddenly be so interested in the view, I'm not sure. Perhaps now I was with Hugh in such a public yet intimate setting, I felt shy. Certainly I showed him little but my profile. At last he touched my cheek.

'You're beautiful,' he said. 'Why don't we go back to your house? We're only ten minutes away.'

High marks for taste, low for subtlety. And then, what about Matt? We'd come over here to rescue him, not to spend the afternoon in my bed, no matter how desirable the prospect might be.

'OK, so we stop off at Rose Road first,' said Hugh. 'And then, come to think of it, at a chemist's.'

We walked back to the car rather more purposefully than we'd come, but still not touching. And drove in silence to Rose Road Police Station.

'I suppose,' Hugh said, pulling the handbrake on, 'that as a writer I ought to be grateful for the experience. But I'd rather be parking out here than be taken through those gates.'

We were in the parking area in front of the police station. A couple of pandas were in the spaces reserved for disabled drivers. A motley collection of civilian cars filled the others. Civilian! But we had a civilian police force, not a military one. And where on earth had I picked up such awful lingo anyway?

Hugh walked not towards the entrance, but towards a heavy set of gates: that was where they must have taken him. He stared grimly at the TV camera scanning us, but said nothing. I touched his hand – apology? Comfort?

After a moment, he turned and smiled at me. 'Hope Matt doesn't suffer from claustrophobia. When I heard those shut behind me, I nearly shat myself. And then the airlock where they make you wait until they can have you in and charge you – Christ!'

'I'm sorry.' Even if I wasn't quite sure what for.

At last he turned. He took my hand and we walked back to the main entrance.

On the whole I was glad he had let go my hand by the time Chris arrived at the front desk. But perhaps Chris wouldn't have seen anyway. We were sitting in the little waiting area, from which you can't see what's going on, and Chris called me before actually lifting the flap and coming out. Perhaps he didn't want to know if we were holding hands.

He ushered us both into the small interview room our side of the reception desk where Hugh and I had been reunited before.

'A more tasteful shade of paint than the room I was invited into,' said Hugh, grinning to show he bore no ill will.

Chris grinned back. Then he stuck out a hand. They were going to do the macho no-hard-feelings bit. And then Chris moved into mine-host mode. Coffee. Proper cups for visitors, please. Sorry about the stains on the carpet – and the place only two or three years old.

At last we settled down. Us one side of the table, Chris the other. Business.

'Why have you arrested Matt, Chris?' I asked.

'Matt hasn't been arrested. He's helping us with our inquiries, that's all.'

I gave him an old-fashioned look.

'He's answering some questions,' Chris corrected himself.

'Not necessarily friendly questions, however?' Hugh suggested.

Chris leaned forward and put his forearms on the table. I had never seen him look so authoritative. 'This is a murder inquiry. One woman is dead, another missing. I'm concerned with the welfare of the other women on the course.' He smiled grimly: no, he wouldn't want any emotion to show. 'Unpleasant things are happening to innocent people –' now he smiled at Hugh – 'in a case like this. We shan't be trying to trick Matt, or roughing him up to extract a confession. Sophie knows me well enough to believe me.' Another smile at me. It was a professional smile, like the one he'd directed at Hugh. Almost.

'Why pick on Matt?' Even to my own ears my voice

sounded petulant. 'I mean, why choose today to decide to ask him questions?'

'Evidence has come to light which justifies bringing him to a place where we can all concentrate.'

'Evidence?'

'Sophie, you know I can't talk about such matters.'

'It'd do his marriage a lot of harm if he were charged with –' Hugh began.

'It didn't do Nyree a lot of good being murdered!' I objected.

'I mean, accused falsely. If Matt did it – and I don't need to remind you I find the whole idea inconceivable – have his hide and welcome. But I don't think his marriage would survive the implication that he'd had such a relationship with either woman that he might wish to kill her,' said Hugh. He too sounded authoritative. I could see him in some boardroom making tough decisions – if, that is, I'd ever seen a boardroom. But I was more interested in what he was saying about Matt. He'd never mentioned his wife as far as I could remember, not even the conventional quasi-humorous moans married people often seem to make about their partners. Some not even quasi, come to think of it.

'We shan't be phoning Mrs Purvis to tell her about our conversations. I assume you won't be either?'

Hugh shook his head.

'Off the record,' said Chris, 'is the marriage on the rocks?' He judged his tone nicely – interest, compassion, apology. And authority again.

I thought of the tensions between Matt and Kate. The expression on Kate's face when she'd watched Nyree in action. Other moments when they had appeared very close without needing to put anything into words. I knew she was attracted to him; I hadn't needed Matt's telling me about their glass of whiskey and the subsequent humiliation of finding himself put to bed by the woman he'd planned to take to bed to persuade me of that.

Hugh shook his head. 'They bark at each other. Bark at the kids. So do other people, but . . . She's in the same line of country as me,' he added.

'Which is?'

'Imports, exports. We're working on developing links with the Far East, among other areas. Huge market potential there. That's how I met Matt – at one of these sponsored do's one has to go to. I knew her slightly, thought of head-hunting her at one point. Brilliant negotiator. Hard as the devil's head.'

'And Matt?'

'Sort of towed around in her wake until he found I wrote poetry. And then we became friends. I made sure he got tickets for any sporting functions at grounds where we had hospitality boxes. Likes his football and his cricket, Matt.'

'D'you offer free tickets to *all* your friends?' I asked hopefully.

He cuffed me, very gently.

It was obvious that Chris wanted to terminate our meeting. He also wanted me to make a statement about my morning's adventures. I was beginning to find tedious the whole business of regaling people with things I'd rather forget. But I could quite see that such matters ought to be recorded.

'Tell me,' I said lightly to Chris as he held open the door for me, 'when are you going to come up with some rabbit out of the statement hat? Find some flaw in someone's account, like they do on TV, and publicly pounce!'

'We do go through the statements,' he said. 'Exhaustively. Exhaustingly.'

'Nothing yet?' asked Hugh, who would also have to tell his story.

Chris shook his head. And yawned.

I completed my statement very quickly. I'd just signed it when Chris popped his head round the door to say goodbye.

'Any news of that Mercedes my Japanese friends were using?'

'Not yet.'

'Surely – I'd have thought communications in the police would be very speedy?'

'Come along here a minute,' he said, and ushered me through the now familiar smart corridors.

'Here' proved to be the control room. One woman, a computer and a headset. There were messages scribbled all over a white-board, and a constant surge in and out of uniformed officers in a hurry.

'And it's exceptionally quiet now,' said Chris.

'Point taken. No matter how quick your response, it can't be instant. Consider yourself forgiven.'

As we retraced our steps, he said quietly: 'I'd give a lot to find out what's happened to our other oriental friends.'

I nodded. 'So would I. Chris, what information could be worth so much money? Drugs?'

'Could be. But I'd expect a Chinese, not a Japanese connection. Have you heard from your friend Kenji?'

I shook my head. 'No time, really. I slept like the dead last night, and got rather overtaken by events this morning. By the way, a strip of my asthma tablets seem to have disappeared now. I hope you don't mind – I asked Ian to phone Agnes to see if she'd got them.' I wouldn't tell him about the jogging yet. With a little luck he'd assume that my conversation with Ian Dale had been my first of the morning. 'I suppose I could always phone him from here. But don't tell me your colleagues in Japan aren't beavering away.'

'This CNN reporter of his might have picked something up that hasn't reached them yet. It's worth a try. Come up to my office: I'll get the call put through for you.'

His room was as disgustingly tidy as when I'd first seen it last spring. True, there were as many files on my desk at William Murdock, but they were relegated to a side table. And the stacks didn't look as if they were about to cascade to the floor. He now had a small TV and a video player by his desk, and a ghettoblaster on a filing cabinet.

While he spoke to the switchboard I stared at Harborne through his windows. When the number stated to ring, he passed the phone to me and left the room. It was a terrible anticlimax to have to call him back in again. I wanted to tell him how I appreciated his tact: perhaps smiling would do. I passed him the handset: he'd just be in time to hear the last of Kenji's voice asking me to leave a message on his answering machine and the tone that told me to start. I left a message, though my accent was already rusty, and rang off.

'Jesus! That sounded impressive.' He perched on the edge of his desk.

'I just asked him to phone me. And told him to pat his

rabbit.'

'Is that some ancient curse?'

'Just his elderly angora. Cuddlier than a rat, but much worse at shedding hair. And it gave me asthma when it moulted.'

Hugh had plainly been waiting some time when Chris returned me to reception, but he seemed to accept that life in police stations has its own immutable pace and shook hands courteously enough with Chris.

Back in his car, he turned to me, a delightful gleam in his eye. 'A chemist's? And then – afternoon tea, perhaps?'

'Boots is just back there,' I said, pointing.

Harborne may be part of a big city but it prides itself on having a village atmosphere. Amid the estate agents and building societies there are still some privately owned shops where the staff make it a point of honour to greet you by name. This is delightful when you are buying meat and vegetables but for various reasons I didn't want my local pharmacist, who always provides exactly the right remedy for teacher's throat or end-of-termitis, to help me select condoms. Hence Boots, nicely anonymous and in the same block as the restaurant we'd eaten at earlier in the week. Parking was a problem – Friday afternoon, of course – but at last Hugh insinuated the big car into a space. He looked at me inquiringly.

If I sat and waited in the car, I suspected I might feel too passive. So I decided to accompany him. But I didn't know if our relationship was up to giggling over the wild names on the packets. It seemed it might be: I'd been lurking discreetly by the vitamin pills when he turned to me, two rival packets in hand.

'At least I shan't be needing this sort,' he said, pointing to the name – Arouser.

I was just about to suggest that I'd always thought there should be a brand called Toughasoldboots, when I realised that the girl smiling from the far side of the counter was this year's star GCSE student. 'Hi, Marietta,' I said exuberantly. 'I can't seem to find the earplugs.'

* * *

We had just parked in front of my house when his car phone rang. I started to get out, but he gestured me back, and sat idly stroking my ear with his free hand.

'Shazia,' he mouthed at me. His voice became steadily less gentle. 'For God's sake! That's totally unreasonable . . . OK. Can't you? I suppose not. Bloody hell, I was just helping out – it's really nothing to do with me.' Then there was a long pause while he listened. Finally he snarled, 'OK. In about half an hour, I suppose, traffic permitting.' And hung up. If that's the term for car phones.

He released my ear, and stroked my cheek with his index finger in a curiously valedictory way.

'Trouble at t'mill?' I prompted.

'Bloody right. Jesus, what do these people want? Blood?'

'I'd have thought they'd had enough of that.'

'That, my sweet Sophie, is where you'd be wrong. They want a teacher. They paid for two teachers, remember? One of the teachers is taken ill, so Matt arranges a substitute. The substitute carelessly disappears. And with appalling insensitivity to the needs of the deprived students, Matt gets arrested. The fact that he conned me into taking Kate's place for a few hours now swims into the students' consciousness: why am I derelicting my duty and not teaching them now?'

'But you did it out of the goodness of your heart, not out of some contractual obligation!'

'"Goodness of your heart,"' he repeated, starting the car. 'What a lovely pre-Thatcherite phrase!'

'So where are we going now, Hugh?'

'Where do you bloody well think? Back to Eyre House, blast and bugger them all! Because if they don't get taught, they're going to fucking sue. That's why.'

Chapter Nineteen

Hugh parked, not very neatly, in the tutors' car park and cut the ignition. Feeling the same awkwardness as before, I jerked my head at the steadily darkening horizon.

'Getting a bit dark over Bill's mother,' I said, in my Oldbury voice.

'Ah,' he replied, Quarry Bank. 'Be a bit damp for another run.'

We nodded sagely, like two old codgers.

He half turned to me. 'Any road up,' he began, half laughing, 'you will –' he hesitated just the right amount, and abandoned his Black Country accent – 'come up for a drink tonight? I hate to expose you to . . . But those student rooms aren't very . . .'

I smiled and put my hand on his, palm to palm. 'What time will you throw out the last of your clients?'

'Oh, half ten. They can't expect me to go on much later than that, surely? Or shall I put you down as the last one? For ten thirty?'

'Hugh, everyone knows I've not written a word!'

'But you'll come up? Later?'

'About eleven. Perhaps later than that. They're bound to overrun their slots.'

'Even with me teaching.'

'Especially with you teaching,' I said, letting my eyes hold his and laughing.

Our hands gripped slightly before we released them. Even that made the muscles in my stomach tighten in anticipation.

I was sprucing myself up for supper when someone tapped on my door.

'Chris! You're the last person I expected to see. I thought you were stuck in sunny Harborne.'

He came in, shutting the door quietly behind him, and smiled bleakly. 'I should be. And I shouldn't be here asking you to do this.'

'But you are here. And what are you asking me to do?'

He sat heavily on the bed and opened a file he'd been carrying. When I sat down beside him, he passed me a photocopy of a letter.

'The original,' he said, 'was printed by an ink-jet printer. Probably Canon. We can't find a similar one on the premises. In Eyre House,' he corrected himself. 'Any ideas?'

'About the typeface or the contents?'

'Either or both. Try the contents first.'

I didn't want to read the letter at all. I certainly didn't want to read it with Chris looking on, all that weight of unexpressed emotion on his shoulders.

> My dearest love,
>
> After what has passed between us surely you can deny our love no more. It is time to speak out and acknowledge our passion to the world. I've got enough money for the both of us, I will happily support you while you strive for the success you deserve. I cannot bear the thought of you touching that woman, she is so beautiful, and all the things I am not. Please, please, stop, or I shall have to find a way of stopping you and do not speak to me of your wife! Every word you utter in her defence is a crime against love. I want to tell you to tell me how beautiful I am, my body rises to yours when you touch me. When we fuck, your beautiful cock raises me to the heights of passion and I gasp for more, I want to fuck and fuck . . .

I stopped reading. Chris was watching me when I looked up.

'Well?' he said.

'What do you want me to say?'

'How authentic do you think it is?'

'What's its provenance?'

'For Christ's sake, Sophie, stop hedging. I have photocopied the first piece of serious evidence we may have found, and all you do is fend me off. Do you think Kate might have written this letter to Matt?' he asked, speaking very slowly, as if to an idiot.

'It would seem odd to me – but remember, I'm still a neophyte as far as computers are concerned – to write a love letter using a word processor or whatever. But I'm sure other people use them. You could polish each phrase, couldn't you? Get it absolutely right. And no spelling mistakes, either. Hey, have you come across that American Christian program which won't let you use rude words? It rejects things like "bastard" and "piss" and –'

'Well, that is a help. We know for certain that this wasn't written using that program, then. I take it the rest of the letter was too fruity for your maidenly eyes.'

'I just don't like the thought of reading other people's letters.'

'Especially if the incriminate their recipients.'

'How does this incriminate Matt?'

'We found it in his room this morning, Sophie. He denies ever having received it, of course, and he says –'

'Go on.'

'No. I want to hear what you say. Do you think Kate would have written that letter to Matt?'

I looked at it again. From the little I knew of Kate I would have expected her style to be economical to the point of self-effacement. And what was that about fixing Nyree? She had dealt more than adequately with Nyree, whose antics had clearly repelled poor Matt. Surely she was too sane to worry about Matt's resistance for a mere week when she had – apparently – longer-term plans for him?

Slowly, I shook my head.

'Why not?'

'Instinct.'

'Bloody hell! Is that all you can come up with?'

'Chris, you know as well as I do it is possible to make a very good guess about the authorship of something by comparing two pieces of work. Experts do it all the time. Lit Crit, it's called. I'm not a lit critic, but I'd say Marlowe didn't write Shakespeare. If I were to read Kate's stories and her novel, I might be happier about speculating. For what it's worth, though, as an English lecturer, I'd say this is not the work of someone who wins prizes for her prose. What do you think?'

He looked embarrassed. 'It did strike me as being . . . not very original.'

'Not even very grammatical.' I sat staring at the letter. The second letter I'd read in this room in the space of a week. 'Have you found out anything else about my little billet-doux?' I asked. 'Like the printer that was used?'

He shook his head. 'No trace of one in Eyre House.'

'How does it compare with this?' I tapped the paper.

The expression on his face was comical. 'Another Canon. Or the same one! Jesus bloody Christ!'

'Careful,' I said. 'You'll have the American Christians on you. You haven't checked? OK, there's still time. And before you start beating your breast and apologising for being inefficient, tell me how much sleep you've had since Tuesday night. And how long it takes to get over jet lag.'

'I should have spotted it, Sophie.'

'Hang on – we don't know yet it if is the same printer. But if it is, it ought to clear Matt.'

'Not necessarily. He might have a printer somewhere else.'

'Like where?'

'Anywhere except Eyre House! He wouldn't need mains electricity – these things run off batteries, don't they? Sophie, I just don't know where to start looking. We've searched the grounds, we've been over the house, we've bloody occupied the stables: still no further forward. Someone nicks tampons and asthma sprays and antihistamines. Biscuits disappear. A rat pops in and out like a jack-in-the-box.'

'And all you want to do is sleep. Chris, did you ever find Kate's notepad and printer? Computer notepad, I mean – not her scribbling block.'

He shook his head again.

'Wouldn't you just bet that these things were printed on it?'

'Is that just a guess, or would you have any evidence?'

'I can't even remember the make of either the computer or the printer. I saw Matt carrying them, and spent about ten minutes sitting beside them. Matt might know the make.'

He heaved himself to his feet. 'Better go and ask him, hadn't I?'

'Why you and not someone on the spot? Why not treat yourself to an early night?'

'You know something, Sophie? When I've asked him, that's exactly what I'll do. I shall go home and put myself to bed.'

I got up and patted his arm. 'That could be the most sensible thing you've said today. Mind you do it, eh?'

'Wild horses couldn't stop me,' he said, and was gone.

Supper must have been the grimmest meal ever taken at Eyre House. Hugh refused to eat with the students, saying he needed time to read the work that had piled up outside his room. Shazia was hardly speaking to what I suspected was the group who'd demanded their rights – Gimson, Toad, Mr Woodhouse and Tabitha.

I thought that if I kept quiet while I picked my way through overcooked beef (they'd been too busy fussing to cook properly), I might pick up the odd smidgen of carelessly dropped information. Would Gimson suddenly weep contrite tears? Or Toad confess that he could keep his secret no longer? Not on your life. All the talk was about writing. What Hugh would say about this paragraph, how he'd feel about the new opening. The sci-fi student was discoursing about Matt's inadequacies in that genre. Tabitha had gone so far as to write a short story and was anxious about it.

I was a complete outsider.

At last, their structures and metaphors and outlines and treatments exhausted, they turned to me for entertainment. But they didn't get it. I quelled any attempts to question me with the erroneous but convincing statement that everything was sub judice.

Eventually Toad got up, saying that since everyone was so bad tempered – I suspect he looked in my direction – he was going to practise his viola for a while. Gimson shuddered and, without leaving the table, ostentatiously started to read a *Times* he'd removed illicitly from the library.

I left the dining room. The two constables in the student corridor nodded courteously. The older one asked if I was all right after the morning's little upset.

'Fine, thanks. Just a bit tired. And I'm stiff.'

'That'll be your bruises coming out from last night. You want to look after yourself a bit, miss.'

I nodded. I was very tired, now I came to think about it. A couple of hours' sleep before going up to Hugh's room was a most desirable prospect. But it was one I'd better turn my back on. Hugh had found Matt a solicitor; I wanted to help find the real murderer.

'I thought,' I said, 'I might go for a quiet walk. Just in the grounds. I might look for Sidney.'

'That rat? Ade was saying one of the students saw him, not far from the stables. Didn't try to catch him, of course. Just called a policeman,' he concluded, in an ultra-respectable voice. 'Make you bloody sick, some of these types.'

He was clearly ready to embark on a quite justified diatribe against people who wanted others to help but were never prepared to do a hand's turn themselves. But I hadn't time to listen. It had just occurred to me what I ought to be doing.

'Quite, quite,' I agreed in the sort of voice I use to soothe irate principals. I almost spoiled it by laughing when I saw the poor man's face – if I had a reputation, it was obviously not for being a quietly acquiescent type.

I popped into my room, collected a jacket and casually set off for my ostensible walk. The constables nodded affably. I didn't immediately leave, however. I slipped into the Library for something to read – today's *Guardian* and a copy of *The Rivals*, a set text for A level next year. If Gimson could ignore house rules, so could I. I tucked them under my jacket and walked at what I hoped was an unobtrusive pace to where George's van was parked.

I got in but made no attempt to start it. I huddled down, wishing for something warm to wrap my hands round. August, yet, and hot and humid enough for thunder, but my hands felt cold. If it got any worse, I'd put on the extra jacket I'd slung over the passenger seat.

Doing obbo was what detective fiction told me was the right term. One day I'd ask Chris what it was really called. Certainly it was boring and cold. When the idea had come to me, it had seemed quite neat. Someone, I was sure, was keeping Kate hidden somewhere not all that far from Eyre House. Someone who stole biscuits and tampons. One of the women? None of them had the sort of build I'd associate with using force, though of course Chris said there was no evidence of violence. To my shame I'd made no effort to get to know any of them, so I'd no inkling of whether they might have any motivation. Dared I narrow the field down to the men in the group?

I could only act on what might be a poor instinct; if one of the men tried to leave the building, I would tail him. I would dearly have loved it to be Gimson, but my reasoning dismissed him. Easier to imagine was Toad. But as I'd passed his door I could hear him starting his practice.

I certainly didn't want it to be Naukez. He was the first out, calling something over his shoulder to Shazia as he set off to the Land-Rover. He reached a giant umbrella from within, shook it at her, replaced it and got in. She waved him out of sight.

I fished out the *Guardian*. That should while away a tedious half-hour. Even at nine, however, it was too dark to read easily. The sky was brown with the gathering storm. A car radio would have been an asset, and a cassette player. George had always insisted that anything electric was an obvious invitation to break in, but I might buy one of those systems you can unplug and carry with you. Not that I'd be doing this sort of thing very often. But company – if you wanted it – was not such a bad thing. Perhaps I wasn't such a puritan as George. No, indeed. Not if I could indulge in a fairly erotic fantasy in which Hugh and I went camping together. I imagined the azure sea, golden sand, blue skies and a brown Hugh. Naked.

And then I saw someone leave Eyre House. In this light, and with the hooded top up, it was hard to tell the gender. Perhaps the walk suggested a man. He walked unhurriedly across the car park. As soon as he could no longer be seen from the house, he broke into a steady jog. I watched him until he merged with the darkness. Then I started the van and headed up the drive. This meant I might overtake him. I'd have to take the risk. If he turned and recognised me, I could simply turn right at the gates and give up altogether.

What I meant to do was not necessarily foolish. All I could hope to do was get some general idea of where he went, and then encourage Chris to concentrate his search there. I certainly didn't mean to tackle him with my bare and bruised hands; I didn't think the rest of my body was up to heroics either. Keeping fit is one thing; being Superwoman at thirty-five is another. Damn it, I teach English, not PE.

I was in luck. Just before the main gates, he struck off left, down the path which runs parallel to the wall, and thus to the lane outside the grounds. If I waited at the end of the lane, perhaps I'd get another sighting. I waved to the duty PC and drove off rather faster than courtesy suggested.

At the end of the lane, where it dwindles into a bridle path, I pulled the van on to a wide verge on the far side, tucking it under some trees. Despite the rain earlier in the week, the ground still seemed firm: perhaps the trees sheltered it from the worst of the rain. It would be embarrassing to have to trail back to Eyre House on foot to demand a tow.

Again, I was in luck. After I'd waited some seven or eight minutes, a figure hauled itself over the wall. The man set off down the bridle track: I wouldn't risk taking the van down that. I valued the sump and springs too much. I could have followed on foot. And done what? I told myself the most sensible thing to do was to stay put.

Instead I got down quietly from the van and followed. And lost him after about thirty yards. A stile one side, a gate the other. At this point I saw sense. If Ade could lift footprints from carpets, he'd certainly be able to follow the prints made in mud by trainers. I turned back to George's van. Sanctuary.

One day I might fit it out as George intended, with a tiny kitchen, even a loo in a cupboard. Since as yet I had no loo, and I did have, what with the fear and the excitement, an urgent need to pee, I squatted behind a bush. As I got up, I sensed, rather than saw, someone by the van. He opened the driver's door and the interior light came on for a second. Darkness again. And movement. What was he doing at the back of the fan? Suddenly I could see him. A torch? The light flickered too much for that. And then I knew. He'd made a firebrand from the paper I'd brought. Or from the book. And he was going to shove it, whatever it was, into the fuel tank.

Diesel. How fast does diesel burn? Petrol, I'd not have a chance. Petrol, he might not have a chance either.

And what, Sophie, did you want a chance to do? Put out the flames? How? Pee them out, like Gulliver? If he found me, he'd throw me into the van, and no one would be there to save me.

While thoughts chased haphazardly through my head, I heard the crepitation of paint burning. Soon the whole thing would be alight. He'd be able to see me.

There were two choices. To stay and wait till I saw where he was before making a move. Or to risk it now, and maybe bump into him.

A sudden whoosh of flame. The driver's seat, perhaps. And there he was, his back to me. A rumble of thunder stopped me hearing him. But I could see his shoulders shaking with laughter.

I picked my way slowly to the lane. As gently as I could, I started to pad away. Over the wall? I had a better chance of dodging across country. Or the lane? Safer, surely, to stick to the smoother surface? And there were policemen at the gate. I could call, I could scream.

I didn't dare look back. I didn't dare. Lightning was now playing closer and closer. If he was looking my way, he must see me. The thunder might be masking his footfall.

There was an almighty bang. Without looking round, I knew what it must be. The explosion woke birds, made copper the sky. It was George's van.

I started to run.

The first police car almost ran me over. I was nearly at the main gate, and staggering with fatigue, when it roared along the lane, klaxon blaring. Perhaps they even saw my face, blue in the flashes of their light. Certainly the next car came more circumspectly, but I had fallen on to the verge by then. I stayed there, feeling the earth shake under the wheels of a quite redundant fire engine.

At last I scraped myself up. Only another couple of

hundred yards. I could crawl it.

And then I thought of Chris's face if I did. I pulled my back straight, made my knees and ankles flex. If I breathed properly I might even manage a feeble jog.

But as I did so, I knew it wasn't pity for Chris that inspired me. It was the thought of the man with the torch, and the knowledge that it would be another two hundred yards before I was in sight of the gate.

The first of the team to arrive at the stables was Tina. The rain was now so intense that the short trek from the car park had left her anorak streaming.

'Fucking hell, our Soph! What you been doing now?'

'Playing Brünnhilde,' I said, and wished I'd saved that response for someone more appreciative, like Chris. I was so tired I could almost feel the little electric sparks making ideas – and count them, they were so few. The police had wrapped me in a duvet, given me thick, sweet drinking chocolate, and despatched a PC to tell Hugh I might be a little late.

'OK, tell us all about it then,' she prompted.

But everyone had heard the explosion, it seemed, and seen the flames, and Hugh had arrived hard on her heels.

'Yes, do just that,' said Hugh. 'Tell us what the fuck you've been up to.'

'When I've had a bath,' I said. And stuck to my guns. The shock had made me dither, I was soaked to the skin, quite literally, and I couldn't identify many places that didn't ache. Both my knees were bleeding properly, not just with gravel rash.

In the end, I made my statement in the bathroom. Tina had come to keep an eye on me, she said. What she really wanted to do was talk about Courtney. There were signs that his coma was less deep. I expressed cautious delight. I could make all the right noises, all except the one she wanted to hear: that Courtney might love her. Courtney was gay. And that wasn't something you could change like a haircut. It was what Courtney was. I didn't say it out loud. I let my silence say it.

Eventually, she pulled herself straight and managed a courageous smile.

‘Right,’ she said. ‘Since we’re in here having a natter, we might as well natter to some purpose. Let’s get down that statement of yours, shall we?’

I agreed willingly. I’d have to correct half her spellings later, of course. While I patted myself dry, Tina went off to hunt for dressings and – at my insistence – some clothes.

I’d unfastened my watch and left it on the windowsill. Eleven twenty, it said. Time for my tryst with Hugh. At least now he’d seen me, he’d understand if I was a little late. Tina patched up my legs, and a surprisingly deep cut on the palm of my left hand, with Melolin and micropore. Then I dragged on my winter-weight tracksuit, the one I’d slept in that first night. My hair was a drooping mess, my make-up had steamed off. If Hugh fancied me now it must be love indeed. I trusted him to be inventive enough not to tangle with the damaged bits.

He certainly looked at me with great tenderness, standing up and putting out his hands to steady me as I strolled with ill-assumed nonchalance into the stables.

Chris turned too, and Ian.

‘Pity about your van, Sophie,’ said Ian, gently.

‘George’s van,’ I said automatically.

And then I understood that there would be no van, no George, ever again. And I started to cry.

Chapter Twenty

I felt bright and well, so I looked out of my bedroom window and found a dazzlingly clear sunny day. Pathetic fallacy, said my English-teacher brain. The view included a constable in shirtsleeves prowling up and down by the rubbish bins. I was being guarded. There was an armed policeman outside my door, too, as I discovered when I set off for the loos.

It did not surprise me particularly to see Chris waiting with him when I returned.

'Two minutes,' I said to him, smiling.

Shutting him out gently, I changed the tracksuit I'd all too obviously slept in for lightweight jeans, a jazzy T-shirt and a sweatshirt just in case the weather wasn't as pleasant as it looked. And some make-up. My face didn't look as well as the rest of me felt.

Then I let him in.

'Never thought you'd be awake this early,' he said awkwardly.

'What time is it, then?'

'About eight. But after last night . . .' He sat down on the chair.

And then things began to come back to me. Gimson, for a start. He'd suddenly appeared, and there'd been a row. And Shazia.

'What did I get up to?'

'I take it you remember the van catching fire? The explosion? George's van?'

I nodded.

'Well, a bit later you started to cry.'

I nodded.

'And you couldn't stop.'

I nodded.

'And eventually we called Gimson in to see if he could give you a shot of something, and . . . shall we say, you didn't want him to treat you.' Chris's intonation suggested a massive understatement.

'My God! Was I very rude?'

'You said something interesting, Sophie. You said he'd threatened Kate.'

'Did I? Had he?'

'You gave us chapter and verse. Overhearing him threaten her. And he denied it, at first. Then we reminded him that though you were not at your articulate best, you had overheard his conversation and, when you were able, you would no doubt oblige us by repeating it. He gave in, not with especially good grace, I have to admit.'

'Go on.'

He smiled and shook his head. 'Confidential, Sophie. Between him and Kate, really. He shouldn't have told us, of course. But he said he'd rather we had the truth than any garbled version you might offer.'

'Did I offer one?'

He hesitated.

'Surely it wouldn't be a breach of confidence if you told me what I've already said. I'll probably remember soon anyway!'

'Bloody Jesuit! OK. He performed some operation. She proved to have a blood clot.'

'That's right! The embolism. It moved. Right?'

'He still insists it developed after the operation. And that Kate was, ah, mistaken. And that his threats were of legal, not physical, action.'

'I hate to admit it, but I suspect they were. He's more of a suer than a strangler.'

'I have a feeling you may be right. Nonetheless, Dr Gimson –'

'*Mr* Gimson –'

'– is now talking to us about his activities this week.'

'Waste of time,' I said, with sudden conviction. 'He was as

surprised as anyone when you told us about Nyree's barbiturate poisoning. And do you see him stealing tampons?'

We started to laugh. I felt happier than I'd felt in his company all week.

'What happened then?' I prompted.

'Shazia came along with some homoeopathic drugs, and she persuaded you to try them. Then you seemed to slow right down, so we carried you back here.'

I wondered who'd done the carrying. Chris, if I knew anything about it. Hugh's knight-errant act in the hospital would have given him the idea. And if Hugh had tried, I reckon Chris would simply have pulled rank. I could ask Shazia later, to satisfy my curiosity. Meanwhile there were other, more important questions: 'How's Courtney?'

Chris shook his head slightly. 'He's a little stronger. But what worries me is Tina. He *is* gay, isn't he? You're sure?'

I nodded.

'Poor Tina,' he said.

We both sighed. But now was not the time to remind him that people don't die of broken hearts. And then I had a pleasant thought.

'You must have let Matt go?'

'It was incontrovertible,' he said slowly, 'that whoever torched your van, it could not have been Matt. So he's been released. He decided he didn't want to come back here last night so we found a hotel room for him. And we'll bring him back here when he's ready.'

'I suppose everyone has an alibi for last night.'

'Every last one. And though you'd have expected someone to come in soaking wet, no one did. Apart from Naukez. No wet clothes in the building, at least.'

'I suppose you couldn't frame Toad for me?'

'Everyone heard him playing that overgrown fiddle of his all evening. He insists on practising with the window open, apparently.'

'That could be a dodge – maybe he'd made a tape of himself so he could go and do his nasty deed.'

'You really don't like him, do you? But the poor man's writhing in agony. He hurt his heel running yesterday and the tendon's inflamed.'

'Oh yeah?'

'Gimson seems to think it's bona fide. He's limping like Long John Silver *sans* parrot, and popping anti-inflammatory pills. From a bubble pack,' he said, grinning.

'Shit! I'd like it to be Toad.'

He laughed. 'No chance! I suppose you couldn't fancy some breakfast?' he added shyly.

'Only with a police escort. And preferably not here. Supper last night was gruesome. I know I'll have to come back, but not on an empty stomach.

I'd never known simple food taste so good. Chris had driven us to a caravan in a lay-by on a scruffy A road running parallel to the motorway. He'd ordered, from a drawn woman he called Eileen, bacon butties: crisp smoked bacon in buttered baps. To hell with cholesterol. The tea she offered us was so strong I'd settled for water, but those butties were grand.

'A lot of the lads who've been on motorway patrol stop off here,' he said, opening the glove box and passing me a box of tissues to mop my greasy fingers. 'Good for food and gossip. Eileen ought to be on our payroll.'

We ate in silence. A heavy lorry pulled up behind us, and then a patrol car in front. I suppressed a crack about fine and private places; I didn't want to be embraced, after all. What I did want was another buttie.

'Your wish is my command,' said Chris, not altogether lightly.

We joined the little queue by the serving hatch. While we waited for the next batch of bacon to fry, he turned to me.

'That van – it was very special, wasn't it?' he said, very gently.

Our turn to order. I waited till we'd been served. Then I walked not to the car, but to a gap in the hedge from which you could see the great sweep of the Birmingham conurbation. Even that looked impressive in the morning sun. It was my home, and Chris's and George's home. But the lay-by wasn't after all a place for the finer romantic feelings: human turds and condoms occupied the foreground.

We walked swiftly back to the car. He opened the door for

me. Then he caught my eye. I hadn't answered his question.

'It was *very* special,' I said.

He walked to his side and let himself in. We sat for a moment in silence.

'What will you get to replace it?' he asked, in a suddenly impersonal tone.

'Replace it?'

'The van. With the insurance money.'

'Insurance money?'

'It must have been insured. For third-party, fire and theft, at the very minimum.'

'Fully comprehensive,' I said, at last picking up his tone. 'I suppose I'd better phone the insurance people and claim. It might be worth quite a bit brand new, after all, in terms of mileage. Only last year's letter in real terms.'

'What'll you get? I must say, I see you in something sporty.'

'On my salary? I might be able to buy it, but I couldn't insure it.'

'Get something second-hand.'

'No: I've always had other people's mistakes.'

'I'll take you round some dealers when we've got this lot sorted out.'

'Great. You'd know the right questions to ask . . .'

'That'll make a change,' he said. And bit into his buttie as if he were still starving.

I felt at a dreadfully loose end, back at Eyre House. My knees were too sore for a jog and I had, of course, no writing to occupy me. Hugh had: other people's writing. There was nothing to stop me interrupting, however.

I trotted up the staff staircase as briskly as I could make my muscles work. If he'd been listening, however, he wouldn't have been impressed by the lightness and delicacy of my footwork. By the time I reached the corridor I could achieve little more than a stagger. I could hardly blame the floor for screaming in protest.

Hugh had pinned up a list of appointments on his door. Now was when he ought to be seeing Gimson. There'd be ten minutes before the next student was due. At the foot of the list, in capitals underlined three times in red, was a reminder that this evening – the last of the course – was when everyone would be reading their work aloud, and students would be well advised to rehearse their piece beforehand.

Everyone except me. I've never failed so comprehensively before. Of course, later in the week I did have other things to occupy my mind, but I had no excuse for the dismal start. I could have relaxed more, I could have jollied up whatever bit of the brain it is that creates.

I tapped the door, and waited. Hugh opened it. He had to put down the *Financial Times* and close the door before he could gather me quite as enthusiastically as I liked, but eventually I had no complaints. He kissed with a delicacy and finesse I found quite irresistible. Fluttering, gentle caresses; passionate, even violent explorations. And then his phone yelled. Why the hell he didn't simply ignore it, I don't know. But he shifted me to one side, turning my face to his shoulder, pressing my ear against his neck so I could both feel the pounding of his pulse and hear his voice, strangely distorted, as he spoke into the phone. He made no attempt to continue our activities. In fact, his body became more remote; he was clearly concentrating very hard on what was being said. I wasn't particularly interested – it was, in the most literal sense, not my business. Plant; cubic tonnes; bents and fescues: God knew what he was talking about.

Suddenly I remembered how tired and stiff I was.

I sat down. The *Financial Times* is not my usual daily, but I might as well read something. As I shuffled it about, my eye caught an advertisement. And another. And a headline. All about Japanese investment.

I started to read. And I resolved to take the paper away accidentally when I left, purely in the interests of academic research.

Then there was a peremptory rap on the door, and in walked Matt. Hugh nodded and then took himself off to the window to finish his call. Matt raised an eyebrow and mouthed something exaggeratedly: '"Mad, bad and dangerous to know."'

I giggled and then flushed: what if I were to be no more than a notch on Hugh's bedpost?

To cover the moment, I gathered up the papers and patted the seat beside me. Matt sat down and rubbed his face. The situation would have been a good deal easier if we'd all known each other properly. Perhaps Matt was thinking the same.

'What we ought to do,' he said suddenly, 'is do what we did the other night.'

'What – fall asleep?'

'Probably. You look pretty knackered.'

'Speak for yourself.'

'I do. The Mondiale's the poshest hotel I'm ever likely to sleep at, but sleep I did not. Haven't slept my full uninterrupted eight hours since God knows when.'

'Tuesday,' I said, desperate not to surprise an idea that was creeping into my head.

'Tuesday. The night that Nyree topped herself.'

'Was topped. They still haven't found the barbiturate bottle, as far as I know. Funny, you know – I slept like the dead (sorry, that was in bad taste) last Tuesday, too. I wonder if anyone else did.'

'No idea. Why?'

'Just an idea. Not even an idea. Just a wonder.' But I would ask Chris if any of the students' statements mentioned somnolence. Just in case.

Then, in an altogether fraternal way, Matt grabbed me and gave me a hug. He smelled as sophisticated as Hugh – no doubt he'd liberated some up-market hotel cologne, and who could blame him? At last Hugh ended the call, and crossed the room, his hand outstretched. Matt got to his feet. And then both men abandoned their stiff upper lips, and hugged. I inserted myself as the third point of the triangle. They probably heard our laughter down in the stables.

At the time I cursed the student who knocked at the door. And it would have to be Tabitha, enriching the day with a skimpier version of the camisole I'd thought slightly risqué even for evening wear. And a very short white cotton and Lycra skirt, the sort that stretches but not enough to be embarrassing. I thought of my scabby knees and suppressed a glower. Nodding impersonally to Hugh, I picked up the paper and raised my eyebrows. He nodded: yes, I could borrow it. Matt followed me into the corridor.

'What's that in aid of?' he asked, pointing to the *FT*.

I showed him. 'I just wondered if it cast any light on those Japanese visitors. They were rather keen to talk to me the other day. My God! Yesterday.' A lot seemed to have happened since. 'Come on – let's have a cup of coffee and you can tell me what Chris did to you.'

But we had no sooner reached the kitchen than Toad spotted him: 'Hey, Matt, I was wondering if you'd have another look at that paragraph you didn't like. I don't think you understood what I was saying . . .'

I handed him his mug and watched him trudge wearily back upstairs, apparently lost in the wonders of what Toad was telling him. I took an extra couple of custard creams, picked up my mug and the *FT* and headed for a bench where I could bask in the sun but be in yelling range of the nearest constable.

I would have liked a two-inch headline to guide me on my way. Japanese industry *per se* is not one of my main interests, despite my relationship with Kenji. But I had to read a lot of smaller print before I located anything that interested me. Japan was poised to invest in Vietnam. But even the *FT* didn't say how and where.

Chapter Twenty-One

The obvious brain to pick about Japan was Hugh's. That would have to wait till lunchtime or a slot in his teaching. But I wanted to explore that other idea, the one about sleep, which was fluttering just outside the part of the brain where it ought to have been.

There was no one within earshot of the public telephone so I used that. What disconcerted me was that I had to look up Carl's number. Two months ago, it had seemed so memorable. And come to think of it, though my heart was pounding quite hard, I couldn't attribute this to Carl. Being with Hugh, perhaps. Trying to walk quickly with bruised knees. But not the thought of Carl's voice. And my telephone voice didn't drop into the more tender vocal range I'd always used to him. Did I use it when I was with Hugh? No need to, of course – with Hugh I was face-to-face. The eyes and body-language would operate. But if ever I were to phone him, I was sure that, unbidden, my voice would take a Dietrich plunge.

Carl's wife Paula answered, on the first ring. She sounded as irritated as she always does on the phone, as if she is in the middle of something urgent and valuable. She sighed hugely when I said I wanted Carl's advice on a murder I was supposed to be trying to write; but she agreed to call him. I heard her footsteps walking away from the phone, and listened in vain for his approaching. At last I heard voices, and fed in a further fifty pence.

'What's this about a murder, then?' asked Carl. Presumably he'd chosen not to mention my previous phone call.

I recapped appropriately – after all, Paula might be within earshot. 'What about mixing sleeping tablets with someone's drink?' I asked at last.

'Very old-fashioned. These days, most doctors are reluctant to prescribe more than a few days' supply. Quite rightly. They only work for about a week anyway. The body gets used to them. What you might do is –'

'No, hang on. Didn't Tony Hancock die because he mixed too many sleeping pills with his booze?'

'They'd be barbiturates. No one has those these days.'

'No one?' I tried to sound disappointed.

'Not for helping them sleep. You have diazepam-, termazepam-related drugs. Quite a different effect.' I could tell he was about to embark on quite invaluable information that was absolutely no use to me. If ever I did get round to writing, I would certainly pick his brain.

'Hang on a minute,' I said. There had been an emphasis on the words 'not for helping them sleep' I should have picked up. 'Do people take barbiturates for anything?'

'Well, they're so old-fashioned. They taste bitter, too, so you'd notice if someone shoved them in your sherry. No good for your plot.'

'Forget my plot for a minute. Do people still take them?'

'Not very many these days – they have side effects.'

'What do people take them for, Carl?'

'One or two doctors may still prescribe them as a preventive therapy for epilepsy.'

'Epilepsy!'

He started to laugh. 'But it'd be a bit of a give-away, Sophie. Find the character with epilepsy and there's the one who dunnit.'

'How would you find out? If you have epilepsy, you don't have your forehead branded or anything.'

'You don't even have to carry a card like you do if you're on certain forms of steroids. You don't actually have to tell anyone. You're supposed to, of course. But there was a case some time ago of a long-haul airline pilot who had an attack – on the ground, thank goodness! – and that was the first time it had come to light in thirty years.' Then he dropped his voice. 'When am I going to talk to you, Sophie? See you? It's been ages.'

'Back at college, I suppose. Only a week away.' I infused commonsense and reality into my voice.

'You know what I mean, my love. She's having her hair done on Tuesday. Any chance we could . . .?'

I'd have to face it and tell him – but to give a man the chop in the same conversation as picking his brain about murder was distinctly bad taste. I temporised: 'I'm sorry, I'm very tied up.' My voice must have given me away.

'You mean – God, you're not saying . . .? And then his voice became public again. 'I'll look up the dose for you. Can I call you back?'

'It's a public phone,' I said. 'I'll phone you. Just as a matter of interest, how long do traces remain in your system – while you're alive, that is? I mean, if I took a tablet today?'

'About two or three days, depending on the dose.'

'And – Carl, how does it make you feel? Sleepy?'

'In a dose sufficient to make you sleep.'

'And it gives you a hangover?'

'I've never taken it. But I'll check.' His voice dropped to a furtive whisper. 'When will you call me? Sophie?'

'As soon as I get a moment. But I'm having quite a trying time, Carl. I can't promise anything.'

There was something wrong with me. I sat on the bed, my head in my hands. I was a grown woman. In the spring I had fancied myself in love; in June I had embarked on an affair with a married man; now I was lusting after Hugh.

Worst of all, I realised, as I stood up and stared at myself in the mirror, I hardly knew myself.

I should have stayed where I was, and embarked on a period of self-examination. But that would have been a luxury that perhaps others could not afford. I had to persuade my stiff and weary body to the stables, and talk to Chris, if he was still there. I suspect that if I'd asked, one of the constables on duty would have summoned him for me, but I preferred to talk business on his territory.

By now it was very hot and unpleasant, like being in one of the Botanical Gardens' hothouses. My jeans were sticking to me; a loose cotton skirt would have been far more comfortable. I felt for the men and women in the stables: all that blue serge must be intolerable. There was no sign of Chris, but Tina was poking a computer, apparently quite at random. When she saw me, her face lit up and she came straight over.

'He's better,' she said. 'They think they can take him off the critical list if he goes on like this. Soph, they reckon as how he'll live!'

I hugged her. After a moment, she hugged me back.

'I'm going round to see him as soon as I get off this afternoon.'

'Send him my love,' I said. And meant it. Though perhaps it wasn't the most tactful thing to say to Tina.

'Was it Chris you was wanting to see, Soph? 'Cause you'll have to watch the midday news for that.'

'Eh?'

'TV personality, our Chris. Press conference,' she explained.

'Going to tell them what?' I asked dourly.

'Load of bullshit to shut them up.'

Although I laughed, I was in fact quite distressed. I needed someone to act as midwife to that elusive idea, and somehow, after our close contact in the spring, I couldn't quite cast Tina in that role. But Chris had always insisted that she was a good officer, so I ought at least to ask her.

'Tina,' I said quietly, 'is there somewhere we can talk? There's something niggling away at the back of my mind, and I need to bounce some ideas off you.'

'Sure. Shall I bring Ian too? How d'you fancy a half down the Miner's Lamp while we talk? Less chance of being interrupted there than here. If we take two cars, then Ian can bring you back here and I'll hop off into town.'

We were sitting round a cast-iron table in the lounge of the Miner's Lamp contemplating the remains of our meal and finishing halves of mild when I decided to put forward my theory.

If someone wanted to lay someone out cold, they could feed them something to make them sleep. If everyone shared meals, it would be almost impossible to slip anything to an individual. What you would have to do is give some to everyone. Barbiturates are bitter. So you would have to disguise the flavour in something bitter. Like chocolate pudding. We had chocolate pud for supper on Tuesday. Nyree ate a great deal. Then she hit the bottle. She died of a mixture of alcohol and barbiturate. QED.

For two such different people, the expressions on Tina's and Ian's faces were so similar as to be comical. But they could not see why I should laugh.

'You're out of your mind, Sophie,' said Ian, simply.

'Been watching too much telly, if you ask me,' said Tina, draining her glass. 'Any road up, why should anyone want to kill Nyree?'

I sighed. I hadn't got that far. But when you teach you have to think on your feet. 'Ask the person who did it, of course.'

'Who is?' asked Ian.

'Whoever has to take barbiturates. Probably someone who suffers from epilepsy. So all you have to do is find out if anyone does, and there you are, Bob's your uncle.'

My confidence was entirely false. I think my doubts had started when Carl was so dismissive. Now I was beginning to see that the theory was simplistic to the point of being naive.

'Do you seriously suppose that anyone is going to tell us if they're epileptic if it will incriminate them to that extent?'

'No. But surely you can find out? Ask their doctor,' I said, right out of my depth now.

'Whose doctor?' Ian's voice was getting more and more exasperated.

'Well, everyone's, I suppose.'

Tina and Ian fell into each other's arms in mock hilarity.

'What's the problem?' I asked.

'So I phone up your family doctor, right? And say, we've got this murderer who may or may not be epileptic, right, and we want you to tell us if Ms Rivers is epileptic. D'you see any problems? Like confidentiality? Or I could phone up and ask if you were on the pill or had had an abortion or had a history of mental illness. You'd like that, Sophie.'

I flushed. There are times when I can be remarkably stupid. This was undoubtedly one of them. My theory lay in shreds.

'What about documents in the public domain?' I hazarded,

faint but pursuing. 'Like his driving licence?'

'Might be worth a try. Assuming he drives. Or she.'

'Just to shut you up, mind,' said Tina, 'when I'm back – Monday morning, that'll be – I'll get on to Cardiff, just to see who's got a licence and who hasn't. OK?'

'Monday!'

'We're allowed to go home at weekends sometimes, Soph,' she said resentfully, pushing away from the table and picking up her bag. 'In any case, there's one other thing you don't seem to have thought of. It doesn't have to be the epileptic who fed the pills to Nyree. Someone could have nicked them – that old guy said people were always leaving things in the bathroom. The owner might have been too embarrassed to own up. Got to think of everything. Can't go jumping to conclusions. And if I were you,' she added, with a touch of venom, 'I wouldn't go telling Chris all this. He'd have bloody kittens. All these theories of yours!'

I nodded. She was referring obliquely, wasn't she, to my belief that Courtney was gay? Apologising would only make it more awkward. And, in Courtney's case, no less true.

'You going to see that young man?' asked Ian. 'Send my best wishes.'

'And mine,' I added quietly.

Ian always enjoyed driving: when he was at the wheel his face softened and his hands were relaxed. So I felt no guilt when I asked him to take me the long way back. I wanted to see once again the corner of the grounds with the ruins of the home farm, and I didn't see myself jogging that far for another couple of days. And the course ended after lunch tomorrow. Ian turned the car obligingly, and we followed a succession of lanes so narrow you wouldn't believe you were within ten miles of the city centre, and two of the M5, under which we eventually plunged.

He parked where the driver of that red car had parked on Wednesday morning.

'Don't worry,' he said, as I opened my mouth. 'Ade and his mates have already checked on the tyre tracks. Chris thought you were panicking unnecessarily but he's a stickler for detail. Especially where you're concerned.'

'I suppose you wouldn't dream of telling me what sort of tyres they were and whose car they belonged to.'

'No, I wouldn't.' Then he grinned. 'But I dare say Chris will if you ask him.'

'They do match one of the students', then?'

'Didn't say that.'

Inside the car, the noise was bad enough. When we got out, it enveloped us. Ian stood aside to let me over the stile first. Seeing how slow I was, he stretched out a matter-of-fact hand to help. Then he got over himself, surprisingly lightly for a man in his late forties. If he grunted with the effort no one would have heard. We walked up to the ruins as quickly as my cuts and bruises would allow. Then on to the ice house. There the noise was bearable, but still intrusive.

Ian peered down. 'Chris reckons they'd store ice in this for the big house.'

He sounded doubtful.

'That's right. I'd have thought this one a bit too exposed to be successful. Perhaps there used to be trees round it but they've been cut down.'

'They'd really keep ice back from the winter?'

'No other way of getting it, I suppose.'

He went slowly down the steps and gave the door a perfunctory rattle. Then he came and stood beside me again.

'We looked all over this lot, Sophie,' he said at last, his voice heavy with forbearance.

'I'm sure you did. And it's too hot to be doing all this haring about now. I'm sorry, Ian. I don't know what I'm doing or why.'

'You think Kate's still alive, don't you? The gaffer does, too. He thinks someone's keeping her alive. That asthma spray and what have you.'

'It has to be someone on the course. There've been so many of you people around, no one else would have had access to the things. But the course ends tomorrow. So what will whoever it is do then?'

We stood side by side, staring at the ice house, absorbed in thoughts that were for me, at least, very disturbing. What would I do, if I'd kept someone for a week without a ransom demand? Or had one been made, without Chris telling me?

'I suppose no one's been in touch with your people?'

'Lots of them, Sophie. Cranks anonymous. People knowing where she is, and by the way, is there a reward? A couple of clairvoyants: one of them says she's dead and buried in the Mendips, and the other says she's alive, "somewhere". But there haven't been any proper ransom demands.'

'So what happens tomorrow? Does the kidnapper set her free? Or kill her? Or go home and leave her to starve to death?'

'Your guess is as good as ours. The problem is, he's no fool, this villain. He obviously knows you're on to him.'

'I wish I bloody were!'

'Thinks you're on to him, then. Sophie, this isn't the time for do-it-yourself detection, you know. If you've got any ideas, for God's sake tell me. Or Chris.'

'I've told you the only thing I can think of. And I know there's some Japanese trade connection with Vietnam – it's in this morning's *FT*, nothing secret. That's why the Japanese wanted Nyree, no doubt – something to do with some deal her husband's involved in. No idea what, though. And no idea at all how that would involve Kate. Unless you've come up with things in her past?' I paused hopefully.

'Not a bloody thing. She was good at her job, then she picked up a legacy – yes, all bona fide, we checked it – and took premature retirement. Like that Matt said, she was positively vetted. Jesus, Sophie, this is a crazy spot to stand talking in. No shade for miles. Nowhere to sit. And it's so humid you'd think you were in Viet bloody Nam itself.'

'That's what she called it,' I said. 'Nyree. She didn't want to go.'

'Don't blame her.' He turned and scanned the expanse of parkland, which shimmered back, blandly. 'All this space, and all within spitting distance of Brum. I'm surprised someone's not developed it properly. This side of the motorway, you know, this'd make a good golf course. And that marshland across the way – I'm surprised no one's got round to dredging it. Make a nice little water-park, that would. Ever done any windsurfing, Sophie?'

'It's a nice thought, in this weather.'

We turned together and walked slowly back to the farm. We paused there long enough for another cursory check.

Nothing.

The air pulsed in the sun. We walked as quickly as we could towards the gate, Ian putting his hand to my arm if he thought I was stumbling.

'When I was a kid,' he said, 'I had this book about India, I think it was. How when they wanted to get a tiger for the sahibs to shoot, they used to tether this goat where the tiger could see it or smell it or whatever. In this heat, in this noise, stuck up there on that hill, I reckon I knew what that goat felt like. Come on,' he added in his normal voice, 'I need a cup of tea.'

We spent the journey back putting together a team for the MCC's winter tour. It was too short for us to get beyond the opening batsmen and the possibility of a specialist wicket-keeper. I'd have been happy to spend the rest of the afternoon talking cricket. It would certainly have been preferable to hanging around waiting for someone to do something, possibly to me. He must have seen my expression as we pulled into the area the police had appropriated for their car park.

'Come along with me – I reckon you need some tea, too. Any response to the gaffer's press conference?' he asked the room at large, as we entered the comparative cool of the stable.

There was a gloomy murmur. He pointed to the chair beside the desk and went to make the tea himself. No one else would make it the way he likes it: Earl Grey so pale as to be gold; no milk; a paper-thin slice of lemon. He didn't speak until we'd drained our cups. Then, as I heaved myself up from the chair, he said quietly, 'I'll have another look at those statements, Sophie. See if anyone else was sleepy after that pudding. In the meantime,' he added, raising his voice, 'no more heroics, eh? Remember that goat!'

Chapter Twenty-Two

Two thirty. The kitchen was still empty. I was so out of touch with the course I couldn't even remember who was supposed to be cooking? Was it Gimson? And wasn't there some rumour that he was refusing to take his place in the roster? I suppose, since he was no doubt considering the joys of Harborne, or that part of it that comprised Rose Road Police Station, the whole issue was academic anyway.

I put on the kettle for another cup of tea. I'd been foolish to drink beer in such heat, especially at midday: it had left me feeling very second-hand. My clothes were sticking to me, the sweat defying my deodorant, and my hair was wilting. The whole of me was wilting, come to think of it. I could do with a nap. But the fear that it would turn into a whole afternoon's sleep put me off the idea, and I joggled the teabag in the hot water rather longer than usual. I needed to raise my caffeine level a bit.

At this point Shazia pushed open the door, banging down a couple of Sainsbury's carrier bags on the table. She didn't speak to me, but ostentatiously emptied the bags, putting a load of salad stuff into the sink. Without asking I boiled the kettle and made another mug of tea. I passed it to her. She pushed it away. Oh, God: I'd made another enemy. I'd wanted Shazia as a friend but I suppose my offhand attitude to the course had irritated her. Funny, I'd thought we were on the same wavelength at supper last night. I ought to ask her what I'd said or done, and explain or apologise.

Suddenly she turned. 'I know it's not your fault. I'm being unfair,' she said. She picked up the tea. 'But they've taken

Naukez now.'

'Why on earth?'

'Just for questioning, they say, but – oh, Sophie, what did you say? To make them suspect him?'

'I just said I'd seen him leaving the house. But it wasn't him I followed, Shazia. I followed someone else. I don't know who. You could hardly see your hand in front of your face before that storm. They can't think it was anything to do with Naukez!'

'It's because he's out on his own such a lot. No alibi. And they reckon he must know the park better than anyone. And, of course, he had that problem with Nyree. Horrible woman!'

'What problem, Shazia?'

'Didn't you know? You must be the only one who doesn't, then. She followed him up to our flat, the first morning she saw him. The Monday, I suppose it must have been. I seem to have lost all track of time. And then that afternoon she kept on pestering him to take her to see the badgers. Oh, Sophie, what if he had? If she'd been with him when she died?'

I shook my head. I didn't want to interrupt her: she plainly needed to talk to someone.

'If his family find out . . . They've never liked me. They'll blame me for not being a good wife, or something.'

'They can't do that! You've done nothing wrong!' But then I remembered families didn't necessarily employ logic when it came to making judgements. And I had interrupted her flow.

She started tearing viciously at the lettuces. I reached across for the watercress and started picking it over. If I waited, perhaps she would start again.

She did; but not as I'd expected.

'And then there's this course. These students, I mean. It was all wrong from the start. All that hostility. I know Nyree was responsible for most of it, but no one seemed to want to be part of a group. All you individuals going in separate directions. Not you especially – you don't even want to be a writer. But no one's trying to help anyone else like they do in other groups – it's all self, self, self. I thought things might change after Nyree's death. I suppose they did. For the worse. Fancy,

Sophie, threatening to sue because there wasn't a teacher. And now –' she turned the tap on – 'now here they are wanting a barbecue tonight. I ask you, a barbecue. No one wants to prepare it, of course, because somehow they'll all be too busy preparing their piece for tonight.'

'Are they going to get one?'

'They are not! Salad and Sainsbury's flans, that's what they're getting, and ice cream to follow. Full stop. I'm supposed to do the lunch tomorrow – that's part of the contract, that and the first supper. And I suppose I'm being a bit ungracious not wanting to do more.'

'Nonsense. You've had more than enough to put up with. Any idea who fingered Naukez, by the way? Since it wasn't me.'

She shook her head. 'All they'd say was they wanted to ask him some questions. Sophie, what shall I do?'

'Trust Chris. He's got to investigate, because if he didn't he'd be in the shit. But he won't accuse anyone falsely. He wants to find Kate. He won't mess around trying to frame an innocent man.'

Shazia nodded, and then seemed to go up a gear: 'What d'you think you're doing with that watercress? You'll get your dressings wet.'

'Only one cut. I can stick another plaster on it. And I shall get it wet anyway when I wash my hair – I mean, look at it!'

She looked: she didn't try to pretend it was a pretty sight. She burrowed in a drawer. 'Better use these and keep the dressing dry, if you ask me.' She passed a wad of thin polythene gloves stapled together at the wrist. 'Tape them on: there's no point in taking unnecessary risks.'

I nodded. I tore one free, put it on and started on the watercress. It made a fiddly job fiddlier, but perhaps she was right.

'Thanks, Sophie,' she said, as I rinsed a colanderful under the tap. 'But you're supposed to be washing your hair, remember – and you've already prepared one meal. Mostly on your own. It won't take me long to finish this lot.'

I tore off another glove, but she picked up the rest and thrust them at me. 'Go on, take them all – they're not very strong.'

* * *

I managed to shower and wash my hair without soaking through the dressing, but drying my hair was tricky. I had to use the wrong hand for the dryer because the cable pressed to hard against the cut, and I kept blowing hot air not at my hair but down my back and on my breasts. If only Courtney – but if I thought about him I might start to cry again.

I was sitting naked on my bed wondering how long make-up might stay on in the heat when someone tapped on the door. I slung my dressing gown on and held it round me while I opened the door. I didn't want to embarrass any passing policeman.

But it wasn't Chris. It was Hugh.

My dressing gown fell open of its own accord. His shirt and trousers took a couple of minutes of delightful fumbling. He'd even brought condoms – had intended, perhaps, a pastoral seduction under some Eyre Park trees.

But a bed, even the hard, narrow variety, was probably more comfortable.

OK, it was lust. But it was very high-quality lust.

He was a considerate and expert lover, as careful not to assault my damaged places as he was to give pleasure to the others. Perhaps the earth didn't move for either of us, but there was a sense that it might next time. We sat naked on the floor while we recovered: it was too hot and sticky to lie in each other's arms, but he would touch my hair or my skin, very gently, from time to time, as if in appreciation. I felt like a contented cat, and smiled back at him, wondering whether it was too soon to prompt that beautiful body of his back into action again. I suspected it wouldn't take much coaxing. For the moment, however, we played an interesting game of tracing into all sorts of delightful places little trickles of each other's sweat.

And then he saw the *Financial Times* open on the desk. His *Financial Times*. His glance was uncomfortably hard.

'What I can't understand,' he said, starting his car and turning on the air conditioning, 'is why no one thought of asking me. A medical problem and they send for Gimson. All these Asians sloshing round the country kidnapping my woman and no one bothers to mention it to me. Damn it it all,

I've more information on Southeast Asia in my office than the average library.'

My woman. I wasn't sure about that. Not yet. But it sounded good, and I liked the tenderness with which he touched my hand as he said it.

'They think of you as a poet, not an expert on international relations,' I said mildly, waving to the PC on duty by the gates.

Hugh prepared to pull away, but the PC flagged us down and walked round to my side. I looked for the window winder but, of course, the windows descended electronically in response to a touch on another button.

'Just wondered how you were, miss. You looked a bit of a mess last night.'

'Fine. All patched up now.' I raised my hand as evidence. 'Look, some of your colleagues have the idea that messages are best transmitted mystically between those concerned. I've told everyone I could think of I'm going into the city with Mr Brierley to look up material on our Asian friends, but now I'm telling you too, and if Chris Groom dashes round like a headless chicken when he finds I've left Eyre House, you will tell him I'm OK, won't you?'

He gave a half-salute. Hugh put the car into gear, and I screamed, 'Sidney! Hugh, stop! I think that was Sidney!'

Hugh stopped.

We all threshed around in the undergrowth for four or five minutes, but in vain. Possibly it hadn't been Sidney at all. Or possibly all our efforts had merely scared him away.

We were both silent as we set off again. Apart from my sneezes and wheezes: a hedgerow is an excellent source of allergens.

'You really do care for that rat, don't you?' said Hugh eventually.

'I suppose I do. Funny really – I'm not so keen on animals in general. But despite his smell, he has a certain charm. And I suppose I see myself as his guardian in Kate's absence.'

'Absence or –'

'Absence. I still think she's alive. Hope, perhaps, would be a better word. Hence, after all, this expedition to town on an afternoon that could be much more pleasantly spent elsewhere.'

He took my hand again.

'Sophie, I have an air conditioned office. And very thick carpets.'

I was grateful for both.

I was sitting on the floor of Hugh's office, surrounded by old-fashioned paper files. He was at his desk – a suitably huge executive one – poring over computer files, tutting occasionally in irritation.

It was a very smart office. I'm used to William Murdock, remember, probably the most grossly underfunded college in the country. We have a foyer, true, and a reception desk, but there the resemblance ends. Our potted plants expired years ago, under a steady deluge of empty Coke cans and fag ends. Hugh's flourished almost as thickly as the carpet. It comes to something, too, when the corridors of your companion's office are infinitely better carpeted and furnished – pictures on the wall that might well be original, and none of them covered in graffiti – than your staffroom. And there was none of the tedious business of hunting for your key – no, everything done by electronics. Hugh's personal sanctum opened to the sound of his voice.

More plants, vertical blinds, furniture that looked as if it might be wood. And space. At William Murdock we'd have had to fit six or eight people into the room: Hugh was able to work in splendid isolation. What did disconcert me a bit was the way he swept a couple of things from his desk before I could see them; but I suppose that he didn't yet know me well enough to trust me absolutely, and if there was money to be made in exports, there was no doubt money to be lost, too.

Eventually he poured two plastic beakers of water from a chiller and came to join me. He pulled me to my feet and led me to the air-conditioner vent. The current was strong enough to ruffle our hair, and he lifted and played with a tendril from near my ear. But it seemed we were to talk business for a while. I would have to try very hard to concentrate.

'Recap,' he said. 'Just what do we know?'

I ticked off the items on my fingers. Japanese visitors to

our relaxation class. Japanese abductors who were courteous to the sick. Less polite visitors (possibly Vietnamese?) who'd been rude to me and Shazia. Kenji's sudden inadequacy. ('Why not phone him from here?' Hugh put in.) Nyree's husband, about whom I knew little except that he'd been a diplomat who liked his golf.

At this point Hugh abandoned my hair and reached for his jacket. But he didn't put it on.

'Were are you going?'

'We. We're going to Eyre House, of course. For our supper and the exciting students' reading. They tell me there'll be a party afterwards.'

'Hugh? Why now?' What I wanted to say was what my body was already saying, quite urgently. That it wanted Hugh, now.

'Because I think I may have some ideas. I think I may – here, give me those papers. Did you keep them in order?' He started to stuff them back into the filing cabinet.

'I think so.' I padded over to the computer. 'Did you find anything?'

'Do you know anything about golf?'

'Absolutely nothing. My cousin tried to teach me, but I found hunting for that stupid little ball interrupted my country walk. And I couldn't deal with the clothes.'

He laughed, locked the cabinet, and came back and kissed me.

'Golf is as addictive as sex,' he said, peeling off my T-shirt and undoing my bra. His shirt and trousers and my jeans rapidly joined them on the floor. Our pants entwined on the top of the pile. 'Once you find you like it, you can't get enough.' He kissed my breasts, making my nipples stand to attention. 'Like sex,' he said, bending for his trousers again and burrowing in the pocket, 'golf is big business. I'm into business, and thus, almost by necessity, into golf. Golf courses, to be precise.' He pushed aside his computer and lifted me so I was sitting on the desk. 'Hmm. Hole in one.'

And then he did not speak for a few minutes. Neither of us did. But I moaned so satisfactorily I afterwards hoped the room was soundproofed.

The discovery that his office furniture included a fridge

was unexpected, but then I was hardly surprised at all when I found it contained champagne. The glasses were there chilling beside it.

'We'll get some more on our way back to Eyre House,' said Hugh. 'I must say the idea of a party with that lot doesn't grab me. I suggest we adjourn somewhere comfortable for our own little party.'

We were naked in that wonderful cool air again. It meant we could hug and caress without sticking together.

'Seems a bit mean to leave Matt to cope with them all,' I said, without enthusiasm. The thought of an all-night party – waking up to find Hugh still beside me – woke up my nipples again.

'Into troilism, are you?'

'Let him cope,' I agreed.

Chapter Twenty-Three

Eventually we'd torn ourselves away from each other and from the air conditioning, and had plunged through the canyon of heat that was Hugh's car park into the air conditioning of his car. We said little until he'd found an off-licence, whence he returned with three bottles of Moët. When he stroked my hair back and lightly tickled my cheek, I was ready to purr.

But I had to be firm with myself; there were questions I had to ask. I hoped he'd be ready to answer them.

'Tell me about golf, then, Hugh,' I said, smiling contentedly at the memory of his hole in one.

'You mean golf-the-game or golf-the-business?'

'Whichever is more relevant to Nyree.'

'How much do you know?'

'I know the Japanese – with the exception of Kenji, by the way – are fanatics. I've seen pictures on TV of golf ranges teeming with men practising their drives.'

'Get you: "drives"! Got the jargon already!'

'And I know they have silly terms like "birdie" and "eagle".'

'Almost as silly as "square leg" and "gully".'

'*Touché*. And I know from your *FT* that the Japanese are keen on making money – or would you prefer the term "overseas investment"?'

'Same thing in their case. But it's not always a bad thing for the country invested in. Where would the British car industry be without Japanese investment?'

I smiled to acknowledge the hit. 'But I take it they want to invest in other countries too?'

'Of course. Wherever there's a chance of getting a good return on their money. China, Vietnam – the Pacific Rim countries. Some of my colleagues are busy trying to persuade the Chinese, for example, to buy prestige cars. I'm more interested in something a little more permanent. I want them to buy golf courses.'

'Buy golf courses?' I repeated.

'Buy them. You don't suppose a golf course is a natural phenomenon, do you? Funny clothes apart, golf involves all sorts of other things. Take grass, for example.'

'Grass is pretty natural,' I objected. 'It's green, isn't it? The sort of thing I have in my lawn.'

'Is yours bent or fescue?'

'It needs cutting every week.'

'Sophie, Sophie, this is science we're talking. Science and money. There's work being done at Sheffield University – we're thinking of sponsoring it – on the bounce of golf balls. What balls bounce on –'

At this point we started to giggle, and the lecture ended.

But it occurred to me, with a vicious, insidious niggle, like a tooth that doesn't quite need filling, that if the Japanese and Vietnamese might consider using force to persuade people to do business with them, Hugh might do the same. Plainly you don't inhabit offices like his without a certain amount of effort, possibly even ruthlessness. How ruthless would he be? Any moment now, I would have to ask whether it was him I'd seen driving swiftly from the main gates, he who had explored the derelict farm.

And I wasn't especially looking forward to hearing the answer. But for the time being I was spared.

There was so much activity outside the gates, I thought for a moment that Chris hadn't received a single one of my messages. Then a couple of police cars shot out. Cursing mildly, Hugh had to pull right on to the verge to let them pass. They looked very full, come to think of it, but I couldn't see more than that. Plainly the drivers didn't expect the passengers to be waving graciously to bystanders.

As we parked, a policewoman in shirtsleeves bounded over with a message from Chris. Would I be kind enough to pop into the stables for a couple of minutes? It was possible there might be something to celebrate.

Slowed by the bruises and some muscles in my lower back protesting about a position they hadn't been called on to use for some time, I staggered rather than sprinted to where Chris was waiting, like a benign Victorian father, beaming at the stable door. Perhaps he was less keen to see Hugh reaching a hand to steady me, but he was too polite, too professional, to switch off his smile.

And then the sober side of his professionalism asserted itself. He invited us in, found us chairs, yelled for someone to make tea and finally seated himself with that air of authority I'd liked in him before.

'The name Nguyen mean anything to you?' he asked briskly.

'Most of our Vietnamese students are called Nguyen,' I said.

'Brierley?'

Hugh shook his head. 'Wrong bit of Asia for me. I'm a Chinese-mainland man. But I do have some contacts who might . . .'

I thought of that office, those files. Damn right Hugh would have contacts.

Chris nodded.

Ian came over with the tea – a repeat order of the lunchtime Earl Grey. Hugh looked at it, then at Ian, with disbelief. I grinned up at Ian. One day I'd like him to talk sherry with Hugh. And then I found myself smiling. This was the first time I'd projected my relationship with Hugh into the future.

I looked up to find Chris's eyes on my face.

'OK,' I said. 'This 'ere good news, Chris. These 'ere celebrations we've heard so much about. Come on. Give.'

He shuffled a couple of papers back into their file, and then looked at me again.

'You remember the morning – dear God, was it only Tuesday? – I came into the lobby and found you having a little difficulty with an Asian gentleman?'

I nodded.

'He came back this afternoon, with a couple of friends. But

he found the young woman on reception he tried to rough up had one or two unexpected resources.'

'Like backup from a number of highly trained officers,' Hugh said.

'Exactly so. So the gentlemen were duly apprehended –' Chris's eyes sought mine as he teased me with the officialese – 'and are going to help us with our inquiries.'

'And I wasn't there to see the fun!' I wailed, not entirely seriously.

'Haven't you had enough fun? You'll be picking scabs off your knees for the next few weeks as it is. They said something weird. In fact, it was so weird we've sent for an interpreter, although their English seems perfectly good. Something about fescue.'

Hugh started to laugh.

'Fescue?' I repeated. 'Wasn't that what you were telling me about?'

'And bent,' Hugh said. 'What about fescue, Chris?'

First-name terms, eh? And how would Chris respond?

'Why should you and Sophie be discussing fescue?'

'Because – at Sophie's instigation – we have just spend this beautiful afternoon, practically the only beautiful afternoon we've had all summer, incarcerated in my office searching for eastern connections. And come up with –'

'Golf courses?' asked Chris, coolly. But his crow's-feet were twitching. He'd set us up.

'How the hell did you know?' said Hugh, who didn't recognise the signs.

The crow's-feet were at their most pronounced. And then he smiled. Any moment we would all be laughing.

'Because of Sophie's friend Kenji. He phoned Rose Road – why on earth did you leave that number, Sophie? You had the poor man dreadfully confused – and the switchboard had the sense to take his number and tell the duty officer, who passed it on to me. And when I called him back – he doesn't seem to like having his beauty sleep disturbed –'

'Beauty sleep, nothing. He'd be having it off with that American journalist.'

'Well, she came into it, I admit. But only as far as her investigations are concerned. No high-level corruption, not as far as she can find out. But a lot of strife over who builds what for whom. Some nasty people involved both in Vietnam and in Japan. And in England.'

I don't know what my face showed. But the niggle of suspicion suddenly exploded as if I'd lost a major filling. I said nothing.

'Hence your unwelcome visitors, Sophie. Of both nations. I suspect we'll find Nyree's husband was brokering the deal, perhaps even Nyree herself. When we've spoken to our Vietnamese friends.'

'But why kill the goose – the gander – laying golden eggs?' I asked, trying not to sing aloud with relief.

Chris shrugged. 'We'll have to wait and see.'

'And how would they do it? And why remove Kate?'

'Patience never was your strong suit, was it, Sophie? Maybe it'll come out when we talk to them. I must say,' he added more thoughtfully, 'I'd like to get my hands on that Japanese-driven Merc. It just seems to have left the face of the earth.'

His face and body sagged. He looked the way I felt at the end of a hard term.

Perhaps we all did. We ought to have laughed at the anticlimax, but none of us had. We ought to be congratulating Chris on his quick-thinking, quick-acting colleagues, but neither of us had. Hugh looked surprisingly grim, and I felt a sudden urge to weep. Post-coital *tristesse*, I told myself.

'So what now?' I asked.

'I'm off to Harborne to talk to the Vietnamese. I shall have everyone mobilised in case what they tell us leads to Kate.'

'What about the people here? Do you no longer suspect any of them?'

'I wish I knew. What I'd like to do is bloody tag you all so I know where you are. Or tail you all. But –'

'So you think there's someone else involved?'

'I don't know. I don't bloody know. Of course there must be. Logic tells me someone must be.'

'The bod who torched my van,' I said.

He nodded.

'The bod who thinks I was following him to wherever he's keeping Kate.'

'Thinks! You bloody were!'

'If he's frightened, isn't there a danger he'll abandon Kate?' said Hugh.

Chris and I turned simultaneously. We'd forgotten he was there.

'And maybe leave her to die of hunger or exposure?' he continued.

'What d'you suggest? We just let you all go quietly home?'

'That's what you promised. We could all go home provided your people knew where we were,' I said.

Chris nodded. 'Right. But you don't leave till after lunch tomorrow, and I'd dearly love to get it wrapped up by then.'

'Hercule Poirot lives,' I said dourly. 'Now who's been reading too many detective stories?'

For reply, he stood up and reached into his pocket for his car keys. 'I can't speculate any longer. I can't hope. I can only work. See you later. I'll let you know of any developments, of course. In the meantime, for God's sake take care, Sophie. OK?'

'No! Not OK! Naukez. You haven't mentioned Naukez. What on earth did you want with him?'

'To ask him some questions. Literally. He must know this area as well as anyone and I just wanted to talk to him about it. Ask him where anyone could hide or be hidden. He and Shazia got a bit worked up. I thought it was best to get Naukez on his own. I got someone to drive him round talking about the place.'

'And –?'

'Not and. But. It seems that though he knows Eyre Park inside out, he's not explored much beyond the boundaries yet. After all, he and Shazia have only been here for about six months.'

He nodded wearily. Hugh started to say something, but Chris turned his back and was gone.

Ian came over. He looked at me, then in the direction Chris had gone. He shook his head slightly.

'Needs a good break with these Vietnamese buggers,' he said.

I hadn't the heart to ask how he was getting on with

rereading all the statements.

Supper would have been a chilly affair, had it not been for the weather. As it happened, the flans and salad were just right: no one could have eaten a hot meal. And a barbecue would have been spoiled by the constant glances at the horizon to see how long the thunder might hold off. I ended up sitting between Matt and Hugh, and although both men responded courteously enough to other people when they were addressed, they made it their business to entertain me. In fact, our attempts to resuscitate the curry poem led to considerable if half-suppressed hilarity, and people kept glancing disapprovingly at us, as if we were naughty kids at the back of the class. And certainly I was cheating; but my friends had apparently decided that I too must have a poem to read out in half an hour's time.

It was a terribly depleted group in the lounge, of course. No Agnes, no Thea. I realised, to my shame, I'd given neither a thought since Thursday. No Courtney. No Kate.

Shazia was still arranging chairs. There were a couple of bottles and some empty glasses on a small table. Naukez, looking sullen as much as shaken, put his head and right arm round the door and waved a corkscrew at her. She took it. He looked at us all and withdrew.

All this took place in silence. The footfalls and scraping of chair legs were unnaturally loud. No one was talking. Guilt or first-night nerves? I rather thought the former.

I smiled at Shazia and reached for the corkscrew. She was only at this appalling event out of courtesy. Normally, I should imagine, she might get quite involved with those she considered her guests. But after the insensitivity over litigation and the barbecue – did no one realise she might quite reasonably object to cooking pork sausages even for other people? – I should think she'd be relieved to see the back of us.

Perhaps some wine might defrost the atmosphere. I poured and passed round and was cut by Mr Woodhouse and by Jean, the only remaining grey lady. Gimson nodded silently. Toad took his glass with absolutely no expression on his face. Tabitha and the sci-fi freak were so busy reading their manuscripts that I put their glasses beside them and left them to it. The giggly girl giggled and crossed her legs to show even more fat thigh. The brace-girl moved her lips and kept her eyes closed as if she were praying. Matt and Hugh came in together and sat down together. Red for both of them: they looked up and smiled as I approached.

This time there was no need for Matt to cough for silence, but he coughed for attention. He stood up portentously and raised his glass. 'Absent friends,' he said.

We responded. And then seemed a good moment for me to ask: 'How are all our absent friends? Agnes? Thea? Courtney?'

'You don't class Kate as a friend?' asked Tabitha.

'I took it as read that no one here knows how or where she is,' I said.

Shazia jumped in: 'Thea's going home on Monday. They're very pleased with her. Her husband used to be a doctor, and both her sons are GPs. She reckons she'll be safer there than in a hospital.'

There was a little stiff laughter. Gimson did not join in.

'And Agnes has got to go into her local hospital for a check-up. Something about regularising her drugs. And Courtney – they were hoping to move him out of intensive care today, but I gather they may leave it till tomorrow, now.'

I didn't like the sound of that. Poor Tina. Poor Courtney. Poor Kate . . . Yes, absent friends.

There was a great deal of coy demurring on the order of reading, at last cut short by Matt, who asked Toad to start. Toad was writing a screenplay on the subject of Jack the Ripper. What he needed was enough copies for each character, plus a narrator, but he chose to read all the parts himself, including the action and camera shots. He complicated it somewhat by abbreviating 'interior' and 'exterior' in a way which would of course have been clear enough on the page but which lost me altogether.

'"Ext. Night,"' he began. '"A mysterious alley, no, London alley, probably in Soho." I'll have to check that out of course, find out exactly where it all happened.'

'You could always watch one of the many films on the subject,' said Gimson.

'"Fog swirls round in a mysterious figure, dressed in typical Victorian clothes."'

'A crinoline?' put in the giggly girl.

I felt a sudden distaste. I always hate it when students bait one of their colleagues, and if I felt vulnerable at the moment I was sure even Toad must. I did what I would do in class – shot a cold look at the offender. She blushed and subsided. I didn't expect to have any trouble with her for the rest of the evening. I also caught Gimson's eye, but he responded only with a supercilious lift of one nostril, a movement I would no doubt find useful in boring meetings if only I could emulate it.

'"A rat moves in the gutter. Diving under a cabbage leaf, a cheaply dressed young lady, young woman, I should say, screams and lifts her shirt, sorry, skirt. The mysterious man lifts his cane and with devilish accuracy swipes and kills the rat. He then scoops it up on the end of his cane, shows it her and throws it in the gutter. Man: If you're afraid of rats, my dear, you should not be out alone at night. Young woman: Sir, you are too kind. I haven't a mama or a papa, I'm just a poor working girl. Man: I cannot believe that such a beautiful young girl as you is poor, there must be many men as would like to make you rich . . ."'

I set my face into lines of severe concentration. My lips would not pucker in amusement nor would my jaw sag into a yawn of boredom. Then I allowed my thoughts to swan off where they would. Hugh, of course: I thought a great deal about Hugh. Tomorrow was the last time we'd be together unless we wanted to push the relationship further. It went without saying I did. There can't be many such attractive young men in Birmingham. Intelligent, funny, sexy. Rich. Oddly that could be a problem. Almost all of my friends are politically on the left, and I couldn't see Hugh criticising the hand that nurtured business.

But then my attention surged back to Toad. What was he saying? Something about punishment? His reading had certainly changed – from that awkward monotone to something approaching liveliness. But even as I cursed myself for not concentrating, Matt interrupted: 'I'm sorry to cut you off there, Garth. But we agreed ten minutes maximum, if you remember, and I'm afraid I've let you do nearly twenty already. Thanks. There's a lot of potential there. Now: Jean?'

Fifteen minutes of a nice lucid story.

'Thanks, Jean. I'm sure we'll be hearing that on Radio Four soon. Remind me to give you a list of *Short Story* producers before we leave tomorrow. Ted?'

Ted was the sci-fi freak, thin, in John Lennon glasses. From him, read in a series of staccato stutters that made my heart bleed for him, a very short story about the plague striking modern-day Manchester.

Mr Woodhouse's sonnet.

Tabitha's erotic story, which sounded to me more like an expedition into a particularly foul-mouthed building site.

A two-hander from the girls – a pilot for a sitcom series. It made everyone laugh, politely.

Then Gimson: a reminiscence of his childhood, so rich in colour and smell and taste I was jealous. It wasn't fair that he should write like that when I could offer nothing of my own. After that it would be cheap to read the cooperative curry poem. I caught Matt's eye and shook my head as unobtrusively as I could. A tiny nod in return – point taken.

'Those that can, do, and those that can't, teach,' said Toad with a vicious mixture of accuracy and complacency. 'You'll have to stand in the corner, Sophie.'

'Another drink, I should think,' said Matt, jovial as Falstaff. 'Come on, Sophie – get busy with that wine!'

Shazia hunched her shoulder away from Toad as I filled Matt's glass. 'I'll be glad when *he*'s gone. I reckon it was he who fingered Naukez.'

I shook my head.

'Well, he threatened to. And . . .' Her eyes filled with tears.

'It's OK; take your time.'

She straightened her shoulders. 'It was when I was killing the weeds on the terrace. He said it'd hurt my baby.' She pressed her hands to her still flat stomach.

I put my arm round her shoulders and kissed her cheek lightly. 'He's lying. Surely he was lying.'

'That's what my GP said. But he wanted me to believe it, he wanted me to be afraid.'

'Take no notice,' I said bracingly. 'What you've done today was above and beyond the call of duty. Why don't you slip away and go and rest – take care of Junior?'

She looked wistfully at her watch, but shook her head. 'Like the man says, I've started so I'll finish. Only a few more hours. Come on, Sophie, you too – into battle!'

Chapter Twenty-Four

For such a small number of people they contrived to make an enormous amount of noise. Reaction, I suppose, like the noise outside the exam hall after the last paper. Even the comments were similar: 'I never thought I could do it but of course I just had to.'

Matt and Hugh were mixing conscientiously, making serious and constructive comments on everyone's efforts. No one would miss me for a few moments.

Except Hugh. As I slipped past him, he touched the inside of my wrist and slid his finger delicately down into the palm.

'Don't forget we have a date with a bottle of champagne,' he whispered.

'I'll be back in a couple of minutes.'

It turned out to be rather longer than that.

I suppose I shouldn't have expected anything other than blank disbelief from Ian Dale when I propounded my theory. It sounded hollow enough, in all honesty, but something inside me was nagging viciously. He sat back in his chair in the stables, his shirt wet with sweat, and laughed when I expanded on it.

'Let me get this straight, Sophie. Mr Kerwin has been very nasty to Shazia – which I don't for a minute condone – and he looked and sounded evil when he was reading his piece tonight. I am therefore required to get a search warrant and do his flat over. Right? Oh, and I am to have him tailed wherever he goes. Unobtrusively. No. And before you ask, I won't phone Chris and ask him to. And neither will you. He's got one of his heads. His migraines.'

'But he wanted to get everything tied up for tomorrow,' I said.

'I know you mean well, Sophie. Don't think I don't. But you can't do that sort of thing in the police, any more than you can check on someone's medical files. He'll be back on his pins tomorrow, with a bit of luck: leave it till then.' He gave an indulgent and avuncular smile. 'Tell you what, Sophie. I've been doing a bit of reading, like I promised. You know, the statements. And I'll tell you something: several people remarked on how deeply they'd slept. There. No –' he put up a hand to stop me – 'no, there's nothing I can do about it tonight. But it's the first thing Chris'll see tomorrow when he checks his electronic mail.'

Ian would expect me to raise an eyebrow at such a sophisticated form of communication, so I did. And I smiled so blithely I hoped to allay any suspicions.

I formulated my plan as I returned to the lounge. The worst thing about it, apart from its illegality, was that it would involve other people, directly or indirectly. I hoped it would be the latter.

Everyone was still milling round the drinks table and Hugh, so I managed to winkle Matt out into the corridor. We stood side by side. If anyone had emerged, we'd have been able to shut up at once – my reputation couldn't, in any case, be any more tarnished.

'Matt, I want you to do something for me. Keep Shazia talking for a moment.'

'With pleasure – but why?'

I repeated what I'd said to Ian.

'You could be right. He's weird. But the fuzz'll sort him out if he is.'

'But not quickly enough. It's urgent. I'm going to check out his place myself.'

'Break into his house!' Matt sounded shocked enough, but then smiled. 'How d'you know where he lives? How will you get there?'

'I don't know yet. But I want you to talk to Shazia for five minutes while I get his address from her files. OK?'

He nodded. 'Better do that first,' he said. 'Or the rest of the mission will have to be aborted. Go on, off you pop.'

So I trotted off to reception. I'd forgotten there'd be an officer on duty. I didn't want to push my luck too far. I smiled innocently and reached, not for the course list, which was presumably confidential, but for the Birmingham telephone directory.

'Were you the one the Vietnamese had a go at?' I asked, while I thumbed through.

Kerwin, G!

'No. Me Mate Trace,' she said. 'Ever so good, she is. Karate and that. Mind you, so were they. Good job she can holler, our Trace.'

I agreed, of course, and walked off with the phone book to the telephone. I even dialled the number, just in case he didn't live alone. I let it ring on and on. But there was no reply. I memorised his address and returned the directory.

Winson Green. He lived in Winson Green. Inner-city Brum. A canal; a railway line; an overcrowded prison; a big mental hospital; pretty new developments alongside the urban decay that reminded you that Handsworth wasn't far away, nor the Lozells Road, scene of the riots a while back.

Back in the lounge I managed to speak to Matt again. He scooped me outside, making an inaudible comment to Hugh that everyone would think was ribald. Possibly it was.

'I'm in luck. He lives in Winson Green. It'll only take me twenty minutes at the outside to get there. What's the time now? Give me twenty minutes there, twenty back, and twenty searching his house – I should be back before eleven, with a bit of luck.'

Matt laughed. 'Great. Only a couple of problems, as I see it. Getting there and getting into the house.'

'Your car. You will lend me your car? I'll use a credit card to get in. And before you mention fingerprints, Shazia gave me some plastic gloves – I'll wear those. Hang on.'

The door was opening. Whoever was coming out would see me and Matt in enthusiastic but spurious embrace.

It must have been effective as camouflage goes because Hugh didn't seem very happy. But he listened while Matt outlined my plan. Then Matt made an important amendment. The Fiesta wasn't up to it, Matt said. It had been stationary so long it wouldn't start when he'd tried it earlier. He'd have to get the RAC to get him on the road tomorrow.

'I suppose you couldn't lend me yours,' I said hopefully to Hugh.

'You suppose right. It's only insured for me and – named drivers,' he said. 'But I could always act as your chauffeur. Provided Matt promises to keep Garth here. Oh, go over his screenplay, for goodness' sake. And throw in a quick lesson on apostrophes while you're at it. He uses them like other people use pepper.'

What had seemed so simple when I was full of adrenalin now seemed a crazy enterprise. How could I imagine that I'd be able to break into a man's home – me, a more or less respectable college lecturer? It was simply outside my experience, outside my imagination, outside my moral code. Then I thought of Kate, and of Toad's eyes, and I stiffened whatever resolve I had left.

Hugh was driving without saying much, but as we reached the outer-circle route I could feel him getting tense.

'Are you sure about this?' I asked.

'Have you noticed all those little knots of youths?' he said. 'They look like trouble to me. Have we much further to go?'

'Couple of miles at most. How d'you mean, trouble?'

'Just a feeling. A hot night like this. All these disaffected kids. Can't wait to get back to Eyre House, to be honest.'

He flicked the radio on, switching from Radio Four to Radio Three and then off altogether.

'Can you navigate from here? There's an A-to-Z in the door pocket.'

So we picked our way through mean streets towards meaner. At traffic lights an XR3 tried to drift us into the kerb. I heard the click of the central locking. Then Hugh shoved the car into gear and flung it forward on to the pavement.

'They got my secretary that way last week. Luffed her into a telegraph pole. Stole her handbag and shoes and make-up. Good shoes, you see – dresses well, Katya. I've had her a car phone fitted now. Shutting the stable door, of course.'

We bumped free on to the road again and set off fast, in the opposite direction to the one we wanted. I waited till he paused for directions to tell him so. And I found a circuitous route back.

And, all of a sudden, we were there.

The street was old, full of two-up, two-down houses. There was scaffolding up to some of the roofs: the old slates were being stripped. Skips marked the builders' progress. There were miniscule front gardens, even smaller than mine, reduced further by tiny bay windows. I'll swear the odd one still showed off an aspidistra. The front doors were wood, once solid, but now in many cases scuffed and broken. Instead of having an entry for every pair of houses, there was one for every six. There would be a path along the back of all the houses separating them from their gardens, if that wasn't too grand a word.

What I prayed now was that Toad didn't live in the middle of a block but at the end. Householders aren't supposed to put gates across the back path, but those with dogs or children or even a natural preference for privacy often do. And I didn't want to meet gates or dogs, whether vociferous or sneaky nippers of ankles.

Parking was going to be a problem too. No garages, of course, so the only place anyone could park was on the street. Hugh drove slowly, scanning for house numbers. Most front doors were completely bare. And I hardly wanted to burgle the wrong house. But we could find number 7 and number 9, so we could guess Toad's house with a reasonable degree of accuracy. And although it didn't have an entry at the side, there would be only one gate or dog to deal with.

'The omens are improving,' I whispered to Hugh as he squeezed into a space at the kerb about thirty yards from number 11.

'I don't like it,' he said flatly. 'I think you're taking too many risks. It's such a wild shot.'

If he'd said that before, he might have dissuaded me. I rather wished he had.

I turned my up collar – I'd changed into a dark shirt – and pulled on the plastic gloves. Then I reached for my torch. My Barclaycard was in my pocket.

Hugh swore.

'What the hell are you doing with those gloves?' I

demanded.

'Trying to put one on without tearing it.'

'But you're not coming with me,' I said.

'Try and stop me. Someone's got to keep an eye on you.'

'But not in the house. From the car, Hugh. You're my get-away driver. And if you're not in the car, how shall we make sure there's still some wheels left on it?'

'Car alarm,' he said.

'Some of my students can kill those in twelve seconds. And I want you to start moving towards me as soon as you see me coming. And if the police turn up, just get the hell out of it and leave me –'

'Oh, yes. And have you mugged? Raped? OK, I stay here. And I give you ten minutes. Not a second longer. Not because you're scared but because I am: right? Here.'

He kissed me on the lips: brisk, businesslike and tender.

I could have been sick as I walked up that entry. As something brushed my legs I had to swallow down the bile. But when I realised it was only a cat I allowed myself to relax, slightly. There was no dog barking at the cat. There was a gate, but it was well oiled. Then the path ran straight through to Toad's house. His kitchen door had a Yale lock. I'd never actually used a credit card to force a lock. I'd seen it done on TV, of course, and Chris had given me a demonstration. I did what I thought he'd done: slide the card in and jiggle, authoritatively. Nothing happened. Nothing at all. I tried again. Nothing. I could have sworn aloud with frustration. All my precious time oozing away. But then I saw the gods might after all be on my side: one of the windows wasn't properly shut. It was a narrow one, running at the top of the frame. One of the larger, lower windows might just open too, with a bit of luck. The glass was frosted – presumably it had been cheaper to fit a bathroom into the old scullery than into an upstairs room. At any rate the wood had warped, and I was able to prise it open with a bit of slate someone should have put in a skip.

I lifted the dustbin – empty and plastic – to where I thought I could reach. Up and in. Nearly. My fingers screamed with the pain from Thursday's bruises, and I caught my breath.

If I stood on the windowsill, and if the rotten-looking

wood didn't give way under my feet, I might just be able to reach through the upper window and lift the catch on the lower one. Just. Just!

I moved the collection of aftershaves and half-squeezed toothpastes and sickly-smelling sponges to one side. Just room for one foot on the sill. And the left knee. I would have to turn and let myself backwards into the bath. Feeling terribly professional, I swilled my muddy footprints down the plughole. Should I leave my shoes on? The thought of fumbling with laces convinced me I should.

I wouldn't use the torch in the bathroom. Might have to in the kitchen – there were too many mats and shoes to fall over. What on earth would someone like Toad eat? But I didn't want to shine the torch much above floor level.

There were two living rooms. The back one opened directly off the kitchen. There were two doors. One led to a minute corridor and thence to the front room. The front door opened directly onto this. I needed to establish an escape route so I looked quickly at the door – yes, there was only a Yale lock. I turned the knob and the door opened. But if I was in a hurry to escape, I might well fumble. Hadn't I read somewhere that burglars would leave the door on the latch but held to with a book? I latched it, then wedged it shut with Toad's telephone directory.

Right. Upstairs.

There were two bedrooms. One was just a junk room. Did he never throw anything away? Old clothes. Several pictures turned to the wall. An ironing board. Nothing obvious.

His bedroom. It smelled of male sweat. His laundry lay in an unwashed heap.

Come on, Sophie. Think. Hugh's sitting out there in a Winson Green crawling with violent youths – more at risk than you. Get a move on.

Back into the junk room. Piles of magazines. A lot of sickening porn. Two photo albums. Some old records. A music stand. A scrapbook. I opened it at random. Postcards of fluffy kittens. I was about to throw it down when I noticed newspaper cuttings in the back. Some hunt sabbing. The liberation of mink from a fur farm. A whole wad about Patti Hearst. I didn't throw it down.

Back to the bedroom, which was at the front. Men's voices were getting closer.

The stairs were too steep to run down. I slipped and slid without hurting myself. But I dropped the scrapbook. It skidded under a heavy sideboard. I burrowed, coming up filthy but successful. And there was something else, another pile of magazines. I flicked quickly through: *True War Stories*, *True Crime*, *Real-Life Crime*, *A Weekly Encyclopaedia of Crime*.

Halfway down, there it was. Lesley Whittle. The Black Panther.

And I was on my feet and at the front door.

I was so busy slipping the catch back and closing it silently behind me, picking up the torch and trying to get my night vision, I didn't notice the youths. Not at first.

It wasn't me they were after. It was Hugh. Whitey in his big flash car.

Hell and hell and hell!

Once upon a time, Andy had taught me to whistle through my fingers, very loudly. I could try that. But Hugh'd have the windows shut and mightn't hear. I could scream. Everyone would hear that. But burglars didn't *want* everyone to hear.

I inched closer – through the front garden and a few yards along the road to Hugh.

He could have got rid of them – by driving through them – but that meant losing me. He was staying where he was as they rocked the car from side to side. I prayed it was too heavy to turn over.

And then I got angry. How dare they! I strode closer: they were no older than my students. If I could deal with students, I could deal with them. Possibly. At least the moment's shock of being harangued by a schoolmarmish voice might give us the chance we needed – me to get into the car, Hugh to get moving. I wondered why the engine wasn't running already. Because someone had stuffed a potato up the exhaust, that was why. I bent and pulled it free, pressing my souvenirs to my chest with the other arm.

And then I got really furious.

'Elvin Morris,' I said very clearly. 'What the hell d'you think you're doing?'

The tallest youth turned. So did the others.

Did Elvin have sufficient clout in the group to risk losing face? I no longer taught him, so I didn't have much leverage myself. But Hugh saw what I was up to, started the car and shoved it into reverse. I could only reach the back door. I wrenched at it. Nothing. Suddenly it opened under my hand. I nearly fell back, and overcompensated – I ended face down on his back seat. He threw the car forward now, heaving it out of the too-short space. You could hear the grind as he removed a layer from his and the other car's bumper. The force was sufficient to swing the door inwards. But it was at the end of the street before I could scrabble up and slam it. And the youths had almost caught us.

He swung wide into the main road, going much too fast to stop at the slow sign. A family saloon swerved so hard to miss us I braced myself for the sound of his crash. But both cars steadied. At last Hugh dropped to a more sober speed. I didn't want to know what it was, though, not in these streets where the corner shops were still doing brisk business and children with plastic carriers popped up without warning from between parked cars. I fastened a seat belt round me.

Perhaps two blocks away, something burned out of control. We could hear the sirens, but couldn't get any sense of movement. And when we drove to the end of the street we found out why. A hundred or maybe two hundred black and Asian kids were celebrating the biggest bonfire this year by overturning cars and smashing windows.

He swung left. It was a cul-de-sac. Halfway down, a gang of white skinheads was rolling a car.

Reverse, as fast as he could. But it was too late. They had spotted us.

Chapter Twenty-Five

It was the rain that saved us, not the 999 call. The storm which had threatened all evening broke with staggering intensity, hailstones the size of hazelnuts lashing into the kids' soft flesh. One by one they broke away. The police would have come eventually – we could just hear the sirens over the drumming on the roof. There was one more crash when someone stopped just long enough to kick in Hugh's tail-lights.

Silently he reversed, the tyres crunching over glass, and started to pick his way back to Eyre House. The roads were littered with videos and hi-fis bursting out of their cardboard boxes, and glass from the storefronts from which they'd been stolen. There were blue-flashing lights wherever you looked. I put through a call to tell them we were safe.

I felt that Hugh was a long way from me, and sensed that he did not want me to take his hand. But when he'd parked, back at a now dark and silent Eyre House, it was to his room we took my booty.

'Safer than yours,' he said. 'And you'll be safer with me.'

At last we kissed and undressed, and then talked about dancing naked on the lawn in the rain. But neither of us moved. We simply stood side by side at the window, watching the rain course down. It was two thirty. The air was suddenly so cold I started to dither.

I wondered how long Hugh had been shivering too. Gently I turned him and pushed him towards the bed. He sat down on the edge.

'What's the matter, Hugh?'

He reached for the champagne and topped up my glass, passing it to me. Then he filled his own glass. But he didn't drink.

'Hmm?' I prompted.

'How did you do it? Break into that house?'

He didn't mean it literally.

I touched his hand. Funny that he should be more upset than I was.

'I don't know,' I said honestly. 'I had to do something to find Kate, and that was the only thing I could think of. And once I'd started, when I thought I'd be peeing myself with fright, I was quite OK. Methodical. Sensible. Actually, it was probably easier for me than for you. I'd rather be up and doing than sitting waiting any day. And you didn't have very attractive company. Here.' I passed him his glass.

He swung his legs into bed, and I got in beside him – to get warm, as much as anything. Then I pulled the duvet up. All very televisual, of course – the attractive young couple, covered from waist down, sitting up in bed quaffing from elegant glasses.

'I thought they'd kill me. And I kept thinking, There's a mistake here. I'm a respectable businessman. I don't belong here. And they're going to kill me.'

I held his hand.

'And then you came and told them off and –'

'Could have got us both killed. And I wasn't much good second time round. Sitting there stuffing my hands into my mouth so I wouldn't scream.'

'Reaction,' he said, squeezing my hand. 'And seeing that fire. I wonder how many more there were by the end of the evening.'

'Not many. Not once the rain had come. Pity, really – I could have done with having Toad's house burned down. I don't fancy Chris and his colleagues finding traces of me all over it.'

'You said you'd got gloves on!'

'Hair. Skin flakes. Prints from my trainers. Fibres from my clothing.'

'What'll you tell him? In the morning?'

'The truth, I suppose. He won't like it.'

He gathered me to him and switched off the light. I don't think either of us had the energy for sex, but it was nice to have him close. But he lay tense and obviously sleepless. Suddenly he flung back the duvet and stumbled towards the sofa.

'Hugh?'

'I'm sorry, Sophie, I hate to say this, but I'm no good at sharing beds. Not if I want to sleep. There are plenty of blankets.'

By now I was out of bed. 'Don't be silly. I'll fit that far more easily than you will. You get back in there. Go on: five foot one doesn't need a full-length bed.'

With no further protest, he obeyed. Soon I could hear his breathing, deep and regular. I didn't sleep until dawn, though – excitement or champagne or something. But I sat for a long time watching the shape on the bed, and found myself smiling. Yes, despite everything, I might be happy.

Eight thirty in the stables, and I was very far from happy. I'd dressed quickly and quietly, leaving Hugh asleep, his head vulnerable on the pillow. I'd wanted to kiss him but was afraid I might disturb him. Fortunately the door was quiet, but the corridor relished every noisy footstep. Once in the student area I'd showered and dressed in fresh clothes, and even my make-up suggested girlish innocence.

Chris wasn't fooled.

I'd meant to find some story about the magazines and scrapbook. As it was, I merely plonked them on his desk.

Perhaps deep down I wanted him to yell at me. It would be an assertion that there was a morality that forbade the law to break the law. It would remind me that I knew I'd done wrong. And then I wanted him to smile at me and say thank you, that I'd done what he wished he could have done.

'Toad's,' I said baldly. 'A history of liberating animals and an interest in imprisoning women.'

'Did you never set animals free when you were young?'

'I set fire to fur coats in posh shops – or at any rate my friends did,' I said. 'And I interfered with my fair share of hunts when I could. But this is different.'

'And is this crime magazine the only one in his collection?'

'No, there were lots –'

'And how did you get hold of them? Did he offer them to you?'

'I – Chris, you'd rather not know how I got hold of them.'

'I'm sure I would. Defence counsel would want it chapter and verse, and I don't think you'd be very good at perjury. And it would blow any case to buggery, Sophie, don't you see that? Jesus Christ, you can't keep your itchy little fingers out of anyone's pie, can you? You spoil Tina's lunch harassing her over checking people's medical files, you make Ian waste his afternoon off looking through statements, you try to make him tail members of the public, and then you try a bit of breaking and entering. What's the matter with you, woman? PMT or something?'

'How dare you!'

'You should know better than this!'

I thought for a moment he was going to hit me. So did he. Instead he picked up the evidence. But he didn't throw it down, as he planned. He turned a page.

I turned and left as unobtrusively as I could. There's more than one way of skinning a cat, after all.

Downstairs there was still no sign of Hugh or Matt. I made a pot of tea and carried two cups up to Hugh's room. He lay where I'd left him, but his eyes were open and he hitched himself on to his left elbow, reaching for the tea with his right hand.

'This is not to be taken as a precedent,' I said. It was the wrong thing to say.

Last night he'd have laughed and reached for me. This morning he merely nodded and looked away.

I put my tea down and went over to the sofa. I folded the blankets and put them back in the cupboard where I'd found them. I glanced at him occasionally but he made no attempt to speak. Still reaction to last night, perhaps – the violence, the lawlessness. Maybe distaste for what I'd done. On the whole, perhaps, I preferred Chris's open anger. When I'd finished the blankets, I went and stood by the window. The rain was drenching down, no longer dramatic with thunder but steady and insistent. The whole world was a bleary grey.

Nothing from Hugh yet.

Perhaps he was a man not at his best in the morning. Perhaps I should simply let him go back to sleep, and tiptoe out. That seemed pretty supine to me, however. I'd let Chris get away with bad temper because I thought it might be more productive to do so. But what had seemed a promising relationship was now visibly dwindling.

'What's the matter, Hugh?' I said, in a tone I tried to make neither brisk nor apologetic.

'Guilt, I suppose.'

'But you didn't do anything: you just aided and abetted me!'

'Isn't that bad enough? In a court of law it would be.'

I wished I could work out how his voice had changed. I looked at him. Then he grinned apologetically. 'Wet Sundays. I've always hated them, ever since I was a kid. Such a waste! You'd get all your homework done to have the day free and then you couldn't go out. Funny, this was one of the places I used to come for a treat then. Years back. Strange, isn't it, I wasn't quite sure I could find it the other day. Not by car, not the way they've messed around with the roads. And I was nervous about the reading. No, really nervous. It was the first time I'd done one, you know.'

I smiled and shook my head. But I didn't want him to talk about that.

'D'you know what I did? What my dad used to do when he didn't know the way. I came the day before, just to case the joint, you might say. Found the lane. Later I found – d'you know what I found? The old farm. I can remember it – just – when it was still working. We stopped there one day to look at some chicks and the farmer threatened to set his dogs on us. Then my dad turned up, and things quietened down a bit. There's an old ice house up there too – you could get in then. Terribly dangerous, of course. They've sealed it up now. Have you seen it?'

I nodded, though I wanted to sing with joy: here was Hugh telling me what I'd been dreading asking him. I hoped my voice was normal when I said: 'I went for a run that way the other day. Didn't like it. The noise.'

'Like a physical presence, isn't it?'

'I may actually have seen you. There was someone on the ice house while I was at the farm. Wednesday morning, that must have been.'

'Good God! It could well have been me. Once I'd found the place I checked in at the Post House for the night. And then I was hours too early, of course, so I explored a bit. Then I went to the Wasson. With the Sand Well in the grounds. But they don't call it the Wasson now. We used to come with Dad, once in a while. You probably came too – you're an Oldbury girl, aren't you, our kid?'

'No car. And my dad was too busy playing cricket and coaching me to waste valuable weekends exploring. I'd have given my teeth –'

'Tomboy, were you? There was a lot to explore, too – pockets of wasteland all over this side of the Black Country then. There were some mines – you could get into them.'

'Mines! Weren't there fences and guards and –'

'Not on these.'

'And how would you get down? Don't you need winding gear?'

'Not on drift mines. That sort you just walk into. You must have been to that one in the Black Country Museum? Some abandoned years ago, maybe even in the nineteenth century, but never filled in or blocked up. Bloody dangerous, of course. Remember that child getting stuck in a hole on Cannock Chase a few years back? Nearly died? And that mine wasn't even on anyone's map.'

'What are they like?'

'Any other day I'd take you. But not in weather like this.'

I laughed. 'Come on, they're underground, mines.'

He shook his head. 'Dad used to take us in. But he made us promise never to try it on our own. We did, of course, but one day we learned the hard way why we shouldn't. A day like this, pissing with rain. And we thought we'd rather be dry than wet so we found ourselves a mine. Lunch. Torches. Bit scary without Dad. Then the water rose, so fast we panicked. I can still remember it: the cold, the dark, not knowing which way to run . . .'

His voice blurred with the remembered fear. I wanted to comfort the child in his memory. But suddenly there was something else.

'That's where he's got Kate. Down a mine.' I said it with absolute certainly. Because I knew.

And I must have convinced him. Suddenly he was out of bed, standing beside me.

'Jesus, if you're right – but which one?' Already he was pulling on his clothes.

I sat on the bed. I had to use my head. I had to think clearly and logically and fast.

He came and stood beside me and touched my hand. Nothing amorous; more to show he understood what I was trying to do. Then he left the room, closing the door quietly behind him.

Chapter Twenty-Six

Kate. I must flood my mind with images of Kate. Maybe her technique of lying on the floor would help. It had taken me to Courtney when he needed me, after all. I stood up and found a pile of paperbacks for my head on Hugh's desk.

I gathered them up: *The Writer's Handbook* must be nearly thick enough on its own. Certainly it would be with his *thesaurus*. I stood weighing them in my hands, staring not at them, but at the rain overflowing from a blocked gutter on to Hugh's car. He'd been surprisingly calm about the damage, considering how new the car was. Certainly hailstones had saved it from a much worse fate. Maybe the RAC could help with the tail-lights when they came to start Matt's poor Fiesta, humbled first by the gloss of Kate's little Peugeot and now dwarfed by this red, if battered, machine. The Peugeot was no doubt tucked up in Harborne, waiting to be called in evidence. Poor car – orphaned before its time. I wondered what would happen to it, and had a fantasy, either macabre or sentimental, I wasn't sure which, that I might buy it with the money from George's van. I'd give it a good home – it would fit into the garage – and I would remember to sing every time it had a mileage birthday.

The mobile phone, our safety link with the police control point, was on the desk. I jabbed the number.

Chris answered, first ring. 'What's up?' I could hear the panic in his voice.

'Nothing. Just tell me how many miles Kate's car had done.'

'Why?'

'Please, don't ask. Just check.'

'OK.'

I could hear the tap of a computer. Some meticulous person had even bothered to write that down, to enter it onto the computer records. And Chris bothered enough to do as I asked.

'One thousand and eighteen point two miles.'

'Ah!'

I put down the phone.

It rang immediately.

I let it.

Since Kate had given me that lift from the village, the Monday morning I went to buy a torch, the morning she had had to fetch supplies from the chemist's for Toad, her car had done one thousand miles. I had heard a car late on Tuesday night. On Wednesday I was sure her car had been parked at a different angle. The car was removed by the police on Wednesday night. Dare I conclude that someone had used her car to take her away on Monday night? And perhaps used it again, perhaps to take food to her, on Tuesday night? Someone who had been able to visit her on foot on Wednesday and Thursday nights? But it would mean a long trek, a round trip of nine miles on foot.

'Here!' I could see the OS map he was carrying even before I could see Hugh. Hardly pausing to close the door, he opened it and spread it on the floor.

'There's Eyre House and Park,' he said.

'But what about mines? Nature reserves and a rifle range, for God's sake, but no mines!'

'They don't have to mark them. Look, Baggeridge Park had mines – not a sign of one on the map. Perhaps we need a larger scale.'

'No, we don't – I need glasses. Here!' I jabbed the map. 'And here.'

'So which do we head for?'

I explained.

'So we need to know which are about four and a half miles by road, preferably less on foot. We need string – no, give me your trainer.'

I unlaced it and passed it to him. He pulled out the lace and held one end on Eyre House. Then, holding it taut, he swung it in an arc across the map.

'Won't work. Better to trace the road with it,' he said, easing along the road to the main gates and then to the right.

'But he'd turned left when he torched George's van,' I said.

'OK, trace that footpath and see if we meet up.'

Our index fingers moved hesitantly together.

'Yes!' I said, on my feet and folding the map. 'Got to be, hasn't it?'

'Now what?'

'We go and look.'

'What about Groom – shouldn't you tell him?'

'If he takes any notice, he'll refuse to let us go too. Or,' I said, more reasonably, 'we could talk to him on your car phone as we go.'

'I've a feeling Matt might want to go with us,' said Hugh.

'Course he would. Is he awake and dressed?'

'I doubt it.'

'Tough, then. We go without him. He can go with Chris.' I was rethreading the lace. 'We'll need kagouls and a torch at very least. Any tools in your car? He won't have tied her up with string.'

'Enough. Get your things – I'll meet you at the car.'

At reception we went our separate ways. I hardly nodded to the officer on duty in the student corridor, as I pushed into my room grabbing torch and kagoul and, as a hopeful afterthought, my asthma spray. All the other students would be busy packing – Shazia's cleaners would want the rooms vacant by nine thirty. Toad was not packing: I could hear the sound of Bach being played not at all badly. A bourrée from one of the cello suites. I found myself humming it under my breath as I sprinted out through reception. Hugh had brought the car round. I flung myself in.

Half the time I'll swear we were aquaplaning, Hugh was forcing the car so fast down the waterlogged roads. He passed the car phone to me.

I hesitated. 'How d'you use one of these?'

'Jesus!'

'I haven't got one on my bike.'

'Sorry. Same as any other phone.'

As I tapped, I could see his knuckles white on the gear lever. He was there, with Kate, knowing from experience the fear she was going through. If she was still alive.

'What the fuck are you up to this time?' Chris asked.

'Trying to find Kate. Hugh remembered a mine he got trapped in as a kid. It ties up with the Black Panther keeping that poor child down the sewer. We've found a mine.'

'Where?'

I read out the map reference, as accurately as I could guess in the bucking, sliding car.

'I'll come.'

'Bring some friends. And Matt.'

At last Hugh swung the car towards a gap in the hedge. There were some other tyre marks. But I don't think he was worrying about preserving evidence.

He was out and over a stile well before me. I had to run to catch up, slithering over the long, wet grass. The ground was hummocky, water already flooding some of the dips. Then there was a strip of ash-covered path. I set off down it. Hugh followed. After a hundred yards or so it branched into two smaller tracks. Right or left?

'You take this one. I'll go down here. But when we've looked we come back here. No heroics!' I said.

'OK.'

I took the left-hand path. The grass was so coarse it was impossible for me to tell if anyone had used it recently. There was a strange, isolating blanket of sound – the motorway, never far away, the rain, the pad of my feet, my increasingly rough breathing. A minute for a drag at the Ventolin. Must be stress, not the exercise. I told myself I had nothing to worry about. Toad was working his way through Bach. Chris knew where I was heading. I was linking up with Hugh again, as soon as we'd checked the possibilities.

I had nothing to worry about.

There was nothing here, anyway. The path just petered out in a scribble of thin broom and bracken. There was a little gorse up to the right.

I turned back. Better report to Hugh. He'd be worrying

about me.

And then I saw him. Sidney. As wet as I was. Thin. A cut down one flank. But Sidney nonetheless.

If only I had something to offer him. Some chocolate, anything. I couldn't imagine him coming to me without a bribe. I inched closer to him but he pursued a dogged course, skirting me. I followed, gaining unobtrusively on him. Perhaps I'd risk calling him.

'Sidney! Sidney?'

If anything, he scuttled on rather more quickly. I stripped my kagoul off. I was wet enough, anyway, for a bit more rain not to matter, and I'd be less visible without it. And the thought crossed my mind that I might even be able to throw it on top of Sidney and catch him that way. Catch him! I had to catch up with him first.

He made his way purposefully towards the bracken. And disappeared.

I followed.

A wooden beam, presumably once a lintel, now leaned crazily. The gap it left was scarcely larger than me. I squeezed through.

I knew it would be dark inside. I wasn't prepared for absolute blackness. But perhaps it wasn't absolute. My eyes weren't used to it yet. Perhaps it wouldn't be so bad. And I had my torch.

I switched it on in time to see Sidney's tail disappearing. There were two routes, one high enough to follow at an awkward walk, the other a hands-and-knees affair. He chose the hands-and-knees one.

I followed.

I don't know how long for. There was no easy way to carry the torch. I knew I mustn't lose that torch. It was my lifeline. And I mustn't bang my head on one of those lumps of rock – or coal? – that formed the roof. I ought to have had a hard hat with a light, a miner's helmet.

As I crawled, the noise started. A low rumble. It got louder and louder. I must be close to the motorway. I had to go back. I couldn't get any closer. The noise was a solid black wall I couldn't penetrate. I banged my fists on it. And I knew it was solid, and that it was coal.

So where had Sidney gone?

The noise hurt so much I found myself crying. I couldn't hear myself, but I knew I must be. If you cry you blow your nose and wipe your eyes. My handkerchief was in my kagoul.

So was Sidney.

If I started to laugh I'd soon be hysterical. Somehow I had to turn round – my God, had the miners been a race of midgets? – and feel my way back. First I'd zip Sidney into the big front pocket. He didn't like being grabbed, and struggled. So did I. As I shoved him, tail first and wriggling, down into the pouch, I must have hurt him. He bit me. I shoved harder and zipped. I'd better leave a gap for him to breathe. Just enough for his nose, no more.

Because I'd no idea how far I'd come, I'd no idea how far back I had to crawl. And my torch was getting dimmer. Long-life batteries, indeed. If I came out of this alive, I'd never buy that brand again.

I shouldn't have thought of that. Of not getting out alive.

I tried common sense. Perhaps the batteries were loose. I gave an experimental shake. Nothing, either better or worse. But the beam was very dim, now. Perhaps it would be better to wear the kagoul. I might be hurting Sidney as I dragged it along. So I propped the torch between my knees and struggled in. I'd buy one with a front-opening next time. Of course there'd be a next time.

The torch slipped and went out.

I groped for it, and found it. It was wet and slippery. I fumbled for the switch, and pushed it. Light again. I rubbed a sleeve over the lens: that improved things. Not the batteries but grime on the glass. It would be all right.

I made good progress for the next few yards, but the tunnel was now very wet indeed. Water was dripping from the roof, quite audible even above the rumble of the road. But I couldn't have far to go, not now. Any moment I would hear a furious Hugh yelling for me. Any moment.

And then I saw the roof tremble. Not much. Enough for me to stop, and then wish I'd rushed forward. And, quite delicately at first, then more persistently, a little black avalanche cut me off from the entrance to the mine.

I was screaming.

If I screamed much longer, my voice would give out. But if I sang, I could keep that up for an hour or more. And I might give myself courage to start picking the lumps from the heap that had trapped me.

'Voi che sapete'. 'Three little maids from school'. 'Summertime'.

And then I heard another voice.

'God Save the Queen'.

A woman's voice. Kate's. I had found Kate.

Chapter Twenty-Seven

I ought to sit tight and wait for them to come – Hugh, Chris and the rest. They'd be out there, looking for me. Hugh knew where I'd gone. Roughly. Chris would come with a posse of men and women trained in all sorts of rescue work.

But I wanted to get out and I wanted to find Kate. Now.

I knelt and reached and lifted and pushed back. A rhythm, I needed a rhythm. A long time ago, at school, a teacher more inspired than most taught us George Orwell, 'Down the Mine', all about these men who worked in confined conditions heaving coal. She'd made us all kneel under our desks and pass piles of dictionaries back, back, back, until our knees and backs and arms screamed. About five minutes. Then we'd giggled and dusted ourselves off and gone back to our desks and never quite forgotten about miners.

The pile was smaller, but the beam from the torch was dimmer. I shoved it between my knees so I couldn't possibly lose it, switched it off, and worked in the dark. Occasionally I would stop and sing again. 'The Ash Grove', 'Londonderry Air', 'Greensleeves'.

'Rule Britannia' and 'I vow to thee, my country' came back. Much more clearly. I was winning. And then it occurred to me that scrabbling sounds were coming from the far side of the roof-fall. Someone was helping.

I don't know what order the thoughts came in. That whoever it was was not trying to call to me. That Toad had been playing Bach uncommonly well. That it was not Toad and his viola but a professional musician playing a cello. A recording. That I had nowhere to run to. That as long as I had my torch, I had a weapon – I shoved it up my left sleeve. That, overriding everything else, I was very frightened indeed.

The last of the coal was nearly cleared. A very bright light dazzled me. I couldn't see who was speaking. I didn't need to. Trust Toad to have acquired a torch as viciously powerful as his ghettoblaster.

I dragged the kagoul-pouch zip completely closed, and prayed Sidney'd have enough air. I wanted to deal with Toad without the complication of rats.

But it was he who was dealing with me. Shazia hadn't mentioned any knives going missing from the kitchen. But Toad had one. And I didn't doubt he'd use it.

He grabbed my hair and inched me forwards. Forwards until I could stand upright. And then he threw me off balance, and caught me by the arm as I lurched. I ought to thank God it was the arm not holding the torch, but all I could do was scream as he wrenched it behind my back. Then he jerked it again. The message was clear: shut up or he'd dislocate it. I shut up. I would concentrate on keeping my balance. I could see reasonably clearly where I was going in the light from Toad's torch. From the angle it fell, he must have fastened it somehow or other to his waist. Now we slithered down the other tunnel, our feet sometimes covered by black water. The smell became rank: foul lavatories and menstrual blood. We were brought up against thick stakes of wood – old pit-props, perhaps. They'd been hammered in vertically to form a crude cage. The floor was solid wood – it looked like the bottom of an old railway wagon, but Toad didn't give me time to look properly. He'd found a metal-barred gate from somewhere, hingeing it crudely with chains and fastening it with another, padlocked chain. A cage.

And in the cage was Kate, naked except for a disposable nappy and a sheen of coal dust.

At least there were now two of us.

Two of us together – we must be able to deal with him. Two of us.

He'd have to let go of me to unlock the padlock. Maybe I could bolt then. But that would mean leaving Kate. I hesitated. He held the knife to my neck. Then he passed the key.

'Open it.'

I fumbled and dropped the key. He sliced my ear. I could feel the blood warm on my neck.

'Pick it up and don't drop it again.'

I did as I was told.

He thrust me inside the cage. The water was to my knees.

'Two for the price of one,' he said.

'Garth,' I said, trying to sound cool and reasonable, 'could you tell me what's going on? I came in out of the rain and got trapped and –'

He hit me hard across the mouth.

Kate stood up. I dared not hope she'd seen the bulge in my left sleeve. But she was going to distract him.

Her chest was heaving. 'Asthma,' she gasped. 'A spray.'

'You know what you have to do,' he said, pointing to the bottom of the cage, swirling with water. He lifted his left foot. And she knelt in the foul water to kiss it.

I hit him very hard. He sagged forward, but then started gently twitching.

I grabbed Kate's hand and pulled her up and towards me. I pushed the key into her hand.

The gate swung open, desperately slowly. Water was now to our thighs. And the floor was tilting.

At least she was out. But the gate was pushing me back towards Toad, and he was already staggering to his feet.

And then I heard voices, and I knew I could swing on the gate, like a monkey if I had to, and wait for them to help me. But nothing would help Toad. He was no longer twitching, but threshing in huge convulsions, literally foaming at the mouth. And by the second he was going deeper into unconsciousness and closer to death by drowning.

Getting me out hadn't been as easy as I'd thought. Eventually I had to let go, wait for the gate to swing, and literally swim out. Chris was there to pull me up.

I was afraid for a moment that I'd drowned Sidney. He was very quiet inside that pouch. But maybe the fabric had kept enough air in.

I pulled off the kagoul and helped pull it over Kate. And I made them wait while I gave her my jeans. I could cope with a blanket. She deserved more dignity.

Chris and Ian would have carried her. But she found the strength to stagger out, a comic, grotesque parody of a woman, and when she saw Matt she broke into a tottering run. Neither said anything. You couldn't tell what streaked the coal dust on her face, tears or rain. Matt tried to pat her face clean with his handkerchief. He said something and pointed to the movement in the kagoul.

And then we heard them laugh.

'God knows how Casualty will cope with a rat,' said Chris, watching the ambulance drive away along the ash-covered track.

'Send a squad car with his cage,' I said briefly. 'And, while they're at it, some clothes for me.'

I was very cold, now I came to think about it, and I would have to succumb any moment now to Chris's insistence that I have my ear stitched. But I couldn't have gone in the ambulance with Kate and Matt. It wouldn't have been fair. They had Sidney to play gooseberry in any case.

Hugh was still white. When I emerged he hadn't hugged me as I'd expected: he'd grabbed my shoulders and shaken me until Ian Dale had stopped him.

'No heroics, you said,' he was shouting. 'No bloody heroics! My God! And look at you!' He turned from me, not to weep but to vomit in the gorse.

Ian silently hitched up my blanket and led me away. Without asking, he fastened my seat belt for me. And then he passed me a mint.

I don't think we spoke all the way to the General. I didn't really want to anyway. My mouth was throbbing viciously and my nose insisted on streaming. Eventually Ian passed me a box of tissues. I left black fingerprints on the packet and on every tissue I touched. I reached for the mirror on the sun visor. The face I saw might have been Kate's. I wondered if the National Health would run to showers.

As we approached the city centre, Ian slowed and pointed. Down side streets we could see the fire service still at work, and bulldozers were clearing wrecked cars. The rain hadn't come early enough for some.

As he parked in an 'Ambulance Only' space, I said, 'I'm not staying in, you know.'

'Of course you're not. You're going back to Eyre House for lunch. I promised Shazia. And Chris. He'll want to talk to you.'

'Yet another statement?'

Ian grunted, and came round to my side to help me out. A wheelchair appeared. I rejected it. Ian sniffed and offered his arm. As we started our dignified progress, a police car screamed into view, slowing sharply as the driver recognised Ian, no doubt. The driver parked with care and scurried after us, a rat cage in one hand and a polythene carrier in the other.

'For the lady,' he said, thrusting the cage at me.

'Wrong lady,' I said, taking the carrier instead.

The National Health ran to a student nurse with sponges and warm, soapy water. I asked him to leave me to it for a couple of minutes, and managed to dunk my hair too. I longed suddenly for the privacy of my bathroom at home. It would be good to be back, to lie and soak. Perhaps a little Haydn on the radio. Maybe a drop of single malt. And then the nurse came back with the casualty officer, a young woman with designs on my ear. A difficult place to stitch, she admitted at last. We settled on a butterfly dressing. More Melolin for the worst of the abrasions: I looked at the messes that constituted my knees and wondered why they'd not hurt when I was crawling on them. She tutted over the puncture marks Sidney had left, but at least I was spared another tetanus shot. I signed myself out this time, but asked to see Kate before I left.

'Two minutes,' said the student nurse, leading the way.

There is nowhere to knock on a curtain, of course. Ian and I looked at each other quizzically, coughed in unison, and he waited for me to put my head round the curtain.

They'd been cleaning her up, too: her hair had been tied back, and her face was no longer bizarre with coal dust. But there were dark circles under her eyes, and her face, once plumply middle-aged, was gaunt, with cruel lines around the mouth. She wore a hospital-issue gown, and was obviously about to be admitted – there was a name tag on her wrist.

Matt was holding her right hand against his cheek. He seemed completely oblivious of us, and of the streams of tears that ran down his cheeks, plunging into the forest of his beard. As we watched, she drifted into sleep.

Sidney might have been observing with interest since his future was no doubt involved, but someone had bought him a Kit-Kat and he was more concerned with that.

'I was wondering if you could use a lift,' said Ian.

'I'm staying here,' said Matt. 'Say goodbye to everyone for me, OK?'

I nodded.

'I'll be in touch, Sophie – I take it Hugh has your address.'

I could feel Ian stiffen. I'd have asked him for a page from his notebook but I'd an idea they were sacrosanct, and I didn't want to make an issue of it.

'What about yours?' I asked.

He suddenly noticed his tears, and rubbed his face with a fistful of NHS tissues. 'Wherever Kate is, for a bit. And then I've got to sort out – everything.'

'If you need a base in Brum, I've got a spare room,' I said. And bent to kiss him.

He laid Kate's hand down on her chest for a moment. Then he got up to meet me, and held me. Eventually the nurse came back, and we patted each other's backs affectionately – time to let go.

I turned to Ian and propelled him from the cubicle as fast as I could. For I knew what the nurse was going to say: 'And what about the rat? Can't your friend look after him?'

Ian heard too. And we did the nearest I could manage to a scamper.

I was running out of clothes, of course, and my tracksuit was hardly the festive garb demanded by our last lunch together. I was suddenly hungry, and wondered what Shazia might have managed to produce, given all the comings and goings. Whatever it was, she wasn't wearing an apron when she pushed into reception to hug me.

I excused myself for a couple of minutes to see what make-up might do to the ravages of my face. Someone had shifted all my clothes on to the desk so they could make the bed. But they hadn't packed. I shoved the lot willy-nilly into my case. I couldn't even lift it.

The officers outside thought it was a great joke. One grabbed the case with one finger. The other grabbed me and carried me to reception. End of term for them too. I'd better get into the swing of things.

What I did not expect to see, when I picked my way into the lounge, was a bottle of champagne, and Gimson pouring it. He saw me and bowing with only the minimum of irony, presented me with a glass. At the sight of my ear he tutted professionally and then said, quite quietly, so no one else could hear: 'The bruises will heal fast enough. But you may be encumbered with unpleasant memories for some little time. Travel might help – a peak in Darien, perhaps.'

I nodded and smiled. We would never like each other but we could at least observe the proprieties.

I toasted him vaguely, and looked about me. No Chris, but he'd be busy tidying up ends. No Hugh. No Tabitha. My God, I couldn't be about to discover jealousy.

Laughter from the corridor: yes, I could. But as soon as he came into the room he looked for me. When our eyes met, he abandoned Tabitha and stood over me proprietorially until Shazia urged us into the dining room.

Christmas had come early, courtesy of Fortnum and Mason. It was fortune for someone's bank balance that there had been so few of us to cater for. Mr Woodhouse demurred that game pie was too rich for him; Jean urged him to take a little more caviare, and the sci-fi freak picked negligently at olives. But the rest of us weighed in. Gimson passed plates with enthusiasm. Mr Woodhouse cleared his throat as if to make a speech. I didn't want a speech to listen to: there were still far too many goodies left.

'I'm sure we would all like to thank –' he began.

Hugh popped a canapé into my mouth and held his fingers to be licked.

' – Mrs, er, Shazia for her kind hospitality and for maintaining the highest standards when chaos was trying to reign.'

Another *bonne bouche*. I fed Hugh several grapes.

'And Matt and Hugh for being patient teachers.'

Hugh's smile was necessarily tight. Perhaps the others thought he was modest and embarrassed.

'And Sophie for finding Kate.'

I bowed my head in acknowledgement, wondering when I might chew on the lobster vol-au-vent.

'And lastly I would like to express my – our – appreciation to Mr Gimson for providing this delectable luncheon.'

Gimson!

Due applause from everyone. Mostly it was the rattling of glasses against dishes – no one wanted to stop yet. And as Hugh and I embarked on drumsticks, the memory of that sixties film of *Tom Jones* came bubbling to the surface of my mind.

There was enough left to fill plates for Chris and Ian when they appeared, both looking grimmer than I expected. Suddenly I felt sick: was it news of Courtney? But Ian shook his head. Courtney might not be much better but he certainly wasn't any worse. It was losing Toad that was their problem. It was better for all if justice could be seen to be done, and neither anticipated a very favourable reaction from those in power when it became generally known that they had allowed an epileptic to drown.

'Tough,' said Hugh. 'At least Sophie'll be spared the pressures of a trial.'

'And Kate and Matt, of course,' I added.

Hugh looked at me. We both knew, didn't we?

'Jesus: what about his wife and family?' he said at last.

I shook my head. 'He's not budging at the moment. So presumably he'll have to tell his wife something.'

'Bloody hell! Twenty years of marriage. Just like that.'

I couldn't work out his tone. I drank another glass of champagne, not to clear my brain but to stop it worrying.

Chris watched with concern, and poured mineral water ostentatiously.

'Maybe you shouldn't drink too much, Sophie. I'll be needing a statement from you this afternoon. And from Hugh. I take it I can rely on you to give her a lift to Harborne? Maybe a couple of my lads to keep an eye on you? See you at about three, then.'

Chapter Twenty-Eight

At last, there was a general and rather hypocritical leave-taking. People who'd hardly spoken to me during the course now decided I was worth hugging and kissing; Gimson kissed no more than my hand, true, but Tabitha and the two girls clutched me as if I were suddenly precious.

'I hope you'll keep in touch,' said Shazia, sounding as if she meant it.

'Of course,' I said, sounding as if I did too.

I never bothered to check whether Hugh had had his tail-lights repaired, not even when I was watching him stow my luggage in his boot. Chris had assumed he'd be taking me to Harborne, and found I was too tired to argue. Not that I wanted to, especially.

'You need a bit of pampering,' said Hugh, glancing at me as he pulled out of the gates. There were police cars fore and aft to discourage the press. Chris had mentioned a press conference later. Much later, I'd insisted. Probably tomorrow.

'A sauna. That'd be nice,' I said eventually. I wondered how long he'd been waiting for me to speak.

'And a massage?' he said, with a pleasantly suggestive smile.

I nodded. First, perhaps, I ought to make him explain his rather extreme reaction to my activities. Maybe later. I'd see how much energy I could summon. I eased myself back in the seat and winced.

'You're sure you're all right?'

'A bit sore. Must be heaving all that coal. You know,' I

added, 'if I were a multimillionaire I would invest all my money in light industry in Yorkshire and wherever to ensure no one would ever have to go down a mine again. Never mind – I dare say government will do it for me. Without the investment, no doubt.'

He didn't speak. My God, with that office, this car, he was probably a card-carrying Tory! What did I really know about this man? Now wasn't the moment to ask. And I wasn't going to apologise for my views either.

We drove on in silence. I felt my eyelids drooping.

I couldn't help crying aloud. Toad was slicing my ear, in the darkness of the mine.

'What is it, Sophie?' Hugh stopped the car and took my hand.

Safe on the surface. I shook my head.

'Sophie?'

'Flashback, I suppose. I was down there again. Toad.' I didn't want to go on.

Suddenly Ian, who'd been in the leading police car, was at the window. Hugh pressed a button to wind it down for him.

'OK?' Ian didn't wait for an answer, but dug in his pocket. I knew what was coming. Extra-strong mints. I took them, and managed a grin.

The convoy set off again.

But the peppermints didn't cheer me up, not this time. For what I couldn't conceal from myself was that I had killed someone.

'Nonsense,' said Chris briskly, when back in Rose Road I put it to him. 'You may have walloped him quite hard, but not hard enough to kill him.' He smiled at me across his desk, and poured more coffee.

'But that twitching. And then that awful fit. And then – then . . .'

Suddenly I was there. Seeing it all happen.

'Let's start a little earlier in the proceedings, Sophie. Let's start when he pulled your arm up your back. Or when he sliced your ear. Or implied he was going to imprison you with Kate. In fact, why don't we kill two birds – sorry, I really didn't . . . My God, I'm so sorry.'

He looked so contrite I managed a laugh.

'I mean, if we could get this together as your statement – and we could really do with yours, Hugh. Could we decamp to an interview room? Ian, will you take Hugh's? Then we'll meet again up here, and I'll tell you about the oriental gentlemen I spoke to last night. But first things first, I suggest. The sooner Sophie's told us everything, the sooner she can start to forget it. Until the inquest, at least.'

We all exchanged smiles. Chris used his phone to request two extra officers. We all trooped off through the civilised corridors to our respective interview rooms. I was introduced to a WPC – Claire. Tina was off for the weekend, of course, and I suppose I accepted Claire as her substitute. But it transpired that Claire was one of the team of women trained as counsellors that I'd met during my afternoon in the rape suite. She'd be prepared to keep in touch with me for months, if necessary – as long as I had problems with the incident. Kate, she said, had also been assigned an officer to support her, she'd be at the hospital on call when Kate came round.

So that was what Chris was doing. Reminding me that if I had killed Toad it was for Kate's good. I looked at him ironically, but he merely looked serious and alert. Between them they took me through the morning's events as briskly and unemotionally as I wanted. I baulked at the torch episode. I had concealed it, intending to use it as a weapon.

'Why did you think you'd need a weapon?' asked Chris.

'Because anyone else would have called out to reassure me. I was sure that the voice I had heard was Kate's. I suppose I put two and two together.'

'And made exactly the right total,' said Chris dryly.

'Chris, I could do with a loo. All this coffee.'

Claire accompanied me, chatting as if we'd just met socially. I suppose they don't let people wander round anyway, but I'd have been happier with a 'take the first stairs on your left and it's just on your right' approach.

She used the other cubicle herself, and I was out and washing my hands before she was. It's automatic, isn't it? Swill your hands and peer across the washbasin into the mirror while you're doing it. But I didn't. I concentrated on my hands. There was still some coal dust under the nails. No nailbrush, of course. And my nails didn't take kindly to being picked with the other nails. I stood staring at them, my hands stretched in front of me.

'All the perfumes of Arabia,' I murmured, embarrassed that Claire had emerged to find me still staring.

'Bad luck to quote the Scottish play,' she said, standing beside me. She tipped the soap dispenser.

On the way back she talked about her degree in drama. Then she turned. 'You ought to be in a better room than this,' she said. 'But they've just brought in a kid who got caught up in that affray down the Lozells Road. Asian girl, fourteen. Gang of skinheads found her on her own. Gang-bang, they call it. And she was too ashamed to go back home. Thought it would bring disgrace on her family.'

'Skins?' I interrupted her. 'I wonder if they might go in for smashing car tail-lights too.'

After that it was easy. It was as if getting sidetracked like that got my brain into a higher gear, one which enabled me to think, not just react. I wanted to get on to the business of describing our skinheads, and Chris wouldn't let me until I'd got, as he put it, the Toad scenario out of the way. One day I'd ask him if he'd set up the conversation with Claire.

The officer in charge of the Photofit was a jocular man in his thirties, and the atmosphere became surprisingly carnival. Chris left Hugh and me to it. One or two things to see to, he said.

Five thirty on a wet Sunday night, and we were still at Rose Road, but back in the comparative luxury of Chris's office. It was cold, though, with those two sides of windows for the rain to drive at. He saw me shivering and produced a fan heater, which purred away in the background while he poured more tea and offered us fruitcake. I could have eaten the lot.

'Let me tell you what I've established so far,' he said, passing me the last piece of cake. 'Now we're not intruding on someone's personal life –' he looked at me sternly, but without rancour – 'I have been able to speak to Kerwin's GP. It seems that Mr Kerwin was indeed unfortunate enough to suffer from epilepsy, but that it was controlled very satisfactorily by regular medication.' This time, when he looked at me, he smiled. 'This medication was phenobarbitone. We found an empty bottle where Kate was imprisoned. Blood tests show she has been taking regular doses: no doubt she'll explain why he gave them to her when she's able to talk. I suspect, though it's too late to verify it now, that he intended to kidnap her on Monday night, and thought the drugs would make her sleepy and more docile.'

'Why should he want to kidnap a perfectly innocent writer?' asked Hugh.

'Maybe,' I said, 'there's some answers in the stuff I, er, liberated the other night. In his eyes she was wicked because she kept Sidney incarcerated. A rat deserves his liberty, not life on a lead. I wonder if he saw Sidney's cage. He might well have done; we all visited the tutors' rooms. And he was one of those helpful people – according to the cuttings he'd kept, those in the back of that scrapbook – who released a load of mink into the wild, thus buggering up the habitat for the local fauna, incidentally.'

'But – Jesus, that cage thing!' Hugh covered his face, as if to shut out the memory. Chris must have let him see it for himself. Perhaps that might explain his behaviour.

'I suppose he might see it as justice,' I said. 'Tie it in with his love of real-life crime stories. I dimly remember he had an argument with Matt about all fiction being derived from fact, too.'

Chris nodded, and then looked at me interrogatively. No, I had no more to say. He resumed. 'Perhaps you'd like to look at these.' He spread some papers. 'We took them off the notepad computer. The printer was a Canon, by the way, Sophie, and the print remarkably similar to that on the letter to you and the one purporting to come from Kate.'

'I wonder if he made her write it – and she used that lousy style to alert Matt?'

'We'll find out when she's ready to talk. Meanwhile –' He gestured at the papers on his desk.

Hugh and I peered: Toad had prepared a set of press releases. He'd planned to make Kate set her name to them – a road-to-Damascus conversion, just like Patti Hearst. I shook my head wearily. It all seemed so much effort just to make his point. Somewhere there must be a deeper reason. Perhaps his press cuttings would show it.

Hugh rubbed his face in disbelief. 'Can we go back to Kate being sleepy?'

'To administer the drug would be difficult. I borrow Sophie's theory here. I think, though it's too late to check now – it doesn't stay in the body that long – that he ground it up and put it in the chocolate pudding. So many people reported sleeping deeply that night that I think the theory holds water.'

'And greedy pigs like me who had second helpings had vicious hangovers,' I said.

'Serves you right.'

'At least I didn't lick the plate,' I said virtuously, 'like Nyree did. Chris, do you have the same idea as I have?'

'Probably a couple of hours ago,' he said.

The fan heater developed an irritating rattle. Chris kicked it gently and it subsided.

'I think that Nyree's excess of chocolate-flavoured phenobarbitone coupled with the whisky she consumed led to her death. I think it was entirely accidental. The conversations I've had with various oriental groups suggest that they wanted her alive, not dead. Dead women can't broker profitable deals. Her husband seems to have combined a love of golf with a desire for a comfortable retirement. Possibly his sojourn in Vietnam has rekindled some capitalist light in his breast. I don't know. If that Mercedes the Japanese drove ever comes to light, we'll find out more.'

'I shan't press charges,' I said. 'But I do wish I'd taken that money.'

Chris gaped.

'For a car. A holiday. A spell in a health farm. That sort of thing. Instead of which it's back to work on Wednesday. Enrolment,' I added.

Chris continued to stare at me.

'Do you reckon our friend planned to kidnap Kate in advance? I mean, that cage –' said Hugh.

Chris shrugged. 'I suspect he might have been thinking about holding someone to ransom. We've had a look at some of his reading matter, too. There was a Dick Francis thriller about kidnapping beside his bed at Eyre House.'

'Brilliant book,' I said.

Chris looked at me with distaste. 'You call a book brilliant that puts that sort of idea into someone's head?'

'Or was it Madame Tussaud's that put it into his head?' asked Hugh. 'I recall having a long conversation with him about the Chamber of Horrors. Do you remember, Sophie? My first evening?'

I nodded. The day of the rat in the fridge. I thought of the penknife in my pillow, the knife through my overshirt. 'Why should he have picked on me? I hadn't a clue who was up to what.'

'You must have said something.'

'I went for that run. If anyone seemed threatening, it was Naukez, actually.'

'Could anyone else have known?'

'Everyone! Shazia drew me a map on the kitchen blackboard,' I said, light dawning at last. 'And I suppose he saw my reluctance to run with him as being fear, or something.' I yawned. I couldn't stop. I wanted to go home, dig a curry out of the deep-freeze, and retire to the comfort of my duvet.

I put the idea of a curry to Hugh when we emerged into the chilly evening.

'Harborne Tandoori,' I said, with growing enthusiasm. 'They know me there. It's a place a woman can eat alone without being patronised or tucked away at a duff table. Then a dram afterwards. And I'll switch on my central heating.'

He seemed less than enthusiastic. But since he had to get me and my case home anyway, he didn't argue. He didn't follow me into the house, however. He grinned suddenly and announced he had an idea or two of his own, and he'd use his car phone to follow them through.

It didn't take him long. I'd done no more than switch on the water-heater and tip all my clothes into the washing machine. I remembered in time to fish out my silk camisole; the overshirt was still with the police. Evidence.

The Mondiale, that was his idea. We'd use their jacuzzi and their sauna, then have dinner in our room. I liked the sound of 'our'. *En suite* bathroom, of course. He sat on my bed and watched me putting clothes into an overnight bag. He pulled my nightdress out.

'Won't be needing that,' he said, dropping it on the floor.

Perhaps a sexy couple of days was just what the doctor would have ordered.

He had to help me out of my tracksuit and into the slacks and top I thought more in keeping with the Mondiale. At least its foyer. The rest of the time I didn't expect to have too much to do with the other guests. He even had to brush my hair back, I was so stiff. When I winced at a button, he kissed the finger better. 'Is that where that rat bit you?'

I nodded. 'A good job it was a tame one, not a wild one. Rats carry all sorts of nasty diseases,' I said helpfully. I suppose I was talking too much because I was embarrassed by my bedroom – it's always been the room I intend to decorate next year.

He returned to the bed. With me, this time. Perhaps we wouldn't be going to the Mondiale just yet.

On Sundays you don't have to pick your way through back streets to avoid city-bound traffic jams. You can risk the main road straight into the centre. He drove easily, and dived into the underpass at Five Ways, emerging into Broad Street. Normally this is where you start wondering where on earth you'll park, but he drove straight to the Mondiale's entrance. A doorman appeared by magic to help me out, but Hugh was there himself. And it did take two of them. Then the car disappeared, almost of its own volition. By the time we had checked in, particularly if we stopped off at the bar first, our luggage would be in our room. All very efficient.

There was a chirrup from Hugh's portable phone while we were still in the foyer. When he'd finished the call, I'd tease him about his plethora of communications technology. Meanwhile I drifted over to the fountain. But I found the movement of water too chill, and turned back again.

His face was very serious. His whole body showed concern. He asked a couple of impatient questions. Then he snapped the phone shut and stowed it in his pocket.

'Problems?' I said mildly.

He nodded. 'Marcus. My eldest. Mumps. And Fi – my

wife thinks Claudia may have them too. I'll have to go straight back home. I wonder if we can intercept our bags.' He pushed his way to the front of the queue.

'Get them to call me a taxi,' I said, over his shoulder.

I'm not sure how long it took to sort things out. A porter arrived eventually, and I reached for my bag.

'Madam's taxi,' he said, keeping hold of it. He gestured to the entrance.

'No need for that. Harborne's on my way,' said Hugh.

'I'd rather.'

'What the hell's the matter with you?'

I looked at him. Couldn't he understand? Perhaps I didn't even want to go to the trouble of explaining. It wasn't so much that he was married – I suppose I ought to have guessed that, and I would probably have taken no more notice than I did of Carl's having a wife – but that he hadn't considered it necessary to tell me. Indeed, now I came to think of it, he'd probably gone to a lot of trouble to conceal the fact.

I walked with as much dignity as I could muster across the foyer and through the automatic doors. The doorman opened the taxi door for me. The porter stowed my case. After a moment's hesitation, Hugh ran down the steps after us.

'When –' he began.

But I tapped the window for the driver to start.

What a pity tomorrow was Bank Holiday Monday. It meant it'd be Tuesday before the shops would be open and I could go and buy a rat.

If you have enjoyed *Dying To Write*, NOW READ:

***Dying Fall* by Judith Cutler**

Sophie Rivers, inner-city college lecturer and amateur singer, has a satisfying life: a job she enjoys, a close circle of friends. Then, suddenly, things go badly wrong. One of her students is murdered on college premises; worse still, her best friend George meets a tragic end on the site of the newly built Birmingham Music Centre.

Everyone believes his death was an accident – everyone except Sophie. Determined to find his killer, she starts asking questions. And soon she knows they must be the right questions, because now someone is trying to murder her . . .

Set in present-day Birmingham, with all its conflicts and tensions, *Dying Fall* is a tautly plotted criminal debut.

Piatkus Paperback
0-7499-3000-4

Eve Of Destruction
by Martin Edwards

When Liverpool solicitor and amateur detective Harry Devlin takes on a client with matrimonial troubles, he becomes entangled in an intrigue which will have deadly consequences. His new client has been recording his wife's telephone conversations with her lover; the first mystery for Harry to solve is the identity of the woman's boyfriend.

Harry's own personal life is currently complicated by the enigmatic behaviour of both his partner in law and the woman he longs for. And soon he finds himself trapped in a maze where nothing is quite what it seems. Even when he discovers a conspiracy to commit murder, he cannot be sure who is the culprit and who the true victim . . .

'(Martin Edwards) . . . writes terrific crime novels'

– *Guardian*

Piatkus Paperback
0-7499-3003-9